Praise for *Letters from an Imaginary Country*

"World Fantasy Award winner Goss (the *Athena Club* trilogy) delivers a wonderfully atmospheric collection of stories set in 16 distinct fantastical worlds. In 'England Under the White Witch,' a permanent winter settles over Britain after the eponymous sorceress raises an army of women who find empowerment in her icy dominion. 'Beautiful Boys' takes the form of a scientific treatise on an alien race whose sole purpose is reproduction. The pageantry and politics of 'Child-Empress of Mars' makes it a standout, as an immortal child ruler engineers a grand heroic quest for a mysterious newcomer, unaware that her 'chosen one' is actually a bewildered ranch hand from Earth. Across the collection, Goss blends fantastical premises with meditations on history, identity, and the art of storytelling, often drawing from her own Hungarian childhood. There is a distinctive undercurrent of wonder and menace to the tales, each one told with lush prose and sly wit. Readers willing to linger in Goss's intricately wrought landscapes will find themselves amply rewarded."
—*Publishers Weekly*

"Literary, lyrical, lovely. An elegant waltz through history and literature, with a fantastical turn."
—Marie Brennan, author of *The Memoirs of Lady Trent* series

"Theodora Goss's luminous collection explores duality and liminality in identity, belonging, and setting. Goss's formidable powers as an observer and storyteller are showcased in these beautiful stories."
—Fran Wilde, Nebula-winning author of *A Catalog of Storms*

"Wildly imaginative, gloriously sneaky, delicious tales of monsters and the terrible and beautiful sublimity of the imagination."
—Cory Doctorow, author of *Red Team Blues* and *Walkaway*

"The worlds in Theodora Goss's wondrous collection *Letters from an Imaginary Country* are tantalizingly, dangerously close to our own. Or, rather, they are our troubling world, as refracted through our most treasured stories' secondary characters, a keen feminist lens, and the products of a feverish imagination. These love letters to storytelling are sharp-witted and illuminating."
—David Ebenbach, author of *How to Mars*

Praise for Theodora Goss

"In the tradition of great modern fantasists like Angela Carter and Marina Warner, Theodora Goss's sublime tales are modern classics—beautiful, sly, sensual, and deeply moving."
—Elizabeth Hand, winner of the Nebula and World Fantasy Awards

"The elegance of Goss's work has never ceased to amaze me."
—Catherynne M. Valente, winner of the Mythopoeic and Hugo Awards

Letters from an Imaginary Country

THEODORA GOSS

TACHYON
SAN FRANCISCO

Introduction copyright © 2025 by Jo Walton
Interior and cover design by Elizabeth Story
Cover art "The Novel" copyright © 2023 by Catrin Welz-Stein
Author photo by Matthew Stein Photography

Tachyon Publications LLC
1459 18th Street #139
San Francisco, CA 94107
415.285.5615
www.tachyonpublications.com
tachyon@tachyonpublications.com

Series editor: Jacob Weisman
Editor: Jaymee Goh

Print ISBN: 978-1-61696-440-5
Digital ISBN: 978-1-61696-441-2

Printed in the United States by Versa Press, Inc.

First Edition: 2025
9 8 7 6 5 4 3 2 1

Also by Theodora Goss

Collections

The Rose in Twelve Petals & Other Stories (2004)
In the Forest of Forgetting (2006)
Songs for Ophelia (2014)
Snow White Learns Witchcraft (2019)
The Collected Enchantments (2023)

The Extraordinary Adventures of the Athena Club

The Strange Case of the Alchemist's Daughter (2017)
European Travel for the Monstrous Gentlewoman (2018)
The Sinister Mystery of the Mesmerizing Girl (2019)

Novella

The Thorn and the Blossom: A Two-Sided Love Story (2012)

As editor

Interfictions: An Anthology of Interstitial Writing
(with Delia Sherman, 2007)
Voices from Fairyland: The Fantastical Poems of Mary Coleridge,
Charlotte Mew, and Sylvia Townsend Warner (2008)
Medusa's Daughters: Magic and Monstrosity from Women
Writers of the Fin-de-Siècle (2020)

CONTENTS

INTRODUCTION
Jo Walton

THERE ARE THREE KINDS OF PEOPLE reading an introduction to a short story collection. There is also an extra kind of person who isn't reading it, who is skipping straight ahead to the stories because who wants to read a boring introduction when the stories are waiting, but that's fine. We don't have to worry about them. Have fun in there, people, the stories are great.

The first kind of people who are reading this are people who already love Goss's work and want to hear me say how great she is, how great her work is, and how these stories are a splendid addition to what she's written before. I don't have to worry about you people either, because we're all on the same page. I agree with you. Theodora Goss is a significant writer, who is doing something different from everyone else, writing things only she can write and things that are absolutely the lifeblood of the fantasy genre. People don't tend to think of her that way, because much of her work is fantasy and fairy tales and we valorize SF over fantasy, and because some of it has been published as YA and we take work for adults more seriously, and perhaps also because she's a woman. But it's true. She's not just an elegant poetic writer; what she's doing is vital, important, alive. In retelling fairy tales she's going right at the root of what fairy tales are and why they've been important to every human culture. Now go read the stories. They're stellar, really.

The second kind of person reading this has read a little Goss but doesn't know much about her, and isn't sure whether to buy a whole collection or not, and maybe trusts me to tell the truth about this particular set of stories. Well, believe me, people, she's not an uneven writer, and everything here is powerful and worth reading. No, seriously, trust me, you won't be sorry. This is a really terrific collection. And maybe what you want is for me to compare these stories so you can triangulate to other writers, maybe to Jane Yolen or Lord Dunsany, maybe to John M. Ford or Isabel J. Kim, maybe to really unexpected people like Ted Chiang or Jan Morris, or even David Graeber. You can make a good case for Goss being like all these people, especially in this collection, which was deeply enjoyable to read. While I read it I kept wanting to read bits aloud, and talking to my friends about the ideas in the stories. It's in conversation with a whole bunch of nineteenth-century fiction, and with the whole idea of what it means for characters to be real.

But the main thing I thought, reading all this in one gulp, is what a European writer Goss is. I don't mean "European" in the faux-medieval way, but directly, how steeped she is in the culture and history of the continent of Europe, not just her native Hungary, though that does run through everything, but all of Europe. These stories are engaging with many countries and many centuries. Maybe it would be more useful to compare Goss to a European writer like Karin Tidbeck or Latin American writers like Angélica Gorodischer or her beloved Borges than to contemporary American fantasists like Peter Beagle or Nisi Shawl. But even in saying this and trying to pin down what I mean, I start to think no, there is an American sensibility there too, like with Terry Bisson. She's standing between both. And that's interesting, because one of the themes of this collection is doubling, reflection, having things both ways.

In one story here, Goss imagines a shadow-twin who stayed in Hungary when she was taken to America as a child. She goes beyond what anyone else would have done with this story and writes about them meeting as adults when Hungary opens up again and forging a relationship as history happens around them. I've never read anything like it. It haunts me. I'm sure everyone has thought of the forking points of their own lives and what they'd be like if . . . but generally as an alternative, not an addition, not as if your other self was someone you could share an apartment with. In two other stories she writes about imaginary anthropology, making up a country and then having the country become real, Ruritania rubbing shoulders with other parts of Eastern Europe. She's working with the world out there on the edges, coming into being with imagination, and then integrating, interacting, being realized. She's so deft as a writer—she moves so smoothly you can almost miss what a punch she packs with this kind of thing.

The third kind of people still sticking around are the people who haven't read any Theodora Goss before, and picked this up on a whim because it has an interesting title, who know nothing. Oh, people, oh my people, this is your lucky day. Stop reading this introduction right now and go ahead and read the stories. Read them in order. There is such a joy of reading and delight of discovery ahead for you! It makes me so happy to imagine you and what a wonderful time you're about to have.

So the thing is, now that nobody is reading this anymore, I first encountered the work of Theodora Goss like that. I was at the Worldcon in Boston in 2004. I was a fairly new and obscure writer then, with just four novels out. Seeing my books on a shelf was still exciting. I'd recently moved to Canada, and I was broke and doing Worldcon on an absolute shoestring, sharing a room with a bunch of friends, and eating as cheaply as possible. However, there was one thing I was keeping money aside for, and that was the new Geoff Ryman collection from Small Beer, a small press that at that time had almost no distribution in Canada. Even though I'd read nearly all the stories in magazines or Year's Best collections, I really wanted it. So, on my second day, in the dealer's room, I sought out the Small Beer table to get my Ryman collection. I found it, and I was about to pay, when the person assisting me saw my name badge. It was Kelly Link (*Kelly Link!*) and she knew who I was. She'd read and loved my most recent book, *Tooth and Claw*, and indeed she'd loved it so much she insisted on *giving* me the Ryman, and also loading me up with other gift books Small Beer had published that she thought I'd like. It was a wonderful thing to do, I was over the moon, not just saving the money so I could afford another meal, but being given books because another writer liked my book. It was like a dream. Not just like a dream come true for the fifteen-year-old in me, but really just like a wonderful dream. And the best of those books Kelly gave me that day was Theodora Goss's chapbook *The Rose in Twelve Petals*.

I'd never heard of her. But you know, being handed a free book because someone liked my work, I was going to read it whatever it was. So I did, and it absolutely blew my head off, the poetry and the stories and the power and assurance Goss brought to what she was doing. She's so amazing. I'm proud to be writing an introduction to her collection.

Jo WALTON has published fifteen novels, most recently *Or What You Will* (2020). She has also published four poetry collections, two essay collections, and a short story collection. She has won the Astounding, World Fantasy, Hugo, Nebula, Locus, and Otherwise awards. Walton comes from Wales but lives in Montreal where the food and books are much better. She is a columnist at *Reactor*, and founded International Pixel-Stained Technopeasant Day.

THE MAD SCIENTIST'S DAUGHTER

In London, we formed a club. It's very exclusive. There are only six members. Five of us live on the premises. Helen, who is married, lives in Bloomsbury, but she comes to have dinner with us twice a week. We need each other. None of us has sisters, except Mary and Diana in a way, so we take the place of sisters for each other. Who else could share or sympathize with our experiences?

I. The House Near Regent's Park

Mary created a trust that holds the deed to the house. We are all listed as beneficiaries:

> Miss Justine Frankenstein
> Miss Catherine Moreau
> Miss Beatrice Rappaccini
> Miss Mary Jekyll
> Miss Diana Hyde
> Mrs. Arthur Meyrinck (née Helen Raymond)

But it is her house, really. Her father left it to her, along with a moderate fortune. She is the only one of us who has inherited any money. Science does not pay well; mad science pays even worse.

From that fortune, she created a fund out of which we can draw for emergencies, but we all work. Mary paints on porcelain. Justine and Beatrice embroider vestments for the church. I write potboilers for the penny press. Diana is on the music-hall stage. She can't, she says, stand the dull, ladylike sort of work the rest of us do. She must have excitement: the footlights, the greasepaint, the admirers. We don't judge. Who, indeed, are we to do so? We have all done things of which we are not proud. The club is a haven for us, a port in a particularly stormy world.

Helen does not work, of course: she has a household to run, a daughter to raise. She is also her husband's model. You might remember her as Helen Vaughan, although she also went by Herbert or Beaumont, at the time of what the newspapers called the West End Horrors. I have seen paintings of her at the Grosvenor, as Medusa with snakes for hair, or a lamia. I envy her sometimes, living in the midst of an artistic ferment, participating in the world. But then I curl up on the sofa by the fire in the clubroom, at peace with the world and myself, and think about how lucky I am to be here, out of the tumult of life, and I am content.

II. How We Live and Work

Beatrice lives in the conservatory. We had it built especially for her, at the back of the house where the laboratory used to be. Looking in through the glass, from the garden, you would think we were growing a jungle. Vines grow up the posts of her bed, orchids and passion-flowers hang down over her as she sleeps. I can see the table where she hybridizes her flowers, but only dimly, since there is always a mist on the glass. Some of the plants I recognize: jasmine, oleander, castor bean, hellebore, laburnum, all part of her poisonous pharmacopeia. And plants that she has created, plants only we have seen, and only in glimpses, since it is deadly for any of us to stay in the conservatory too long. She pollinates them herself, since insects can't live in the conservatory. She breathes in their fumes, and they give her a particular luster.

Beatrice is the only one of us other than Helen with any claim to beauty, but it is the beauty of a poisonous flower. Sometimes when she has been sitting with us in the clubroom too long, she tells us that she feels faint, and must return to the conservatory. The powders she makes and sells to the medical school supplement our income.

Apart from Beatrice, only Justine can visit the conservatory for any length of time. Nothing seems to harm her physically, although eventually, breathing those poisonous fumes, even she will begin to feel faint. But she is the most sentimental of us: the pigeons roo-cooing on the roof, the first flowers on the cherry tree outside her window, a book of poetry will all bring her to tears. Reading Wordsworth will depress her for a week. I can't help laughing sometimes, to myself of course, when I look out my window and see her sitting in the garden, sighing like a sad giantess.

Justine lives in the attic. She says that she likes to be close to the sky and the pigeons, but really I think it's the only room in the house where the ceiling is high enough for her. When you're seven feet tall, even a ten-foot ceiling feels cramped. All of her furniture had to be made to order: the long bed, the wardrobe tall enough to accommodate her dresses, the looking glass that we bought from a magician, who used it to perform tricks. We've offered to help her decorate, to paper the walls, hang lithographs. I've offered to sew her curtains. But no, she says. She prefers the spartan simplicity of whitewash, a bedstead and a single chair, sunlight streaming through the windows. A cross hanging over her bed and a miniature of her grandmother on the dresser are the only decorations. And books. Piles and piles of books.

Mostly religious, but also a great deal of poetry. Too much, I think, to be entirely healthy for her.

Mary, Diana, and I live below her, on the second floor. Mary and Diana share a room. We've told them it's not necessary, that we can convert the library into a room for one of them, but they prefer to live together. I think it took so long for them to find each other, they do not want to be parted, even for a night, although they constantly disagree. Mary: tall, slender, fair, a quiet girl who is always either embroidering or reading philosophical works. Diana: short, dark as a gypsy, as temperamental as I imagine all actresses are. When we found her, she was working in a brothel. We are not entirely certain that she has given up her less respectable pursuits. When she comes home, smelling of gin, it is Mary who sits with her and bathes her head while she lies on the sofa, moaning. I suspect Mary has, on more than one occasion, paid Diana's debts.

Mary's side of the room: blue wallpaper with a pattern of white flowers, blue-and-white checked curtains, a brass bed with white linen, a small desk on which she has put daffodils in a vase. Diana's side of the room: Indian silks in reds and pinks and oranges, like an exotic sunset. A divan covered with pillows beside a table carved to resemble an elephant. Clothes strewn all over the floor, because she is incapable of keeping anything neat. Everywhere: statues of Hindu gods, buddhas with fat bellies, an onyx dog from Africa, a collection of brass bells, dyed baskets, the detritus of Empire. A vanity inlaid with ivory and strewn with cosmetics that, Mary tells her, will eventually ruin her complexion. Mrs. Poole refuses to clean Diana's half of the room. "Let her learn to pick up after herself," she says, uncharacteristically.

What would we do without Mrs. Poole? Her father worked for the Jekylls, and his father before him. She takes care of us all, makes certain that Justine isn't starving herself on a diet of lettuce and parsley, that Diana gets up by noon so she can make her curtain call. She feeds my cats.

My room is not very interesting. I was born in Argentina and then reborn on my father's island in the South Seas. Perhaps that is why my room is as English as possible. Roses on the wallpaper, a rose chintz on the armchair. A mahogany suite: bed, dresser, wardrobe. A bookshelf filled with Jane Austen, the Brontës, George Eliot. A desk where I write my potboilers.

The Mysteries of Astarte
The Adventures of Rick Chambers
Rick Chambers and Astarte
Rick Chambers on Venus
Invasion of the Cat Women

I look down at the page in the typewriter:

"No mortal man can resist me," said Astarte, pulling back her veil. The eyes that looked at him shone like twin stars in the night sky, dark and yet luminous in her white face. The perfect mouth, with lips curved like the famous bows of the Phoenicians, laughed.

Harold fell down before her, worshiping her beauty. Even Professor Hardcastle wiped the sweat from his brow. Only Rick remained calm.

"Your beauty, Madam, is most impressive. But I am an Englishman, and I prefer justice."

That will be *The Death of Astarte*. I have already been paid for *The Resurrection of Astarte* and *Rick Chambers, Jr. in the Caverns of Doom*.

On the bed, three cats lie purring: Alpha, Omega, and Bess. I found them one morning, three ragged kittens mewing by the kitchen door. Poor things. How difficult it must be, to be a kitten in London, always running from dogs, always in danger of being run over by cart wheels. Of course we took them in. The club is a refuge for them as well, and I am particularly fond of cats.

III. What We Talk About

Sometimes we talk about our fathers.

Justine: "My father loved me. He made me from the corpse of a girl who had been a servant of the Frankenstein family. She had been hanged for a crime she did not commit, and he had preserved her body, anticipating that someday he might be able to once again give her life. He even gave me her name, to commemorate her innocence.

"I can't begin to tell you what a wonderful childhood I had! My father guided me gently through the various stages of knowledge. He taught me the words to describe the world around me: the birds, the plants, the phenomena of nature. He taught me to read, and in the evenings we would read together: *Paradise Lost*, *The Sorrows of Werther*, *Plutarch's Lives*. But he was always haunted by the memory of the creature he had created, and eventually that creature came for him. At his death, I lost my father and my only friend. Until," she looks at us, sitting and listening to her, the firelight on our faces, "until I found you." And we look away politely, while she blows her nose into a handkerchief.

Beatrice: "For so many years I was angry at my father. I thought he had no right to make me poisonous, to make my only playmates the plants of his garden."

Helen: "He *had* no right. Seriously, Beatrice, you're too forgiving. You need to learn to stand up for yourself."

Mary: "For goodness' sake, let her finish. You're always interrupting."

Helen: "That's because I can't stand to see any of you justifying them. I mean, seriously. They were abusive bastards, and that's all there is to it."

Catherine: "I have to agree with Helen. Abusive bastards seems, you know, fairly accurate. I mean, look at my father."

Beatrice: "I don't think you can compare my father to yours, Cat. No offense, but your father was a butcher. Mine brought me up himself, in a beautiful garden—"

Mary: "I agree that there are relative degrees of—well, although I don't like to say it, abusive bastardhood. But Bea, he never taught you anything. All that time on his hands, and he never took any of it to sit you down, teach you about your own biology. So you ended up poisoning the man you loved, basically by accident—"

Beatrice: "I should have known."

Diana: "Why in the world would you blame yourself? I'm with Helen. They were bastards, the lot of them, even Justine's sainted Papa Frankenstein. Look at me, born in a brothel. My mother died of syphilis."

Mary: "You can't generalize your story to all of us."

Diana: "Oh, right, now you're taking the other side. My story is *our* story, or have you forgotten, *sister?*"

Justine: "For goodness' sake, why are we arguing? I know perfectly well that my father wasn't perfect. But why should I remember all his faults? Why can't I remember the good times we had together, how kind he could be?"

Helen: "Because that's like lying to yourself. We've all been lied to. Do we really want to lie to ourselves as well?"

And then we are all quiet, and stare into the fire.

"My father," Helen continues, "was a scientist, like yours. He took my mother from the gutters, where she was starving, fed her, educated her, seduced her, and then experimented on her. She had a vision. She saw something she could not, or perhaps did not have the guts to, understand—the god Pan, source of all order and disorder, Alpha and Omega, to whom all things in the end will come. Nine months later I was born, daughter of the respectable Dr. Raymond and of Pan. It's not hard to understand why, as a teenager, I tried to destroy the world. Sometimes I wish I had. I mean, look at it. The other day, a man tried to steal my pocketbook. He was drunk, red-eyed and reeking of gin, and I turned and started hitting him with my umbrella. I thought, I could have destroyed you all—the beggars, the bankers, the filthy streets of London."

Catherine: "So, why didn't you?"

Helen: "Well, I married Arthur around that time, and then Leda was born. I would have had to destroy Regent's Park, and ice cream, and prams. It just didn't seem practical. Besides, I didn't want to give my father the satisfaction."

Mrs. Poole comes in. "Would any of you ladies like some tea?"

IV. A Peaceful Domestic Scene

Sometimes when Helen comes, she brings her daughter, Leda. She's a solemn child, with black hair that curls past her shoulders, genuinely hyacinthine. When she smiles, you can faintly hear the clashing of cymbals, the strings of the lyre plucked, the chanting of Bacchantes. You pause, thinking, *I must be imagining it*, and then you realize that no, you really are hearing something otherworldly. Once, I saw her in the garden, playing with a boy who had horns on his head, and the legs and hooves of a goat.

"She can't control it," says Helen. "She's too young. I couldn't control it either, at her age."

Leda is only twelve. But we can see in her, already, what we all seem to have, what I would describe as a mark, if it were not so variable.

I look in the mirror. I am, everywhere, golden brown: brown hair, brown skin, golden eyes. If you look at them too closely, you will begin to feel strange. You will realize that my pupils are slitted, except in the dark. That I do not blink as often as I ought to. And my face, although well-shaped, is seamed with scars.

We all have the mark, but in different ways. Mary, our golden-haired English girl, sits too still, is too placid for human nature. If you sit with her long enough, you will start to become nervous. Justine, willowy, elegant, is too tall for a woman, or even a man. Diana, lively and laughing, suffers from attacks of the hysteria. She will, suddenly, begin to pull out her hair, cut her arm with a dinner knife. Once, when she was younger, she almost bled to death. Beatrice, beautiful Beatrice who moves through the house like a walking calla lily, kills with her breath. When we gather together for dinner, she sits at the far end of the table. She has her own dishes and plates, which Mrs. Poole collects wearing gloves.

You could, I suppose, call us monsters. We are frightening, aren't we? Although we are, in our different ways, attractive. When we walk down the street, men look, and then look away. And then perhaps look again, and away again. Some of us don't leave the house more than we have to. The butcher delivers, and Mrs. Poole goes to the grocer's. But not even Justine can stay inside all the time. Sometimes we have to just, you know, get out. Go to the library, or the park. Personally, I'm sorry that veils are going out of fashion.

Imagine us in the evenings, sitting by the fire in the clubroom. I am reading from *The Yellow Book*. Justine is darning a sock. Mary is sketching Beatrice, who is posing by the window, which is open at the bottom despite the autumn chill.

"When will Diana return from the theater?" Beatrice asks.

"I really don't know," says Mary. "She has a new hanger-on, some sort of viscount. I just wish she'd be more careful."

"Well," I say, "if he does anything to hurt her, we'll sic Beatrice on him."

"Or Justine," says Beatrice.

"Me?" says Justine. "You know I wouldn't hurt a fly."

"Yes," I say, "but he wouldn't know that. You look frightening enough."

"I couldn't. I mean, it would be terrible . . . ," says Justine.

"Oh, for goodness' sake," I say. "When the villagers come with pitchforks, what are you going to do? Hide in a hayloft? We should be ready to—I don't know, tear their throats out." This is London, but how far away are they ever, the villagers with pitchforks?

"Let's get back to the story," says Mary, the conciliator. "I want to know whether what's-her-name is going to have an affair with Lord—what's his name?"

"That was the *last* story," I say. "Haven't you been listening?"

"You know I don't like that modern stuff, except your books, of course." I happen to know she never finished *Rick Chambers and Astarte*. "I just want you to stop bothering Justine. Can't you see she's upset by all this talk of violence?" She turns back to her sketch. "Bea, hold your head up a little. You're drooping."

A peaceful domestic scene. An ordinary evening among monsters.

V. How I Joined the Club

I knew Justine before we joined the club. We were in the circus together, the Giantess and the Cat Girl. The manager was a good man, a Polish Jew who called himself Lorenzo the Magnificent. When I joined his Traveling Circus of Marvels and Delights, Justine had already been there for two years. She sat outside the sideshow tent, taking tickets from the patrons. She also had an act with two dwarves dressed as clowns and a pony that kicked on command.

There is an etiquette in the circus. Everyone is polite to one another, but still, the performers have a certain contempt for the sideshow, and vice versa. The performers were proud of their tricks, walking the high wire, riding bareback, being shot from a cannon. But we needed no tricks in the sideshow. We were the tricks. We could perform without moving a muscle.

I was Astarte, the Cat Girl from Egypt. I have no tail and my ears are almost normal, just a little pointed at the tips. But you should have seen me in my costume! Cat ears, cat tail. I certainly looked the part. I would growl with fury and show the customers my claws. I even purred for the gentlemen who paid extra to stroke me. Atlas, the Strong Man, stopped them if they went too far. I was always a respectable cat.

Atlas was in love with Justine. He even asked her to marry him.

"Why don't you?" I asked her. We had become friends, in part I think because of our similar family histories. Her father had made men out of corpses. Mine had made men out of animals. They were, in a sense, in the same profession.

"I just can't," she said.

"Is it your sainted Papa? Are you afraid that you'll never find a man with his charm, his erudition? It's true that Atlas is not exactly literate . . ."

"You're making fun of me. Please don't, Cat. No, it's something else."

I waited.

"You have to promise that you won't tell anyone."

"Who would I tell? It's not as though anyone else would understand."

"All right. The creature—the one my father made. He wanted me to be his mate. One day, he attacked me. You think I'm strong, but he was so much stronger. He had his hand around my throat . . . If he had wanted to kill me, I'm sure he would have. But that wasn't what he wanted, at least not then. I can't . . . I really can't talk about it anymore." Tears were streaming down her face.

"Oh, Justine . . ." I said.

"So you see," she said, finally blowing her nose on a handkerchief. She seemed to have an endless supply of them. "I'll never marry any man."

I put my arms around her, and we sat together on one of the packing crates, listening to the elephants trumpet.

With the circus, we toured the provinces. That was when I fell in love with England, its greenness, its freshness. That was when I created Rick Chambers, the quintessential English gentleman, Eton and Oxford and cricket and the sun never setting and all that. Astarte will never defeat the English gentleman, no matter how many times she lures him into her bed. Of course, he'll never defeat her either. It would be boring if the English gentleman ever won.

Those were happy days, more or less, with Justine, and Lola the Bearded Lady, and Harold the Wolf Boy, and the two dwarves, Pip and Squeak. The pay was low, but we were like a family. However, they were destined to end. Lorenzo was in debt, and even the Traveling Circus of Marvels and Delights could not pay the full amount.

"If only I had the Black Widow!" he said mournfully one evening as we were eating our supper together around a campfire. The Black Widow was a new marvel, a beautiful girl whose breath was as deadly as the deadliest poison. She was not in a circus, but at the Royal College of Surgeons. Medical men were attempting to determine what made her so toxic. It was Beatrice, of course, but Justine and I didn't know that then. We knew of her only from newspaper articles.

"Poor girl," Justine would say, reading them.

"Why? It says that even the Queen has gone to see her. Imagine the price people would pay, if she were in the sideshow."

"To kill everything you touch! I think that must be terrible."

"If you say so. Personally, I think it would come in handy sometimes."

Two days before the circus was to break up, when Justine and I were wondering what we were going to do with ourselves, a woman came to see us. She was dressed in black, and heavily veiled. When she drew back her veil, we saw a beautiful face, with an olive complexion and black eyes, obviously foreign looking, yet it would have been difficult to tell what country she came from. She looked so completely exotic, yet at the same time so ordinary, like an English lady. Aha! I thought. If I ever write a book about Astarte, I'll make her look just like that.

"Miss Frankenstein, Miss Moreau," she said. "I'm delighted to make your acquaintance." Her voice was deep, musical, and I almost imagined that I heard the sound of lyres as she spoke. "I understand that your employment is almost over. I've been authorized to offer you membership in a very exclusive club."

VI. The Reports of Our Deaths

The reports of our deaths have been greatly exaggerated.

Justine: believed dismembered, her body parts thrown into the sea.

Beatrice: believed poisoned by a toxic antidote.

Helen: believed strangled by a hangman's rope.

Catherine: believed killed by Moreau's hand.

And yet, as you see, we survive.

VII. The Stories We Tell

Mary: "People often don't know that my father had a wife. She was left out of the case history that was written shortly after his death, I suppose to protect her privacy. Poor Mother! She was only eighteen when she married, and he was in medical school. She was so proud to have married a doctor. My grandfather was a country vicar, and she had been educated at home by my grandmother, taught to sew and sing hymns and keep hens. She didn't understand when my father began refurbishing the laboratory, conducting experiments. When I was fifteen, shortly before she died, she told me, 'Your father was a good man. Never forget that, Mary. It was his science, his fatal science, that ruined him. If only it had been a woman! Read your Bible, Mary. In it you'll find everything you ever need to know. Never give in to the curiosity that killed your father.'"

Beatrice: "There's nothing wrong with science. In itself, it's neither good nor evil. It's simply a way of looking at the world."

Mrs. Poole: "Well, then why does it lead to all those nasty mad scientists, I want to know? No, Miss Beatrice, I think all that science and experimenting should be left alone, especially by young ladies like yourselves. Mrs. Jekyll was a good, upstanding woman, and she was right. Everything you need to know, you'll find in the Good Book."

Beatrice: "Science saved me, Mrs. Poole. When I recovered from Professor Baglioni's antidote, it was late afternoon. Where could I go? I loved my father, but I didn't want to return to his garden, which had been my prison for so many years, or to the lover who had so cruelly rejected me. Instead, I wandered around Padua, trying to find the university. When I finally found the front gate, I asked to see Professor Baglioni.

"He was startled to see me. I think he had, in an indirect way, tried to kill me, absolving himself of blame because he had not been sure of the result. I told him, 'If you don't help me, I'll go to the authorities and accuse you of attempted murder. I may be a monster, but I'm also the daughter of the famous Dr. Rappaccini, who has cured many of the townspeople, including the mayor's wife. Do you think they'll ignore me?' I don't know, really, if the authorities would have listened to me, but he was already frightened and uncertain of his position, so he did what I asked.

"He took me to his villa and brought me all of his books on natural philosophy, particularly botany. When those weren't enough, he brought me books from the university library. I spent months studying them, trying to understand my own physiology. I wanted to remove the poison from my system. I think part of me still hoped I could return to my Giovanni and say, 'Look, I'm a normal woman now.' I still wanted him to love me. But I could find no way to alter my condition.

"One day, he told me of my father's death. My father had continued his studies, but without me to tend the garden for him, he had slowly been poisoned by its fumes. How I cried! All the anger I had felt toward him melted away, and I felt only an emptiness. I was now alone in the world. I left the seclusion of the villa and offered myself to the learned men of the university for study. When they could give me no answer, I went to another university, and then another. I traveled from city to city, from Padua to Milan, Geneva, Paris, and finally London, always hoping that someone would find a cure. Without that hope, sometimes I think I would have lain down on the earth and simply died. Finally, I decided that I would become a scientist myself. If I could not find an answer in books or from learned men, I would have to experiment. So I followed in my father's footsteps. I wonder if he would have been proud of me?"

Mary: "I'm certain he would have. You're doing wonderful work."

Diana: "How do you do it, Mary? You always agree with everyone. You never say anything mean or lose your temper. Honestly, I think it's creepy. Sometimes I think you're a doll that a magician brought to life and taught to behave from a good conduct book. I have no problem with Bea making potions, but we shouldn't pretend that any of us will ever be normal. Sometimes when I'm with the viscount, all I want to do is bite him until he bleeds and lap up the blood. Cat knows what I'm talking about."

Catherine: "I often want to bite someone. The butcher looks so delicious, carrying those glorious hunks of meat!"

Diana: "Exactly. Well, you girls know my history. My mother was a whore, who didn't know she was with child until after my father died. She figured out what was what quickly enough, and Mrs. Jekyll paid through the nose—until my mother died of syphilis at twenty-one. I was sent to an orphanage run by nuns. How sick I became of their pieties! At night, when they thought all the girls were sleeping, I cut their habits to shreds and pissed in the communion cup. I rang the bells at the wrong hours. Finally, they decided the orphanage was haunted and brought in a bishop for an exorcism. But it was all me, of course. When I was old enough, I left to follow my mother's trade. Don't tell me that any science is going to make me normal."

VIII. The Stories We Tell, Continued

Catherine: "I killed my father. I bit him and bashed his head in. And when a ship finally came close enough to the island, I pretended to be in distress so the captain would take me aboard. He believed I was an English lady whose ship had been captured by pirates, and who had finally been left to starve on a deserted shore. That was the only way he could explain my scars, and of course I told him that I could not remember anything before my time on the island. He brought me to England, and his wife cared for me. She taught me how to dress, how to eat with a knife and fork, all the things my father had not taught me. She wanted to adopt me as her daughter—they were childless— but one day when I was sitting in the parlor, darning a sock, her little dog came by, a yapping little dog that had never liked me, and bit me on the ankle. So I bit it back. When she came in, its corpse was dangling from my jaws. She started screaming . . . I left with only the clothes on my back. I begged in the streets for months before Lorenzo asked me to join his circus."

Justine: "Those were good days with the circus, weren't they?"

Beatrice: "How did you join the circus, Justine?"

Justine: "Do we have to talk about it?"

Beatrice: "I'm sorry, I didn't mean to distress you. I was just curious."

Justine: "All right. But it's hard for me to talk about—I'd rather forget. The creature my father had made wanted a wife, so my father made me. But after he had completed me, he realized that he could not give me to the creature. So, he made the creature believe he was destroying me by rowing out and throwing a sack full of stones into the sea. Then, he took me to a cottage on the coast of Scotland, even more remote than our previous location had been. 'I won't give you to that monster,' he told me. 'You have the ability to reason and to appreciate the beautiful. You are not like him, and you will not belong to him.' The creature, supposing I had been destroyed, did not follow us. And so for a few years, a few happy years, we were left in peace.

But one day, the creature found our cottage. He was determined once more to have my father make another like himself. And there, on the shore by that northern sea, he saw my father playing with me, the bride who had been meant for him. We were throwing a ball back and forth, one of my favorite games at that time—remember that although I was full-grown, I was only three years old. He was in such a rage that he ran toward my father and strangled him with his bare hands. And then he attacked me. . .

"He forced me to live with him in that cottage, to read him the books my father and I had read together, to sit by the fire with him as though we were man and wife. But one night, as he lay asleep after drinking the last of the whisky in the house, I stuck a kitchen knife into his heart. And then I ran, sobbing, because I had killed the man who had been both brother and husband to me, the only one, as far as I knew, of my kind. I lived on berries, the bark from trees, and what I could steal from farmyards—the slop left for the pigs, the grain scattered for the hens. Once, a man tried to shoot me with a gun. Another time, boys threw stones at me. Finally I came to a town, and there was a circus. It was, of course, Lorenzo's Traveling Circus of Marvels and Delights. The tent was so bright, so cheerful, scarlet and yellow in the middle of a field. And I heard music . . . Although I was sick and starving, I walked closer to see where the music was coming from. But there, just by the tent, I fainted. When I came to again, I was in Lola's caravan, and Lorenzo was looking at me, smoothing his mustache. Cat, you remember what a black mustache he had. We were convinced he dyed it. 'Young lady,' he said, 'I have a proposition for you.' I was terrified! I had never spoken with a human being before, except my father. But I accepted his offer to join the sideshow. What choice did I have? I had no way to earn my living in the world. I had only the knowledge my father had given me, and the fact that I was, you know, different."

Beatrice: "Why do we always die in the stories?"

Catherine: "Because we're not the ones who write them."

IX. The Secrets We Tell Each Other

Justine: "Once, I killed a man. I put my hands around his neck and strangled him. I didn't mean to—he threatened to shoot me with a gun."

Mary: "Once, a man tried to kiss me. He was a clerk at the attorney's office, when I went to hear the provisions of my mother's will. That was when I learned about Diana—it was my mother who had placed her in that orphanage. The front hall was narrow, and as he was handing me my coat, he suddenly leaned down . . . But then, at the last moment, he drew back. There was a look on his face, as though he had smelled something repugnant. I don't know what it is—I don't think I'm unattractive. But no man has tried to kiss me since."

Helen: "I don't know how many men I've slept with—I never kept track. They were all respectable men, the kind you meet in drawing rooms or at balls during the season. You have no idea what strange tastes some of them had . . ."

Beatrice: "Well, please don't tell us. I don't think I have any secrets. Does that make me boring?"

Diana: "I've had an abortion. And I would do it again, if I had to."

Catherine: "Some days, when I look in the mirror, I just wish I looked normal."

X. Our Plans for the Future

Helen is the only one of us who has ever been married. Arthur Meyrinck is her second husband. Her first husband committed suicide.

Men have a way of doing that around Helen. But Arthur is an artist. Nothing she does can shock him. If he comes down in the morning to find that the parlor has turned into Arcadia, with naked woman dancing to the sound of Pan pipes, he eats his breakfast in the kitchen. Most men are not so tolerant. Most men do not want a wife who is stronger than they are, like Justine, or who can bite through their necks, as I can, or who, like Beatrice, can kill them with a breath.

That, I suppose, is why we rather spoil Leda, sewing her dresses, letting her borrow whatever books she likes. Mrs. Poole makes her cakes and biscuits and tarts.

Justine has said, "Why don't we make a child of our own? We could make her out of corpses, or a large dog. Or," looking at Beatrice, "some sort of shrub? Maybe a rhododendron?"

I say, "Do you really think it would be a good idea to create another one of us? Aren't there enough of us in the world already?"

I know that Justine disagrees, that she thinks there's nothing much wrong with us, that the problem is with the world, which has no place for us in it. Except here, in this house. She has the confidence that comes from having once been loved.

Helen says, "Why just one? Why not start with three—plant, animal, corpse, and see which one works best? Then go on from there. We could make any number of daughters, if we wanted. What none of you, except Diana, realizes is that we're powerful. Not just because we're strong or deadly or have sharp teeth, but because of everything we've endured. We're our fathers' daughters in more ways than one. We could control this society we live in, rather than hiding from it."

Ever since we joined the club, Helen has tried to convince us to take over the world.

Helen: "*Plan A.* Beatrice creates a poison that we can introduce into the water supply. We make all of London sick. We offer to release the antidote, but only if the government pays us a certain sum of money. That's if we need money."

Mary: "We always need money."

Catherine: "Bea, could you actually do that?"

Beatrice: "It wouldn't be particularly difficult, scientifically. But I wouldn't want to harm anyone."

Helen: "That's why we'd have an antidote. *Plan B.* We kidnap Queen Victoria. She shouldn't be too difficult to extract from Balmoral. Justine snaps her neck and then reanimates her in a remote location, perhaps the cottage her father used to own on the coast of Scotland. The reanimation erases her memories, creating a blank slate for us to write on. Over the course of a month, we teach her to trust us, do what we tell her to. We return her to a grateful nation, saying that we found her wandering, suffering from amnesia. And then through her, we control the government."

Justine: "How do you expect me to reanimate her? And you know how well that worked for my father—the creature he created was uncontrollable, destructive."

Beatrice: "But wasn't he made from the corpse of a criminal? I've met the Queen—she's a kind and gracious woman. I'm sure her corpse would be much more amenable to suggestion."

Mary: "For goodness's sake, don't let Mrs. Poole hear you. She has a picture of the Queen hanging over her bed. Where do you think we could get another housekeeper?"

Diana: "We know you still have your father's notebooks. They're in the bottom drawer of your dresser, under your chemises."

Justine: "I can't believe you would go through my personal things!"

Catherine: "You are talking about *Diana* here. I'm sure she's gone through all of our drawers. She doesn't take your clothes because they're too big for her, but I'm constantly missing stockings . . ."

Helen: "*Plan C.* Catherine creates an army of beast people. We use them to terrorize London."

Mary: "How would that lead to world domination?"

Helen: "Honestly, I haven't thought that far ahead. I just think it would be fun. Imagine, we could make horse people and dog people and rat people . . ."

Diana: "Well, what does Cat think?"

Catherine: "I don't know. On one hand, it would be nice to have more of us. On the other, I don't think any of you understand my and Bea's and Justine's position. At least you were born rather than made. Do we really want to manufacture beings like ourselves? To create monsters, as our fathers did? Although making beast people does sound easier, scientifically, than concocting a poison and its antidote, or reanimating corpses. I mean, it's just sewing the parts together. Any of us could do it."

Justine: "But why? Would we make society any better?"

Helen: "We could, if we wanted to. We could put Mary in power. She's so orderly and logical. Imagine what sensible rules she would make. At least the trains would run on time."

Justine: "I suppose we could do it for the greater good. We could clean up the East End, especially those dreadful areas around Whitechapel. We could find homes for the children in orphanages, and employment for the women who flaunt their wares on the streets . . ."

Helen: "There, you see? I'm not saying we should spend all of our time planning to take over the world. I have other commitments myself. But I do think we should start giving it some serious consideration."

Diana: "Helen's only being practical. You know they're going to come after us eventually. They always do—scientists, other monsters, the police. So why not take control first?"

Helen: "Whether or not you agree with me now, there's going to come a day when all of you, except perhaps Mary, will want children. You'll want them to live safely in this world, and then you'll realize that it's time for us to seize power. You'll see."

Maybe she's right. I do sometimes think about how nice it would be to have a daughter of my own, not just cats.

———

XI. Why I Wrote This Sketch

Someday, I would like to write a book that isn't about Rick Chambers or Astarte. It would be the sort of book George Eliot could have written, about life in a country town and the people who live there, their jealousies, their ambitions, the minutiae of their lives. How they fall in love with the wrong people, or the right people at the wrong time, or lose the mercantile business on which their fortune is built. Or misplace wills. You know, *literature*.

But I've never experienced any of those things myself. All I know is monsters.

So I decided to write about us. Just a sketch, no heroic Englishman journeying into the heart of a dark continent, no idol with rubies for eyes. No Caverns of Doom. Just us, sitting and talking. A story that George Eliot could have written.

We are as ordinary, in our own way, as the inhabitants of a country town. In the morning we rise and make our beds, except Diana. We eat breakfast (toast and eggs for Mary, steamed turnips for Justine, raw chicken for me, and for Beatrice a cup of mossy water). Then Justine and Mary take up their work, while Beatrice helps Mrs. Poole, who has found mice in the pantry. (Poor Beatrice. How she hates exterminator duty. But it's an easier death for the mice than Alpha's claws.) I curl up in the rose chintz armchair and start my chapter. In the afternoon, Mary will go around to pay the bills, Diana will rise and go to the theater, Beatrice and Justine will play a game of chess, and I will help Mrs. Poole polish the silver.

We will worry about where the money's going to come from for a summer dress, how to make a cake with only one egg in it, who left the back door open, the plumbing, whether the cherries on the tree in the back garden will ripen this year, and growing old. I think George Eliot could have made something of us, don't you?

XII. An Application for Membership

Yesterday, I received a letter. "Dear Miss Moreau," it began.

> My friend Mrs. Jonathan Harker (née Mina Murray) suggested that I write to you. Until a month ago, I lived in an asylum in Wittenberg, caring for my mother, whose health and sanity had been destroyed by certain experiments in blood transfusion performed by my father, Professor Abraham Van Helsing, whose work may be familiar to you from a variety of scientific journals. My own health was affected while I was yet in the womb, for her pregnancy did not alter his research.
>
> I suffer from an acuteness of hearing, an antipathy to light and to strong scents, and persistent anemia, as well as other medical symptoms that I can describe to you in more detail if required. After my mother's death, I could not bring myself to live with my father, so I have been staying with friends or in boarding houses for the past month. I have no independent income, but I make a little money by giving singing and piano lessons. Mrs. Harker has described for me the club you have formed in London for the daughters of mad scientists, and I wonder if my parentage and experiences might qualify me to join you? I would certainly be grateful to have a good home and find companionship with others in my circumstance.
>
> Yours sincerely,
> Lucinda Van Helsing

Justine: "Yes, of course. Write to her immediately and tell her that she can come, poor dear."

Mary: "We can turn the library into her bedroom, and put the books in the clubroom. We may also have some room for shelves in the front hall. I'll start sewing her curtains to block out the light."

Diana: "It will be nice to have some music around here. It's so deadly quiet sometimes. I wonder if the piano is still in tune?"

Mrs. Poole: "I've heard terrible things about this Professor Van Helsing. He killed a girl by driving a stake through her heart!"

Beatrice: "But that's terrible! How can society allow such things?"

Helen: "You know what I think—the more of us the better. All right, any objections? We have to be unanimous, you know." We all shake our heads. "Well, write to her then. Leda and I have to go now. We have to prepare for a Walpurgisnacht party in the studio. Artists! You can't imagine the mess they make. A troop of satyrs is nothing to it. Mrs. Poole, have you seen our umbrellas? We're going by bus, and I think it's starting to rain."

I say, "I'll write to her tomorrow. It will be nice to have a new member of the club."

Then we sit by the fire, reading or sketching or embroidering, just us monsters.

DORA/DÓRA:
AN AUTOBIOGRAPHY

DÓRA MUSZBEK was born on September 30, 1968 in Budapest, Hungary. I know because I have her birth certificate. It's on thick beige paper, with designs and letters in green ink, and folds like a booklet. On the front it says "Születési Anyakönyvi Kivonat," above a ten-forint stamp. Inside, the green lines are filled with information in fountain pen. Her birthplace is listed as Budapest, her father as Dr. Muszbek, her mother under her maiden name although she is married and a doctor as well. Inside the booklet, on both sides, is an escutcheon in green ink: the Hungarian flag, with sheaves of wheat on either side, topped by a Soviet star.

What I know about her early years comes from black-and-white photographs. Here she is in a cotton romper and bonnet, looking at the camera and laughing. Here in an inflatable swimming ring, floating just off a wooden platform on Lake Balaton. Here she is walking down a street in Budapest, holding her father's hand, perhaps on her way to the swings in the park. That must have been before the divorce. Here she is in her grandparents' apartment, sitting on the sofa next to her mother, with one arm around her mother's neck and the other holding a stuffed bear. That must have been after, when her mother had moved back in with her parents.

Their apartment was on Múzeum utca, across the street from the Magyar Nemzeti Múzeum, the museum of Hungarian history. Her grandparents had moved there after the war, into a building that had once been the city palace of an aristocratic family but had long ago been divided into flats. The building was arranged around a central courtyard, where carriages had driven in and out. Their apartment was on the second floor, up a stone staircase. You opened the front door with an ancient key and walked down a hallway to the living room, one half of what had been a double parlor divided by a set of doors with panes of pebbled glass. The ceiling was eighteen feet high; the tall windows looked down onto the park that surrounded the museum. The other half of the parlor was her grandparents' bedroom. Dóra and her mother slept in the living room on beds that during the day became sofas. Both rooms were heated by ceramic stoves that had to be fed with coal kept in the building's cellars. Off the hall were a bathroom, a WC, and a small kitchen with a pantry where Dóra's grandmother stored preserved plums and cherries. The stove had to be lit with a match, a procedure that always scared Dóra a little. I have a photograph of her at Christmas, beside a tree on which real candles are burning. There is a bucket by the tree, just in case.

Those photographs are all I have left of her, except a few children's books with titles like *Kisgyermekek Nagy Mesekönyve* and the stuffed bear, named Dani. He is almost as old as I am, and has lost much of his fur.

After that, the photographs are in color, and no longer in Hungary. Here is one of her at the zoo in Brussels, with an elephant. Another of her eating ice cream in front of the Atomium. By that point, her mother had moved to Brussels, leaving on a visa that allowed her to visit for two weeks, with a suitcase, a small child, and the equivalent of twenty dollars in foreign currency. The visa expired, but by then she had found work as a doctor. I have been told that when he realized she was gone, her father searched for Dóra frantically, banging on her grandparents' apartment door, petitioning the Red Cross. But

I don't know. So much has been lost, to secrecy and the inevitable passage of time, to forgetfulness and lies.

In Brussels she learned to speak French and brush her teeth twice a day. She had not realized the importance of toothbrushing, but in school all the children were asked to form three lines: those who did not brush their teeth, those who brushed their teeth once a day, and those who brushed their teeth twice. Having gone to the middle line, she quickly realized her mistake: good Belgian children brush their teeth both in the morning and at night. Perhaps that is why, after all these years, I am so attentive to my teeth, going to the dentist twice a year, flossing before I go to sleep every night. When the dentist tells me how clean my teeth are, I feel a small moment of triumph at being in the right line.

It was in Brussels that Dóra first lost herself. I have a certificate of name change, Dóra Muszbek to Dora Méliès. Why Méliès, I once asked her mother. "I wanted to be French," she said. "There was no point in being Hungarian, not then." Years later she added, "The Embassy kept calling, telling me that I should go back, that I was a traitor to my country. But I did not want to go back. There was nothing for me there. So I changed our names and telephone number. At the time, I thought we were going to stay in Belgium." Sometimes conversations such as this one will go on for years, punctuated by long silences. By the time they resume, I will have forgotten what question her mother is answering.

Despite half a lifetime in the United States, her mother still speaks with a strong Hungarian accent. She still exhibits the tendency I have noticed, in Hungarian and Chinese speakers, to confuse gender—he for she and vice versa. Hungarian has no gender—male or female, you are ő. This has not resulted in any greater equality between the sexes.

So Dóra became Dora. She brushed her teeth twice a day, spoke French, and wore sweaters knitted by her mother in red or brown wool. From that time, I remember only three things: the toothbrushing line, the sweaters because they itched, and walking down the street in a blue-and-white checked dress that Dora's mother had sewn for her, an exact copy of the dress she was wearing. A policeman who passed them asked if they were sisters, smiling, flirting with her mother, whom Dora thought was the prettiest woman in the world.

And then, the lights of New York through a circular plane window. Her mother had received an offer to continue her medical research at the National Institutes of Health, and who could pass up an opportunity like that? Her daughter would be American.

In the United States of America, the 1970s meant Wonder Bread, bell-bottom jeans, and watching *Speed Racer* on Saturday morning television. Dora developed a crush on the mysterious Racer X. She had to repeat first grade, because her English was not yet fluent enough for second. Then she skipped second grade and went directly into third. She had a green girls' bike, a Ballerina Barbie, and a friend named Angela, one grade ahead of her, whose father kept *Playboy* magazines under his bed. She wore bell-bottom jeans and sweaters knitted by her mother, which she would stuff into her backpack as soon as she was out of sight because they itched, and anyway they were stupid. No one wore handmade clothes.

By that time, Dóra—no, Dora—had no idea who she was anymore. She would dream that she was trying to speak, but no one could understand her. Even she did not understand the language she was speaking.

They lived in a house with a yard in which there was a pine tree taller than the house itself. Throughout elementary school, Dora would climb the pine tree up to a place where three branches made a sort of floor. That was her nest. She would live there, the Dora-bird, the girl with wings. When she was a bird, she would speak bird language, which all the birds understood. Birds can fly anywhere. They can see anything. She would be able to as well. She never thought of flying back to Hungary, because it was lost forever behind a curtain of iron, like a country in a fairy tale. Once you left, you could never go back.

Every once in a while, she received letters from her grandmother in stilted, textbook English. She would have to write back. "Write back to your grandmother," her mother would say, "but remember that the Secret Police will read it."

What could she write? "Dear Nagymama: Today I was a bird. I have a crush on Racer X, who is secretly Speed Racer's brother. I have forgotten how to speak Hungarian."

In school, she committed two crimes that she would remember for the rest of her life. In first grade, she stole a sticker from another girl's locker, and in third grade she plagiarized a story for a writing assignment. Both times she was caught, and the humiliation of the experience, of being "talked to" by a teacher, made her particularly cautious not only to do no wrong, but to be perceived as doing no wrong. She reformed, and became both Student Council secretary and a patrol, with a badge on an orange plastic belt. At lunchtime, she and the other patrols would escort kindergarteners home after their half day. If a car had come careening down the road, threatening to run over one of her charges, she would have leaped in front of it, putting herself in danger, like Robin Hood in the Disney animated version, or Nancy Drew.

For she was Responsible. Every day, after school, she walked home and let herself in by the key that hung on a string around her neck. She got herself a snack and did homework until her mother came home. Sometimes her mother would tell her to come directly to the NIH, so she would walk up the broad avenue to the main research building and take the elevator up to her mother's laboratory. In those days, you could still play with the lab animals: rats and rabbits and mice, all bred specifically for experiments, soft and inquisitive and ticklish, smelling of their feed, and poop, and the wood shavings that lined their plastic bins. Sometimes she was allowed to give them more of the thick green pellets they fed on, or change their water. But most days she just waited, sitting at her mother's desk, turning around and around in the revolving chair. She came to recognize the distinctive smell of laboratories.

She made a friend named Amy, the best friend she'd ever had. Amy's parents were also divorced. After school, the two of them liked to go to the playground, sit on the swings, and talk about the books they were reading: mostly Anne McCaffrey's Pern series. Someday, a dragonrider would appear in the sky and touch down near the kickball field. He would take them to Pern, where they would become dragonriders as well. It seemed a more logical ambition than being a doctor or lawyer. But she lost Amy forever when her mother decided to repeat her residency so she could practice medicine in America. They moved to a school district in another state.

One day Dora, now in middle school in Virginia and exceptionally lonely, found a letter from her grandmother that had fallen behind a bookshelf. What was she looking for? I suspect the big book of Indian art that had explicit pictures in it. That and Judy Blume novels, passed around in school, carefully hidden in lockers and under desks, the important pages turned down at the corners, were her introductions to human sexuality, for the *Playboy* magazines had been less than instructive. The letter was in Hungarian of course, so she could not read it, having lost that part of herself entirely. But tucked into the envelope was a photograph—of her grandmother, with a tall girl in a school uniform standing behind her. On the back of the photograph was written "Nagymama és Dóra."

Dora knew at once what had happened. When her mother had taken her from Hungary, she had left Dóra behind. Not her twin—she had no twin, she knew that perfectly well. No, the part of herself that had been Dóra had somehow been left behind. While she was growing up in the United States, trying to persuade her mother to buy her designer jeans, Dóra was growing up in Hungary.

She did not ask her mother about Dóra. She had learned early on that when she asked her mother questions, her mother responded with answers that were only partly true. Dora could not always tell which part.

"Why did you divorce my father?"

"Because he expected me to iron his underwear."

"Why did we leave Hungary?"

"Because I wanted to give you the opportunities I never had."

"Why can't I wear earrings?"

"Because you will look like a gypsy."

"What does that word mean? The one you say when you're angry."

"It doesn't mean anything. Don't repeat it to anyone who speaks Hungarian."

She imagined asking her mother, "Why is Dóra still living in Hungary?"

Her mother would say, in her heavy accent, "Don't be ridiculous." She would roll her r's: r-r-ridiculous. So instead, Dora imagined what life would be like for Dóra, living with her grandparents in a Communist state. Growing up in the 1970s in America, here are the things she knew about Communism:

1. Communists were not allowed to practice their religion. Dóra had been baptized in a Catholic church. Did she ever sneak into a church service? Did she, secretly, surreptitiously, take communion? In moments of stress and confusion, did she, like Dora, say a Hail Mary—although her mother had told her, in no uncertain terms, that religion was the opiate of the masses?

2. Communists owned no property. Her grandparents' apartment, where Dóra presumably lived, was owned by the state. Dóra would sleep in the living room, on one of the beds that were sofas during the day. In the morning, she would be woken by the light that came through the tall windows facing the park and a cacophony of song from the birds in the linden trees. Then she would have

breakfast in the tiny kitchen.

3. What would she eat? Communists were poor and had to wait in long lines. Her grandmother would wait in line for food, first for bread at the baker's, then for vegetables at the market, then sausages . . . For breakfast, Dóra would have bread and butter, a tomato with salt, and slices of ham. Then she would go into the ancient bathroom and put on her school uniform.

4. Communists wore red kerchiefs and addressed each other as Comrade. Dóra would tie a red kerchief around her neck and go to school, where she would be called Comrade Muszbek. Did she ever see her father? Perhaps on holidays. Once, when Dora had asked about him, her mother had said, "He has remarried. His second wife is a schoolteacher. He has two other daughters now." So he would not have much time for his first daughter. Anyway, he had become a professor at the University of Debrecen, in the medical school. Would Dóra sometimes go there during the holidays, to spend time with her sisters? Did she even think of them as her sisters?

5. Subversive literature was banned. But knowing Dóra, she probably wrote subversive literature. After all, Dora wrote, so Dóra probably wrote as well—subversive poetry. It was subversive because it did not glorify the state. Rather, it was about a young girl's search for herself, her thoughts on life, the world . . . She kept it in a notebook under the mattress of her bed, which was also a sofa. If her grandmother had ever found it, she had never said so.

6. She also read banned literature. Her copy of *1984* was hidden inside the dust jacket of an edition of Grimm's fairy tales that had been destroyed when she dropped it into the bathtub.

7. Like all Communists, Dóra would do anything for a pair of American jeans.

Dora wished she could send Dóra a pair of her own American jeans, not bell-bottoms now but straight, and so tight at the waist that she had to lie back on her bed to zip them—or just talk to her. But if she sent a letter, the Secret Police would see it, and what then? Perhaps the Secret Police would send agents for Dóra, and even for Dora sitting comfortably watching television in her American living room. They would both be put in a prison, perhaps in the same cell. Dora wondered what sort of conversations they would have.

Dóra would tell her about school, which her mother had assured her was much more difficult than an American school, and about writing poetry, like an ancestor who had been a famous Hungarian poet. She would talk about going to Lake Balaton for vacations, about swimming in the muddy water among the reeds, sleeping in the house her grandfather had built after the war, watching her grandmother paint the shifting light on the lake from her upstairs studio. She would talk about eating fried fogas, a fish that lived only in the lake.

"And what is it like when you meet our father for ice cream in Budapest?" Dora would ask. "Do you like our sisters? Do you wish you had American jeans? Or your own bedroom? Are you popular in school?"

Dora would tell her about being in the Gifted and Talented Program, and definitely not popular. About reading novels and trying to write them, and never being satisfied with what she had written. "For vacation we go to Ocean City, on the Atlantic Ocean, and eat crabs in a restaurant where you have to break the shells and take out the meat yourself," she would say. Dóra would want to know whether she listened to Michael Jackson, what Americans thought of Hungarians ("They mostly don't," Dora would have to admit), what it was like to grow up with a mother.

Would they be executed? If so, they could stand in front of the firing squad together, holding hands.

By the time Dora went to high school, her mother was no longer at the National Institutes of Health. Now she was in private practice as a physician. When Dora said she felt sick, her mother would say, "You're not sick. Get up and go to school." Except the one time she had appendicitis and her mother drove her to the hospital for an appendectomy. Ever after, she knew there were two responses to feeling sick: either you were on your way to the emergency room, or you were not sick and it was time to get up.

In high school, Dora was on the Honors track, which was essentially the same as the Gifted and Talented Program—fifteen students who spent the entire day, except homeroom and gym, going from class to class together. She tried to wear what the popular girls were wearing, the ones who were on the cheerleading squad and made homecoming court, but her mother did not think clothes were important. What you had in your head was important: it was the only thing you could take with you when the Russians invaded. Did Dora think it couldn't happen here? Then Dora was naïve.

Perhaps that is why I have always assumed that everything can be destroyed in a moment. Perhaps that is why my basic attitude toward life has always been fear.

Dora rebelled by painting her room cherry blossom pink and hanging lace curtains over her bed. She read Barbara Cartland and Willa Cather and *ElfQuest*. She dated high school boys, and even one college freshman, partly to feel wanted, partly to feel that something in her life could be other than ordinary. It took years for her to realize that boys were actually quite ordinary—not that different from other human beings. At the time, they seemed to her like a fascinating alien species. She was always in love, sometimes with one of the boys, but more usually a film or literary character. Her most serious crushes were Sherlock Holmes, the Scarlet Pimpernel, and the Disney animated fox Robin Hood. She tried to smoke clove cigarettes, but never quite learned to inhale. She drank peach wine coolers that her friend Susan stole from her parents' basement refrigerator. One day, she pierced her own ears with ice and a safety pin. Once they healed, she wore silver hoops. When she shook her head, she could feel them swinging against her cheeks. This was her Rebellious phase.

Meanwhile, in Budapest, Dóra was writing poetry. She wrote it in secret, and when it was published, it was in an underground literary journal, mimeographed and handed around the secondary school. She had fallen in love with a teacher at her school who had once been a poet, but who had been labeled subversive and sent to a prison camp. After such restrictions eased, he was released and assigned a job as a teacher of literature. In his teaching, he was always careful to be correct. He taught Hungarian translations of *The Grapes of Wrath* and *The Jungle*, denouncing the evils of capitalism. But it was he who had started the school's underground literary journal. Sometimes when he read Dóra's poetry, he told her that she was a genius. He wore a sweater with a hole in the elbow and smoked Sobranie cigarettes, which she could smell in her hair. They met in his apartment, a single room in a building on Rákóczi út, to talk about poetry and make love, or what Dóra assumed was love. It was very much how the popular novels described—filled with endearments and recriminations. "You are so beautiful, little bird," he would tell her. "Someday, you will fly away and leave me forever." Then he would become moody and pace around the apartment, as though he were still in prison.

Sometimes, walking home from his apartment, she would stop for ice cream, csokoládé és citrom, and feel guilty that she was enjoying walking along Üllői út licking ice cream as much as she had enjoyed being with him.

Her grandmother still made all her dresses, except her school uniform, following patterns that had been popular in the 1960s. Only the wealthiest girls in school had clothes from Austria or Italy. She still slept in the living room of the apartment on Múzeum utca and did not imagine that would change, unless someday she got married and her husband requested an apartment. But she did not know if she would ever marry—look at her stepmother, who complained about being the wife of a university professor in a provincial city like Debrecen. Women had to put up with a great deal, in marriage. No, she was going to university, to study literature. Her grandfather did not want her to go—his daughter, Dóra's mother, had gone, and look at what had happened! She had left her husband, her daughter for them to take care of . . . and for what? So she could boast about her big house in America? Who was going to take care of them in their old age? But her grandmother said that nowadays girls must become educated. And as a professor, Dóra could travel to international conferences. Her father did that all the time, spending more time out of the country than in it. Perhaps someday, she could go to America and meet her mother.

She was not surprised that her mother wrote so rarely. After all, she had Dora, her American child. And her father had his two younger daughters. She was the one who had been abandoned, who had been left in Budapest with her grandparents. Of course, once she was a famous poet, they would realize that they should never have forgotten about her. That's who she was: the forgotten one. She wrote a poem with that title, and it won first prize in the school poetry competition. The prize was a medal, which her grandmother hung in the glass cabinet where she kept her most precious possessions, including the miniature of an ancestress who had been a noblewoman and hosted Napoleon at her country house. In America, Dora entered an essay contest. She submitted an essay about leaving Hungary and coming to America, about losing herself. When she won and the essay was reprinted in the local paper, her mother told her that she had put them both in danger: the Secret Police might read it, find them, and take them back to Hungary. There were things her mother told her that Dora no longer believed: that wearing makeup made you look like a prostitute, that politicians were always corrupt, that American children were spoiled and ungrateful. She seriously doubted that the Secret Police read the *Loudoun County Gazette*.

Dóra's examination scores were good enough to get her into Eötvös Loránd University. She would still be living with her grandparents, but now she would be a university student. In high school, she had studied English, German, French, and of course Russian. I have noticed that in Hungary, although everyone over a certain age took compulsory Russian in high school, no one admits to speaking Russian. Everyone says, "Oh, of course I took Russian—it was compulsory. But I don't remember any of it." It's a sort of linguistic amnesia. Dora had studied French and Latin so she could do well on the SAT. When she opened her acceptance letter from the University of Virginia, she was both delighted and relieved. Yes, that was where she would go. For one thing, it was in-state and she would not have to take out loans. For another, she had been to visit, and fallen in love with its red brick, white columns, and green lawns. It was one of the oldest universities in the country—the oldest part of the university had been designed by Thomas Jefferson himself. She had only recently become a naturalized citizen. Maybe going to UVA would make her feel American, as though she belonged. And it had a good English department. She could study literature, maybe even go on to get her PhD.

At the university, Dóra studied Faulkner, Proust, and Hesse in the original languages. She read Chekhov, remembering Russian for the sole purpose of studying literature. ("I can't speak conversational Russian, of course," she would say. "I've forgotten it all.") Every morning, she would wake up, make herself breakfast—muesli and yogurt because she had become a vegetarian, which her grandmother insisted would cause her to die of starvation. She would get dressed, walk down the stone stairs of the apartment building, and cross Kálvin tér. Then it was only a few blocks to the main university building. She would take classes, meet with her professors. For lunch she would go out with her friends or eat brown bread, curls of smoked cheese, and slices of tomato in the park, under the linden trees. She no longer saw the literature teacher. She assumed he had taken on another student, female of course, as his acolyte.

Six years of university, and she would have a Master's degree. Then she would teach or go on to get her PhD. The laws were so much more permissive now that she might even be able to teach elsewhere, in Austria perhaps, where you could make more money. Her father had been permitted to form a private consulting company, and her sisters Judit and Eszter were going to Vienna regularly to buy clothes. Dóra could not afford such luxuries, but went to the secondhand stores that students frequented on Rákóczi út. There she could find jeans and sweaters, and if they were a bit torn, that only made them more fashionable. She wore bright red lipstick and Chanel No. 5, from a bottle her father had given her after a conference in Paris. They were her trademark, you could say. She had cut her hair short and looked a little, she thought, like Claudette Colbert.

Dora wore pearls to class. She had a set of pearls that her mother had given her on her eighteenth birthday. They were supposed to be for special occasions, but the other girls wore pearls to class, so she did as well, with ripped jeans, a twinset, and ballet flats. She wore pink lip gloss, and Charlie on her neck and the insides of her wrists. Every morning she would put her hair in hot rollers so it fell in curls down her back, then hairspray it so it would stay curled. She took classes on the history of English literature, from Chaucer to Joyce, and one on magical realism in which the professor introduced the students to Allende and Márquez. After class, she would go back to the French House, where she had a room so small there was space only for a bed, a desk, a wardrobe, and a square patch of carpet on which she could turn around and get dressed. She would eat with the other students in the communal dining room (French was compulsory), then go to a meeting of the literary and debating society she had joined. She still wanted to study literature, and maybe someday be a writer, although she scarcely understood what that meant. But it had been decided, mostly by her mother, that after college she should go to law school.

Her mother had taught her three things:

1. Life is hard.
2. People are out to get you.
3. Literature and art are fine as hobbies, but you need a *real* profession. Like law.

In the summer of 1990, Dora sat on the floor of her boyfriend's apartment, in front of the television, watching German teenagers break off and carry away pieces of the Berlin Wall. They had met a few months ago, through a mutual friend. On their first date, he had taken her to his parents' house in the hills above Charlottesville— horse country. The house was old, surrounded by a hundred acres of pasture merging into forest. They walked out to the barn, saddled the horses, rode along a forest path. It had been years since her brief experience with riding lessons—nothing, like riding or violin or ballet, had lasted long. Her mother would move, or money would run out. Writing was the only thing she had been able to keep up, all that time. Would she have married him if he had taken her to the movies rather than to such an obvious symbol of the stability and wealth she had never experienced in her life? One of his ancestors had fought with Washington at Valley Forge. Three years later, when she walked down the aisle of the Episcopal church in her white silk Laura Ashley wedding dress, she wondered if now, finally, she was becoming a real American.

Dóra watched the wall coming down on her boyfriend's television as well. He was an East German studying in Hungary, and eventually, although he did not know it then, he would have a German passport and travel freely throughout the EU as a financier. Dóra would see his name long after in a newspaper article covering his indictment for fraud, but she would have lost touch with him by then. She had decided that she would never marry, after seeing her best friend Ildikó finish her graduate degree, marry a dentist, immediately get pregnant, and take a government job that offered two years of maternity leave. Now when Dóra visited her suburban house, all she did was complain about her swollen ankles. Her other best friend Anna was going to be an actress, and they had decided together over the Tokaji served at Ildikó's wedding that they would never get married, never put husbands ahead of their ambitions or careers.

Her first year at Harvard Law School, during the misery of a long-distance relationship and the realization that she hated law the way she hated calculus, although calculus had a moral purity that the study of law lacked, Dora received a letter:

Dear Dora:

I hope you will excuse my English, which is probably quite awkward. I have not studied it formally since high school, or what we call gymnasium. Our grandmother received a letter with your address in it, so I thought I would write and say hello. Hello! Do you know about me? Has our mother told you? Perhaps you have seen photographs.

I have seen photographs of you, and I think we look very much alike, except for the hair. Mine is much shorter, and I think yours is lighter? Perhaps you have lightened it. Mine is very practical, for with university classes I do not have much time to take care of my appearance. I think yours is more pretty!

When I learned that you were at Harvard, I was most impressed! I am at Eötvös Loránd University, which I think is the best university in Hungary, perhaps like Harvard in the USA. I am studying comparative literature. When I finish my degree, I hope to become a teacher, but really I would like to write. I have had some of my poetry published already. I would send you some, but I think you do not speak Hungarian.

I hope that you will write back to me, and also that perhaps someday we may meet, now that the political situation has changed.

Puszi (that means I kiss you),

Dóra

It took Dora three days to write back.

Dear Dóra,

It's good to hear from you. Strange, but good. Harvard is a lot less impressive than you would think. To be honest, I kind of hate law school. What I really want to do is be a writer. Coincidence, hunh? I'm writing a fantasy novel—it's like *The Chronicles of Narnia*, but from the White Witch's point of view. It's in my desk—sometimes I work on it when I'm supposed to be studying.

I have a boyfriend—his name is Jefferson (no joke, it's one of those Southern names, his father and grandfather both have the same name so he's actually "the Third") but I call him Jeff. We're engaged, but he's down in Virginia, in medical school.

Yes, I know about you—not much, though. Tell me about yourself. Do you like school? What do you do in your spare time? What is our grandmother like?

Do you know Mom changed my name? You wrote Muszbek on the envelope, but it's been Méliès for a long time now. No one knows how to pronounce it, and in middle school some of the kids called me Smelly. And then in high school it was "Hey, Malaise!" Sometimes people think it's Mexican and start talking to me in Spanish.

I have to go study for my crim exam—my professor is a famous criminal defense lawyer. He's always on talk shows. Yesterday, he told us that if we ever found evidence implicating our clients, we should hide it. Which is, um, illegal? Anyway, sorry if I sound really spacey. I just don't feel like I belong here, you know? Write again, and I hope to meet you some day.

Love,
Dora

p.s. Tell me about Dad?

Every couple of months, Dora would get a letter on thin blue airmail paper. Every couple of months, Dóra would receive the same. Dora would sit at her desk in the Cambridge apartment she shared with a roommate, and then in her apartment in Brooklyn, New York, with a cat on her lap. Dóra would sit at the kitchen table in the Budapest apartment, and then on the sofa in her own tiny apartment in the same building. And they would read . . .

I am very sorry to tell you that our grandfather is going to a home for old people. He has Alzheimer's disease (I hope that is the right word) and cannot remember whether he lit the stove or where his shoes are. Our grandmother is afraid he will hurt himself. I am very sad to see him go. I remember when I was little, and I walked holding his finger. Sometimes he does not remember who I am.

We've planned the wedding for the summer after I graduate. I'll take the bar exam in July, and then we'll get married in August, which is a little crazy. But Jeff got a residency in New York, so I've taken a job at one of the big firms there. It's not what I want to do, but I'm $80,000 in debt (!!!) so I have to figure out a way to pay it off. Mom said she would help me, but instead she bought another house.

I had a wonderful visit to Prague with my boyfriend. I mean my new boyfriend, Attila—I met him after Dietrich, who decided to move back to Germany. Attila is a filmmaker and also a photographer. He took a photograph of me that I like very much. I am hoping that if I can have this poetry book published, I can use the photograph on the back cover. It is very difficult to publish anything in Hungary nowadays because of the economic situation.

It's not very good, but here's the story I mentioned: "Swan Girls." I've given up on the novel—I don't have much time to write anymore, and anyway, I don't think I'm ready to write one. So I'm going to focus on finishing short stories and sending them out to magazines. Meanwhile, I've started taking the Kaplan course for the bar exam. Kill me now.

I spent a week in Balaton with our grandmother. I do not know if you remember the house our grandfather built. I hope someday you can come see it. It's not very luxurious, for there is no heating or hot water.

But there is a large plum tree in the garden. We made a great deal of lekvár (plum jam). I am enclosing a little embroidery that our grandmother asked me to send you. She is very sorry that she cannot write to you herself, but nowadays she has a pain in her hands—rheumatism, I think you say?

Here are some pictures of the wedding. I wish you could have been there—you could have been my bridesmaid, instead of Jeff's sister! In the end, Mom didn't show up. She even called Jeff's dad, the cardiologist, to tell him that he should call it off—as though he could have. Basically, she doesn't like Jeff, she doesn't like the fact that we got married at his parents' house (as though we could have afforded anything else), she *hates* the fact that I took his name and refuses to call me by it. At this point, you probably have a better relationship with her than I do, despite the fact that you're on the other side of the Atlantic.

I am sad to write that our father's mother has died. She was a very sweet woman who lived in a village near Debrecen. I did not know her well, because I was only able to visit a few times, but she always sent me Christmas gifts she made herself. Last year she knitted me a hat that I like very much, with a pattern of roses. I remember she had a garden full of beautiful roses, red and pink and yellow. I do not think our grandfather will last much longer. It is so hard losing the old people. They have seen so many things, and when my life is difficult, I remember how much more difficult it was for them, living through the war.

The truth is, New York scares me. I'm working on the forty-second floor of a skyscraper in Manhattan, and all I can think about is what would happen if I fell out the window. One day the window cleaner came and actually *opened the window and leaned out and cleaned it*. He had on a harness, but I was watching him through the doorway and I swear I had to go to the bathroom and throw up. All I want to do is leave here, as soon as Jeff finishes his residency.

Here it is, my poetry book! I am so sorry that you cannot read it in Hungarian, but I have translated one of the poems for you. Of course a translation can never be as good as in the original language, but I hope you will think it is not too rotten. I do like the cover, and I think the photo Attila took of me is very good. It has even been nominated for a small poetry prize for emerging European writers!

I'm really lonely. Jeff has to be at the hospital all the time, and when he's not working he's sleeping. So when I'm not working it's just me and Cordelia. This is Cordelia! (In the picture—she's such a fluff-ball!) I found her wandering around the apartment house parking lot, mewing at me and running away whenever I got close to her. I watched her for a few days, then caught her in a Havahart trap baited with tuna. For a couple of days she hid under the bed, but then she started letting me pet her. Right now, she likes to knead my lap and chew on my finger, both of which *hurt*. Meanwhile, I'm trying to re-pay my law school loans as fast as I can—we're basically living on Jeff's salary so I can pay them off. I have a plan, but I don't want to say anything about it yet, because I'm not sure it will work. If it does, I'll have time to write, and I'll be doing something I've wanted to do for a long time . . .

I met our mother. It was a strange meeting, as you told me it would be. I am sorry you have not spoken to her in some time. She told me how disappointed she was that you are leaving the law and going back to graduate school. I tried to explain how much you dislike being a lawyer, how tired you are, working late every night. But she said I was a typical Hungarian. She thinks socialism has ruined Hungary, that we are all lazy, only wanting to be comfortable. She says that in the family, she is the only entrepreneur. I know she makes a lot of money, but is she truly happy? She does not sound like a happy woman. She and our grandmother quarreled a great deal, so I often went to my own apartment, or to see Attila. I do not know why they quarrel so much, but it is all about the family, about how our grandfather is being taken care of at the nursing home, and some of his cousins I have not seen in many years because our grandmother does not like them and tore up their pictures.

So first of all, today a billionaire threw a pen at me! He's a client of the firm, and I was at his company's office doing the legal work for a complete reorganization of its subsidiaries. He needed to sign something, so he borrowed my pen, and then he didn't want to walk all the way back to me, so he threw it. At least the cap was on—it hit me right in the chest. He's a Swedish media mogul, with blond hair combed over his balding head, and he can only be in the US a certain number of days a year for tax reasons. I'm pretty sure I'm going to use this in a story someday . . . In the meantime, here's a copy of the magazine! They sent me two. Ignore the babe in chain mail on the cover. I think my story's actually pretty intellectual, definitely not genre fantasy. It's on p. 12, "Tale of the Rose." My first professional sale!

Attila wants me to live with him—he has a large apartment in Buda and is doing very well for himself. My friend Anna says he would make a good husband—he is handsome, hardworking, very talented at his photography. Yesterday we went to my favorite restaurant, the Építész-pince Étterem, at the Architectural Institute behind Múzeum utca. I had hortobágyi palacsinta, which is very filling, but I am a little thin just now because I have been working so hard. He talked to me about the future, about how he would like to build his business. He said someday we should be married and have children, a boy and a girl. Or two boys, but at least one boy for him. Anna says I am foolish not to move in with him, that life as a single woman is very hard. But I want to stay in my little apartment and write poetry. Is that foolish, do you think?

I'm glad I met him while he was here, although it was pretty awkward—I didn't know what to call him. I couldn't just say "Dad" after all these years. He didn't have much time because he was one of the keynote speakers at the conference, but I took the subway up to Columbia and we found a cafeteria where we could sit and talk. You're right, he does look sort of like one of those old film stars. I still don't understand what happened between him and Mom, and I probably never will. He showed me pictures of Judit and Eszter. They both look just like him, very blonde and blue-eyed. I suppose I take after Mom. He said he hoped someday I would be able to meet them. He also said he was proud of you—he called you "very clever, and really a good writer." I thought you would like to know that! Sometimes I wonder . . . but it's not really worth thinking about how life would have been different if I'd been someone else. I'm not, that's all.

I am very, very sorry to tell you that our grandfather has died. Here is a little sketch that our grandmother did for you, so you can remember him. It is of him as a young man, when she first knew him. It makes me very sad to look at . . .

We're leaving New York on Sunday! We gave away almost everything we've accumulated here—anyway, most of it was from thrift shops, because it's not as though we can afford real furniture. We're only taking as much as we can pack in the car—books, clothes, and Cordelia, who's probably going to drive us crazy, mewing the entire way to Boston. It's hard to believe we've been here three years. Everyone at the law firm stared at me incredulously when I told them I was leaving to go back to grad school. I didn't even mention that my loans are COMPLETELY paid off. I'm really glad Jeff got that fellowship at Mass General. It will be nice being back in Boston, or at least better than New York.

I have been offered a position as a teacher at the university—I am what you might call a "lecturer." I thought of finding a position abroad as Attila wants, but if I leave Hungary, who will take care of our grandmother? She is getting old now, and it is difficult for her to carry groceries up the stairs. I am grateful that our mother is sending money, but grandmother needs someone to live here, to make sure she is taken care of. I go almost every night to have dinner with her, so she will not be alone. Dora, I feel as though there is something missing from my life. Is it a husband? A child? Another book? I look at the future and I cannot see it as any different from now, living in this little apartment, teaching classes at the university, having dinner with grandmother, quarreling with Attila. Perhaps I am one of those people who will never accomplish anything?

I'll be in Hungary for a whole month. It's not as though I have any money, but I'm going to use part of my student loans for the year (loans again! I'll never get out from under them). I'll fly to Frankfurt, and from there to Budapest. Can you tell me how to get from the airport to the apartment? Honestly, I'm a little scared. But if I don't do it now, I don't know when I'll be able to. After this summer, I have to start writing my dissertation, and Jeff and I have been talking about having a baby . . . Anyway, my life seems to consist of doing things that scare me—I don't know, maybe that's very American, or maybe it's just me. SO, SEE YOU IN JUNE!

I wondered what would happen when Dora and Dóra met for the first time. Would it be like a science fiction movie? Would they merge into one another, or create some sort of space-time anomaly, or combust? I was apprehensive.

But no. They just went out for ice cream.

Dora's Lufthansa flight landed at Budapest Ferihegy International Airport, which was so small that passengers walked from the landing strip to the terminal. She went through customs, showing her American passport almost with a sense of shame, and announced the reason for her visit: tourist. Then, as Dóra had told her, she took the airport shuttle into the city, to Kálvin tér. She pulled her wheeled suitcase over the cobbled intersection to Múzeum utca, found the apartment building, and rang the bell for her grandmother's apartment. When she heard the front door buzz, she pushed it open: it was a small door cut into the larger one that had once opened to admit carriages into the building's central courtyard.

Budapest was changing. On the streets, in the late 90s, you could see Mercedes and Peugeots, but still some Trabants, looking like toy cars next to the French and German models. Slowly, building by building, the soot of the Communist era was disappearing, although some of it remains even now, a reminder of the past. Buildings were being repainted in the distinctive colors of Budapest: lemon yellow, pale rose, pistachio, burnt umber. The old Hungarian flag, with the crown of Szent István at its center, was flying again. There were beggars on the streets, and rich Russians and Germans going to the casinos that had sprung up and would be gone by the end of the decade. The buildings on Kálvin tér were being either restored or replaced by modern contraptions of steel and glass. Soon, next to the bakery and antiques store selling Zsolnay and Herend, there would be an international hotel. Soon, not too soon but in the foreseeable future, Hungary would join the European Union. There would be a California Coffee Company on the corner of Múzeum utca, selling Italian coffee, a Hungarian interpretation of American sandwiches, and sour cherry brownies. But that was in the future for Dora and Dóra. That is in the future you and I know.

"Hello!" Dóra called out, standing by the apartment door, as Dora made her way up the stairs. "Do you need help with your luggage?"

"No, I'm fine, thanks."

"Did you have a good flight?"

"Yes, but I think Frankfurt airport is the most confusing place in the world." Their voices echoed off the stone walls.

Dora reached the second-floor landing. This is when I might have expected a combustion, a space-time vortex, or something equally spectacular. Instead, there was the awkward dance of an American who goes in for a hug and a Hungarian who tries to kiss you on both cheeks—like two people waltzing who are both trying to lead.

Dóra helped Dora with her suitcase. For the first time since she was a child, Dora walked down the hallway of her grandmother's apartment. It had not changed. The ceilings were still high, although not as impossibly high as they had once been. The walls were still painted a pale yellow, faded now. They were still covered with her grandmother's paintings of flowers, boats on Lake Balaton, a few friends. The tall windows still opened onto the park around the museum.

"Ah, Dóra! Nagyon szép vagy!" Her grandmother was several inches shorter than her, with white hair in a sensible cut, wearing a housecoat. What would it have been like growing up here, in an apartment with furniture that had no doubt been bought cheaply in the 1950s and was beginning to fall apart, and doilies crocheted by her grandmother on every surface, and the clear light of Budapest coming through the windows? What would it have been like growing up with a woman who called her nagyon szép, very pretty? Well, she had only to ask Dóra.

"Would you like something to eat? Nagyi is making dinner, but perhaps I can give you a little something beforehand. Do you like pogácsa?" Dora nodded. For parties, her mother had made the small biscuits, spreading butter on the dough, folding it over, letting it rise, rolling it and spreading butter and folding again. Dóra put several on a small plate.

She looked curiously at her American self, the one who had gone away and grown up across the ocean. Dora was the same height, but a little heavier than she was, almost chubby. Her hair was longer, lighter in color. In a letter, she had mentioned getting "highlights." She wore makeup, but it was less visible, unless you knew how to look for it: the colors more natural, the application subtler. Her clothes were newer, more fashionable, and her suitcase was heavy. What did she have in there? (A curling iron, among other things.) Also she seemed more confident than Dóra, as though she wore invisible armor that she never took off.

They sat in the living room, which had once been Dóra's bedroom as well. Their grandmother had gone into the kitchen to finish cooking dinner, but she had left old family photographs. Dóra explained who they were, the men in wool suits, the women in silk dresses trimmed with lace, the babies of either gender in christening gowns of white lawn. "Your grandfather's father was a schoolteacher. And here is his wife, your great-grandmother, holding your grandfather." How strange that this toddler, looking distinctly feminine in an embroidered cap, would grow up to become an engineer, and live through the Second World War, and finally forget the life he had known, dying in a home for old men, most of them veterans. Dora felt time pressing down on her, time and tragedy, the way she never did in America, where even the air seemed new. Time and tragedy were, she would discover, as much a part of Budapest as the sunlight and the ice cream vendors. "And there is the home that our grandmother grew up in. It was a farm, a very large farm, owned by the church, and her father was the . . . manager, you say? Or supervisor? It was a hereditary position, but he had no son, and anyway the Communists took it. Now it is a museum. Our grandmother went to art school in Szeged, and that is where she met our grandfather."

Dóra wanted to talk about more than the past, more than black-and-white photographs. But now was not the time, and anyway dinner was ready. They ate at the kitchen table: a pörkölt with noodles and cucumber salad. Dora realized that all the dishes her mother had made, her signature dishes at dinner parties, had been only an imitation of Hungarian food, like a ghost. This was the real thing, with the right ingredients: beef from the local butcher, paprika grown in Szeged or Kalocsa. It was like the Hungarian language, both familiar and utterly alien. She felt a sense of dislocation that had nothing to do with the food or jet lag. When she had last tasted these flavors, she had been a child.

"Nagyi, that is what I call her, like grandma, it is an affectionate term. She says that she missed very much seeing you grow up. She says you are very tall and pretty, like me. These plums came from our house in Lake Balaton. Perhaps you would like to go down there? During the summer we go down almost every weekend to pick the plums. There is a train that takes us to Szántód, that is where the house is located. She says she will do a painting of you. After dinner, she wants to show you all her paintings, but perhaps you would like to go for a walk and see Budapest? We could get ice cream."

Dora nodded and smiled at the little old woman who was nodding and smiling at her, talking in rapid Hungarian. She was sure Dóra was not translating, could not translate, it all—and it was coming back to her, just a little. No, Dóra was saying, I will not tell her again how sorry you are that you do not speak English. She knows. She already knows. Dóra felt the strange irritation of being in two worlds, translating between her grandmother and her American self. Why could Dora not have learned Hungarian? Then they could all speak comfortably, but here she was, trying to think in two languages at once. She saw something in Dora, an unconscious arrogance in how she carried herself, that she both disliked and envied. Dora ate the pörkölt and noodles— called nokedli—and cucumber salad as though she would never taste them again, as though that particular complexity, the hot sweetness of paprika, the coolness of cucumber in vinegar and sour cream, would once again be lost to her. Was she really here? She swallowed the last bite of pörkölt and wished she could lick her plate clean.

After dinner, Dóra washed the dishes and Dora dried. Then Dora put on a jacket, for it was growing chilly—the evenings are often chilly even in summer, said Dóra. Be careful, be careful, said their grandmother behind them, as though they were still children. Together they walked down to Kálvin tér, then turned left onto Vámház körút, a large commercial street that led toward the river. "I'll take you to Váci utca," said Dóra. "There are many places on Váci utca to eat ice cream." They passed a pharmacy, clothing stores, restaurants with signs that said "Traditional Hungarian Dinner 2500 Ft." And there was the Nagy Vásárcsarnok, the Central Market Hall that had been built a hundred years before, where the tourist buses stopped and their grandmother liked to buy vegetables, doing her marketing each day with a string bag.

Across the street was Váci utca, and yes, right there in the square was an ice cream vendor.

If you want to know what Hungarian ice cream tastes like, from any ordinary street vendor in Budapest, go to the best Italian gelato shop you can find in New York City. That's what it tastes like, except some of the flavors are distinctly Hungarian, such as somlói galuska, which is the ice cream version of a Hungarian dessert that involves sponge cake, raisins, and walnuts soaked in a chocolate rum sauce.

Dóra asked for scoops of chocolate and citron, Dora asked for scoops of hazelnut and raspberry. Dora insisted on paying. "Would you like to walk down Váci utca?" asked Dóra.

But across the square . . .

"Is that—" said Dora.

"Yes, that is the Duna," said Dóra.

There it was, the river over which so many armies have fought, down which so many ships have sailed: the Danube. They walked to the embankment and stood looking over the railing at the stone steps that went down into the water. It was as green as jade. Dora vaguely remembered a Hungarian swinging song in which someone was thrown into a river. "Hinta palinta," it started, but she could not remember the rest. She felt like crying. Instead, she bit into her ice cream cone.

Dóra looked down at the river she had seen so many times, crossed so many times in her life. Attila's apartment was on the other side. Usually, she took the trolley over. For the first time, she saw it as something immensely old, immensely powerful, and she wondered if she would ever get away from it. Perhaps she ought to marry Attila and move to Germany? Or even France? But then what about Nagyi? For a moment, she hated Dora, who would stay for a month in a city she obviously thought was magical, eating magical food, going to all the museums, trying her best to speak the language, laughing when she could not wrap her tongue around it. And then she would fly away on an airplane, waving a passport with an American flag on the cover.

That was another kind of magic. Dora thought she had never had such good ice cream in her life. She was beginning to feel better: perhaps it was the air? It seemed so light, not like the heavy air of Boston. She finished the bottom of her cone, into which she had pushed the last of the raspberry with her tongue.

There we stood, the one or two or three of us: Dora, Dóra, and Dora/Dóra, separately and together, looking down into the jade-green water of the Danube as it flows through Budapest.

There were things neither Dora nor Dóra knew, but I will tell you. Dora did not know that she would have a child, a red-haired girl named Cordelia with eyes blue and green and gray as the Atlantic, who would never wonder whether she was truly American. She did not know that she would get divorced or become a professor at a university, although it would take her longer than she wanted or had planned. Dóra did not know that Attila was already having an affair with a model, and that he would move to France without her. Before she was entirely over that betrayal, she would meet an Englishman who was teaching at the International School. With him she would move to England, and it would all be easier than she imagined because Hungary had joined the EU, and also because Nagyi had died at the respectable age of ninety-six. The apartment was left empty, with paintings curling on the walls and dust gathering on the furniture, although she would try to go back as often as she could. But by then she was doing a graduate degree at Oxford, and also she would have a little boy named after his father, although she and Arthur would never marry, because who got married anymore? They were committed to each other—that was enough.

Dora and Dóra kept in touch by email, and they became Facebook friends. They "liked" and commented on each other's posts. When Dora was going through the divorce, it was Dóra she turned to. When Dóra lost the second baby and learned she could not have another, she texted Dora and they talked for hours, despite the time difference. Dora traveled to England. Dóra traveled to the United States. Their children got into a fight about which Doctor Who was the real one, the ninth or tenth.

One summer, they both returned to Budapest, to the apartment. They were in their forties now. Dora was a college professor, in a beige linen Ralph Lauren skirt she had bought at a thrift store, which she liked to wear when she traveled because no one expected linen to be ironed, right? And a black t-shirt, a scarf with large orange poppies. The days of ripped jeans were long behind her. Coincidentally, Dóra was also wearing a black t-shirt, but with black leggings and a long cardigan. She had brought three pairs of leggings, three t-shirts, and two cardigans that could be combined into various outfits. Whenever she could, she avoided checking luggage on Ryanair because it cost so much, and it was so much of a hassle waiting afterward at the carousel. Anyway, nowadays she could buy almost anything she needed in Budapest.

"I think Mom doesn't want to take care of the apartment anymore," said Dora. "The heater in one of the rooms needs to be repaired—honestly, I think it hasn't been serviced since it was converted to gas. The bathtub needs to be replaced, and really the whole bathroom needs to be updated. It's got to be forty years old. The problem is, I was hired full-time in September—finally! It's great—I'm tenure-track, I get health insurance, a whole benefits package. But I have almost no savings. This apartment is worth what, probably around $80,000?"

"But you said she was willing to work out a payment plan? I don't have that sort of money either—Arthur and I can barely afford to live in London. Thank goodness Artie can go to the school where he teaches for free. But working for a university press—I don't know, perhaps it was a mistake. I've thought about moving back to Budapest, but Arthur wants Artie to grow up in England." Dóra pushed her hair behind one ear. Sitting cross-legged on the sofa, she certainly didn't look forty-six. Dora would have to ask about her face cream. "I don't know why I keep writing poetry. It's not as though I'm ever going to make money at it. I'm invited to these conferences—come to

Finland, they say. Do a reading, speak on a panel. We will pay your registration fee. But I still have to pay the travel and hotel. I'm not sure it's worth it."

"When is your book coming out?" Dora put her plate on the table. When Dóra had arrived from the airport, she had fixed them a snack: bread and körözött, since Dóra was still vegetarian. Her own book, the second to be published, was coming out in September, just in time for their forty-seventh birthday. Her first book, a short-story collection, had been published ten years ago, to good reviews. But the publisher had gone out of business during the recession, and it had fallen out of print. There were still copies floating around on Amazon and eBay. It felt so late to be publishing her second book—and first novel. She should have done it years ago, but there had been her daughter to raise, and a graduate degree to finish, and Jeff had made so little during the long years of a cardiology fellowship with a specialty in heart surgery that she had gotten good at mending the holes in her underclothes so she would not have to buy new ones. And then trying to find a full-time teaching job, and the divorce. *I am*, she reminded herself, *doing the best I can*. Now, for the first time in a long time, the ground seemed solid under her feet.

"Next month," said Dóra. "I'm pleased with it, but who will read it? So few people read poetry nowadays. I have to beg for reviews!"

"But you win prizes. Actual important ones."

Dóra shrugged. "At any rate, the problem is that neither of us have much money. How much would she be willing to take a month in a payment plan?"

"Three hundred. Dollars. I don't know what that is in pounds, but I could google it on my phone. I have an international data plan. Could you afford half? And then we could fix it up, little by little. Kicsi by kicsi! I swear, that Hungarian class is going to kill me." She had been in Budapest for two weeks, and would be here another two, taking intensive Hungarian. So far she had figured out that Hungarian was the complete opposite of English, and that it made her brain hurt. "But honestly, I think my pronunciation is pretty good. I'm going to set the second book in the series here in Budapest. Monsters in Budapest!"

"See, you will have readers. That is what people want nowadays, an adventure story to read on an airplane or at the beach. No one wants poetry."

"They mostly watch videos on airplanes." On the Swissair flight, Dora had watched *John Carter* with Chinese subtitles because she had not known how to turn them off, a British comedy starring Judy Dench, and a Bollywood musical. "I think I could afford one fifty. But I don't know, do we even want to own an apartment together?"

"Yes," said Dóra. "Yes, we do. We spent our childhoods here, remember? Me more than you, of course, but there are so many memories here. It will be about a hundred pounds a month—I can afford that. And I would like Artie and Cordelia to have this, someday." She put her plate down and wiped her mouth with the paper napkin. "We should buy a washing machine . . ."

Dora put their dishes in the sink, and then they walked around the apartment, talking about paint colors and how to clean out the pantry, which still had jars of lekvár in it put up twenty years ago. Dora had long hair in a braid, darker now that she was dyeing it. Dóra had short hair, going gray, in a bob that swung around her chin. They were both on diets because, as Dora said, as soon as you set foot in the US or UK after having been in continental Europe, you gain five pounds. Dóra sometimes went to church, to Catholic Mass—more often since this new Pope, who seemed more liberal and enlightened than his predecessors (just look at his encyclical on climate change). Dora was vaguely spiritual in a way that combined mindfulness and pop quantum mechanics. She thought of herself as a pantheist: surely spirit was everywhere, in everything? Also, string theory. Both of them believed, more than anything else, in the power of the written word, in the sacredness of literature. Both were afraid of growing old. Dora was afraid of growing old alone. Dóra sometimes felt as though her relationship with Arthur was a miracle. At other times, when she saw that he had left the breakfast dishes on the table for her to clean up, she imagined different ways she could murder him without being caught. Perhaps, instead of poetry, she should write murder mysteries? "We'll have to replace most of the furniture," said Dora. "At least everything is cheap here, since the recession. I think we should make it look the way it's supposed to, nothing modern. As though it were still a palace, filled with antiques."

"Then I think we've made a decision," said Dóra. "We can call our mother later. Right now, I would like to go for a walk. I have been on the tube, and then an airplane, and then the shuttle bus all day!"

"I need to buy vegetables at the Nagy Vásárcsarnok. See, isn't my pronunciation good? Let me get the shopping bag."

They walked down the stone stairs, out the passageway and into the light of the summer afternoon. The linden trees were in flower and releasing their fragrance. They passed the California Coffee Company and the Hotel Mercure Korona, then headed down Vámház körút toward the river.

I'm not sure who said it, Dora or Dóra: "Fagylalt!" It could have been either of them, calling for ice cream.

"There's a new ice cream place called Levendula, right across from the Nagy Vásárcsarnok," said Dora. "I pass it every morning on my way to the language school. It has all sorts of unusual flavors, and the cutest shop. Painted lavender!"

They stopped for ice cream: one cone of lavender citron and chili dark chocolate, one cone of pear ginger and caramelized fig. Then, carrying their cones, they walked down to the Liberty Bridge—the Szabadság híd, Dora reminded herself—which had recently been repainted, and looked over the railing at the river, as they had twenty years before. It was a darker jade now: to their right, the sun was beginning to set, sending fingers of pink and orange over the water.

"It's so different, and so much the same," said Dóra.

Up the river, they could see Castle Hill, that palimpsest of historical periods and styles, going back a thousand years. It was already lit up for the night. Downriver, to their left, were new apartment and office buildings, many unoccupied because the effects of the recession still lingered. This was a Budapest with no Trabants in it, with Tescos on the street corners, where Dora could withdraw money at the OTP Bank out of her American bank account using an ATM that told her the exchange rate. Of gay pride parades and right-wing political parties that talked about a Greater Hungary. Tomorrow morning, Dóra would go to the California Coffee Company, order a kicsi latte, and find a quiet corner where she could use the free Wi-Fi to Skype with Arthur and Artie.

And yet here was the Danube, flowing as it had flowed when Szent István was crowned the first king of Hungary in 1000 AD. With embankments and bridges, but the same river.

"Váci utca?" said Dora, finishing the bottom of her ice cream cone, into which she had pushed the last of the pear ginger with her tongue. "You know, I think Budapest has the most beautiful light in the world. Van Gogh would have loved it here."

"Yes, I need to find some perfume," said Dóra. "I hope the perfume shop is still there. Everything changes so quickly nowadays."

Twenty years earlier, she had turned to Dora and said, "Would you like me to show you Café Gerbeaud? It is a very famous coffeehouse, dating from the nineteenth century. It's a little bit of a walk to Vörösmarty tér, but I think perhaps you would like to walk after being on an airplane." She and Dora had walked slowly up Váci utca, going into the antique stores, agreeing that they both preferred Zsolnay to Herend, which they found a little kitschy. Agreeing that they did not like the shops that catered to tourists, discovering they shared a taste for the desert called madártej, that their favorite holiday was Christmas—Karácsony in Hungarian. Becoming friends.

They would not always like each other, they would not always agree—Dora said it was stupid not to have a clothes dryer and Dóra maintained that air-dried clothes smelled better, and also Americans were spoiled. But in years after, whether they were twenty-six or forty-six, when either of them felt that sick sense of darkness and despair that comes upon you at 3 a.m. or in the middle of a cocktail party, they would call or email or text. And the sense we get, that we are after all alone in the world, would go away, for they were not alone—they had each other.

I cannot tell you any more of this story, for I do not know it myself. I am Dora and Dóra, not a fortune-teller. The future is always a series of threads that we cast ahead of us, with only partial control over how they are woven. Our lives are a collaboration with fate, and the best we can hope for is a hand to hold in the darkness, a voice on the other side of uncertainty—another who, when called, will answer "I am here."

CIMMERIA:
FROM THE *JOURNAL OF IMAGINARY ANTHROPOLOGY*

REMEMBERING CIMMERIA: I walk through the bazaar, between the stalls of the spice sellers, smelling turmeric and cloves, hearing the clash of bronze from the sellers of cooking pots, the bleat of goats from the butchers' alley. Rugs hang from wooden racks, scarlet and indigo. In the corners of the alleys, men without legs perch on wooden carts, telling their stories to a crowd of ragged children, making coins disappear into the air. Women from the mountains, their faces prematurely old from sun and suffering, call to me in a dialect I can barely understand. Their stands sell eggplants and tomatoes, the pungent olives that are distinctive to Cimmerian cuisine, video games. In the mountain villages, it has long been a custom to dye hair blue for good fortune, a practice that sophisticated urbanites have lately adopted. Even the women at court have hair of a deep and startling hue.

My guide, Afa, walks ahead of me, with a string bag in her hand, examining the vegetables, buying cauliflower and lentils. Later she will make rice mixed with raisins, meat, and saffron. The cuisine of Cimmeria is rich, heavy with goat and chicken. (They eat and keep no pigs.) The pastries are filled with almond paste and soaked in honey. She waddles ahead (forgive me, but you do waddle, Afa), and I follow amid a cacophony of voices, speaking the Indo-European language of Cimmeria, which is closest perhaps to Old Iranian. The mountain accents are harsh, the tones of the urbanites soft and lisping. Shaila spoke in those tones, when she taught me phrases in her language: Can I have more lozi (a cake made with marzipan, flavored with orange water)? You are the son of a dog. I will love you until the ocean swallows the moon. (A traditional saying. At the end of time, the serpent that lies beneath the Black Sea will rise up and swallow the moon as though it were lozi. It means, I will love you until the end of time.)

On that day, or perhaps it is another day I remember, I see a man selling Kalashnikovs. The war is a recent memory here, and every man has at least one weapon: Even I wear a curved knife in my belt, or I will be taken for a prostitute. (Male prostitutes, who are common in the capital, can be distinguished by their kohl-rimmed eyes, their extravagant clothes, their weaponlessness. As a red-haired Irishman, I do not look like them, but it is best to avoid misunderstandings.) The sun shines down from a cloudless sky. It is hotter than summer in Arizona, on the campus of the small college where this journey began, where we said, let us imagine a modern Cimmeria. What would it look like? I know, now. The city is cooled by a thousand fountains, we are told: Its name means just that, A Thousand Fountains. It was founded in the sixth century BCE, or so we have conjectured and imagined.

I have a pounding headache. I have been two weeks in this country, and I cannot get used to the heat, the smells, the reality of it all. Could we have created this? The four of us, me and Lisa and Michael the Second, and Professor Farrow, sitting in a conference room at that small college? Surely not. And yet.

We were worried that the Khan would forbid us from entering the country. But no. We were issued visas, assigned translators, given office space in the palace itself.

The Khan was a short man, balding. His wife had been Miss

Cimmeria, and then a television reporter for one of the three state channels. She had met the Khan when she had been sent to interview him. He wore a business suit with a traditional scarf around his neck. She looked as though she had stepped out of a photo shoot for *Vogue Russia*, which was available in all the gas stations.

"Cimmeria has been here, on the shores of the Black Sea, for more than two thousand years," he said. "Would you like some coffee, Dr. Nolan? I think our coffee is the best in the world." It was—dark, thick, spiced, and served with ewe's milk. "This theory of yours—that a group of American graduate students created Cimmeria in their heads, merely by thinking about it—you will understand that some of our people find it insulting. They will say that all Americans are imperialist dogs. I myself find it amusing, almost charming—like poetry. The mind creates reality, yes? So our poets have taught us. Of course, your version is culturally insensitive, but then, you are Americans. I did not think Americans were capable of poetry."

Only Lisa had been a graduate student, and even she had recently graduated. Mike and I were postdocs, and Professor Farrow was tenured at Southern Arizona State. It all seemed so far away, the small campus with its perpetually dying lawns and drab 1970s architecture. I was standing in a reception room, drinking coffee with the Khan of Cimmeria and his wife, and Arizona seemed imaginary, like something I had made up.

"But we like Americans here. The enemy of my enemy is my friend, is he not? Any enemy of Russia is a friend of mine. So I am glad to welcome you to my country. You will, I am certain, be sensitive to our customs. Your coworker, for example—I suggest that she not wear short pants in the streets. Our clerics, whether Orthodox, Catholic, or Muslim, are traditional and may be offended. Anyway, you must admit, such garments are not attractive on women. I would not say so to her, you understand, for women are the devil when they are criticized. But a woman should cultivate an air of mystery. There is nothing mysterious about bare red knees."

Our office space was in an unused part of the palace. My translator, Jafik, told me it had once been a storage area for bedding. It was
close to the servants' quarters. The Khan may have welcomed us to
Cimmeria for diplomatic reasons, but he did not think much of us,
that was clear. It was part of the old palace, which had been built
in the thirteenth century CE, after the final defeat of the Mongols.
Since then, Cimmeria had been embroiled in almost constant warfare, with Anatolia, Scythia, Poland, and most recently the Russians,
who had wanted its ports on the Black Sea. The Khan had received
considerable American aid, including military advisors. The war had
ended with the disintegration of the USSR. Ukraine, focused on its
own economic problems, had no wish to interfere in local politics, so
Cimmeria was enjoying a period of relative peace. I wondered how
long it would last.

Lisa was our linguist. She would stay in the capital for the first
three months, then venture out into the countryside, recording local
dialects. "You know what amazes me?" she said as we were unpack-
ing our computers and office supplies. "The complexity of all this. You
would think it really had been here for the last three thousand years.
It's hard to believe it all started with Mike the First goofing off in Professor Farrow's class." He had been bored, and instead of taking notes,
had started sketching a city. The professor had caught him, and had
told the students that we would spend the rest of the semester creating
that city and the surrounding countryside. We would be responsible
for its history, customs, language. Lisa was in the class, too, and I was
the TA. AN 703, Contemporary Anthropological Theory, had turned
into Creating Cimmeria.

Of the four graduate students in the course, only Lisa stayed in
the program. One got married and moved to Wisconsin, another
transferred to the School of Education so she could become a kin-
dergarten teacher. Mike the First left with his Master's and went
on to do an MBA. It was a coincidence that Professor Farrow's next
postdoc, who arrived in the middle of the semester, was also named

Mike. He had an undergraduate degree in classics, and was the one who decided that the country we were developing was Cimmeria. He was also particularly interested in the Borges hypothesis. Everyone had been talking about it at Michigan, where he had done his PhD. At that point, it was more controversial than it is now, and Professor Farrow had only been planning to touch on it briefly at the end of the semester. But once we started on Cimmeria, AN 703 became an experiment in creating reality through perception and expectation. Could we actually create Cimmeria by thinking about it, writing about it?

Not in one semester, of course. After the semester ended, all of us worked on the Cimmeria Project. It became the topic of Lisa's dissertation: *A Dictionary and Grammar of Modern Cimmerian, with Commentary.* Mike focused on history. I wrote articles on culture, figuring out probable rites of passage, how the Cimmerians would bury their dead. We had Herodotus, we had accounts of cultures from that area. We were all steeped in anthropological theory. On weekends, when we should have been going on dates, we gathered in a conference room, under a fluorescent light, and talked about Cimmeria. It was fortunate that around that time, the *Journal of Imaginary Anthropology* was founded at Penn State. Otherwise, I don't know where we would have published. At the first Imaginary Anthropology conference, in Orlando, we realized that a group from Tennessee was working on the modern Republic of Scythia and Sarmatia, which shared a border with Cimmeria. We formed a working group.

"Don't let the Cimmerians hear you talk about creating all this," I said. "Especially the nationalists. Remember, they have guns, and you don't." Should I mention Lisa's cargo shorts? I had to admit, looking at her knobby red knees, above socks and Birkenstocks, that the Khan had a point. Before she left for the mountains, I would warn her to wear more traditional clothes.

I was going to stay in the capital. My work would focus on the ways in which the historical practices we had described in "Cimmeria: A Proposal," in the second issue of the *Journal of Imaginary*

Anthropology, influenced and remained evident in modern practice. Already I had seen developments we had never anticipated. One was the fashion for blue hair; in a footnote, Mike had written that blue was a fortunate color in Cimmerian folk belief. Another was the ubiquity of cats in the capital. In an article on funerary rites, I had described how cats were seen as guides to the land of the dead until the coming of Christianity in the twelfth century CE. The belief should have gone away, but somehow it had persisted, and every household, whether Orthodox, Catholic, Muslim, Jewish, or one of the minor sects that flourished in the relative tolerance of Cimmeria, had its cat. No Cimmerian wanted his soul to get lost on the way to Paradise. Stray cats were fed at the public expense, and no one dared harm a cat. I saw them everywhere, when I ventured into the city. In a month, Mike was going to join us, and I would be able to show him all the developments I was documenting. Meanwhile, there was email and Skype.

I was assigned a bedroom and bath close to our offices. Afa, who had been a sort of under-cook, was assigned to be my servant but quickly became my guide, showing me around the city and mocking my Cimmerian accent. "He he!" she would say. "No, Doctor Pat, that word is not pronounced that way. Do not repeat it that way, I beg of you. I am an old woman, but still it is not respectable for me to hear!" Jafik was my language teacher as well as my translator, teaching me the language Lisa had created based on what we knew of historical Cimmerian and its Indo-European roots, except that it had developed an extensive vocabulary. As used by modern Cimmerians, it had the nuance and fluidity of a living language, as well as a surprising number of expletives.

I had no duties except to conduct my research, which was a relief from the grind of TAing and, recently, teaching my own undergraduate classes. But one day, I was summoned to speak with the Khan. It was the day of an official audience, so he was dressed in Cimmerian ceremonial robes, although he still wore his Rolex watch. His advisors looked impatient, and I gathered that the audience was about to begin—I had seen a long line of supplicants waiting by the door as I was ushered in. But he said, as though we had all the time in the world, "Dr. Nolan, did you know that my daughters are learning American?" Sitting next to him were four girls, all wearing the traditional headscarves worn by Cimmerian peasant women, but pulled back to show that their hair was dyed fashionably blue. "They are very troublesome, my daughters. They like everything modern: Leonardo DiCaprio, video games. Tradition is not good enough for them. They wish to attend university and find professions, or do humanitarian work. Ah, what is a father to do?" He shook a finger at them, fondly enough. "I would like it if you could teach them the latest American idioms. The slang, as it were."

That afternoon, Afa led me to another part of the palace—the royal family's personal quarters. These were more modern and considerably more comfortable than ours. I was shown into what seemed to be a common room for the girls. There were colorful rugs and divans, embroidered wall hangings, and an enormous flat-screen TV.

"These are the Khan's daughters," said Afa. She had already explained to me, in case I made any blunders, that they were his daughters by his first wife, who had not been Miss Cimmeria, but had produced the royal children: a son, and then only daughters, and then a second son who had died shortly after birth. She had died a week later of an infection contracted during the difficult delivery. "Anoor is the youngest, then Tallah, and then Shaila, who is already taking university classes online." Shaila smiled at me. This time, none of them were wearing headscarves. There really was something attractive about blue hair.

"And what about the fourth one?" She was sitting a bit back from the others, to the right of and behind Shaila, whom she closely resembled.

Afa looked at me with astonishment. "The Khan has three daughters," she said. "Anoor, Tallah, and Shaila. There is no fourth one, Doctor Pat."

The fourth one stared at me without expression.

"Cimmerians don't recognize twins," said Lisa. "That has to be the explanation. Do you remember the thirteenth-century philosopher Farkosh Kursand? When God made the world, He decreed that human beings would be born one at a time, unique, unlike animals. They would be born defenseless, without claws or teeth or fur. But they would have souls. It's in a children's book—I have a copy somewhere, but it's based on Kursand's reading of Genesis in one of his philosophical treatises. Mike would know which. And it's the basis of Cimmerian human rights law, actually. That's why women have always had more rights here. They have souls, so they've been allowed to vote since Cimmeria became a parliamentary monarchy. I'm sure it's mentioned in one of the articles—I don't remember which one, but check the database Mike is putting together. Shaila must have been a twin, and the Cimmerians don't recognize the second child as separate from the first. So Shaila is one girl. In two bodies. But with one soul."

"Who came up with that stupid idea?"

"Well, to be perfectly honest, it might have been you." She leaned back in her revolving chair. I don't know how she could do that without falling. "Or Mike, of course. It certainly wasn't my idea. Embryologically it does make a certain sense. Identical twins really do come from one egg."

"So they're both Shaila."

"There is no both. The idea of both is culturally inappropriate. There is one Shaila, in two bodies. Think of them as Shaila and her shadow."

I tested this theory once, while walking through the market with Afa. We were walking through the alley of the dog-sellers. In Cimmeria, almost every house has a dog, for defense and to catch rats. Cats are not sold in the market. They cannot be sold at all, only given or willed away. To sell a cat for money is to imperil your immortal soul. We passed a woman sitting on the ground, with a basket beside her. In it were two infants, as alike as the proverbial two peas in a pod, half covered with a ragged blanket. Beside them lay a dirty mutt with a chain around its neck that lifted its head and whimpered as we walked by.

"Child how many in basket?" I asked Afa in my still-imperfect Cimmerian.

"There is one child in that basket, Pati," she said. I could not get her to stop using the diminutive. I even told her that in my language Pati was a woman's name, to no effect. She just smiled, patted me on the arm, and assured me that no one would mistake such a tall, handsome (which in Cimmerian is the same word as beautiful) man for a woman.

"Only one child?"

"Of course. One basket, one child."

Shaila's shadow followed her everywhere. When she and her sisters sat with me in the room with the low divans and the large-screen TV, studying American slang, she was there. "What's up!" Shaila would say, laughing, and her shadow would stare down at the floor. When Shaila and I walked through the gardens, she walked six paces behind, pausing when we paused, sitting when we sat. After we were married, in our apartment in Arizona, she would sit in a corner of the bedroom, watching as we made love. Although I always turned off the lights, I could see her: a darkness against the off-white walls of faculty housing.

Once, I tried to ask Shaila about her. "Shaila, do you know the word twin?"

"Yes, of course," she said. "In America, if two babies are born at the same time, they are twins."

"What about in Cimmeria? Surely there is a Cimmerian word for twin. Sometimes two babies are born at the same time in Cimmeria, too."

She looked confused. "I suppose so. Biology is the same everywhere."

"Well, what's the word, then?"

"I cannot think of it. I shall have to email Tallah. She is better at languages than I am."

"What if you yourself were a twin?"

"Me? But I am not a twin. If I were, my mother would have told me."

I tried a different tactic. "Do you remember the dog you had, Kala? She had two sisters, born at the same time. Those were Anoor's and Tallah's dogs. They were not Kala, even though they were born in the same litter. You could think of them as twins—I mean, triplets." I remembered them gamboling together, Kala and her two littermates. They would follow us through the gardens, and Shaila and her sisters would pet them indiscriminately. When we sat under the plum trees, they would tumble together into one doggy heap.

"Pat, what is this all about? Is this about the fact that I don't want to have a baby right now? You know I want to go to graduate school first."

I did not think her father would approve the marriage. I told her so: "Your father will never agree to you marrying a poor American postdoc. Do you have any idea how poor I am? My research grant is all I have."

"You do not understand Cimmerian politics," Shaila replied. "Do you know what percentage of our population is ethnically Sarmatian? Twenty percent, all in the eastern province. They fought the Russians, and they still have weapons. Not just guns: tanks, anti-aircraft missiles. The Sarmatians are getting restless, Pati. They are mostly Catholic, in a country that is mostly Orthodox. They want to unite with their homeland, create a Greater Scythia and Sarmatia. My father projects an image of strength, because what else can you do? But he is afraid. He is most afraid that the Americans will not help. They helped against the Russians, but this is an internal matter. He has talked to us already about different ways for us to leave the country. Anoor has been enrolled at the Lycée International in Paris, and Tallah is going to study at the American School in London. They can get student visas. For me it is more difficult: I must be admitted at a university. That is why I have been taking courses online. Ask him: If he says no, then no. But I think he will consider my marriage with an American."

She was right. The Khan considered. For a week, and then another, while pro-Sarmatian factions clashed with the military in the eastern province. Then protests broke out in the capital. Anoor was already in Paris with her stepmother, supposedly on a shopping spree for school. Tallah had started school in London. In the Khan's personal office, I signed the marriage contract, barely understanding what I was signing because it was in an ornate script I had seen only in medieval documents. On the way to the airport, we stopped by the cathedral in Shahin Square, where we were married by the Patriarch of the Cimmerian Independent Orthodox Church, who checked the faxed copy of my baptismal certificate and lectured me in sonorous tones about the importance of conversion, raising children in the true faith. The Khan kissed Shaila on both cheeks, promising her that we would have a proper ceremony when the political situation was more stable and she could return to the country. In the Khan's private plane, we flew to a small airport near Fresno and spent our first night together at my mother's house. My father had died of a heart attack while I was in college, and she lived alone in the house where I had grown up. It was strange staying in the guest bedroom, down the hall from the room where I had slept as a child, which still had my *He-Man* action figures on the shelves, the Skeletor defaced with permanent marker. I had to explain to her about Shaila's shadow.

"I don't understand," my mother said. "Are you all going to live together?"

"Well, yes, I guess so. It's really no different than if her twin sister were living with us, is it?"

"And Shaila is going to take undergraduate classes? What is her sister going to do?"

"I have no idea," I said.

What she did, more than anything else, was watch television. All day, it would be on. Mostly, she watched CNN and the news shows. Sometimes I would test Shaila, asking, "Did you turn the TV on?"

"Is it on?" she would say. "Then of course I must have turned it on. Unless you left it on before you went out. How did your class go? Is that football player in the back still falling asleep?"

One day, I came home and noticed that the other Shaila was cooking dinner. Later I asked, "Shaila, did you cook dinner?"

"Of course," she said. "Did you like it?"

"Yes." It was actually pretty good, chicken in a thick red stew over rice. It reminded me of a dish Afa had made in an iron pot hanging over an open fire in the servants' quarters. But I guess it could be made on an American stovetop as well.

After that, the other Shaila cooked dinner every night. It was convenient, because I was teaching night classes, trying to make extra money. Shaila told me that I did not need to work so hard, that the money her father gave her was more than enough to support us both. But I was proud and did not want to live off my father-in-law, even if he was the Khan of Cimmeria. At the same time, I was trying to write up my research on Cimmerian funerary practices. If I could publish a paper in the *Journal of Imaginary Anthropology*, I might have a shot at a tenure-track position, or at least a visiting professorship somewhere that wasn't Arizona. Shaila was trying to finish her premed requirements. She had decided that she wanted to be a pediatrician.

Meanwhile, in Cimmeria, the situation was growing more complicated. The pro-Sarmatian faction had split into the radical Sons of Sarmatia and the more moderate Sarmatian Democratic Alliance, although the Prime Minister claimed that the SDA was a front. There were weekly clashes with police in the capital, and the Sons of Sarmatia had planted a bomb in the Hilton, although a maid had reported a suspicious shopping bag and the hotel had been evacuated before the bomb could go off. The Khan had imposed a curfew, and martial law might be next, although the army had a significant Sarmatian minority. But I had classes to teach, so I tried not to pay attention to politics, and even Shaila dismissed it all as "a mess."

One day, I came home from a departmental meeting and Shaila wasn't in the apartment. She was usually home by seven. I assumed she'd had to stay late for a lab. The other Shaila was cooking dinner in the kitchen. At eight, when she hadn't come back yet, I sat down at the kitchen table to eat. To my surprise, the other Shaila sat down across from me, at the place set for Shaila. She had never sat down at the table with us before.

She looked at me with her dark eyes and said, "How was your day, Pati?"

I dropped my fork. It clattered against the rim of the plate. She had never spoken before, not one sentence, not one word. Her voice was just like Shaila's, but with a stronger accent. At least it sounded stronger to me. Or maybe not. It was hard to tell.

"Where's Shaila?" I asked. I could feel a constriction in my chest, as though a fist had started to close around my heart. Like the beginning of my father's heart attack. I think even then, I knew.

"What do you mean?" she said. "I'm Shaila. I have always been Shaila. The only Shaila there is."

I stared down at the lamb and peas in saffron curry. The smell reminded me of Cimmeria, of the bazaar. I could almost hear the clash of the cooking pots.

"You've done something to her, haven't you?"

"I have no idea what you're talking about. Eat your dinner, Pati. It's going to get cold. You've been working so hard lately. I don't think it's good for you."

But I could not eat. I stood up, accidentally hitting my hip on the table and cursing at the pain. With a growing sense of panic, I searched the apartment for any clue to Shaila's whereabouts. Her purse was in the closet, with her cell phone in it, so she must have come home earlier in the evening. All her clothes were on the hangers, as far as I could tell—she had a lot of clothes. Nothing seemed to be missing. But Shaila was not there. The other Shaila stood watching me, as though waiting for me to give up, admit defeat. Finally, after one last useless look under the bed, I left, deliberately banging the door behind me. She had to be somewhere.

I walked across campus, to the Life Sciences classrooms and labs, and checked all of them. Then I walked through the main library and the science library, calling "Shaila!" until a graduate student in a carrel told me to be quiet. By this time, it was dark. I went to her favorite coffee shop, the Espresso Bean, where undergraduates looked at me strangely from behind their laptops, and then to every shop and restaurant that was still open, from the gelato place to the German restaurant, famous for its bratwurst and beer, where students took their families on Parents' Weekend. Finally, I walked the streets, calling "Shaila!" as though she were a stray dog, hoping that the other Shaila was simply being presumptuous, rebelling against her secondary status. Hoping the real Shaila was out there somewhere.

I passed the police station and stood outside, thinking about going in and reporting her missing. I would talk to a police officer on duty, tell him I could not find my wife. He would come home with me, to find—my wife, saying that I was overworked and needed to rest, see a psychiatrist. Shaila had entered the country with a diplomatic passport—one passport, for one Shaila. Had anyone seen the other Shaila? Only my mother. She had picked us up at the airport, we had spent the night with her, all three of us eating dinner at the dining room table. She had avoided looking at the other Shaila, talking to Shaila about how the roses were doing well this year despite aphids, asking whether she knew how to knit, how she dyed her hair that particular shade of blue—pointless, polite talk. And then we had rented a car and driven to Arizona, me and Shaila in the front seat, the other Shaila in back with the luggage. Once we arrived at the university, she had stayed in the apartment. Lisa knew, but she and Mike the Second were still in Cimmeria, and their internet connection could be sporadic. I could talk to Professor Farrow? She would be in her office tomorrow morning, before classes. She would at least believe me. But I knew, with a cold certainty in the pit of my stomach, that Anne Farrow would look at me from over the wire rims of her glasses and say, "Pat, you know as well as I do that culture defines personhood." She was an anthropologist, through and through. She would not interfere. I had been married to Shaila, I was still married to Shaila. There was just one less of her.

In the end, I called my mother, while sitting on a park bench under a streetlamp, with the moon sailing high above, among the clouds.

"Do you know what time it is, Pat?" she asked.

"Listen, Mom," I said, and explained the situation.

"Oh, Pat, I wish you hadn't married that woman. But can't you divorce her? Are you allowed to divorce in that church? I wish you hadn't broken up with Bridget Ferguson. The two of you were so sweet together at prom. You know she married an accountant and has two children now. She sent me a card at Christmas."

I said good night and told her to go back to sleep, that I would figure it out. And then I sat there for a long time.

When I came home, well after midnight, Shaila was waiting for me with a cup of Cimmerian coffee, or as close as she could get with an American espresso machine. She was wearing the heart pajamas I had given Shaila for Valentine's Day.

"Pati," she said, "you left so quickly that I didn't have time to tell you the news. I heard it on CNN this morning, and then Daddy called me. Malek was assassinated yesterday." Malek was her brother. I had never met him—he had been an officer in the military, and while I had been in Cimmeria, he had been serving in the mountains. I knew that he had been recalled to the capital to deal with the Sarmatian agitation, but that was all.

"Assassinated? How?"

"He was trying to negotiate with the Sons of Sarmatia, and a radical pulled out a gun that had gotten through security. You never watch the news, do you, Pati? I watch it a great deal. It is important for me to learn the names of the world leaders, learn about international diplomacy. That is more important than organic chemistry, for a Khanum."

"A what?"

"Don't you understand? Now that Malek is dead, I am next in the line of succession. Someday, I will be the Khanum of Cimmeria. That is what we call a female Khan. In some countries, only male members of the royal family can succeed to the throne. But Cimmeria has never been like that. It has always been cosmopolitan, progressive. The philosopher Amirabal persuaded Teshup the Third to make his daughter his heir, and ever since, women can become rulers of the country. My great-grandmother, Daddy's grandma, was a Khanum, although she resigned when her son came of age. It is the same among the Scythians and Sarmatians." This was Lisa's doing. It had to be Lisa's doing. She was the one who had come up with Amirabal and the philosophical school she had founded in 500 BCE. Even Plato had praised her as one of the wisest philosophers in the ancient world. I silently cursed all Birkenstock-wearing feminists.

"What does this mean?" I asked.

"It means that tomorrow we fly to Washington, where I will ask your President for help against the Sarmatian faction. This morning on one of the news shows, the Speaker of the House criticized him for not supporting the government of Cimmeria. He mentioned the War on Terror—you know how they talk, and he wants to be the next Republican candidate. But I think we can finally get American aid. While I am there, I will call a press conference, and you will stand by my side. We will let the American people see that my husband is one of them. It will generate sympathy and support. Then we will fly to Cimmeria. I need to be in my country as a symbol of the future. And I must produce an heir to the throne as quickly as possible—a boy, because while I can legally become Khanum, the people will want assurance that I can bear a son. While you were out, I packed all our clothes. We will meet Daddy's plane at the airport tomorrow morning. You must wear your interview suit until we can buy you another. I've set the alarm for five o'clock."

I should have said no. I should have raged and cried, and refused to be complicit in something that made me feel as though I might be sick for the rest of my life. But I said nothing. What could I say? This, too, was Shaila.

I lay in the dark beside the woman who looked like my wife, unable to sleep, staring into the darkness. Shaila, I thought, what has happened to you? To your dreams of being a pediatrician, of our children growing up in America, eating tacos and riding their bikes to school? You wanted them to be ordinary, to escape the claustrophobia you had felt growing up in the palace, with its political intrigue and the weight of centuries perpetually pressing down on you. In the middle of the night, the woman who was Shaila, but not my Shaila, turned in her sleep and put an arm around me. I did not move away.

You are pleased, Afa, that I have returned to Cimmeria. It has meant a promotion for you, and you tell everyone that you are personal assistant to the American husband of the Khanum-to-be. You sell information about her pregnancy to the fashion magazines—how big she's getting, how radiant she is. Meanwhile, Shaila opens schools and meets with foreign ambassadors. She's probably the most popular figure in the country, part of the propaganda war against the Sons of Sarmatia, which has mostly fallen apart since Malek's death. The SDA was absorbed into the Cimmerian Democratic Party and no longer presents a problem. American aid helped, but more important was the surge of nationalism among ethnic Cimmerians. Indeed, the nationalists, with their anti-Sarmatian sentiments, may be a problem in the next election.

I sit at the desk in my office, which is no longer near the servants' quarters, but in the royal wing of the palace, writing this article, which would be suppressed if it appeared in any of the newspapers. But it will be read only by *JoIA*'s peer editors before languishing in the obscurity of an academic journal. Kala and one of her sisters lies at my feet. And I think about this country, Afa. It is—it was—a dream, but are not all nations of men dreams? Do we not create them, by drawing maps with lines on them, and naming rivers, mountain ranges? And then deciding that the men of our tribe can only marry women outside their matrilineage? That they must bury corpses rather than burning them, eat chicken and goats but not pigs, worship this bull-headed god rather than the crocodile god of that other tribe, who is an abomination? Fast during the dark of the moon, feast when the moon is full? I'm starting to sound like a poet, which will not be good for my academic career. One cannot write an academic paper as though it were poetry.

We dream countries, and then those countries dream us. And it seems to me, sitting here by the window, looking into a garden filled with roses, listening to one of the thousand fountains of this ancient city, that as much as I have dreamed Cimmeria, it has dreamed me.

Sometimes I forget that the other Shaila ever existed. A month after we returned to Cimmeria, an Arizona state trooper found a body in a ditch close to the Life Sciences building. It was female, and badly decomposed. The coroner estimated that she would have been about twenty, but the body was nude and there was no other identification. I'm quoting the story I read online, on the local newspaper's website. The police suggested that she might have been an illegal immigrant who had paid to be driven across the border, then been killed for the rest of her possessions. I sometimes wonder if she was Shaila.

This morning she has a television interview, and this afternoon she will be touring a new cancer treatment center paid for with American aid. All those years of listening and waiting were, after all, the perfect training for a Khanum. She is as patient as a cobra.

If I ask to visit the bazaar, the men who are in charge of watching me will first secure the square, which means shutting down the bazaar. They accompany me even to the university classes I insist on teaching. They stand in the back of the lecture hall, in their fatigues and sunglasses, carrying Kalashnikovs. Despite American aid, they do not want to give up their Russian weapons. So we must remember it: the stalls selling embroidered fabrics, and curved knives, and melons. The baskets in high stacks, and glasses of chilled mint tea into which we dip the pistachio biscuits that you told me are called Fingers of the Dead. Boys in sandals breakdancing to Arabic hip-hop on a boombox so old that it is held together with string. I would give a great deal to be able to go to the bazaar again. Or to go home and identify Shaila's body.

But in a couple of months, my son will be born. (Yes, it is a son. I've seen the ultrasound, but if you tell the newspapers, Afa, I will have you beheaded. I'm pretty sure I can still do that, here in Cimmeria.) There is only one of him, thank goodness. We intend to name him Malek. My mother has been sending a steady supply of knitted booties. There will be a national celebration, with special prayers in the churches and mosques and synagogues, and a school holiday. I wish Mike could come, or even Lisa. But he was offered a tenure-track position at a Christian college in North Carolina interested in the Biblical implications of Imaginary Anthropology. And Lisa is up in the mountains somewhere, close to the Scythian and Sarmatian border, studying women's initiation rites. I will stand beside Shaila and her family on the balcony of the palace, celebrating the birth of the future Khan of Cimmeria. In the gardens, rose petals will fall. Men will continue dying of natural or unnatural causes, and the cats of Cimmeria will lead them into another world. Women will dip their water jugs in the fountains of the city, carrying them on their heads back to their houses, as they have done since Cimmeria has existed, whether that is three or three thousand years. Life will go on as it has always done, praise be to God, creator of worlds, however they were created.

Reprinted from the *Journal of Imaginary Anthropology* 4.2 (Fall 2013).

Dr. Patrick Nolan is also coauthor of "Cimmeria: A Proposal" (with M. Sandowski, L. Lang, and A. Farrow), *JoIA* 2.1 (Spring 2011), and author of "Modern Cimmerian Funerary Practices," *JoIA* 3.2 (Fall 2012). Dr. Nolan is currently a professor at Kursand University. He is working on *A History of Modern Cimmeria*.

ENGLAND UNDER
THE WHITE WITCH

It is always winter now.

When she came, I was only a child—in ankle socks, my hair tied back with a silk ribbon. My mother was a seamstress working for the House of Alexandre. She spent the days on her knees, saying Yes, Madame has lost weight, what has Madame been doing? When Madame had been doing nothing of the sort. My father was a photograph of a man I had never seen in a naval uniform. A medal was pinned to the velvet frame.

My mother used to take me to Kensington Gardens, where I looked for fairies under the lilac bushes or in the tulip cups.

In school, we studied the kings and queens of England, its principal imports and exports, and home economics. Even so young, we knew that we were living in the waning days of our empire. That after the war, which had taken my father and toppled parts of London, the sun was finally setting. We were a diminished version of ourselves.

At home, my mother told me fairy tales about Red Riding Hood (never talk to wolves), Sleeping Beauty (your prince will come), Cinderella (choose the right shoes). We had tea with bread and potted meat, and on my birthday there was cake made with butter and sugar that our landlady, Mrs. Stokes, had bought as a present with her ration card.

Harold doesn't hold with this new Empress, as she calls herself, Mrs. Stokes would tell my mother. Coming out of the north, saying she will restore us to greatness. She's established herself in Edinburgh, and they do say she will march on London. He says the King got us through the war, and that's good enough for us. And who believes a woman's promises anyway?

But what I say is, England has always done best under a queen. Remember Elizabeth and Victoria. Here we are, half the young men dead in the war, no one for the young women to marry so they work as typists instead of having homes of their own. And trouble every day in India, it seems. Why not give an Empress a try?

One day Monsieur Alexandre told my mother that Lady Whortlesham had called her impertinent and therefore she had to go. That night, she sat for a long time at the kitchen table in our bedsit, with her face in her hands. When I asked her the date of the signing of the Magna Carta, she hastily wiped her eyes with a handkerchief and said, As though I could remember such a thing! Then she said, Can you take care of yourself for a moment, Ann of my heart? I need to go talk to Mrs. Stokes.

The next day, when I ran home from school for dinner, she was there, talking to Mrs. Stokes and wearing a new dress, white tricotine with silver braid trim. She looked like a princess from a fairy tale.

It's easy as pie, she was saying. I found the office just where you said it was, and they signed me right up. At first I'm going to help with recruitment, but the girl I talked to said she thought I should be in the rifle corps. They have women doing all sorts of things, there. I start training in two days.

You're braver than I am, said Mrs. Stokes. Aren't you afraid of being arrested?

If they do arrest me, will you take care of Ann? she asked. I know it's dangerous, but they're paying twice what I was making at the shop, and I have to do something. This world we're living in is no good, you and I both know that. Nothing's been right since the war. Just read this pamphlet they gave me. It makes sense, it does. I'm doing important work, now. Not stitching some Lady Whortlesham into her dress. I'm with the Empress.

In the end, the Empress took London more easily than anyone could have imagined. She had already taken Manchester, Birmingham, Oxford. We had heard how effective her magic could be against the remnants of our Home Forces. First, she sent clouds that covered the sky, from horizon to horizon. It snowed for days, until the city was shrouded in white. And then the sun came out just long enough to melt the top layer of snow, which froze during the night. The trees were encased in ice. They sparkled as though made of glass, and when they moved I heard a tinkling sound.

Then, she sent wolves. Out of the mist they came, white and gray, with teeth as sharp as knives. They spoke in low, guttural voices, telling the Royal Guards to surrender or have their throats ripped out. Most of the guards stayed loyal. In the end, there was blood on the snow in front of Buckingham Palace. Wolves gnawed the partly frozen bodies.

Third and finally came her personal army, the shopgirls and nurse-maids and typists who had been recruited, my mother among them. They looked magnificent in their white and silver, which made them difficult to see against the snow. They had endured toast and tea for supper, daily indignity, the unwanted attention of employers. Their faces were implacable. They shot with deadly accuracy and watched men die with the same polite attention as they had shown demonstrating a new shade of lipstick.

Buckingham Palace fell within a day. On the wireless, we heard that the King and his family had fled to France, all but one of his sisters, who it turned out was a sympathizer. By the time the professional military could mobilize its troops, scattered throughout our empire, England was already hers to command.

I stood by Mrs. Stokes, watching the barge of the Empress as it was rowed down the Thames. She stood on the barge, surrounded by wolves, with her white arms bare, black hair down to her feet, waving at her subjects.

No good will come of this, you mark my words, said Mr. Stokes.

Hush! Isn't she lovely? said Mrs. Stokes.

You have seen her face in every schoolroom, every shop. Perhaps in your dreams. It is as familiar to you as your own. But I will never forget that first glimpse of her loveliness. She looked toward us, and I believed that she had seen me, had waved particularly to me.

The next day, our home economics teacher said, From now on, we are not going to learn about cooking and sewing. Instead, we are going to learn magic. There was already a picture of our beloved Empress over her desk, where the picture of the King used to be.

At first, there were resistance movements. There were some who fought for warmth, for light. Who said that as long as she reigned, spring would never come again. We would never see violets scattered among the grass, never hear a river run. Never watch young lovers hold each other on the embankment, kiss each other not caring who was watching. There was the Wordsworth Society, which tried to effect change politically. And there were more radical groups: the Children of Albion, the Primrose Brigade.

But we soon learned that our Empress was as ruthless as she was beautiful. Those who opposed her were torn apart by wolves, or by her girl soldiers, who could tear men apart with their bare hands and were more frightening than any wolves. Sympathizers were rounded up and imprisoned, encased in ice. Or worse, they were left free but all the joy was taken from them, so that they remained in a prison of their own perpetual despair.

Her spies were everywhere. Even the trees could not be trusted. The hollies were the most dangerous, the most liable to inform. But resistance groups would not meet under pines, firs, or hemlocks. In many households, the cats were on her side. Whispers of disloyalty would bring swift retribution.

And many said, such traitors deserved punishment. That winter was good for England, that we needed cold, needed toughening. We had grown soft after the war, allowed our dominions to rebel against us, allowed the world to change. But she would set things right. And so the resistance movements were put down, and our soldiers marched into countries under a white flag that did not mean surrender. Those who had tried to be free of us were confronted with winter, and sorceresses, and wolves. Their chiefs and rajahs and presidents came to London, bringing jewels and costly fabrics to lay before her feet, and pledged their loyalty.

Our empire spread, as indeed it must. A winter country must import its food, and as winter spreads, the empire must expand to supply the lands under snow, their waters locked in ice. That is the terrible, inescapable logic of empire.

I was a Snowflake, in a white kerchief with silver stars. Then, I was an Ice Maiden. The other girls in school nodded to me as I walked by. If they did not wear the white uniform, I asked them why they had not joined up yet, and if they said their parents would not let them, I told them it was their responsibility to be persuasive. I won a scholarship to university, where I was inducted into the Sisterhood of the Wolf.

My den mother encouraged me to go into the sciences. Scientists will be useful to the Empress in the coming war, she said. Science and magic together are more powerful, are greater weapons, than they are apart. And there is a war coming, Ann. We hear more and more from our spies in Germany. A power is rising in that part of the world, a power that seeks to oppose the reign of the Empress. Surely not, I said. Who would oppose her? A power that believes in fire, she said. A fire that will burn away the snow, that will scorch the earth. That does not care about what we have already achieved—the security, the equality, the peace we will achieve when her empire spreads over the earth.

When I graduated, the Empress herself handed me a diploma and the badge of our order. My mother, who had been promoted to major general, was so proud! All of us in the Sisterhood had been brought to Buckingham Palace, in sleighs drawn by reindeer with silver bells on their antlers. We waited in a long room whose walls were painted to look like a winter forest, nibbling on almond biscuits and eating blancmange from silver cups with small bone spoons. At last, we were summoned into her presence.

You have seen our beloved Empress from far away, from below while she stands on a balcony, or from a sidewalk as she is drawn through the city streets in her sleigh. But I have met her, I have kissed her hand. It was white and cold, with the blue veins visible. Her grip was strong—stronger than any man's, as she was taller than any man. Her face was so pale that I could only look at it for a moment without pain. Her black hair trailed on the floor.

You have done well, she said to me, and I could hear her voice in my head as well as with my ears. To hear that voice again, I would consent to being torn apart by wolves.

You have never seen, you will never see, anything as magnificent as our Empress.

Where did she come from? Some say she came from the stars, that she is an alien life-form. Some say she is an ancient goddess reborn. Some say she is an ordinary woman, and that such women have always lived in the north: witches who command the snows.

The question is whispered, in secret places where there are no hemlocks, no cats: does human blood flow in her veins? Can our Empress die?

I met Jack in the basic physical training program required for all recruits to the war effort. My mother had used her influence to have me chosen for the Imperial Guard, the Empress's personal girl army, which could be deployed throughout the empire. After basic training, I was going to advanced training in the north, and then wherever the war effort needed me. He was a poet, assigned to the Ministry of Morale. He had been conscripted after university—this was in the early days of general conscription. He was expected to write poetry in praise of the Empress, and England, and those who served the empire. But first, we all had to pass basic training.

We stayed in unheated cabins, bathed in cold water, all to make us stronger, to bring the cold inside us. Each morning, we marched through the woods. The long marches, hauling weapons and equipment through the snow, were not difficult for me. I had been training since my university days, waking at dawn to run through the snow or swim in the icy rivers with the Sisterhood. But he was not as strong as I was. He would stumble over roots or boulders beneath the snow, and try to catch himself with chilled, chapped hands—the woolen gloves we had been issued were inadequate protection against the cold. I would help him up, holding him by the elbow, and sometimes I would carry part of his equipment, transferring it into my pack surreptitiously so the Sergeant did not see me.

Why are you so kind to me, Ann? he asked me once. Someone has to be, I said, smiling.

The other girls laughed at him, but I thought his large, dark eyes were beautiful. When he looked at me, I did not feel the cold. One day, I sat next to him at dinner. He told me about Yorkshire, where he was born—about the high hills, the sheep huddled together, their breaths hanging on the air.

Perhaps I should have been more like my father, he said. It was my headmaster at school who first read my poems and told me to apply for a scholarship. There I was, a farmer's son, studying with the children of ministers and generals, who talked about going to the palace the way I talked about going to the store. I kept to myself, too proud or ashamed to approach them, to presume they might be my friends. But my tutor sent my poems to the university literary magazine, and they were published. Then, I was invited to join the literary society. I thought it was an honor—until we all received letters from the war office. So here I am, losing my toes to frostbite so I can write odes for the dead in Africa—or for the war they say is coming.

We all believed that war was coming. The newspapers were already talking about a fire rising in the east, burning all before it.

It's a great honor to write for the Empress, I said.

Yes, of course it is, he said after a moment. He looked at me intently with those dark eyes. Of course, he said again, before finishing the thin broth with dumplings that we were told was Irish stew.

We spent more and more time together, huddled in the communal showers when we could, telling each other about our childhoods, the foods we liked, the books we had read. We wondered about the future. He hoped that after his compulsory service, he could work as a schoolteacher, publish his poems. I did not know where I would be assigned—Australia? South America? There was always unrest in some part of the empire.

One day, the Sergeant said to me, Ann, I'm not going to tell you what to do. I'm just going to warn you—there's something not right about Jack Kirby. I don't know what it is, but Thule—who was her wolf—can't stand him. I don't think a general's daughter should show too much interest in that boy. You don't want anyone questioning your loyalty, do you?

Her words made me angry. He was going into the Ministry—wasn't that good enough? That night, we met in the showers. I don't want to talk, I said. I kissed him—slid my hands under his jacket, sweater, undershirt. His body was bony, but I thought it had its own particular grace. He told me that I was beautiful, breathing it into my neck as we made love, awkwardly, removing as few layers of clothing as possible. You're beautiful, Ann—I hear it in my mind and remember the warmth of his breath in that cold place. There had been others, not many, but he may as well have been my first. He is the one I remember.

During our week of leave, he asked me to come home with him, to Yorkshire. His father met us at the train station. He was a large, quiet man who talked mostly of sheep. Look at these pelts, he told me. Feel the weight of them. Didn't use to get wool like this, in Yorkshire. It's the perpetual winter as does it. Grows twice as thick and twice as long. But he grumbled about the feed from the communal granaries—not as nourishing as the grass that used to grow on the hillsides, never seen such sickly lambs. And the wolves—not allowed to shoot them anymore. Those who complained were brought before a committee.

We had suppers of Yorkshire pudding and gravy, and walked out over the fields holding hands. I asked Jack about his mother. She had died in the influenza epidemic, which he had barely survived. That was before the coming of the Empress. I could see, from the photograph of her on the bureau, that he had inherited her delicacy, her dark eyes and thick, dark hair. Late at night, when his father was asleep, he would sneak into the guest room and we would make love under the covers, as quietly as possible, muffling our laughter, whispering to one another.

The day before we were to return from leave, his father told him that a ewe was giving birth in the snow. She had become trapped in a gully, and could not be lifted out in her condition. There was no chance of bringing her into the barn, so he and his father, one of the two farm hands, and the veterinarian went out, grumbling about the cold.

I wandered through the house, then sat in his room for a while, looking through the books he had read as a child. Books from before the Empress came, and from after—*Prince Frost and the Giants*, the Wolf Scout series, the *Treasury of English Poems* we had all studied in school. I can't tell you why I chose to look through the battered old desk he had used as a schoolboy. It was wrong, a base impulse. But I loved him, and on this last day before we went back to the camp, I wanted to feel close to him. I wanted to know his secrets, whatever they were—even if they included love letters from another girl. I tortured myself for a moment with that thought, knowing how unlikely it was that I would find anything but old schoolbooks and pens. And then I pulled open the drawer.

In the desk was a notebook, and in the notebook were his poems— in his handwriting, with dates at the tops of the pages indicating when they had been written. The latest of them was dated just before camp. They spoke of sunlight and warmth and green fields. Next to the notebook was a worn copy of one of the forbidden books: *The Complete Poetical Works of Wordsworth*. I opened to the page marked with a ribbon and read,

> I wandered lonely as a cloud
> That floats on high o'er vales and hills,
> When all at once I saw a crowd,
> A host, of golden daffodils . . .

I slammed the book shut. My hands were shaking. I remembered what the Sergeant had said: You don't want anyone questioning your loyalty, do you?

By the time Jack, his father, and the other men returned, I was composed enough to seem almost normal. That night, he came to my room. We made love as though nothing had happened, but all the time

I could hear it in my head: *I wandered lonely as a cloud—a host of golden daffodils.* I remembered daffodils. I could almost see them, bright yellow against the blue sky.

The next morning, as Jack and his father were loading our bags into the sleigh that would take us to the train station, I told them I had forgotten something. I ran back into the house, up the stairs and into Jack's room, then quickly slid the notebook and book into my backpack.

When we arrived back at camp, I went to the Sergeant and denounced Jack Kirby as a traitor.

I told myself that I was doing the right thing. He would be sent for reeducation. He would become a productive citizen, not a malcontent longing for what could never be. Perhaps some day he would even thank me.

He was sent to a reeducation camp in the north of Scotland. I graduated from basic training, went on to advanced training for the Imperial Guard, and was eventually given my wolf companion, Ulla. Together, we were sent to France, where the war had already started. We were among the first to enter Poland. We were in the squadron that summoned ice to cover the Black Sea so our soldiers could march into Turkey. My den mother had been right: science and magic together created powerful weapons. It took five years, but the fire in the east was defeated, and our empire stretched into the Russian plains, into the deserts of Arabia.

When I returned to England, I asked for Jack's file. It told me that he had died in the camp, shortly after arriving. The causes of death were listed as cold and heartbreak.

During the Empress's reign, England has changed for the better, some say. There is always food in the shops, although it has lost its flavor. Once, carrots were not pale, like potatoes. Cabbages were green.

They were not grown in great glass houses. The eggs had bright yellow centers, and all meat did not taste like mutton. Once, there were apple trees in England, and apples, peaches, plums were not imported from the distant reaches of our empire, where winter has not yet permanently settled. There was a sweetness in the world that you have never tasted. There was love and joy, and pain sharp as knives, rather than this blankness.

Our art, our stories, our poems have changed, become ghosts of their former selves. Mothers tell their daughters about Little White Hood and her wolf companion. About Corporal Cinder, who joined the liberation army and informed on her wicked sisters.

Our soldiers move on from conquest to conquest, riding white bears, white camels. Parts of the world that had never seen snow have seen it now. I myself have sent snow drifts to cover the sands of the Sahara, so we could deploy our sleighs. I have seen the Great Pyramid covered in ice, and crocodiles lying lethargic on ice floes in the Nile.

Our empire stretches from sea to sea to sea. Eventually, even the republics that now fight against us will come under our dominion. And then perhaps the only part of the world that has not bowed down to our Empress, the wild seas themselves, will be covered in ice. What will happen to us then, when there are no more lands to send provisions to the empire? I do not know. Our Empress has promised us a perfect world, but the only perfection is death.

You have heard stories of primroses and daffodils, and you do not believe them. You have heard that there were once green fields, and rivers that ran between their banks, and a warm sun overhead. You have never seen them, and you believe they are merely tales. I am here to tell you that they are true, that in my childhood these existed. And cups of tea that were truly hot, and Christmas trees with candles on their branches, and church bells. Girls wore ribbons in their hair rather than badges on their lapels. Boys played King Arthur or Robin Hood rather than Wolf Scout.

I'm here to tell you that the fairy tales are true.

And that, sitting in this secret place, looking at each other in fear, wondering who among you is an informant, you must decide whether to believe in the fairy tales, whether to fight for an idea. Ideas are the most powerful things—beauty, freedom, love. But they are harder to fight for than things like food, or safety, or power. You can't eat freedom, you can't wield love over another.

You are so young, with your solemn faces, your thin bodies, nourished on pale cabbage and soggy beef and slabs of flavorless pudding! I do not know if you have the strength. But that, my children, you will have to find out for yourselves.

Your leaders, who have asked me here tonight, believe that winter can end, if you have the courage to end it. They are naïve, as revolutionaries always are. Looking at your faces, I wonder. You have listened so intently to an old soldier, a woman who has seen much, felt much, endured. I have no strength left to fight, either for or against the Empress. Everyone I have ever loved—my mother, Mrs. Stokes, Jack Kirby, Ulla—is dead. I have just enough strength to tell you what the world was once, and could be again: imperfect, unequal, and in many ways unjust. But there was warmth and light to counteract the cold, the darkness.

What do I believe? Entropy is the law of the universe. All things run down, all things eventually end. Perhaps, after all, she is not an alien, not a witch, but a universal principle. Perhaps all you can do is hold back the cold, the darkness, for a while. Is a temporary summer worth your lives? But if you do not fight, you will never feel the warmth of the sun on your cheeks, or smell lilacs, or bite into a peach picked directly from the tree. You will never hold each other on the embankment, watching the waters of the Thames run below. The old stories will be forgotten. Our empire will spread over the world, and it will be winter, everywhere, forever.

FRANKENSTEIN'S DAUGHTER

To Mrs. Saville, England
May 27th, 17—

My dear Margaret,

You know with what high hopes I set out once again on this third of my expeditions into the Arctic Circle. This time, I told myself, I would not be defeated by ice and the dreadful cold of those latitudes. This time my sailors would not rebel, this time my ship would not become trapped among icebergs. This time, finally, I would break through into that temperate northern sea I had dreamed of, and sail upon it to the other side of the globe, returning with riches from Africa or the Americas. This time the North would not defeat me.

But I return to you a broken man, more broken this time than in my previous endeavors. I am weakened by a long illness, but it is not that which has made me, in the space of six months, a bent wreckage of my former self, my hairs gray—or rather grayer than they once were, particularly about the temples, although I confess that when I look into the mirror, I remain youthful of countenance, and not unattractive. No, it is that most common and yet mysterious of human ailments, a shattered heart.

How I shattered it—or how she did so, the woman to whom I

offered it, and who cared about it no more than she cared about jewels, fine clothes, or such other feminine adornments, you shall hear. I shall sit down again at your fireside in Hampshire, where I shall return to nurse my wounded heart. I know that you, most affectionate of sisters, will welcome me into your parlor, and gazing at me in your particular way, both loving and admonitory, say "Seriously, Robert" at this account of my adventures. But I assure you, dearest Margaret, that they are all true, or as true as memory may recollect, for my mind was touched as well by the illness I suffered, and there are things I remember only as fever-dreams. Yet her, and her dreadful father, I remember as clearly as though they stood before me—alas, if only she were here with me now! But I lost her, or rather I never had her, and therefore I return to you alone, with hopes and dreams dashed.

How fortunate I am that you, my sweet sister, are one of those women sent to be a comfort to man! It will be a pleasure to see your face again, with its calm gray eyes, and feel the warmth of your solemn smile, and taste the wonderful cakes that Mrs. Asher makes, the ones with the apricot jam centers.

But now to my story!

You know how I have dedicated my life and fortune to the exploration of the Arctic Circle, and how in that attempt I have been thwarted again and again! You yourself have been a generous supporter of these endeavors, when the audacity of my dreams has been greater than my income. On my first attempt, I was able to purchase the services of an English ship and captain. We made our way to a northern sea that glitters with icebergs, under the almost perpetual light of the Arctic summer. But alas, the ice closed in on us, and in the end, fearing for the safety of his ship and crew, the captain determined to turn back. It was on this trip that I encountered my friend Victor, of whom I have often spoken—a nobler gentleman never walked upon this earth. It was then, too, that I met the fearful shadow that pursued him—that fiend in human form, the destroyer of my friend's health and happiness. Of him, more anon.

On my second attempt, I was not able to get so far—waylaid by a fever in Archangel, I was confined to a sanatorium for three months, and finally ordered home for my health. I still remember with what devotion you nursed me, dear sister, during my long convalescence. "Robert," you said to me then, "surely this is enough. Surely now you will leave off this vain pursuit and live a sensible life. There are sciences you may pursue here, without going off to the ends of the earth, that will benefit mankind." Or some such. I cannot exactly recall your words, as to be honest, I did not then mark your advice. I remained desirous of scientific renown for opening up regions that had been hitherto hidden from man. Surely any gentleman who has been educated in what science can do, in its limitless potential to transform our understanding of this earthly realm, if not indeed the heavens themselves, will understand my ambition.

I still remember what a serious child you were, with your long brown ringlets, eternally sketching wildflowers, catching insects in jars and creating the most enchanting displays pinned on cards, prattling about the gradations of species as though you were an infant Linnaeus! And how you grew into a very pretty girl, the picture of sense and propriety, hiding your muddy boots under the hem of your skirt so our uncle would not know you had been out on the downs, collecting what have you—fossils, I think it was? You, with your feminine modesty, cannot understand the desire for glory, for the conquest of new realms, whether of land or knowledge, that drives men on— or some men. My friend Victor was such a man, and I myself have not been able to resist similar lofty ambitions. But alas, this third attempt was to prove my most disastrous, and I do not think that I shall ever again make the attempt.

Once again I hired a ship, but I was known in Archangel, and said to be bad luck, so no captain would work with me except one, a Russian named Ivan to whom others had given the soubriquet of The Madman. This madman, so-called, said he would work for me, and he assembled a crew. The men were not prepossessing—I suspected that some of them were smugglers or even pirates rather than honest whalers—but I had no choice in the matter.

We set out in late summer, later than I would have liked, but it had taken longer than I expected to equip our expedition. There was no enthusiasm for my project in Archangel. There was no wealth to be gained from sailing so far north, men said—they did not believe in my dream of a northern sea that would allow us to travel over the top of the globe itself, to the other side, and establish new routes to the riches of the Orient. They insisted that to the north was only ice. Alas that the mass of mankind is so shortsighted.

Nevertheless, the voyage started more propitiously than my last one. The weather was relatively balmy for those climes, the water remained clear of ice, and we sailed without impediment farther than I had been able to sail on my first ill-fated voyage.

But then, almost a month after we set out from Archangel, on a course headed northwest into the sea beyond Nova Zembla, we encountered storms so severe that I was in despair, expecting every day that my crew would insist on turning back, and I would once again have lost my chance at renown. Indeed, I believe they were prevented from so doing only because I had laid in a considerable supply of rum, and there was general drunkenness on board although somehow, the captain managed to keep us on a steady course. At last, the sea grew calm—I hoped we were about to enjoy a period of milder weather. But the cold came, suddenly, silently in the night—there was ice on the masts, ice on the sails, frost on the men's beards. We continued to sail northward, but the men began to grumble, and the rum was almost gone. Fights broke out—evidently the quartermaster had saved a private barrel for his mates, and some of the men suggested throwing him overboard. These are the circumstances of a rough sailing life, which would shock a gentlewoman like yourself.

Each day was colder than the last, and the ocean began to freeze around us. Finally, we had only a narrow path northward, and then no path, and the ship was entirely surrounded by ice.

Then began a dark and difficult time. For two weeks we stayed there, trapped in ice like the insects you collect in amber, insisting they reveal the age of the earth—darling Margaret! How your speculations have always charmed me! I am glad that you have never been exposed to the harsh, rough world of such men as these sailors. They fought and drank, and when the rum ran out, they fought the more. Then the biscuits and salted meat ran out, and a dark sort of talk began of salting the quartermaster—of how he would taste pickled and brined, probably like pork. One of the cabin boys disappeared, and I do not know if he wandered off into the white fogs that sometimes swirled about the ship, or whether—but I should not speculate about such things.

I knew that I must do something—so I asked the captain to gather his men on deck, and I spoke to them, as my friend Victor had done on my first voyage. I exhorted them to think beyond themselves: of the good they could do mankind, the fame they would achieve if we stuck to our purpose. Did they not want to benefit their fellow men? Did they not want to expand the field of science, of human knowledge?

Victor must have had some eloquence I lack, or perhaps this crew was much lower than the last in sensibility and ambition, for when I had made this argument, they glowered at me out of eyes that were red and raw from the perpetual light of the north, and in a few moments I found myself trussed like a chicken, tied hands and feet with rope.

Then they put me out upon the ice. None of them wished to kill me himself—there were English trade representatives in Archangel who would make inquiries, and none of them wished to be *more* guilty than his fellows, only *as* guilty so there would be no value to any of them in informing on the others. And besides, some of them were religious—they did not want blood on their hands. But they were willing to let the ice and cold perform the task they shunned. So I found myself out upon the ice sheet, which was in some places blue, in some gray, in some pure white, far enough from the ship so they did not have to witness my inevitable demise. I shouted myself hoarse for them to come back and get me, but to no avail. There I remained, bound hand and foot, protected only by the fur coat and leggings that I had commissioned specially in St. Petersburg.

I do not know how many hours I lay there, alternatively feeling anger and despair, sometimes commending myself to my Lord and Savior, for I expected to die before nightfall, sometimes railing against the men who had so cruelly abandoned me. At last, I lost consciousness from cold, fatigue, and hunger. I had no voice left with which to curse my fate or beg for mercy. My last memory is of the bright northern sky above, the glittering plains of ice around, and two words descending from the heavens as though spoken by God himself. I clearly remember that they were *You fool!*

When next I woke, I found myself in a room—not the cabin of a ship, but a proper room, although somewhat rough, with thick beams overhead. I could feel that I was lying down, and that I was warm. Indeed, I soon found, when I sat up a little, that I was in a bed under a wool blanket, and that the room was spacious, with dark wood furniture and a wide hearth on which a hearty fire was burning.

Where was I? What good angel had brought me here? Whoever he was, he had saved me from certain death.

For some minutes I lay still, wondering, then attempted to rise—but I could not. My head immediately began to spin, and my limbs to tingle as though I were a pincushion, with a thousand pins stuck into me. Indeed, the pain was so great that I once again lost consciousness, but before I did, it seemed to me that an angel came into the room, with a halo of black hair braided around her head, and eyes as gentle and kind as your own, Margaret, although brown rather than gray. She looked down upon me and said something I could not understand, then held a cup to my mouth, from which I drank—and remembered no more.

When I woke again, she was sitting in a chair beside the fireplace, reading a book of some sort. She heard me stir and looked up. By her dress, she was a servant—it was a simple red tunic over loose trousers, such as peasant women sometimes wear in Russia, embroidered at the neck and on the cuffs and hem.

"How are you feeling today?" she asked. To my astonishment, she spoke in English—heavily accented, but nevertheless English! She walked to my bedside and looked down at me—hers were the eyes I remembered from my dream, hers the braid of black hair. This woman, young and beautiful, was my good angel.

"Well, thank you," I said. I was startled by the sound of my own voice, which emerged as a hoarse whisper, as though I had not used it in a long time. I had a fit of coughing then, and she held my head while I drank from the cup that had been placed on a table at my bedside. Her hands were gentle although they held me firmly, and I felt that she was an angel indeed. She did not look like our English notion of an angel—her complexion was what we call olive and associate with the classically Greek, while her eyes turned upward at the corners, like those of a Turkish houri. Nevertheless, I divined it was she who had nursed me through my illness. But who had rescued me from the ice and brought me to this haven? It could not have been this delicate maiden. Such a rescue must have taken a team of intrepid men. I must find out to whom I owed my gratitude.

"If you will take me to your master," I said, "or perhaps your mistress, I will express my thanks for the care that has been taken of me. I do not know how I got here or how long I have been your patient, but someone has saved me from a dreadful fate, and I would like—"

"I am the only mistress here," she said, smiling with what seemed like amusement. "And at present, the only master. My father, who rescued you from the ice, is not expected back for some weeks. You may express your gratitude when he returns. You have been here a month, mostly under the influence of laudanum, my own formulation of it, while you recovered from exposure and dehydration. You will not remember most of that time. And there is no possibility of you getting out of bed, not today or anytime soon. No, don't try to get up—" for I had been in the process of attempting to rise, not aware that I was dressed only in a nightshirt. "I just gave you another dose of the drug. You will be asleep within a few minutes."

That is how I first met Aila, although I did not know her name until later. I was under the influence of the drug for some weeks after— there are days I remember only from moments or perhaps an hour of lucidity. Even now, I blush to think of how she must have cared for me during that time, bathing me, attending to the needs of my body—I vaguely recollect a chamber pot under the bed. And the conversations we had, in which she listened with interest to my accounts of England and my voyages, although she often had to depart before I was finished to perform her household duties. Is it any wonder that I grew to love her, that sweet maid whom I shall never see again? She told me that I had almost lost both legs and one hand to the terrible cold. It was only her ministrations, I am convinced, that kept me a whole man—except two toes on my left foot and my right pinky finger, which could not be saved. You have likely noticed that my handwriting is even more of a scrawl than when Mr. Parsons used to lecture me about it. Do you remember that we called him Parsley-face? You are fortunate, dear sister, that you did not have to listen to the lectures of a tutor, and were put under the guidance of Miss Elliott instead. What a pretty singing voice she had, although a rather large nose, and how nicely she danced! But no woman is a match for my lost angel, my beautiful Aila.

As the days went by, from her answers to my questions, for she never spoke much but answered with amused tolerance, I pieced together her history. She lived in that house with her father, but had not always lived there. The master of the house, who had rescued me from my terrible predicament, was a European, cast out from society for some sin or crime she did not specify. By her account, he was a great explorer, and had performed inhuman feats—climbing mountains no man had climbed, venturing into the inhospitable North farther than any man has yet ventured. At the time, I assumed these exaggerated claims arose from her evident love for her father, which I found admirable. In his journeys through the wilderness, he had encountered the reindeer herders of Lappland, who lived all year in their tents and wander here and there over the high tundra. There he met and fell in love with a woman, the chieftess of her people. By Aila's account, this woman, who would become her mother, was as strong and courageous as her father, but more steady of character. One day, when I was more lucid than usual, because I was beginning to heal and she had lowered my daily dose of the drug, I begged her to tell me more.

"All right," she said, putting down her book—when she entered my room, she was generally carrying a book of some sort, or some implement I could not identify, perhaps for cookery. I could not tell what that day's tome was from the name on the spine, since it was in Hebrew and my education, as you know, stopped at Latin. "I will tell you, if only to stop you from asking interminable questions. I cannot always be attending to you, now that you are getting better. I have my own work. But this once, because I know that otherwise you will not stop asking."

She sat down on the side of my bed—today her tunic was yellow, with the same embroidered patterns, or similar, but I do not have a woman's eye for such fine work—paused for a moment, then began.

"I did not know my mother long," she said. "I was only seven years old when she died, defending our herd from southern hunters. Every year they would come for the sport of hunting the reindeer, from Norway, Sweden, Denmark . . . Every year our tribe guarded and defended our herd. It was more than our source of milk, meat, fur. It was a part of our tribe, and my mother told me that sometimes a person who had died would return as a reindeer, or the other way around. Her own grandmother, a shaman during her lifetime, had been reborn as a leader of the herd, a large female with antlers that grew each autumn like the spreading branches of a tree.

"I asked her how she had met my father, who was obviously not of our people, with his pale face, his long limbs. Our people are short and compact, to conserve heat in winter, at the latitude where we dwell.

"She told me that one day, she had ridden out upon the tundra to find a pregnant female who had wandered away from the herd. She had given birth during the night in a ditch, and wolves had come—five of them, a small pack. The female was obviously sick—that was probably why she had wandered off. She could not care for her calf, who was staggering about, crying for milk. My mother could have fought off the wolves, but she could not do that, and protect the calf, and save the mother at the same time. She did not know what to do. That is when my father appeared at the top of the ditch—he had heard her shouting at the wolves, which often frightens them. But this pack was not frightened off. The three females had begun circling my mother, while the two males approached the calf. My father would have killed the wolves with his bare hands, but she told him to stop and leave them be. He did not understand our language, not then, but her gestures were clear, and he obeyed them. She could see that one of the female wolves had just given birth—her dugs were hanging down. The wolves needed food as much as the reindeer, as much as the tribe itself. The calf's mother was obviously too sick to survive. She told my father to keep back the wolves and, as gently as she could, she cut the female's throat, telling her to come back soon and be reborn as a member of the tribe.

"'Perhaps you are that reindeer, Aila,' she once said to me. 'Perhaps she blessed me for saving her child by becoming mine.'"

Aila was silent for a moment, perhaps considering the notion that she was a reindeer reborn—primitive tribes often have these sorts of ideas, which may seem ridiculous to civilized Europeans, but help them understand the world in the absence of science or theology. Then she continued. "They left the mother for the wolves, and my father carried the calf back to our tents. That was their first meeting. You will meet him soon," she said, glancing at me. "My father. He returns within a few days. Do not be startled when you see him. I used to think that he was ugly because he was European—I thought all of you looked like him. Since I have learned about Europeans from reading their books, I have realized that he would be considered an ugly man anywhere. You are shocked that I speak so of my own father, but you will see—even as a child I knew there was something wrong with his appearance, although his heart is more tender and loving than most.

"But my mother did not consider him ugly. To her, he was beautiful—for his strength, his compassion. She was the chief of our tribe—her father had been chief before her, and his aunt before him. Her brothers and uncles were worried when she chose a foreigner to be her husband, but when they saw how hard he could work, how impervious he was to any hardship, and how quickly he learned our language, they respected her choice. My parents loved each other with a tenderness that I believe is rare, for any couple.

"For some years, they did not have a child—my father told me that he feared he would never be able to have one. But at last I was born. I spent my first seven years with the tribe, sleeping in our tent, running over the tundra, learning the plants there, the signs that foretold weather, the ways of the reindeer. And I would have remained there all my life, perhaps becoming chief myself someday, or following the path of a shaman. But that summer the southern hunters came early, in larger numbers than usual—a Prussian count and his party wanted game. They paid a high price for the best guides and trackers. My father was away on one of his journeys—he could not keep from wandering in the wilderness, and my mother did not try to stop him. He assumed we would be safe until later in the season.

"I was not there when she was shot—she had left me safely back in our tent. But I was there when my uncles carried her back, still alive although dying from wounds we could not heal. There is no herb that will help against a gunshot.

"'Aila,' she said to me. 'Remember that I will always love you. When you look up at the stars at night, my spirit will be there, watching you, until one day it will be reborn again. I think this time I would like to come back as a wolf . . . But you, grow up strong and brave, my daughter. And take care of your father. He is strong but he has wounds on the inside, close to his heart—wounds that will never heal. When I die, he will have another one. He will need a reason to continue living. You must be that reason.'

"And then she died. Three days later, my father returned, in time to place her body on the funeral pyre. 'Aila,' he said to me after her funeral, 'there is something I must do. I will return soon.' It was three months before he returned again."

"Where did he go?" I asked, for she had paused in her narrative. I thought she might have forgotten I was there altogether—she seemed so lost in her own story.

She looked up, as though mentally returning to my sickroom. Then, she smiled. "Even in England, you must have heard of the death of Count von Schmetterling. It was notorious for its gruesome and inexplicable nature—the count was found both drowned and strangled, at the top of a tower that had not been entered since medieval times. He was found only because his horse was tied to an iron ring at its base. The key to the tower had been lost long ago, and it was evident that the door had not been opened for centuries—its hinges were so rusted that it had to be removed entirely before the local magistrate could enter. Under those circumstances, no suspicion could attach to anyone—a supernatural agency was clearly indicated, and rumors circulated of a family curse. His widow inherited his estate and is, I have heard, very happy with her second husband." She seemed amused by this terrible account, which made the hair on my neck stand up and sent shivers down my spine.

Something was beginning to stir in my mind, a memory and a supposition. Perhaps if I had not spent weeks in the Lethe of laudanum, I would have put it all together sooner—perhaps, Margaret, you have already guessed where my letter is leading. You were always good at puzzles and parlor games. But I merely stared at Aila, uncertain what to do with this information.

"Finally, my father returned," she said. "He told me that he could no longer stay with the tribe. There were too many sad memories for him there, too many painful recollections. But I could, if I wished it. I could stay with my mother's people, my aunts and uncles and cousins, learning the ways of the tribe and the reindeer. Or I could go with him, to a house he had built long ago on the coast of Spitsbergen. There he would teach me as best he could, as he had taught himself. But it was my choice to make.

"I remembered my mother's words—that he would need a reason to continue living, and I could be that reason. 'I will go with you, Father,' I said. So he brought me here, where I have grown and learned, alone except for him, when he is here. There is a village where we go for supplies, but it is three days from here by cart in summer or sleigh in winter, so I do not go often."

I took her hand. "You do not have to be alone any longer, lovely Aila. In these weeks I have grown to love you dearly. You are my sweet angel, a natural gentlewoman to match any in Europe. Come back to England and be my wife. I know my sister Margaret will welcome you into her household. And I will make a good husband for you. I will love and care for you as you deserve."

She looked at me with astonishment, then burst out laughing. "You take care of me? You cannot even take care of yourself. What would I do with a husband who goes off on useless and impractical journeys into the northern snows, who cannot wipe his own behind for a month at a time? You are not the husband for me, Robert Walton."

"Well, that is good to hear!"

Whose voice was that? It echoed through the room and into the depths of my consciousness. And then I knew what voice, not God's but the Devil's, had said *You fool!* on the ice.

It was he, the fiend and murderer of my friend Victor, his nameless creation—the monster.

"You!" I shouted. I believe I would have launched myself at him, despite his superior size and strength, if I were capable of doing so. But in my weakened state, all I could do was glare at his hideous countenance—still crossed by scars, still the pale yellow of a corpse. How could any woman, even one from a primitive tribe, who had never learned the refinements of civilization, find beauty in such features? How could anyone love *that*?

"Hello, Papa," said Aila, going to him and kissing him on the cheek. I shuddered to see it. My love for her did not die, would never die—not even such a gesture would kill it. But I could not bear the sight.

"Yes, it is I," he said, with an expression of lurid glee—or so I supposed, for what else could that embodiment of malice be feeling? He was my rescuer—and now my tormentor! As he had been to Victor himself.

"I thought you had determined to destroy yourself in a conflagration at the North Pole," I said, with contempt.

"That was my intention," he said, with a smile—a ghastly smile, I should say, although it also seemed somehow sorrowful. "But there are few materials with which to conflagrate, at that cold and remote location, and in the end, I wanted to live. Life itself remained precious to me, even after all I had suffered—and I still retained the desire to experience the natural world, to understand mankind. So I lived and traveled, to see sights upon this Earth that you, with your frail mortal body, shall never witness, Walton. To marry the best and most courageous woman who ever walked this Earth, and father a child that even you, with your limited, provincial mind, cannot help admiring, although you understand only a small portion of her worth. But she is not for you. It's time for you to return to your home in England. And God help me, if you ever set foot above latitude sixty degrees north again, I will strangle you myself, which is better than you deserve for all the trouble you cause. As soon as I heard in Archangel that you were back for another of your foolish voyages, I knew where it would end—and in truth, perhaps I should have left you there! I am only glad that the rest of your crew managed to make it back safely, once the ice broke. Aila, can he be ready to travel tomorrow?"

Aila looked at me appraisingly. "I think he is well enough, if he is dosed well and wrapped warmly."

"Good," said the monster. "I want him out of my house as soon as possible. Walton, you will travel by land to a village on the coast, where you will be picked up by a whaler on its way to Archangel. There, you will remain until you are well enough for the long journey back to England. And for God's sake, stay there! This is no place for a gentleman adventurer. Aila would find the Pole more quickly than you could find your own . . . well, I shall not say that in front of my daughter."

Did she understand the nature of her father? Of how he had been created from corpses by my friend, Victor Frankenstein? Alas, my poor Victor, who had suffered so much! It came to me that I should tell her—I should warn her that her own father was a fiend in human form, a daemon of the pit. But as she stood beside him, with her hand in his, her cheek against his arm, so calm and confident, I shuddered at the thought. I could not tell her of her own dreadful parentage. And it came to me, as well, that if I did, the monster might kill me directly afterward. So I said nothing.

And that, my dear sister, is how I ended up, for the second time, at a sanatorium in Archangel—the same sanatorium, where luckily the sisters recognized me and treated me kindly, calling me Walton the Arctic Explorer—admiringly, although some of them did giggle, but then girls do, you know.

I look forward to once again sitting by your fireside, drinking tea out of the Sèvres service that our mother left you, eating Mrs. Asher's cakes and little sandwiches. Please remind her that I particularly like the curried eggs and the watercress. I return to you a broken man— love lost, dreams and ambitions unfulfilled. But I shall henceforth take pleasures in the little things of life, and my own hearth, or rather yours, dear sister, for as I have no home of my own, I hope you will allow me to spend considerable time at Chatworth with you and Charles and the children. Please tell him that I am looking forward to seeing him again, and to continuing our discussions of Roman politics in the time of Julius Caesar.

I almost forgot to mention that before I left, Aila asked me to enclose a letter to you, no doubt some reminiscences of our time together and directions for my care. It is a bit lumpy, I do not know why, most likely because of the quality of the paper. You know she does not have access to fine linen weave in the far North! But I enclose it here. I look forward to seeing you soon, my dear Margaret.

Your loving brother,
Robert

Dear Margaret,

I hope you don't think it rude of me to address you so informally. Your brother Robert told me a great deal about you, both in his delirium and when in his right mind, for the man never stops talking. Forgive me, he is your brother, but the tedium of hearing his stories over and over again almost drove me mad. I do not know how you can stand it. You may recognize my surname, for Robert talked incessantly of his friend Victor—the man my father taught me to call grandfather, although I scorn the lineage. Among other deficiencies, my grandfather seems to have been an inferior researcher, careless in his observations and crude in his methodology.

From what Robert said, or did not say, it seems that you too are interested in the science of Botany. It is one of my fascinations, and I hope that someday I can study in Europe at one of the institutes, or perhaps a botanical garden. I write to you now asking if you would perhaps care to correspond, and I enclose several seeds, with a description of their characteristics and properties, that may interest you as examples of the local flora. I do not believe they have yet been studied by European scientists.

If you write to me at the enclosed address in Archangel, the letter will reach me, although slowly in my present remote location. But I look forward to hearing from you, and to learning that I have a sister in science who is as dedicated to the pursuit of knowledge as I am.

Yours sincerely,
Aila Frankenstein

COME SEE THE LIVING DRYAD

I CAN HEAR THEM WHISPERING.

I cannot see them, not yet. And when the curtain is pulled back, what will I see? Faces, pale and almost indistinguishable in the gaslight. My shows are only at night, for that, he tells me, makes them more impressive.

But I know my audience. Clerks heading home from their offices, tired after a day of crouching over a ledger, wanting to see a miracle. Serious young ladies who would never condescend to the spectacles of Battersea Park, but this is different—a scientific lecture. A tutor shushing his charges, boys who will one day go to university—until they see me, and then they shush of their own accord. They recognize me from their lessons in the classics and wonder, how is it possible? Gentlemen in top hats, headed afterward to more risqué entertainments. An old woman in black who peers at me through her pince-nez, disbelieving. She must have seen an advertisement and become curious—is it real? Or a hoax, like the Genuine Mermaid?

I am improbable, am I not?

Almost, but not quite, impossible.

And when the curtain is pulled back and they see me, sitting on my pedestal, arms raised, branches swaying, they will gasp. As they always do.

COME SEE THE LIVING DRYAD
PROOF THAT THE ANCIENT MYTHOLOGIES WERE
VERITABLE TRUTHS!

YOU HAVE READ OF THEM IN HOMER AND HESIOD.
NOW, TONIGHT, YOU MAY SEE FOR YOURSELF, ONE
OF THOSE "DWELLERS IN THE LOVELY GROVES,"
THOSE DAUGHTERS OF GAIA. LIVING PROOF THAT
THE WONDERS OF THE ANCIENT WORLD HAVE
NOT PASSED AWAY ALTOGETHER IN THIS AGE OF
TECHNOLOGICAL MARVELS.

VIEWING AT 8.30, SPECIAL LECTURE AT 9.00 BY
PROFESSOR L. MERWIN, M. PHIL., D. LITT., LL.D.,
MEMBER OF THE ANTHROPOLOGICAL INSTITUTE OF
GREAT BRITAIN AND IRELAND.

TICKETS TWO SHILLINGS,
HALF PRICE FOR CHILDREN.

Who killed Daphne Merwin? By 1888, she was famous enough that the case was mentioned in the *London Times*:

> A tragedy in Marylebone. On the morning of June 7th, Mrs. Lewison Merwin, who has become famous as Daphne, the Living Dryad, showing nightly at the Alhambra, was found brutally murdered at her home in Marylebone. Her husband, Professor Merwin, is distraught and stated that he does not know who

could have committed such a crime, as she had not an enemy in the world. According to Inspector Granby of the Metropolitan Police, Mrs. Merwin was stabbed in the chest with a kitchen knife. This crime was doubly brutal because, due to her physical peculiarities, Mrs. Merwin was unable to defend herself. Members of the public are urged to bring any pertinent information to the attention of the Metropolitan Police, who promise a swift investigation.

As this edition of the paper was going to press, the man who would be hanged for her murder had already been arrested. Alfred Potts was a pauper and occasional petty thief. That morning, he had come to the Merwin residence. The maid-of-all-work had let him in at Daphne's insistence. According to her account, he had offered to do whatever work needed doing of a heavy nature, in exchange for a hot meal. Daphne, who was habitually charitable, said he could do some work in the garden. After the maid let him in, she returned to the basement kitchen to prepare lunch for the Merwins. Lewison Merwin, who had a meeting with a business associate, was expected back at noon.

She did not leave the kitchen again until she heard the front doorbell. It was Lewison, who had forgotten his latchkey. The maid let him in and returned to the kitchen, expecting to serve lunch. A few minutes later, he ran down the back stairs and told her to come quickly, that Mrs. Merwin had been murdered. When she followed him up to the parlor, she saw Daphne lying on the carpet, with a red stain spreading across her nightgown. Alfred Potts was gone. So was the money for miscellaneous expenses kept in a side table drawer, in the front hall.

It was the nightgown that first struck me about the case, now more than a century old. Why would Daphne Merwin meet a strange man in her nightgown? In 1888, no lady would have done such a thing, and Daphne was trying very hard to be a lady. Potts was arrested in a public house in Spitalfields, where he had been drinking most of the day.

The money that had been in the drawer was found in his pocket. He claimed Daphne had given it to him. He knew nothing about any work in the garden, and indeed there was nothing to indicate he had done any. The gardening tools were still in the shed, and there was no evidence they had been used. After she had given him the money, he had left and gone straight to the pub. He had been sitting there drinking at the time the maid claimed he was murdering Mrs. Merwin. The woman who owned the pub confirmed his story, but since she had once been arrested for prostitution, neither the police nor the jury believed her. The pub being otherwise empty at that hour, there were no other witnesses.

The inspector asked why Mrs. Merwin would give him money, without him having done any work. But Potts, who was drunk, merely cursed and tried to assault him. Then he was taken away in a police wagon.

This was all I could learn from the records of the Metropolitan Police, which had been digitized the previous year and placed online. The online archives of the *London Times* contained an account of the trial, which lasted only three days. During the trial, Potts made an extraordinary claim: that Daphne Merwin was his sister, and that she had given him money several times since he had discovered her address, following her home one night from the Alhambra. But when asked for evidence, he could produce nothing, claiming that any proof of their relationship had been stolen from him long ago. Indeed, the police found few possessions of his in the squalid room he shared with two other men, both dockworkers. Lewison Merwin stated that his wife had been an orphan and alone in the world when he met her. He insisted that he had never seen Potts before in his life, and the maid confirmed that she had never seen him at the house before the day of the murder. Surely, if Potts had come to solicit Mrs. Merwin before, the maid would have been the one to let him in.

Needless to say, neither the judge nor jury believed Potts. Not even his own barrister seems to have believed him. He was poor, sleeping on street corners or in that disreputable boarding house, and an alcoholic. The jury reached its verdict in under an hour. He was condemned to death and hanged on September 27th, 1888.

—*The British Freak Show at the Fin-de-Siècle*,
D.M. Levitt, PhD

Every morning, he prunes me. I sit in a chair in the middle of my bedroom and raise my arms. Carefully, he trims away any small branches that are not aesthetically pleasing.

"We don't want you to look pollarded," he says.

His goal is always beauty, grace, lightness.

I was neither beautiful nor graceful when he found me. The branches had grown from my hands so I could hardly lift them. They had grown on my feet so I could scarcely walk. Bark had begun to grow over my face. I was worried that soon it would cover my eyes, and I would be a poor, blind, crippled girl, a pitiable object.

Every day, my brother would place me on my little cart and pull me down to a street corner near Brick Lane Market. There we would beg for pennies. Some passersby would throw pennies on the ground, pitying my grotesqueness. Some would turn away with a shudder. Sometimes the bric-a-brac sellers would give me bits of their lunch. Sometimes we were spit upon, or a group of boys would throw pieces of pavement and rusted nails.

But he found me and saw what I could become. If you come with me, he said that day on the street corner, I will make you beautiful. I will make it so all men look at you and gasp in admiration rather than fear. I will make you a celebrity.

My brother had gone off—young as he was, he had already succumbed to the Demon Drink. I knew he was spending our pennies at a public house while I sat on the cart, waiting and hungry.

Yes, I said. I will go with you.

Look how my branches rise into the air, so gracefully, so lightly. The bark grows up my arms to my elbows. My feet he prunes more thoroughly, so only a few small branches sprout from my toes. I have no need of shoes, for my soles are hard. The bark grows up to my knees.

There is a little bark on my forehead, but it does not encroach on my eyes. My ears are clear. I can see and hear and speak. A human heart beats in my chest. And yet I am like no other woman. That is why he loves me, he says. Because I am unique.

After he prunes me, Lucy removes my nightgown and bathes me, because of course I cannot bathe myself. She dresses me. And then she brings me the child.

You schoolboys sitting in the front should know, or your schoolmaster should have told you, that the dryads and oreiades were the nymphs of the trees and woodlands. They were associated with particular trees, and when her tree died, the dryad died with it. Woe betide any Greek villager who felled a tree with a dryad, for misfortune would follow him all the days of his life!

The dryads and oreiades sprang from Gaia herself. Who is Gaia, you ask? Surely that learned young woman in the back . . . yes, exactly. Gaia was the goddess of the earth. And their father was Ouranos, god of the sky. So they were born of heaven and earth. There were many kinds of dryads: the meliai, nymphs of the ash trees; the pteleai, nymphs of the elms; the aigeroi, protectors of poplars. The balanis for holly trees, the sykei for figs, and moreai for mulberry. And then there were the orchard trees: the meliades protected apple trees, and kraneiai could be found beneath the cherry boughs. But the most graceful of all were the daphnaie, the nymphs of the laurel trees, and that is what you see before you tonight.

Where did I find such a marvel? Why, in the hills of Arcadia, of course. I was walking through the verdant groves when I came upon her, sitting by a stream, looking down at her reflection in the water, as laurel trees do. Since I spoke the language of ancient Greece, whose study I recommend to those of you who are diligent and have the time, I convinced her to return with me to the greatest city in the world, to London itself. So you, citizens of the age of steam and iron, could see that the wonders of the ancient world are not wholly gone from the earth—nay, they are only hidden from our eyes. But if we have faith, if we listen with open hearts and see with unclouded vision, we may still witness miracles.

Turn, Daphne, so our audience can see the beauty and delicacy of the daughter of Gaia and Ouranos, nymph of laurel trees—a modern wonder!

Lewandowsky-Lutz dysplasia is one of the rarest diseases in human history. In the late twentieth century, two cases brought the disease to public attention: those of the Romanian Ion Toader and the Indonesian Dede Koswara. This hereditary genetic disorder makes the sufferers abnormally susceptible to an HPV (human papillomavirus) infection of the skin. As a result, wherever the skin is cut or abraded, the patient develops macules and papules, particularly on the extremities, such as hands and feet. In extreme cases, these can grow into "limbs" that resemble tree branches and must be removed by surgery. More common are bumps and ridges on the skin that may turn cancerous. Toader was fortunate: he was diagnosed by a prominent dermatologist, who was able to remove most of his growths surgically, and his continuing medical treatment was paid for by the state healthcare system. Since his surgery, the Lewandowsky-Lutz has not progressed, and he has been able to live a normal life.

The second case, that of Dede Koswara, was both more serious and more widely reported. He had a particularly advanced case of the disease, both because he lived far from modern medical facilities and because his immune system lacked an antigen that would have helped him fight the HPV infection. By the time his condition was diagnosed, he was almost completely incapacitated, working in a freak show to support himself, like Daphne Merwin, but without the help of a consummate showman such as Lewison. Once his condition was discovered, he was profiled on various cable television shows, as well as in a *Medical Mystery* episode titled "Tree Man." The show paid for surgery to remove most of his growths, but there was no way to stop them recurring, and he recently passed away from what the internet describes only as "complications." There is still no cure for Lewandowsky-Lutz.

Since the age of twelve, I have developed flat, scaly macules regularly on my hands and feet. Fortunately they have not spread to other parts of my body, and the university provides me with excellent health benefits. I visit a dermatologist monthly to have them removed. Underneath, the skin is lighter, so my hands and feet look mottled. I could cover them with concealer, I suppose. But when I look at them, I remember Daphne. In a small way, they bring me closer to my great-great-grandmother.

—*The British Freak Show at the Fin-de-Siècle*,
D.M. Levitt, PhD

I thought Lucy was my friend.

Of course she is my maid, but where else could she find work, with her disfigurement? I knew her when she was begging on the street corners of Spitalfields: a dirty, hairy girl with wild, scared eyes. It was I who insisted that he hire her. And now?

He says she should not have told me, that he is still negotiating a contract. But she is to come before me . . . before *me*! And thus, he says, he will show them both our evolutionary and mythological pasts. Both the Primitive Eve and the Living Dryad.

But she is not beautiful. No amount of grooming could make her beautiful. She looks like . . . yes, a monkey. A sly, low, ill-bred monkey of a girl that I took off the streets, and clothed, and housed. And this is how she treats me.

I heard them last night, long after he thought I was asleep. I did not drink my laudanum, so I lay awake and heard noises, for her bedroom is above mine. First the two of them talking, although I could not make out the words. And then other noises.

Has he not considered me? Has he not considered our child? Our Daisy, asleep in her cradle. How I love her, and yet it is even more difficult for me to hold her than to write.

COME SEE THE PRIMITIVE EVE
THE MISSING LINK IN MR. DARWIN'S THEORY!

HITHERTO, THE ARGUMENT AGAINST MR. DAR-
WIN'S THEORY HAS BEEN THAT NO CREATURE
HAS BEEN FOUND IN A STATE BETWEEN MAN AND
MONKEY. THE PRIMITIVE EVE IS THAT CREA-
TURE—AN ATTRACTIVE, WELL-FORMED MAIDEN
COVERED ENTIRELY WITH A PELT OF DARK HAIR.

FOUND AS A CHILD IN THE WILD FORESTS OF
BORNEO, SHE HAS BEEN BROUGHT BACK TO ENGLAND
AND TAUGHT THE BENEFITS OF CIVILIZED SOCIETY.
HEAR HER READ FROM THE BIBLE. WATCH HER
PERFORM HER NATIVE DANCES AND THEN CURTSY
WITH THE NICETY OF AN ENGLISH SCHOOLGIRL. ALL
SHOULD SEE THIS LIVING MARVEL!

VIEWING AT 8.30, SPECIAL LECTURE AT 9.00 BY

PROFESSOR L. MERWIN, M. PHIL., D. LITT.,
LL.D., MEMBER OF THE ANTHROPOLOGICAL
INSTITUTE OF GREAT BRITAIN AND IRELAND.

TICKETS TWO SHILLINGS,
HALF PRICE FOR CHILDREN.

My mother first showed me the diary when I began developing Lewandowsky-Lutz. She wanted me to understand where it had come from—why I had bumps on my hands and feet, although evidently it had skipped a generation, because she never developed symptoms. But my grandmother died young of cancer from Lewandowsky-Lutz. My great-grandmother, Daisy Merwin, lived to a hundred and one, although she had to clip the growths on her forearms at regular intervals. It affects us all differently.

After Daphne's death, Lewison sent their daughter Daisy to the United States, to be raised by his sister's family in Virginia. That would free him to travel with his newest marvel, Lucy Barker, advertised as the Primitive Eve. She belonged to the "hairy woman" type of freak show performer, like her contemporaries Krao and Julia Pastrana, both of whom are discussed in Chapter One. Merwin traveled all over Europe with the Primitive Eve, who became particularly popular in France—until she died of a laudanum overdose. Deprived of his major source of income, he returned to New York and worked in the Barnum & Bailey Circus, becoming one of its managers after Barnum's death in 1891. Although he tried to arrange his own shows on the side, he never again attained the success he had with Daphne or Eve.

After his death, his daughter Daisy received a small inheritance, mostly wiped out by his debts, and a box of her mother's effects. They included Daphne's diary, a silver brush and comb set that I still use to subdue my hair, and a necklace of coral beads I wear almost every day.

In the nineteenth century, coral was believed to protect against diseases—that is why children were given coral necklaces to wear. The necklace didn't help Daphne; nevertheless, I find it reassuring. It is an attractive placebo.

We must remember that Lewison was a charlatan. Despite his claims, he was not a university professor, nor had he earned any of the degrees or distinctions listed on his advertisements. He had started his career at a theological seminary in Virginia, training to be a minister. One week, P.T. Barnum's Grand Traveling Museum, Menagerie, Caravan, and Circus, as it was called in the 1870s, came to town. Lewison bought tickets for every show, and finally asked to meet Barnum himself. That was the beginning of his career as a showman. Barnum hired him as an agent and sent him to London to arrange bookings for his various shows. And that is where he found Daphne, the Living Dryad.

Her diary contains no dates. It is rambling and impressionistic, written in large looping letters made by a woman who had difficulty simply holding a pen. There are misspellings, although her grammar is almost self-consciously correct, for which, I suppose, we must thank Lewison: he taught her to write. Nevertheless, the entries are suggestive.

What they suggest is that Daphne Merwin was not killed by Alfred Potts.

—*The British Freak Show at the Fin-de-Siècle*,
D.M. Levitt, PhD

This cannot continue. I will speak to him, I will tell him that he cannot have us both.

Think of the publicity! he says. Think of the money we will make! But I do not care about that.

I would rather be back on the streets of London, begging for crusts of bread. Am I insensate, a piece of wood for him to move about as he wishes? Am I the mythical creature he likes to call me? No, I am human, whatever I may appear to be. I breathe, I feel, I love.

I will not let him treat me like this. I will not let her speak to me as she has in the past few days. She has been boasting about how successful she will be, more successful than I am. She has been wearing my dresses, neglecting the child. My child—who deserves better, who deserves everything. I cannot let this continue.

I will speak to him and tell him so.

WESTERN UNION

MISS LETITIA MERWIN

CLOVERFIELD, V.A.

JUNE 23

SENDING YOU DAISY CARE OF IRISH NURSE ARRIVING
U.S.S. MERRIMACK AT NEWPORT JULY 3RD WILL SEND
CHEQUE FOR EXPENSES SOON AS NEW SHOW OPENS
AT ALHAMBRA LOVE LEWISON

MISS LETITIA MERWIN

CLOVERFIELD, V.A.

JUNE 24

ALSO REMEMBER WATCH FOR SYMPTOMS SHE MAY
BE AS DISTINCTIVE AS HER MOTHER IF SO SEND
WORD IMMEDIATELY IMAGINE THE SENSATION A
CHILD DRYAD

The evidence from the Merwin murder case is collected in a small box in the basement storage facility of the Metropolitan Police. In the summer of 2014, I traveled to London for two weeks on a research grant. I visited the neighborhood in Spitalfields where Daisy Potts, who would become Daphne Merwin, spent her childhood. It is now filled with restaurants—Indonesian, Albanian, Bangladeshi. I stood near the corner of Brick Lane Market, thinking of what it must have been like for Daisy, begging here, almost blind, until Lewison Merwin found her.

I visited the house in Marylebone where she had lived, but it was now a dentist's office, with flats on the upper floors. I visited Leicester Square, where the Alhambra used to stand. Even Newgate, where Alfred Potts was hanged for her murder.

Then I went to the headquarters of the Metropolitan Police. It had been difficult to get an appointment. The head of my department had written a letter describing my research, on university stationery. When that received no response, I asked a friend at Oxford, with whom I had gone to graduate school, to intervene. I thought Oxford would mean more than a regional American college. At long last I received an email from the head archivist: I would be allowed to examine the evidence for two hours, 4:00–6:00 p.m., on a Thursday afternoon. A camera would be allowed, without flash.

The junior archivist who met me in the waiting room was a serious young woman in glasses with thick black frames. Her badge proclaimed her Dr. Patel.

She handed me a similar ID badge, conspicuously marked TEMPORARY, with my name on it: Dr. Daphne Levitt, University of Southern Vermont.

"I've never been to America," she said as we rode down the elevator. "I would be a little nervous, especially in New York. You have so many shootings!"

"Not so many where I live," I told her. "My university is in a small town up north. They mostly shoot deer there. And street signs."

She looked at me as though scandalized that I would joke about such a thing.

"Your job must be so interesting," I said. That is my magical phrase. As an introvert, I've always found it supremely useful at parties. Once I say it, I don't have to talk for the next half hour.

She described it to me enthusiastically, but I only half listened. I was wondering what I would find in the evidence box, and whether it would help me solve the Merwin case. When I started writing this book, I asked my mother to send me Daphne's diary. I had not read it since I was a teenager. Then, I had only been interested in the disease itself, in what might happen to me if the Lewandowsky-Lutz progressed. But something about the newspaper account of the trial kept bothering me, and when I looked at the diary again, I saw it. Daphne had mentioned a brother. Could it be Alfred Potts? If so, Lewison had lied. Why?

I followed Dr. Patel down a long beige hallway that reminded me of middle school, and then into a room filled with shelves, rather like university library stacks except that all of the shelves were filled with carefully labeled boxes. We walked down one of the rows while she scanned them. "There," she said, and took down a box labeled *Merwin, Daphne 1888*.

I had expected an evidence box out of Dickens, yellowed and moldering, but this was thoroughly modern.

"Everything was recataloged in the 1990s," she said, I suppose in response to my expression. Perhaps the Metropolitan Police trained even archivists to read people.

She carried the box to a long table under fluorescent lights. "Just a moment," she said, as I reached for the lid. From a nearby cabinet, she produced two surgical masks and gloves of some artificial material that felt like plastic trying to be cotton. When I was properly outfitted, I sat at the table and opened the box.

In it were the items the police had collected on the day of Daphne's murder. At the top of the box, protected by a plastic sleeve, was a stack of yellowing papers. On the first sheet of paper was written, in a sloping nineteenth-century hand,

> *Evidence in the death of Mrs. Lewison Merwin:*
> *Item 1: Nightgown torn by knife, with bloodstain.*
> *Item 2: Branches broken from the body of Mrs. Merwin*
> *in altercation.*
> *Item 3: Photograph of Mrs. Merwin.*
> *Item 4: Statement of Professor Merwin.*
> *Item 5: Statement of Lucy Barker, housemaid.*
> *Item 6: Statement of Mrs. Polansky, neighbor.*
> *Item 7: Statement of Alfred Potts, suspect.*
> *Item 8: Statement of Alice O'Neill, barmaid.*
> *Item 9: Kitchen knife stained with blood.*

I opened the sleeve and drew out the stack of papers. Beneath the list was the statement of Lewison Merwin, describing how he had found his wife in the parlor, stabbed to death. He had been out of the house all morning, attending a business meeting at the Alhambra, where Mrs. Merwin had shows three nights a week. Under his statement was written, *Husband clearly distraught.* I took photographs of each page with my iPhone. Next was the statement of Lucy Barker, describing how she had answered the door at around ten o'clock and found Alfred Potts on the doorstep. She had not wanted to let him in, but her mistress had insisted, out of the goodness of her heart. She was always one to help the poor. Lucy had given him a meal in the kitchen at Mrs. Merwin's request, at which point he must have taken the knife, and no, she could not have watched him more carefully. She had lunch to prepare, hadn't she? Then he had gone out into the garden. She had heard nothing more until noon, when Professor Merwin rang the bell and she had let him in. A few minutes later, he had run into the kitchen, saying that her mistress had been stabbed. Of course he was upset, Mrs. Merwin had been stabbed, hadn't she? He had asked for a towel and hot water, but by then there was nothing to be done. Mrs. Merwin was dead. No, she had heard no sounds of an altercation in the parlor. The kitchen was in the basement, on the other side of the house, so why should she? And now if he could stop bothering her, she needed to feed the child. Under her account was written *Seems devoted to her mistress. UGLY!* The statement of Mrs. Polansky was short: she had been sitting in her parlor at around 11:30 when she had heard a man and woman arguing next door at the Merwins'. The walls were that thin, to the shame of these modern builders. Yes, she remembered the time because she had a grown son who was a clerk and came home for lunch, so she kept looking at the clock, knowing he would return around quarter till. No, she could not hear what was being said, but one voice was deep, a man's voice, and the other she thought was Mrs. Merwin's. A nice lady, although one couldn't exactly invite her over for tea, could one? Under her statement was written *Not English—Polack?* The statement of Alfred Potts was not much longer. He had gone to the Merwins' house asking for money, had been given money out of the hall table drawer, and had left, that was all. He had gone to the pub, where he had been sitting on this [objectionable language] chair ever since, as Alice could tell you. Asked why he had gone to the Merwins', which was half across town, rather than begging in Spitalfields, where he was no doubt better known. He had assaulted the officer and sworn in the most inventive and objectionable terms. At that point, he had been arrested. Under his statement was written *DRUNK.* The statement of Alice O'Neill was also short: Alfred Potts had come into the pub at 11:00, sat down in that chair right there, and had been sitting there ever since. Under her statement was written *Known to police as Alice O'Connell, Alice Ferguson.*

Dr. Patel sat patiently while I photographed each page. At the bottom of the stack was the photograph that forms the frontispiece of this book. It is the only photograph we have of Daphne Merwin, since in her advertisements she was usually drawn in a way that exaggerated her arboreal qualities. When I first located it on the internet, on a website devoted to freak show history and paraphernalia, I printed out a copy and pinned it to my office bulletin board. But this was one of the original prints. It shows her seated on what looks like a column with a Corinthian capital, about the height of a kitchen stool, wearing a long white gown that leaves her arms bare. She is holding her arms up as though they were a bifurcated trunk with branches and twigs growing from them. Her skin is rough and bark-like to the elbows, but perfectly smooth above. Her hair is done up in the Victorian idea of a classical chignon. The gown is floor-length, but she is raising one foot so you can see the thick, gnarled growths on her toes. They do, indeed, look like tree roots. You have to give Lewison Merwin credit for one thing: he did a good job pruning her. The branches are thinned out, trimmed back in places. Despite their weight, she could lift her arms. She could walk. If you look closely at the original photograph, you can see what is not obvious from the online version: the rough skin on her forehead. But it does not grow down to her eyes. She could see. She could even have a child. She looks off to the side rather than at the viewer, but her chin is raised, elegantly, proudly. If you ignore the growths on her arms and feet, it is the photograph of an ordinary, if very attractive, Victorian woman.

"My God," said Dr. Patel, leaning across the table. "What was wrong with her?" She had been quiet for so long that I had almost forgotten she was there.

"Lewandowsky-Lutz dysplasia," I said. "Or, you know, being murdered. Can I take out the nightgown?" I had now photographed every piece of paper in the stack. I slipped the stack back into the plastic sleeve and set it aside. It was time to look at the physical evidence.

"Yes, as long as you're wearing gloves," said Dr. Patel. Now she was leaning forward, clearly interested. I pulled the nightgown out of the plastic bag. It was made of a thin white cotton batiste, very finely embroidered: an expensive article in the 1880s.

"You see all these buttons on the shoulders," I said, as though lecturing one of my students. "She couldn't have pulled the nightgown over her head. It had to be buttoned up, probably by her maid."

"A wound that deep would have killed her almost instantly," said Dr. Patel, looking with professional curiosity at the place where the nightgown was torn. Around the tear it was bloody, and blood had soaked down one side, probably where it had dripped and pooled. "You see, the knife went right in: the hole isn't ragged. But there's a lot of blood. It would have been a deep, clean wound." She put on a pair of fake-cotton gloves, pulled the plastic sleeve of papers toward her, and started reading through them.

I imagined Daphne Merwin lying on the floor, with a deep, clean wound in her chest, bleeding her life away while my great-grandmother lay in her cradle upstairs. Did she cry out? There is no record of any cry, so maybe she was too startled, maybe she died too quickly. Who stood over her, watching her die? That was the question I wanted to answer. I folded the nightgown and slipped it back inside the plastic bag. It had told me only that Daphne was indeed stabbed—and that the Living Dryad had bled like an ordinary woman.

Below the nightgown were two other plastic bags, both containing pieces of linen. Perhaps wrapped around whatever was inside? I lifted the one on the left, distinguishable from the other only because it was more square than oblong. I unwound the linen. Inside were a bunch of horny, bifurcating growths.

"Some of her branches," I said in response to Dr. Patel's inquisitive expression. "Parts of her, hardened like keratin, almost like your nails? They must have broken off during the struggle."

"There was no struggle," Dr. Patel responded, frowning above her glasses. "Not judging by those bloodstains—just stabbing and bleeding. She wouldn't have had time to fight back. Can I take a look?"

"I'm glad you're here, because bloodstains don't tell me anything," I said. "Then I suppose these must have broken off when she fell, after she was stabbed?" I pushed Daphne's branches toward Dr. Patel and turned to the third and final plastic bag, knowing what it must contain: the murder weapon. While I unwrapped it, she examined the broken growths. It made sense that she would be curious—after all, how often did you hear of a person like Daphne Merwin, a malnourished nineteenth-century orphan with a full-blown case of Lewandowsky-Lutz, turned into a living myth? And then a murder case.

I unwound the final piece of linen. Here was the knife that had killed her. I laid it on the table in front of me.

It was about seven inches long, four of handle and three of blade: a sharp, curved knife that would inflict a particularly vicious wound below the skin. The blade and part of the handle were stained an ancient, rusted red.

"That's a strange-looking knife," said Dr. Patel. She had the branches spread in front of her and was lining them up, like a child playing with twigs.

"It is," I answered. "The Victorians often used very specific tools. I wonder if it had some sort of specialized use in the kitchen . . ."

I took a picture of it with my phone. "Can I use your Wi-Fi? I want to do a Google search, but it says I need a password. I can't get a cell signal down here."

"You won't, in the basement of one of these old buildings," said Dr. Patel. She pulled off one glove and held out her hand. "Here, I'll type in our guest password."

When she handed the phone back to me, I did a Google image search.

And there it was, the same knife, with the wicked curved blade, although without the bloodstains of course. THE ORCHARDMAN'S BEST FRIEND, REGULARLY £35, ON SALE FOR £25 UNTIL THURSDAY, HOME ORCHARD AND GARDEN SUPPLY, BERKSHIRE. BY APPOINTMENT TO HER MAJESTY THE QUEEN.

"It's a pruning knife," I said. I stared down at the image on my screen, then showed it to Dr. Patel. I think, at that moment, the truth was just beginning to sink in. "You see, he used to prune her . . ."

"Well, that makes sense," she said. She held up one of Daphne Merwin's branches. "These ends are cut, not broken. The . . . growths didn't break off during a fight. They were cut off, probably with a blade just like that." She peered at my phone screen, and then at the knife, with the intellectual curiosity of a born scientist who dissects reality for the sheer pleasure of understanding. I could not be quite so dispassionate, but whatever I was feeling, looking down at the weapon that had killed my great-great-grandmother, I put aside for the moment. This was not the right time.

"Let me start at the beginning. You see, she left a diary . . ." I told Dr. Patel everything I had learned so far about Daphne and the Merwin household. "So he's pruning her," I concluded. "They quarrel, and he stabs her with the knife. All it would take is him going out again, maybe through the back door into the alley, then coming back half an hour later. Lucy Barker verifies the time of his arrival, identifies the knife as one of the kitchen knives, and tells the police about Alfred Potts's visit earlier that day. All it would take is Lucy lying for him."

"What happened to Lucy?" asked Dr. Patel.

"She died two years later, of a laudanum overdose. Accidentally—or so it was assumed at the time. Perhaps it was suicide—perhaps she felt guilty for her part in the murder? I suppose you could call her an accessory after the fact."

"Are you sure it was murder?" Dr. Patel tapped the papers piled on their plastic sleeve with one gloved finger. "The statement of Mrs. Polansky describes some sort of altercation. Perhaps he stabbed her on impulse? That would make it a case of manslaughter."

I stared down at the knife. "I don't suppose we'll ever know for sure." Anyway, did that sort of legal distinction matter? Whether he had planned to do it or done it on the spur of the moment, Lewison had stabbed Daphne Merwin. I was sure of it.

"What happened to Professor Merwin after Eve's death?"

"He wasn't a professor—he just claimed to be. And he returned to America." As though nothing had happened, as though he could go on with his life. Yet that was what people did, wasn't it? Go on? Although Eve had not been able to . . .

"He must have been a clever, charming man, to attract two such women," said Dr. Patel. "But unscrupulous. Men like that often are."

"Why didn't the police officer who originally investigated see this?" I asked. "It was right there in front of him."

Dr. Patel smiled—now she was the one lecturing a student. "One of the first things they teach us is that people don't see what's in front of them. They see what they expect to see. It's very hard to get beyond that."

"So we walk through a world already created by our preconceived notions?"

"Precisely."

Precisely was also how she packed all the evidence back in the box. This, I thought, was Daphne Merwin's coffin, as much as the one in which her body lay decomposing.

That was in Highgate Cemetery. It was the next to last place I would visit in London.

"I'll look for your book," said Dr. Patel as we shook hands. Mine felt odd from being inside those gloves.

"I'll send you a copy," I said. And when I do, I thought, you'll see yourself in the acknowledgments. Thank you, Dr. Patel, for showing me what I could not have seen on my own: who killed Daphne Merwin.

—*The British Freak Show at the Fin-de-Siècle*,
D.M. Levitt, PhD

Dr. Daphne M. Levitt, PhD
Assistant Professor, Department of English
University of Southern Vermont, Ascutney Campus
Ascutney Falls, Vermont 05001, USA

Dear Dr. Levitt:

I was so interested in the case of Daphne Merwin that I decided to look into it a little further. I hope you will forgive me, but your great-great-grandmother was a fascinating woman. I did not find anything pertinent in our archives, so I asked a colleague of mine at the British Library to investigate as well. He suggested that if Daphne Merwin, or Daisy Potts, was living in Spitalfields at the time she was discovered by Lewison Merwin, she might be on the rolls of one of the poorhouses in that area. Most of those documents have been lost, so I did not have much confidence that he would be able to find anything. However, after several weeks, he sent me the following scan of a page dated March 1880 from the record books of the St. Joseph Street Charitable Institution. If you look approximately a third of the way down the page, you will find the following entry:

> *Alfred Potts, 17 years of age, able-bodied workman,*
> *and sister Daisy, 15 years of age, cripple.*

I believe this entry refers to your great-great-grandmother and her brother Alfred. It would be a great coincidence if there were an Alfred and Daisy Potts of exactly the right age, siblings and the sister described as a "cripple," in Spitalfields at that time. I hope this helps with your research. I very much look forward to reading your book!

Sincerely yours,

Dr. Devi Patel, MSc, PhD
Junior Archivist II
Metropolitan Police

Dear Daffy,

I read your book, and the chapter on Daphne just made me cry! I recommended it to the book club, and we're supposed to talk about it next Thursday. Honestly, I don't know how I'm going to get through the meeting without starting up again—I'd better bring a box of tissues. She was a remarkable woman, and Lewison was just rotten to her. Though I hate to think he was a murderer—maybe it was an impulse, as Dr. Patel said? Although I don't know if that makes it any better. And I can't help blaming that Eve person for helping him, although I'm sure Lewison was just as bad to her as he was to Daphne. It's too bad we have to be related to him too, hunh? But that's how families are, I guess—a mixed bag.

You inspired me to go through Grandma's boxes up in the attic. I know I should have done it sooner, but it took me a long time just to get over her being gone. Even now, I keep expecting her to be in the kitchen baking biscuits, or in the living room watching her soaps. I guess your mother never leaves you, not really. When your dad comes into a room and catches me just staring out the window, he says, "You're thinking about Judy again, aren't you? I sure do miss her cooking." Even he says she was the best mother-in-law, and I don't know how he could give a bigger compliment than that!

Anyway, yesterday I finally went through all those boxes, and I found an old photo album I'd never seen before, under a prayer book. It's filled with photos from her dad's family, and you know she never talked to him after he forbade her to marry Grandpa. Well, you won't believe what I found, tucked right into the back—it's a picture of Daphne Merwin! That photo you used in the book, the one you found on eBay a couple of months ago and wanted to buy, except you said it was too expensive. Well, here it is! I used a photo envelope so it wouldn't get bent and paid the Earth for special delivery—you know how those postal people are! You send a package through the regular mail, and it's like wolves tore it apart.

It's a real original photo! The name of the studio is printed on the bottom, and on the back you'll see some words—I'm pretty sure Daisy wrote them. It looks like a child's writing, though children wrote so much more neatly back then, and with real ink! It says, *My beloved Mama.* Isn't that sweet? There, I'm going to cry again. I'm glad her daughter remembered her. Seriously, someone should make a movie based on Daphne's life story—except I wouldn't want everyone to know my great-grandpa was a murderer. Your book is fine, of course—it's all scholarly, with footnotes. But seeing it on a screen would be different.

I heard it snowed again up there—down here the crocuses are out, and Dad is complaining that he'll have to start mowing the grass soon! Tabby brought in a baby bird—we put it out on the back porch and half an hour later it was gone. I don't know if it got away, or if Tabby found it again. Drat that cat! That's all the news from down here. I hope you get some time to rest, with all those students—you work too hard, sweetie! Dad sends a big hug, and we're looking forward to seeing you this summer.

> Lots of love, and we're so proud of your book,
> Mom

After meeting with Dr. Patel, I stopped at a Costa for a chai latte and a cheese and chutney sandwich, then took the Northern Line up to Highgate Cemetery, where I knew Daphne Merwin was buried. My visit to the Metropolitan Police Archives had taken longer than anticipated, and I had just enough time to find her grave, then take some photographs for this book. Her gravestone was a simple obelisk, on the pedestal of which was written,

Daphne Merwin
The Living Dryad
1865–1888

Long ago, someone had planted a vine at its base, and it had grown up over the obelisk, almost obscuring it in dense, shrubby growth. That day, the vine was covered in green leaves and small white flowers. I wondered if Daphne would have liked that, if she would have considered it some sort of tribute.

It was getting late: the shadows of gravestones lay dark across the paths. So I took the tube back to central London. In the university dorm room I was renting for two weeks, I typed up the notes from my visit to the archives and started packing my suitcase. The next day would be my last in London.

That night I dreamed I was lecturing my students, back in Vermont. But when I looked down at myself, I realized I had become a tree. They did not seem to notice, typing on their laptops as usual, although I was standing at the front of the lecture hall covered with bark, waving leafy green branches instead of arms. I remember the lecture was about Nathaniel Hawthorne.

The next day, I slept through my alarm and woke up with a headache. I took two Advils and finished packing for that evening's flight back to New York, where I had an appointment at the Barnum & Bailey Museum Archives, which contain a collection of Lewison Merwin's papers and paraphernalia. I had already visited the Barnum & Bailey Museum once: there I had seen a transcript of Lewison Merwin's lecture, taken in shorthand during one of Daphne's performances, as well as letters and telegrams. After his death, Daisy Merwin sent all of his papers to the museum, but she kept the diary—the archivist there had not even known Daphne Merwin's diary existed. (My family has agreed to loan it to the museum for a Merwin exhibit, focusing on both Daphne and Lewison, to coincide with the publication of this book.) Now, however, I would be looking at them from a different perspective. Now I would know how Daphne had died. Perhaps I would see things in Lewison's papers that I had not seen the last time. After that, I would go back to Vermont, where I was scheduled to teach Classics of English and American Literature II during the second summer session. And I had a book to finish.

But that morning, my last in London, I would visit the Royal College of Surgeons.

It was a gray, wet day, typical for summer in London. I got off the tube at Holborn and walked to Lincoln's Inn Fields, then to the imposing gray building with its classical portico and Latin engraving across the front. There was a smaller sign for the Hunterian Museum, where I was headed. Once you enter the Royal College of Surgeons, you go up one flight of stairs, and there, to your right, is the Hunterian Museum: a collection of anatomical specimens and curiosities that dates to the late 1700s. You enter, expecting oak cabinets and dim lighting, as it might have looked in the eighteenth and nineteenth centuries, but no. What you see are glass cases, all around you, brightly lit as though you were in a dissecting room. The cases are filled with glass bottles, as anatomy students would have seen them a hundred years ago. Some of them still have their original labels, with Latin names written in ornate script. They contain animal embryos preserved at every stage of development, tumorous growths of various sorts, the brain of the mathematician Charles Babbage. There are skeletons, from a bat's to the tall bones of Charles Byrne, the Irish Giant. The exhibit is arranged on two floors around a central space that allows you to see from the top of the museum to its bottom, so you can walk around and around that macabre display.

At the back, there is a small gallery, a dark alcove of paneled wood hung with paintings: some of prominent scientists, some of freak show performers. It is an unintentional reminder that to many Victorians, genius was a frightening, freakish quality—as much a deformity, in its own way, as a beard on a woman. Eng and Chang are in that alcove, as is Julia Pastrana. In a dark corner, under a prominent surgeon, are two paintings, hanging side by side. I had deliberately left them for my last day, not wanting them to affect my interpretation of the research. Now here they were, and here I was. Under one, on a brass plaque, was engraved *The Living Dryad*. Under the other, *The Primitive Eve*. Both were by the same artist, both set in an idealized natural landscape that resembled the Royal Botanic Gardens. In one, a woman dressed in a classical Greek chiton held up her arms, which were also branches—recognizably Daphne Merwin, although more arboreal. She even had leaves at the ends of her fingers. In the other crouched a woman dressed only in a loincloth, covered with light brown hair. Lucy Barker had died and been buried in France, but here she was reunited with Daphne. The both of them together, counterparts of each other, as Lewison had wanted them in his show.

I stood there, looking at them for a while . . . not sure, as a modern woman, what to think of that tragedy, long ago. That tangled relationship between two women, and the man who had helped and used them both. Who had been, directly or indirectly, responsible for their deaths. I blamed Lewison for what had happened. His was, after all, the hand that held the knife. But like everything else in life, it was more complicated than I had assumed it would be. History always is.

But I could not stay long. I had a plane to catch, a life in America to return to.

On my way out, the front desk attendant said, "I hope you enjoyed the museum! Bit gruesome for some . . ."

"I enjoyed it very much," I replied, and put my last British coins in the donation jar. I still had ten pounds in notes, which would be enough to buy me coffee and a magazine at Heathrow before I boarded the plane for home.

If we had been living in the late nineteenth century, you and I, we might have paid a shilling or two to see the human wonders of the age: the Bear Woman, the Dog-Faced Boy, the Elephant Man, the Primitive Eve, the Living Dryad. A century later, we must rediscover Julia Pastrana, Fedor Jeftichew, Joseph Merrick, Lucy Barker, and Daphne Merwin: the human beings behind the labels and advertisements. Who were they? What did they think? How did they feel? By and large, they left no records, although perhaps there are papers moldering somewhere, like Daphne's diary. We owe it to them to learn as much about their histories as possible. That has been, in part, the aim of this book: to see beyond social and ideological constructs and recover, to whatever extent possible, the voices of the voiceless. To let the spectacles speak for themselves.

—*The British Freak Show at the Fin-de-Siècle*,
D.M. Levitt, PhD

But do they actually see me?

Or only the creature he has created? To them, I am merely a curiosity, and sometimes I wish that I could speak—he has told me not to speak, that only he is to speak, ever. My speaking would destroy the illusion. But I wish to tell them . . . what? That I am real, flesh and blood, not wood. That I am a woman, not a fairy tale. I have a soul, as they do.

Would they listen?

You, beyond the lights, I would say. When you look at me, what do you see? When I speak, what do you hear?

BEAUTIFUL BOYS

You know who I'm talking about.

You can see them on Sunday afternoons, in places like Knoxville, Tennessee or Flagstaff, Arizona, playing pool or with their elbows on the bar, drinking a beer before they head out into the dusty sunlight and get into their pickups, onto their motorcycles. Some of them have dogs. Some of their dogs wear bandanas around their necks. Some of them, before they leave, put a quarter into the jukebox and dance slowly with the waitresses, the pretty one and then the other one.

Then they drive or ride down the road, heading over the mountains or through the desert, toward the next town. And one of the waitresses, the other one, the brunette who is a little chubby, feels a sharp ache in her chest. Like the constriction that begins a panic attack.

"Beautiful Boys" is a technical as well as a descriptive term. Think of them as another species, *Pueri Pulchri*.

Pueri Pulchri cor meum furati sunt. The Beautiful Boys have stolen my heart.

———————

They look like the models in cigarette ads. Lean, muscular, as though they can work with their hands. As though they had shaved yesterday. As though they had just ridden a horse in a cattle drive, or dug a trench with a backhoe.

They smell of aftershave and cigarette smoke.

That night, when she makes love to her boyfriend, who works at the gas station, the other waitress will think of him.

She and her boyfriend have been together since high school.

She will imagine making love to him instead of her boyfriend: the smell of aftershave and cigarettes, the feel of his skin under her hands, smooth and muscled. The rasp of his stubble as he kisses her. She will imagine him entering her and cry aloud, and her boyfriend will congratulate himself.

Afterward, she will stare into the darkness and cry silently, until she falls asleep on the damp pillow.

Would statistics help? They range from 5'11" to 6'2", between 165 and 195 pounds. They can be any race, any color. They often finish high school, but seldom finish college. On a college campus, they have almost unlimited access to what they need: fertile women. But they seldom stay for more than a couple of semesters.

They are more likely than human males to engage in criminal activities. They sell drugs, rob liquor stores and banks, but are seldom rapists. Sex, for them, is a matter of survival. They need to ensure that the seed has been implanted.

They seldom hold jobs for more than six months at a time. You can see them on construction sites, working as ranch hands, in video stores. Anything temporary.

They seldom marry, and those marriages inevitably end in desertion or divorce. They move on quickly.

They always move on. I believe that on this planet, their lifespan is approximately seven years. I have never seen a Beautiful Boy older than twenty-nine.

Oscar Guest is not his real name.

He had all the characteristics. Tall, brown skin, high cheekbones: a mixture of Mexican and American Indian ancestry. Black hair pulled back into a ponytail, black eyes with the sort of lashes that sell romance novels or perfume. He was wearing a t-shirt printed with the logo of a rock band and faded jeans.

"I hear you're paying $300 to participate in a study," he said.

It's a lot of money, particularly considering our grant. But we choose our test subjects carefully. They have to fit the physical and aesthetic criteria (male, 5'11"–"6'2", 165–195 pounds, unusually attractive). Even then, only about 2% of those we test are Beautiful Boys.

I could tell he was one of them at once. I've developed a sort of sensitivity. But of course that identification would have to be verified by testing.

Sometimes, the Beautiful Boy doesn't move on immediately. Sometimes, he stays around after the dance. He gets a job in construction, starts dating the pretty waitress. If she insists, they might even get married.

By the time he leaves, she's pregnant.

As far as we know, Beautiful Boys mate and reproduce like human males. Based on anecdotal evidence, we suspect they're superior lovers, but that data has not been verified. We are writing a grant to study their reproductive cycle. However, we are still at the stage of identifying them, of convincing the general population that they are here, among us, an alien species.

We always perform the standard tests: blood tests, skin and hair analysis. Beautiful Boys are physiologically identical to human males, but show a higher incidence of drug use. They typically have lower body fat, more lean muscle. I have known some to live on a diet of Cheetos and beer. They don't need to diet or exercise. It's as though their metabolism is supercharged.

What Oscar used to eat: Cocoa Puffs with milk, orange juice from concentrate, peanut butter and jelly sandwiches, leftover pizza, Oreos, beer.

Although I have no statistical evidence, I believe Beautiful Boys need more carbohydrates than human males. Once, at night, I walked into the kitchen and saw him standing in front of the open refrigerator, in his boxer briefs, drinking maple syrup from the jug.

He showed up at my house.

"Hey, Dr. Leslie, it's me, Oscar," he said when I opened the door. "I was wondering if there's anything else I can do for the study. My landlord just kicked me out and I don't have money for another place."

"Why did he kick you out?" I asked. It was 2 a.m. I stood at the door in my pajamas and a robe, trying not to yawn.

"I got in a fight."

"A fight? You mean in the apartment?"

"Yeah," he said. "With the wall."

He showed me his bloody fists. I told him to come in and cleaned his knuckles, then bandaged them.

"How much have you been drinking?" I asked.

"A lot," he said. He looked sober, although he smelled like beer. Beautiful Boys have a higher than average tolerance for alcohol. That metabolism again.

"You can spend the rest of the night on the sofa," I said. "Tomorrow, you'll have to find a new apartment."

The next morning, I woke up to the smell of pancakes. He was in the kitchen, fixing the screen door that had always stuck. "Hey, Dr. Leslie," he said. "I made you pancakes. How come you don't have a man around to fix this door, a beautiful lady like you?"

"My husband decided that he preferred graduate students," I said.

"Seriously? What an idiot. This door should work a lot better now. Anything else you want me to fix around here?"

The pancakes were stacked on a plate, on the kitchen table. I sat down, poured syrup over them, and started to eat.

I have devised a test that identifies Beautiful Boys with 98% accuracy. I believe Beautiful Boys emit a particular set of pheromones to attract human women. I do not know whether this is a conscious or unconscious process.

We put the test subject in an empty room. My research assistant, a blonde Tri Delt, enters the room and asks the test subject a series of questions. The questions themselves are irrelevant: What is your favorite color? If you could be any animal, what would you be? (A statistically significant number of Beautiful Boys identify themselves as predators, wolves or mountain lions.) After he has answered the questions, we inform the test subject that he has been enrolled in the study and give him the study t-shirt, in exchange for the shirt he is currently wearing. We take that shirt and put it in a sterile plastic bag.

Later, three testers smell the t-shirt and rate their sexual arousal on a scale of one to ten. Human males typically elicit no more than a five. Beautiful Boys average in the seven to nine range. Our testers are all female. I have found that the best testers are brunette, a little chubby, nearsighted. They are most responsive to the chemicals that Beautiful Boys emit.

Why have they come to Earth?

For the same reason aliens always come to Earth in old science fiction movies: Mars needs women.

Where is their home planet? I'm not sure even they know.

Sometimes Oscar would stare off into space, and I would say, "What are you thinking about?"

He would say, "Just a place I used to play when I was a kid." Then he would roll over and say, "Hey, how about it? Are you up for a quickie?"

He was a superior lover. I do not, of course, know if that is a characteristic of all Beautiful Boys, or unique to Oscar. I think of him sometimes, when I'm alone at night: his smooth brown skin, mostly hairless, with the muscles articulated underneath. The black eyes looking down into mine. He would grin, kiss the tip of my nose. He was always affectionate, like a puppy. One day he brought me flowers he'd stolen from the college's botanical gardens.

"You really shouldn't have," I said. "I mean, seriously."

"I know," he said. "But that's what makes it fun."

One day, he came to me and said, "Dr. Leslie, I've got to go. My dad down in Tampa is sick, and I need to take care of him for a while."

I didn't tell him, you don't have a father in Tampa. You landed here on an alien spaceship with others of your kind. Where, I don't know.

"Give me your father's address," I said. "I'll send you some books."

He scribbled an address down on a slip of paper.

We made love one last time. It was like all the other times: intimate, affectionate, effective. Like being made love to by a combination of teenage boy, eighteenth-century libertine, and robot. Then I gave him $500 and he drove off in his pickup.

A week later, I missed my period. I was angry with myself, told myself I should have been more careful. Although I suppose my therapist would tell me that I unconsciously wanted this to happen.

I found a phone number for the address in Tampa. It was a bicycle repair shop, where they had never heard of Oscar Guest.

The study has three stages. The first one, nearly complete, involves devising a test to identify Beautiful Boys. That test has been devised, with 98% accuracy. We are in the process of writing up our results.

The second stage, for which we are currently seeking funding, focuses on understanding their reproductive cycle. We believe Beautiful Boys belong to a species that only produces males. To reproduce, they depend on the females of other species. In order to spread their genes and avoid inbreeding, they leave the planet on which they were born and travel to another planet, where they transform themselves into particularly appealing males of the target species. They travel around that planet, implanting their offspring.

The third stage focuses on the offspring they produce with human women. What are these children like? We do not know when Beautiful Boys first began coming to Earth, although we suspect their presence as far back as the early twentieth century. There were probably Beautiful Boys seducing women in both World Wars, in Korea, in Vietnam. There are certainly alien children among us. We should find out as much about them as we can.

———

I'm going to call him Oscar Jr.

I didn't need the ultrasound to tell me that he was a boy. Of course he would be.

What will my Oscar be like? Will he play with Matchbox cars? Will he watch *Scooby-Doo*? Someday, will he ask about his father?

We don't know what happens to the children of Beautiful Boys, which is why completing the third phase of the study is so important. We don't know if some of them have the lifespan of human males, or if they all repeat the reproductive cycle of their fathers. Will Oscar go to college, settle down with a nice brunette, have my grandchildren?

Or, after high school, after we have argued because he's been smoking pot again and he's told me that he needs to find himself, waving a battered copy of *On the Road*, will he drive to the mountains, find the ship with others of his kind, fly to another planet and become whatever the women want there: green, with six arms and gills, like something out of an old science fiction movie?

I don't know. I think I would love him, even with six arms and gills.

I think of them sometimes, all the Beautiful Boys, driven to reproduce as salmon are driven to spawn. Driving across the country like an enormous net whose knots are bars, cheap apartments, college dorm rooms. And because I'm a scientist, I'm comforted by what science teaches us: that life is infinitely stranger than we can understand, that its patterns are beyond our comprehension. But that they tie us to the stars and to each other, inextricably. Like a net.

PUG

> "Pug is flat, like most animals in fiction. He is once
> represented as straying into a rose-bed in a cardboard
> kind of way, but that is all . . ."
> —E.M. Forster, *Aspects of the Novel*

You DON'T KNOW how lonely I was, until I met Pug.

In summer, tourists come to Rosings. The coaches are filled with
them. They want to see where Roger de Bourgh murdered Lady Alice, or where Lady Alice's grandniece Matilda de Bourgh hid King
Charles, in the cellar behind a cask of port, from the Roundheads.
There has always been a rumor that her son, from her hasty marriage
to Walter d'Arcy, resembled the king more than his father. The de
Bourghs have never been known for acting with sober propriety. Miss
Jenkinson relishes the details. "And here," she says, "you will see the
bloodstains where Lady Alice fell. This floor has been polished every
day for a hundred years, but those stains have never come out!" And
indeed there are, just there, discolorations in the wood. Whether
they are the bloodstains of Lady Alice, I can't tell you.

When the tourists come, I go to my room, in the modern wing of the house where even Miss Jenkinson's ingenuity will find no blood-stains, or out into the garden. If, by chance, they happen upon me, I admire the roses, or the fountain with its spitting triton, and they assume I am one of them. Of course, if Miss Jenkinson sees me, she scolds me. "Miss Anne, what will your mother think! Outside on a day like this, and without a shawl." With the fog rolling over the garden. We are in a valley, at Rosings. We are almost always in a sea of fog.

I could hear them that day, the tourists. In the fog, their voices seemed to come from far away, and then suddenly from just beside me, so I ducked into the maze. It is not a real maze: for that, the tourists must go to Allingham or Trenton. It is only a series of paths between the courtyard, with its triton perpetually spitting water, while stone fish leap around him in rococo profusion, and the rose garden. But the paths are edged with privet that has grown higher than I, at any rate, can see. I have called that place the maze since I was a child. When I am in the maze, I can pretend, for a moment, that I am somewhere else.

So there I was, among the privets, and there he was, sitting on his haunches, panting with his pink tongue hanging out. Pug.

Of course I did not learn his name until later, when he showed me the door. The door: inconsistent, irritating, never there when you want it. And at the best of times, difficult to summon, like a recalcitrant housemaid.

But there was Pug. I assumed he had come from Hunsford, from the Parsonage or one of the tradesmen's houses. He was so obviously cared for, so confident as he sat there, so complacent, even fat. And he had a quality that made him particularly attractive. When he looked at you with his brown eyes and panted with his pink tongue hanging out, he looked as though he were smiling.

"Here, doggie," I said. He came to me and licked my hand. I knew, of course, that Mother would never allow it. Not for me, not in, as she called it, my "condition." But as I said, I was lonely. "Come on, then." And he followed me, through the courtyard, into the kitchen garden with its cabbages and turnips, and through the kitchen door.

I had no friends at Rosings, but Cook disliked Miss Jenkinson, and the enemy of my enemy was at least my provisional ally. I knew she would give me a scrap of something for Pug. He gobbled a bowl of bread and milk, and looked up at me again with that smile of his.

"If Lady Catherine finds him in your room, there will be I-don't-know-what to pay," Cook said, wiping her hands on her apron.

"Mother never comes into my room," I said.

"Well, I'll tell Susan to hold her tongue. Only yesterday I said to her, you're here to clean the bedrooms, not to talk. Someday that tongue of yours is going to fall off from all the talking you do. And won't your husband be grateful!"

"All right, Cook," I said. "I'll take him up, and could you have Susan bring me a box with wood shavings, just in case, you know."

"Certainly, Miss." She patted Pug on the head. "You're a friendly one, aren't you? I do like dogs. They're dirty creatures, but they make a house more friendly."

And that's how Pug came to Rosings. I carried him, as quietly as I could, past the gallery. "Every night," Miss Jenkinson was saying, "Sir Fitzwilliam d'Arcy walks down the length of this hall and stands before the portrait of his brother, Jonathan d'Arcy, who chopped off his head with an axe right there in the courtyard and married his wife, Lady Margaret de Bourgh. Visitors who have seen him say that he carries his severed head in his arms." I heard gasps, and a "Well, I never!" The de Bourghs and the d'Arcys. We have been marrying and killing each other since the Conquest.

Later, when I had learned something of how the door works, I discussed it with the Miss Martins.

"Mary had a thought," said Eliza. "She did want to tell you, although I told her, Miss, that you might not like hearing it."

"Please call me Anne," I said. "We share a secret, the three of us—

and Pug. So we should have no distinctions between us. We know about the door. Surely that should make us friends."

We were sitting in the Martins' garden, at Abbey-Mill Farm. I could smell the roses that were blooming in the hedge, and the cows on the other side of the hedge, in the pasture. Eliza had folded her apron on the grass beside her. She was fair and freckled, although she used Gower twice a day. She looked what she was, the perfect English farm girl, with sunlit hair and a placid disposition. Mary was still wearing her apron, as though about to go in and finish her cleaning, but she had woven herself a crown of white clover. She was darker than her sister, with a liveliness, like a gypsy girl from Sir Walter Scott. An inquisitiveness. She had been the scholar, and regretted leaving school.

"Well," said Mary, "this is what I've been thinking, Miss—Anne. Eliza and me, we're the ones to whom nothing happens. There's Robert marrying Harriet, and all the high and mighty folks of Highbury marrying among themselves, and even the servants seem to have their doings. But us—we just milk the cows, and clean the house with Mother, and take care of the garden, day after day, no different. And begging your pardon—Anne, but nothing happens to you either. You read and you go out riding in your carriage, that's all. And what could happen to Pug?" Who was lying contentedly on the grass beside us. At Abbey-Mill Farm, the sun almost always shone. I was glad to escape, for a while, the fogs of Rosings.

"You're right," I said. "Nothing ever does happen to me. I don't think anything ever will."

"Well then," said Eliza, "here's what Mary thinks. She thinks the door is for us. That it was put there just so we could find each other. Do you think that could be true?"

I put a clover flower on Pug's nose, and he stared at me reproachfully before shaking his head so that it fell onto the grass. "We are told there is providence in the fall of a sparrow. Why not in the opening of a door?"

"That's lovely, Miss," said Eliza. "Just like Mr. Elton in church."

When I was a child, I was not allowed to have toys. I slept on a bare bed, in a bare room. Those were the days of Dr. Templeton. He believed in strengthening. If I could be strengthened, I would no longer be sick or small. So there were cold baths, and porridge for breakfast, and nothing but toast for tea. Then came Dr. Bransby, who believed in supporting. If my constitution could be supported, then I would be well. Those were the days of baths so hot that I turned as red as a lobster, fires in July and draperies to keep out drafts, and rare roast beef. I have been on a diet of mashed turnips, I have been to Bath more times than I remember, I have even, once, been bled. Nothing has ever helped. I have always been sick and small. When I walk up stairs, I am always out of breath; when I look in the mirror, there are always blue circles under my eyes, blue veins running over my forehead. I always remind myself of a corpse.

When I was a child, I was not allowed to have friends. Other children, "young horrors," as Mother called them, would be too softening, said Dr. Templeton, too trying, said Dr. Bransby. One day, so lonely that I could have cried, I wandered through the corridors, almost losing myself, and discovered the library. ("Over a thousand volumes," said Miss Jenkinson. "The gilding on the books alone is worth more than a hundred pounds.") Dr. Templeton's regiment had confined me to the schoolroom, but Dr. Templeton had been summoned to Windsor Castle, to attend the King himself. And Dr. Bransby, whose carriage was expected that afternoon, had not yet arrived. Miss Jenkinson, thinking I was asleep, had put her feet up and fallen asleep with a handkerchief over her face. I could hear her snoring.

I tiptoed, frightened, down the endless corridors of Rosings, with de Bourghs and d'Arcys frowning at me from the walls. At the end of one corridor was an archway. I walked through it and saw shelves of books going up to heaven. ("The fresco on the ceiling was painted by an Italian, Antonio Vecci," said Miss Jenkinson. "Although unlikely to appeal to our modern tastes, in his day the painting, of classical gods disporting themselves in an undignified manner, was considered rather fine. If you look in the corner there, up to the right, you'll see where the painting was left unfinished when Vecci eloped with Philomena de Bourgh. He was later shot in the back by Sir Reginald.")

Will you laugh if I tell you that the first book I read, other than my Bible and *The Parent's Assistant*, which Miss Jenkinson appreciated for its edifying morals, was Aristotle's *Metaphysics*? How little I understood of it then! How little I understand still, even after discussing it with Dr. Galt. But Dr. Galt seldom has time for long discussions.

My cousin Fitz teased me about my serious reading matter. "You don't read like a girl, Anne," he said, "but like you're prepping for Oxford. Look, I brought you some grapes from the conservatory." I was not allowed to eat fruit, which Dr. Bransby said were not sufficiently supportive. But how tired I was of soft-boiled eggs and beef tea! "If you won't tell, I'll teach you a little Latin."

From his window, Fitz could see when Dr. Bransby walked to the Parsonage, where he could smoke his pipe without Mother finding out. She did not approve of tobacco. When Dr. Bransby was out of sight, Fitz would say, "Come on, Anne, let's go down to the maze!" We would laugh at the triton, with his absurdly distended cheeks, and crouch among the rosebushes, where no one could see us, feeling the pleasure of being unsupervised and completely hidden.

Of course, I knew why Fitz came, or had to come. Those portraits of the de Bourghs and d'Arcys—they haunted us both like ghosts.

Once, when I was fifteen, I said to him, "I'll never be a beauty, will I?"

"You're distinctive in your own way, Anne," he said.

That wounded me, although he had meant it as a compliment. Was woman ever wooed thus? No, I don't think so either.

Finally, Dr. Galt said, "It's your heart, Miss de Bourgh, and there's nothing to be done about it. You must live as normally as you can." Thank goodness for Dr. Galt.

It was Pug who showed me the door.

"Take that dog out of the drawing room at once!" said Mother. "Can't you see that he's shedding on the cushions? Really, Miss Jenkinson."

She would never, of course, say it directly to me. I was the delicate one, the last of the de Bourghs, who must be coddled and tortured into health. Into marrying and producing an heir. She steadfastly treated Pug as Miss Jenkinson's dog, although every night that he was at Rosings, he slept in my bed, curled beside me, snorting in his sleep. She would never give in to something as vulgar as fact.

I took Pug into the garden. It had rained the night before. I had seen the lightning from my bedroom window, flashing over the avenue of lime trees, over the park where the tourists fed the deer. The triton looked wet and somehow glum. The privets were bent awry, as though they had been engaged in a mad dance. The path through the rose garden was covered with petals, like wet rags. Pug ran over them, toward the lime alley. And suddenly, he was no longer there.

"At first," said Eliza, "I couldn't see the door at all. But now I always see it, that—shiver, when it opens. Mary could always see it better than I can. And she seems to be able to—call it, sometimes."

"I don't know how I do it," said Mary. "I just call, and it comes. But not always. Don't worry, Miss, you'll see it better after a while. And you've got Pug. He seems to be able to smell it, almost. As soon as the door opens, he goes right to it."

That first time, the door opened into another garden. It surrounded a house, modern, not particularly attractive, smaller than Rosings. I wandered around the garden, curious and confused, not certain where I was or what I should do. Finally, I looked in through a window. A woman, stately, placid, as old as Mother but without her appearance of constant activity, sat on a sofa. "Why, Pug," she said, "wherever have you been?" Pug jumped up on the sofa and sat beside her, like a cushion.

"The strangest thing," said Eliza, "is that when you go through the door to another place—or time, no one seems to notice you're there. And when you come back, no one seems to notice you were gone. It's like being a ghost."

"Do you think it's wrong for us to go through it, Miss?" asked Mary. "Perhaps it's a devilish device, as Mr. Elton would say, designed to tempt us." She seemed genuinely distressed. I put my hand on hers.

"Don't be silly," said Eliza. "Miss de Bourgh has already told us that it can be explained naturally, like that machine at the Royal Society. Like lightning. Surely nothing in nature is of the Devil. Surely everything in nature has been created by God. And think of what finding the door has done for us! We've been to London, to Bath. Do you think the Miss Martins of Abbey-Mill Farm would have been able to travel to those places? And thank you again, Miss," she nodded to me, "for showing us around Pemberley. It was a kindness my sister and I will never forget."

"Do you believe, Miss, that the door is created by God?" asked Mary.

"I don't know," I said. "But you said, once, that we are the people to whom nothing happens. I wonder if, perhaps, there is a provision for us. I know this sounds silly, but—a provision for us specifically, for the people to whom nothing happens. Perhaps the door has been sent—to allow us to communicate with one other, so we will not be, you know, lonely."

"But then why only the three of us—and Pug?" asked Mary. "Surely we aren't the only ones to whom nothing happens."

"Don't forget Mrs. Churchill," said Eliza. "Although she did not encourage the acquaintance, after that first meeting in Bath. I think, to her, the Miss Martins of Abbey-Mill Farm were of no consequence. She was not as condescending as you are, Miss. And we have not seen her now for more than a year."

"But that shows there are others," I said. "That we have not found them does not mean they do not exist. Perhaps it's time we started looking for them."

Here are the things my mother wanted me to have. Beauty, in which I failed her completely. Come to the mirror, let us look at my face, so pale, so insignificant. Wit, ditto. Once, when I was a child, Fitz's sister Georgie came to visit. She said to me, after an afternoon during which we were supposed to be playing, "I would like you better, Anne, if you weren't so dull." Accomplishments, of course, I could not have. Dr. Templeton and Dr. Bransby agreed: I must not hold a pencil or paintbrush, must not practice the pianoforte, must not under any circumstances learn to dance. I must not exert myself in any way. Dr. Galt said, "What a pair of quacks." But by then it was too late; I was neither beautiful, nor witty, nor accomplished. I had nothing to recommend me except a fortune.

And of course, Mother wanted me to marry Fitz.

Fitz said to me once, as we were walking in the garden, "Anne, we can talk to each other, can't we? I mean, we used to be friends when we were children."

He looked, as he always looked, sad and uneasy. I think he had read too much German philosophy. Once he had told me that at Oxford he had lost his faith in both humanity and God.

"There's no reason we can't be friends now," I said.

"Then—would you care terribly if we didn't marry?"

I put my arm through his. "Oh, Fitz. Marry that girl, the one who came with the Lucases, who plays the piano so badly." She did play badly, I was jealous enough to say that. I cared, of course. It was difficult not to love Fitz. But I remembered what Dr. Galt had told me.

"It's your heart, my girl. It's like a lake in there, sloshing around. I wish it had a good, steady beat like a piston. Some day, we'll be able to replace the human heart with a machine."

"That doesn't sound at all nice," I said. "How can a machine love?"

There were other things I asked him: "Am I going to die?"

"We're all going to die. And if you're careful, you won't die any sooner than most. But that means no marrying. You must learn to content yourself with the pleasures of an old maid. The first child you have—then you *will* die, Anne. And perhaps the child will die as well. Do you understand?"

"If Mother were here, she would dismiss you at once. Do you know I've been destined to marry my cousin since I was born? It's a sort of dynastic alliance."

Dr. Galt laughed. "It's time the de Bourghs and the d'Arcys had some new blood. You've been marrying each other too long." Then he shook his finger at me. "But I'm serious, Anne. You can live long and well, but you must find another way."

And: "What if there were a door that could take me, in an instant, between two places that are far away from each other, perhaps even far away in time—into the past for instance, or even the future, when Napoleon will be defeated."

"As we all hope he will be!"

"If there were such a door, how would it work?"

"So you've been following my advice."

He had told me, "Most of the women I know waste their lives embroidering on silk and reading French novels. You should hear my own daughters, talking about the regiment! It's soldiers, soldiers all day long. But you, Anne, with your natural ability and the library here at Rosings, can develop the intellect God gave you. Read philosophy, read history. Learn Greek. There is nothing in the field of scholarship that you can't accomplish."

"Despite my broken heart?"

"Because of your broken heart."

"Doors that transport you through space and time are not my speciality," he answered. "But at a meeting of the Royal Society I once saw a mechanical apparatus with two arms, which resembled a headless doll. A spark of electricity jumped from one arm to the other, instantaneously, without seeming to have passed through the space between. Later that day, at a lecture attended by the King, I heard a philosopher say we are all composed of energy. Why should we not, with a mechanical device, or a door as you called it, pass from one place to another, like that spark?"

And he smiled at me, as though I were a clever child. That is what we see in the mirror, a sick child, although I am almost twenty.

"Keep reading, Anne. Keep exercising your mind as much as you can. If you can't have the life other women have, remember you can still have a life that is fulfilling, even in some ways superior to theirs."

This is what I told Fitz: "Marry her with my blessing. And if you accomplish nothing else, you will have made Mother thoroughly angry. That in itself will be an accomplishment, I think. Life at Rosings will be so much more interesting for a while."

He looked down at the path. "I don't even know if we could be happy together. But I can't help loving her. Oh, I'm a fool!" My introspective, morose cousin. Would he make a good husband for anyone? He would, I thought, have made a good husband for me.

"You must get out into the sun more often, Anne," he said. "You look like a fish that has lived in a cave for a hundred years." I was startled and gratified that he had noticed.

"What sun?" I said. "The sun never shines at Rosings."

Once, when I was in London with Mother, I saw a blind man being led by a dog. A black dog, a labrador mostly, and it led him to a street corner where the dog sat, and then the man sat and put his cap on the pavement. The dog lay down beside him, leaning into his ragged coat.

At first, Pug led me. I could not see the door myself. Eventually, I learned to see the shiver, as Mary described it, when it appeared. And eventually, I even learned to summon it—at least, when it wanted to come.

What I liked best was going to Lyme. I would sit on the Cobb, watching the ships come in and the fishermen unloading their nets, the fish gleaming orange and purple in the evening light. The smell of the fish, the smell of the sea, the harsh voices of the fishermen. The feel of rough stone. It was as though I had been transported to fairyland.

I did not like going to London, but the door opens where it wants to. Its intentions are inscrutable, the destination not under our control. And that is where I met the Miss Martins.

They were walking down the street, still with their aprons on, looking into the shop windows as though they had never seen shops filled only with ribbons, or only with ladies' shoes. I knew immediately that they had traveled through the door, as I had. We recognize each other, we travelers through the door.

"Please forgive my forwardness," I said, "but—I am Anne de Bourgh."

It was the first time they had been to London. We went to the Queen's Palace and the park, with its strutting ducks and tubs of orange trees. Mary admired the parterres, which were, she said, "even fancier than at Donwell Abbey," and Eliza laughed at the French fashions. "Imagine," she said, "if I wore that bonnet at home!" We walked down Pall Mall and finally stopped to have cakes at a shop near Marlborough House, although the attendant did not seem to realize we were there. We took what we wanted, and I left some coins on the counter. It was evening and I was trying not to show that I was at the end of my strength when the door appeared again, in the middle of St. James's Square, and took us back to Abbey-Mill Farm. They could see I was not well, so they made me lie on the sofa and bathed my forehead with rosewater. Then there was the door, right in the parlor wall, and it took me home to Rosings.

"What have you been doing?" asked Dr. Galt. "Running up and down stairs? I told you, my girl, you can live a normal life, but within reason. Whatever you've been doing, you must not do it again." I lay sick in bed all that week, and Miss Jenkinson brought me interminable cups of beef tea. But I had found friends.

We have tried to understand the rules by which the door operates.

It appears and disappears unexpectedly. When we step through it, we do not know where we will be, or how long we will be there. When it comes back for us, it usually takes us home. But not always.

At first, only Mary could see it—and, presumably, Pug. Now we can all see it—as a sort of shiver in the air, as though the brick wall, or hedge, or whatever is behind it, were behind a waterfall.

It does not like to be ignored. If we do not step through it, the door sulks. Sometimes it does not come back for days.

Sometimes, when we call for it to appear, it comes. At other times it will not come, no matter how we call. Sometimes, it will take us where we ask. At other times, it will not. "Door, could you please take us to Pemberley?" has worked in the past, as has "Open, Sesame!" As has "Here, door, door, door!"

The door appears to have limits. We have never traveled earlier than the King's reign, nor later than the defeat of Napoleon. (Imagine our relief to learn of Waterloo.) We have never traveled outside England, although Eliza has asked, again and again, to go to Italy.

Wherever we go, we are ghosts. We walk unnoticed. And when we return, we have not been missed. Life seems to flow around us, as though we were pebbles in a stream, eternally still in the midst of motion. Once, Eliza said, "Is it the door, or is it just us? I can go to Highbury for hours, and when I return Mother says she thought I was home all the time, in the garden or with the cows. Perhaps we are just like that, going through life unnoticed."

We call it a door, but is it a door at all? We say that it opens, but can what it does be called opening? What happens when it appears? What determines where it will take us? We do not know.

"I think," I said to Mary and Eliza, "that we should begin attempting to summon the door. I believe it has a purpose, and that we must fulfill it."

"What sort of purpose?" asked Mary.

"I believe we should find others like ourselves. They must exist, and I think the door will take us to them."

We were in Bath, walking along the Crescent. The sun was bright and Mary's nose was beginning to freckle. The door does not wait for one to fetch a parasol.

"You don't know how lonely I was until I met Pug. And if there are others like me, who are also lonely, I want to find them."

I said it with steady conviction, although I was not sure, myself, that the door was not simply a devil, an impish device that had decided to play with us for a while. But there is something I have wondered since the days of Dr. Templeton and Dr. Bransby, while being lowered into a cold bath or drinking beef tea. Is there a force in the universe that understands us, as we long to be understood? And if so, is this force compassionate? Does it, even as it metes out ill, long for our good? If so, it is the force that will give Fitz the girl he wants, the happy ending he deserves. But what about those of us for whom there can be no happy endings? Perhaps it gives us something else, a secret. A companionship that even Fitz would not understand.

So far, we have only found two others like ourselves, apart from the unfriendly Mrs. Churchill. Mrs. Smith of Allenham Court, in Devonshire, is a widow with a heart condition like mine, who cannot travel much. But we go visit her, when the door allows. Mr. Wentworth is a vicar in Shropshire. I said to him once, "It seems, Mr. Wentworth, that you disprove Mary's conjecture. You have a profession. You are married and have children. Surely you are not one of those to whom nothing happens."

"It is true, Miss de Bourgh, that I have more to occupy myself than you do, which precludes me from joining you as often as I would like. But consider, my brother is an admiral in His Majesty's navy. I, too, once longed to become a sailor, but my father destined me for the church. Compared to his, my life is dull indeed."

"Perhaps," said Eliza later, when the three of us were alone, except for Pug, "that is the difference between men and women. Mr. Wentworth's life would be considered full, for a woman. And yet he considers it dull."

"I feel for him," I said. "But I confess, I feel more for Mrs. Smith, lying on her sofa all day long."

The first time we walked through the door into her room, kept as dark as mine in the days of Dr. Bransby, she said, "Good dog! You've brought some friends. Sit down, girls, sit down. Stay and talk with me for a while."

This is what Miss Jenkinson tells the tourists as they walk through Rosings. I have heard it so often I could almost recite it myself: Roman foundations, a Saxon fort, given to Sir George de Bourgh by William the Conqueror.

"In the days of Sir Roger de Bourgh, the cellars contained so much port it was said you could sail on it to China. The requirements of the present Lady de Bourgh are considerably more modest." Laughter.

"Under Lady Anne de Bourgh, a portion of the house burned and had to be rebuilt. As we walk through the house, I will point out the various architectural styles. This hall, as you see, is Elizabethan, although after the fire it required extensive restoration. Only one of the walls is original. It was said that Lady Anne set the fire herself after her lover, William d'Arcy, rejected her for the Virgin Queen. At present, Rosings has forty-two bedrooms, a number considered propitious by Sir Roger de Bourgh, who was believed by some to be a mathematician, and by others to be an alchemist. His wife, Arabella d'Arcy, was accused of assisting in his alchemical experiments. Her grandmother, Isabel d'Arcy, who was the mistress of Henry VI, was afterward tried as a witch. There are twelve bathrooms, of which eight have modern plumbing, put in at a cost of over a thousand pounds." Gasps.

"The de Bourghs hold extensive lands in Kent, including this county and of course the village of Hunsford. In his capacity as magistrate, the late Sir George de Bourgh was responsible for hanging fourteen poachers in one year. Madam, if you could stop your child from kicking that chair. It was presented to Lady Catherine by Queen Charlotte herself. Observe the painting of Sir Edward de Bourgh as a child, which was saved during the Civil War by being buried under a local pigsty."

"Tell us about the Wicked Lord!"

"Edward de Bourgh, the Wicked Lord, as he was called at court, was beheaded for his unwanted attentions to King Charles' mistress, Nell Gwyn . . ."

Pug and I escape to the garden. When we were children, Fitz was made to learn this tale of folly and bloodshed. No wonder he reads German philosophy. The de Bourghs and the d'Arcys: alchemists, rapists, thieves. Let him have his happy ending.

In the garden, I sit on the edge of the fountain, feeding the fish. These are the living fish, imported from China: orange and white, with an exquisite beauty that their stone cousins cannot match. They rise to nibble the bread I drop for them. Pug puts his front paws on the edge of the fountain, looks at them, and barks.

A woman and a boy come into the garden.

"What a bad boy you are, Tom," she says, sighing and sitting down on one of the benches. "Why did you have to kick the furniture? I can't take you anywhere."

"I'm bored," he says, quite reasonably, in my opinion. "I want to see the secret passage. You said there would be a secret passage."

"Well, there isn't a secret passage. That Jenkins woman said so. Now will you behave yourself?"

I have no more bread. The fish rise to nibble my fingers. Pug barks and barks, and turns to me, panting, for approval. He looks as though he is laughing.

Madam, I want to say, there is a secret passage. Miss Jenkinson cannot show it to you. But there is, there is.

A LETTER TO MERLIN

My enemy, my friend:

How many times have I written you this letter? More than ten, perhaps more than twenty. The first time I was sent here, I did not write to you, nor the second time. It was not until the third time that I realized what you must be, where you must have come from. The third time, I wrote to you, from this same desk under this same window. Perhaps I have written to you more than thirty times, I don't know. I have lost count of how many times I have lived this life.

Below me in the courtyard, gray doves are walking back and forth in the herb garden, among beds of thyme and tarragon, marjoram and rosemary. The bushes are softer now, no longer neat and trim as they were earlier in the year. In autumn, everything gets a bit straggly except the lavender, which has just been harvested. The nuns walk back and forth, going about their tasks like gray doves themselves. I like them, these women of God, in their neat habits, with their kind, worn faces. They have been compassionate to me. They do not judge the disgraced queen.

No matter what else happens in this life, it always ends here, in what will someday become Glastonbury, between these stone walls. To be honest, I have come to welcome these quiet years, in which I can grow old and remember.

It was the third time that I began to suspect you were like me, an interloper, a—what shall I call us? An implant, an insertion? I would use the term "secret agent," but I do not know where you are from, exactly. In your timeline, were there governments and corporations to spy on each other? Surely there were. Surely those are endemic to late humanity.

Every time I wake in this body, I breathe deeply. The air here is pure, almost effervescent. It is air a thousand years before factories, and it affects me like wine. Feeling a little drunk, I get up and look in the mirror to find this now-familiar face looking back at me, achingly young and beautiful, with light blue eyes and masses of red hair falling over a linen shift. The beauty is important—it is what will make him fall in love with me, and later facilitate my betrayal.

Do you know that already, on the first day—that I will betray him? When I walk down the steps to the great hall in my blue peplos, with my hair in a long braid down my back, a gold circlet on my brow, and they announce the arrival of Princess Guinevere, do you already know? Do you ever feel sick in your stomach, knowing that the man standing beside you, himself achingly young and beautiful, Arthur, king of a small kingdom that he would like to extend by marriage, will die in agony and we will be the instruments of his death? For I hold you culpable, Merlin—as culpable as I am. Did we not come to this place, this time, to enact a tragedy?

Do you remember the flat gray place where they trained us and fed us and kept us, until we could sleep again? Once, I asked the Chronographer where it was. She said the buildings had been military barracks in an ancient war, when the moon had rebelled against the Earth.

Sometimes at night I could see the full disk of the barren Earth, gleaming in the sky.

Nothing relieved the gray of that place—the buildings made of some concrete composite, the bland food (it reminded me most of liver). Those of us who were temporarily awake were different from one another, yet somehow the same—different colors and heights and ages, yet dressed in identical gray garments that reminded me of medical scrubs, our heads filled with dreams. At least the nuns here have white wimples to relieve the monotony of God's uniform.

Sometimes, in the waking intervals, I made friends. There was a woman named Melina 9—she and I became close for a while. She had also come from North America, although the western coast, before San Francisco sank beneath the waves. Her specialty was assassinations. She said she had poisoned kings, shot presidents. She once told me, "I wish they would stop giving me Lucretia Borgia." But we have little choice of where we go, what life we are given. Once we develop a specialty, we are sent back again and again. How many times have you been Merlin?

If I had a choice, would I come here time after time? Would I continue to play Guinevere? Yes. I would, for him, for those early years.

The first time I saw him, I thought it must be a trick of the light that he seemed to shine more brightly than anyone else in the great hall of Cameliard. Even you, Merlin, with your long gray beard and imposing robes embroidered with stars, was a pale figure beside the young king. He seemed to burn like a flame.

How much of that early love was me, how much Guinevere? The underlying Guinevere, the seventeen-year-old into whose mind I had been inserted, like a cuckoo's egg into a nest, to hatch and take over? Another word for us, I suppose, is usurper. Or parasite. I could feel her there, the pampered daughter of King Leodegrance who had never been denied anything. Privileged, pious, a little vain, a little scared of life, fundamentally conservative. Ten years later, would she betray her husband? I was here to make certain she did.

And there he was before me, standing in the sunlight. Then my father was presenting me, with the air of one showing a prized heifer he was about to offer for sale—the price being an alliance between Cornwall and England, or whatever we are to call Arthur's kingdom, that loose conglomeration of Angles and Britons and Celts that was eventually to stretch from Rheged to the Atlantic. We may as well call it England, although that name will not be spoken for centuries.

Did she love him, that Guinevere? She must have been infatuated and gratified—he was a king, he was handsome, his brown hair cropped in the Roman fashion, although like most men after the withdrawal of the legions he wore a short beard. He must have increased her sense of her own worth. If she was a prize heifer, she was an expensive one. And I-in-Guinevere, did I love him then? Not the first time. It was only after a lifetime of walks in the palace garden, of riding through the forests around Camelot and conversations at night in our bedroom, a lifetime of him calling me Ginny, that I loved him. The second time, when I saw him again, I almost burst into tears. But we do not break character, do we, Merlin?

Where were you born? When were you born? How did your world end?

I was born in New Cleveland, on the north side, near the Towers—a cluster of government projects that jutted into the brown sky. They had been built for the working class when Old Cleveland was leveled and the new city was built, farther inland, away from the encroaching waters of what was then called Lake Erie. The middle class had moved to the gentrified neighborhoods of the south side, protected by the flood wall, or into the Columbus suburbs. The wealthy who had once lived in those suburbs had long ago decamped to the orbiting stations, to enjoy filtered air and a simulated world. I was told there were artificial windows looking out onto a blue sky with white clouds. I had never seen such a sky myself. The tops of the Towers were wreathed in perpetual smog. From our windows, halfway up, all I could see was a landscape of rust and iron. When I was a child and the pollution was not so bad, we could sometimes see the lights of Copernicus City, until the Great Recession hit and the lunar settlements were abandoned.

Both of my parents died in the second wave of Black Spot, leaving me and my sister Angelina. A woman from Child Welfare, Delilah Watson, said there was no more room in the orphanages. She helped me apply for guardianship of Angie and got me a FlexCare account with a dependent child allowance so we could buy groceries in the supermarket on the fifth floor or the bodegas at ground level. Delilah had been born in Detroit and told me what it had been like before the waters of the Huron Sea closed over it. She made sure the Housing Cred for the apartment was transferred to my name, and I arranged with a man named Johnny Duvall that no one would try to take it away from us. You had to pay for protection in the Towers, one way or another. Johnny had an old-fashioned notion of chivalry. He was rapacious with honor, not much different than most of Arthur's knights.

Angie went to the Towers school, next to what had once been a community center but now housed the homeless who were too sick or drug addled to apply for FlexCare, or housing credit, or any of the other benefits that, thanks to Delilah, were coded into my FlexBand, which mostly worked except when we had rolling internet blackouts. On the north side, I could never be sure when my FlexBand or Angie's tablet would connect. I had just turned seventeen, so I dropped out of school and started working as a waitress at a restaurant on the south side, which paid in cash at the end of each week, although by then the federal government in Chicago was in such disarray that I don't think the IRS would have noticed. Ohio was part of the Secessionist movement, convinced it would be better for the northern states to ally themselves with Canada and form a North American Union.

Does any of this sound familiar? Are you from my disaster or another? There were so many, the Chronographer told me. Humanity, she said in her dry, clipped, precise voice, has an infinite appetite for self-destruction. The details are boringly repetitive: war, famine, pestilence.

It was pestilence that got me in the end, despite the yearly vaccinations. I made sure Angie and I got whatever the government was offering that year, wherever it came from—we all knew Indian vaccines were the best, but after the famines, we could rarely get them. Anyway, that year's Black Spot was a new and more virulent variety. It came in a shipment of bananas from the USSA—there had been a bad outbreak in Ecuador. It hit on the East Coast first—Virginia, Kentucky, Tennessee, all around the Gulf of Carolina—then made its way inland. Once I started coughing, once I had difficulty catching my breath, there was no need to see a doctor, even if we could afford one. We knew what an X-ray would show: the telltale black spots on my lungs. I went into the bedroom where our parents had died, shut the door, and told Angie to keep out. It was all I could do for her.

One night, as I was coughing myself to death, I heard the door open. I was about to shout at Angie, telling her to get out, stay away from me, but it was Delilah Watson. She came and sat on the edge of the mattress. "Janelle," she said, "I've transferred your FlexCare and the apartment to your sister. You're going to be dead in twenty-four hours. Would you like to save the world?"

How do you tell a love story without sounding like one of those old Hollywood movies from before the San Andreas earthquake, especially when you have lived it twenty or thirty times already? My memories are a palimpsest—the first time Arthur and I walked alone together in the apple orchard at Cameliard as a betrothed couple, the second time, the third time. Each time was a little different, as each timeline is a little different. It was like acting in a play that required continual improvisation, although the play was my life—Guinevere's life, stolen by me.

"Lady," he said, "would you really like to be wedded to me? I know the king your father commands it, but I would not wish to wed unless you so desire."

Forgive me, I am trying to translate from early medieval Anglish, for I cannot call it English, into a language that only you and I can understand. By the time it is spoken anywhere in the world, this rough paper, made of beaten linen by the nuns for keeping their household accounts, will long ago have disintegrated. Only the vellum codices of the monks will have survived. I am aware that I sound like a bad edition of Shakespeare. (Once or twice, I was Anne Hathaway. It was a relief being the faithful wife.)

"Yes, your Highness," I said, or something like that. "I also desire—" To kiss you again after all the years apart. Of course I did not think that the first time. I knew only my lines, my duty in this lovely teenage body.

How did I fall in love with him, my husband? It did not happen in those early days in Cornwall. I was still playing a part assigned to me by the great computer, if that's what it is, in the Temporal Observatory—those golden strings stretching upward, each representing a timeline. Strings, threads, cables—I don't know what to call them. Streams of information going up and up, all the information for each timeline stretching upward as far as humanity survives, and then going dark where the information ends. Where humanity has destroyed itself again. Every single string, except one—the only one that stretches into the darkness. The final timeline of humanity.

That first time, I had not been a cuckoo long. It was, I believe, only my fifth assignment. Only my fifth attempt to make the timeline stretch just a little longer. All my roles had been young women, I suppose because the Chronographer thought it would be easier for me. Since then, I have played many roles, of many ages—who knows how old I am now, after so many lifetimes? But my best role remains Guinevere. I play it perfectly so they will send me back again.

My wedding coat was embroidered by three Cornish women, like the three Fates, and took two months to complete. It was covered with stylized flowers—lilies for purity, roses for love. Nothing like it had been seen before in Cornwall, and some of the ladies-in-waiting whispered that it was a Frankish fashion. As we stood over my marriage contract, while my father signed it, I could see my beauty reflected in Arthur's eyes. He was not in love with me yet either—perhaps with the princess of Cornwall, but not with me.

On our wedding night, I realized he was not much more experienced than I was. After all, he had spent his life trying to stay alive as the bastard son of King Uther and then consolidating his kingdom. He was only twenty-three, but looked older. He had fought battles, led men. There had been no time for gentler things. We had to find those together, create them between us.

Nights sitting by the fire at the castle in Camelot, he would say, "Ginny, tell me a story, something Cornish. A fairy tale, or something with giants." I would reach into her memory, or remember something in the databases I had studied at the Library, when I was learning as much as I could about early sixth-century Britain—sometimes I could not tell the difference. Which was my mind, which hers? And I would tell him a story. Halfway through, he would close his eyes, tired out from the endless negotiations of being king over a fractious kingdom. I would stroke his hair, his eyebrows, run my finger down his nose. The tenth time, the fifteenth time, I would think, *Remember this, when you believe I have been unfaithful. Remember me like this, when our world has fallen apart.*

I remember a conversation we had in Camelot. The barons were being particularly obstreperous, fighting each other rather than banding together against the Saxon settlements in the south, as Arthur wanted. He knew the threat they posed—they had been mercenaries settled there by the Romans, and made regular incursions into Arthur's kingdom. I could not tell him that one day, Angles and Saxons would fight together against the French.

"Go to the people," I said.

He looked at me, confused.

"Go directly to the people. As the Roman senators did."

Thank you, Merlin, for giving him a classical education. I saw a light in his eyes at the idea that he could bypass the quarreling barons and speak directly to the populace. It became the cornerstone of his diplomacy. This was the early Middle Ages, after all, before feudalism had really taken hold. Britannia was still an island of opinionated freemen. If he could get the people behind him, the barons would have no choice but to follow.

Sometimes he would stroke my hair back from my forehead and look at me with such love in his eyes that I felt as though I might drown in it. "When I married you, Ginny, I received so much more than I expected. My wife, my love, my queen." And then he would kiss me, so tenderly, so completely, as though his soul was in that kiss.

Yes, I could not help thinking. You got two in one, what a bargain. Guinevere and Janelle. The beautiful Cornish princess and the implant from a world in which representative democracy had already failed, where the rich lived in space while the people coughed and stumbled at ground level through brown fog, unheeded and unheard. Forgive me if I sound bitter. I know that he loved me in her, and yet he also loved her in me—her beauty, her grace, her gentility. He would not have loved me as a waitress from the north side of New Cleveland.

Once, I asked one of the librarians what the hosts we entered experienced—whether the underlying Guinevere was aware of me. "Only as part of herself," came the answer. "You nudge her toward different actions, different decisions. You are like an impulse in her mind, a sort of conscience telling her what to choose. But she has no access to your thoughts, if that's what you're asking."

Did he love her or me? I suppose it does not, in the end, make much of a difference.

This is what I remember, this is why I am glad and relieved to be sent back, time after time: sitting together in the garden at Camelot, my ladies-in-waiting sent away for an hour, him reading to me from an ancient, precious scroll from his foster father's library, where Ector saved all the Roman literature he could, while I embroider some random piece of knightly regalia. That, I learned from Guinevere—you cannot learn embroidery from a database. Or at night, lying together in bed by candlelight with my head on his shoulder, his fingers tangled in my hair, talking about his childhood wandering through the forests with Kay, learning to be a knight. Him turning to me, saying, "Make love with me, Ginny." Both of us forgetting politics for a while. Those private moments away from the court and its constant bickering—among knights for precedence, among their ladies for flirtatious attention.

We had seven years. It is those seven years I am glad to come back for.

The first time, I did not understand why you avoided and seemed to dislike me. I understood the rest of Arthur's family, his inner circle. His foster brother Kay resented that as queen, I was a new locus of power at court. I came between him and the absolute control he held over the royal household as Arthur's steward. His half sister Morgan, in her rare appearances at Camelot, resented me for the same reason she resented Arthur. After all, Uther had seduced her mother. She had no love for her young half-brother, and I was simply an extension of him, no more important in her eyes than the spoon with which he ate his soup. Her dislike for me was almost a reflex. She was always a direct, practical sort of person, interested only in power and how she could obtain it. Arthur's nephews, Gawain and Gaheris, both liked and looked up to me, the way teenage boys will idealize an older woman who is comfortably out of their reach. I might as well have been a film star. As for Mordred—I don't wish to write about Mordred, Arthur's son and murderer.

But you—why did you seem to be my enemy? It puzzled me, that first time. Of course I know now. We are alike in so many ways, Merlin.

You loved him too, as a teacher loves his brightest and most promising pupil. Neither of us wanted to be the agent of his destruction.

Seven years. That's what we had, Arthur and I, before he arrived—the Breton knight who would later become Lancelot. I might as well call him by that name. I might as well call us all by the names we will be given in the stories. After all, what matters in the end is the legend we created, isn't it, Merlin, Myrddin, whoever you are? The truth was burned to the ground with Camelot, and out of it grew a tree called the Matter of Britain, and what does it matter how our names were spelled in the beginning?

Have I mentioned yet that once, in another Camelot, I was Jacqueline Kennedy? It was not my best role. I am not good at playing the grieving widow.

We had seven years of love and happiness. Seven years before I had to betray my king, my love, my husband.

It was the third time, as I have said, that I began to suspect you. Arthur was in Mercia, subduing another rebellion. At midnight, I was supposed to meet Lancelot in the chapel, where we would declare our love and make plans to flee Camelot together. He would enter through the chapel door as though to pray. I would sneak in through a back door that opened directly into the sacristy. I had done this twice already, in two different timelines. But this time, the door was locked. The key was missing.

What was I to do? This script had been written long ago—I had only to play my part. But suddenly, I had lost my cue.

That was when you appeared in the stone hall, by the light of my flickering candle, with the key in your hand. "The priest left this in his vestments," you said, handing it to me. I was so astonished that I could not say anything. Without another word, you disappeared into the darkness.

That was when I wrote you my first letter—I mean, after my plans with Lancelot were discovered, after I was tried for adultery and almost burned at the stake, after I retired to this abbey. I remembered something I had almost forgotten, a small detail from the databases in the Library—that Merlin was supposed to live backward through time. And I started to wonder.

I no longer wonder. I am certain. In the seventh lifetime, you brought me a letter from Lancelot that his squire had accidentally dropped in the courtyard. In the twelfth or thirteenth, I don't remember which, you tripped the servant who would have lit my pyre too soon and burned me to a crisp before Lancelot arrived. Time after time, you have corrected glitches in the system, places where the script did not work for one reason or another. You have untangled knots in the timeline.

In other words, my friend, my enemy, you are like me. You are of the tribe of cuckoos.

Tell me if this is true. I have sent you this letter so many times. Each time, I am patient—I wait to write it until we have both fulfilled our tasks. Yesterday, I received news that my beloved is dead and Camelot has fallen again. So write to me, Merlin. Just once, acknowledge my letter. Reply.

"Why?" I asked the Chronographer the first time I met her in the Observatory.

I had already seen the training videos, already been shown the chamber of sleepers—hundreds of them floating in oval tanks that nourished their bodies while their consciousnesses were lost in time, inhabiting the bodies of Genghis Khan, Marlene Dietrich, or countless men and women whose names were no longer remembered but whose actions had changed their timelines in some small but important way.

"Janelle 13," our receptionist had said, "you might be interested to see your recruiter, Delilah Watson, or as she is known here, Ifeoma 7. You will find that you perform best in certain roles. You will develop an affinity for certain eras, genders, nationalities, professions. But Ifeoma 7 can become anyone, at any time. She is equally good as Nefertiti and Sir Francis Drake. Only the best are asked to become recruiters."

I looked down into the tank before me, shaped like an egg and filled with some sort of gel in which floated the woman named Ifeoma 7, her eyes closed in sleep. I did not recognize her. Her skin was darker than Delilah's, and she was younger, more muscular, with long braids of hair floating around her bare shoulders. I looked at all the oval tanks in that room, as large as a sports stadium. Each one was filled with a sleeper living a different life. I could not imagine being one of them.

Someone in our small group of recruits asked a question, but it was in a language I did not understand—at that time I did not speak Mandarin, and even now my understanding is only elementary. The receptionist answered in that language, then explained to the group in two other languages before she said, "Hoda 2 and Janelle 13, Xiang 27 wanted to know about the recruiting process. I told him that each recruiter identifies suitable candidates for this type of work. Intelligent, practical, adaptable, able to put the needs of others before their own—and about to die. At the moment of their death, with their prior permission of course, the recruiter transfers their consciousness here. Only consciousness, what some might call the soul, can cross the barrier between timelines, and only at the moment of physical dissolution. It's difficult to find the right sort of person, particularly from late enough in the timeline to understand the technology we use here. From each timeline, we are able to recruit only two or three candidates. So you see, each of you is precious to us. We have tried to replicate your previous bodies as closely as possible based on your genetic code, although they are not entirely biological. I hope they are satisfactory. They will age very slowly, and there are no pathogens here, but it is possible to injure them. Please tell one of us if you require medical care. In the meantime, we still have a lot to do. Later today you will each meet with the Chronographer—I suppose you could call her the CEO of this place. Tomorrow you will begin your training."

"Training in what, exactly?" asked Hoda 2. I could not place her accent—she told me later that she came from the Republic of Ghana, during the Great Migration that followed the water wars.

"In repairing the timelines," said the receptionist. "Saving humanity."

"Why do the timelines need to be repaired?" I asked the Chronographer, later that afternoon. The training videos had been technical. They had not answered that question.

"Come, I'll show you," she said, waving me forward. We reached a central console and walked around the circular room, whose perimeter was filled with golden threads rising up, up into the darkness. Hundreds of them, perhaps thousands. She stopped.

"This is your timeline," she said. It looked no different to me than any of the others—like a fiber-optic cable, flickering along its entire length as it rose toward the distant ceiling, stopping several meters above my head. "We have already extended it twice. Originally it was destroyed in 1956, during the Cold War. You and your sister could be born because a sleeper named Xandi 11 decided not to push a button when he was ordered. We will never send you back into that timeline—no one ever reenters their own timeline. But there are other timelines, with other Janelles and Angelinas. The work you do here may allow those other Janelles and Angelinas to live. It may give them clear skies and clean water so their parents do not die of Black Spot. It may prevent the Northern Secession. Angelina may not have to fight or die at the Battle of Ottawa. Each time we make an insertion into the timeline, we try to keep humanity alive a little longer." She looked around at all the golden timelines with a weary look on her face. I wondered how old she was—she looked both ancient and ageless.

"Who is we?" I asked. "I mean, who are you? Those of you who are not us—not recruits." I felt as though I had walked into a science fiction movie. "Are you aliens?"

She looked surprised, then broke into a laugh. It made her sound much younger. "There are no aliens. In all the millennia that human beings have survived on Earth and the moon, and briefly on Mars, no alien intelligences have introduced themselves. Perhaps they're avoiding us—I would not blame them. As far as we know, in the darkness of space and time, there is only us." She frowned and gestured at all the golden threads. "Us, destroying ourselves again and again. We—that is, myself and the receptionists who showed you around, the librarians you will meet later, the technicians who keep this place running, all of us working here in the Temporal Observatory, inhabit the last timeline of humanity. Look." She pointed upward, and I could see one golden thread rising above the others, disappearing into the darkness. "We are flickers of light, bits of information dancing at the top of that column. And soon we too will be gone. We have learned to extend our physical lives, but we no longer reproduce. No children have been born in a thousand years. When we die, humanity will be over. The universe will go on without us." Her voice was sad.

"How many of you are there?" I asked.

"Less than three hundred."

I was silent. Here we were, in an ancient military barracks on the moon, high above the uninhabitable Earth. Less than three hundred human beings remained in the universe. This was all that was left of humanity.

I wish I could ask a favor of you, Merlin. I know you were there at the last moment of Arthur's life, when he lay in the mud after the Battle of Camlann, killed by Mordred's sword. I know you will be there again, in the next lifetime. At that moment, I wish you could lean down and say to him, "Guinevere loved you every moment of this life, and she will love you again in the next, and the next, and the next," as many times as they send me back here. But you would not do that, and I will not ask you to. We both have our duty to fulfill, you and I. All I dare, in this lifetime, is to send you this letter, now that our tasks are done and we are waiting for death to free our souls again. Please, if you can, write back to me. This time, next time, the time after, send me a reply so I know that you understand. I need someone, in all the golden streams of time, to understand that I loved him and will love him, as long as humanity lasts.

Or perhaps we will find each other in the Observatory. There is only a small chance that we will be awake at the same time and recognize each other. And after all, perhaps you are not one Merlin but two or three. Perhaps there are a number of sleepers who have been you. But I persist in believing that, lifetime to lifetime, you recognize me. When you awake, come find me—ask for Janelle 13.

I must go to compline. The nuns are waiting for their Abbess, the final role I play in this place and time. I shall walk through the herb garden, scattering gray doves, and crush a bit of thyme or sage between my fingers to inhale the sharp fragrance. Perhaps there will be a final sprig of lavender fallen on the path. Only such small pleasures are left to me—but they are enough.

The next time I see you again, I will be seventeen years old. You will stand beside Arthur in the great hall of Cameliard and stare at me disapprovingly as I curtsy to my future husband, thinking of the days to come, when for a little while I will once again be with my love.

Until then, affectionately,
Guinevere

ESTELLA SAVES THE VILLAGE

I HAVE LIVED IN THE VILLAGE ALL MY LIFE.

Miss Havisham has told me the story over and over again: how, as an infant, I was found in a basket on the front steps of the church, and how Reverend Rivers asked the villagers gathered for service on Sunday morning which of them would be willing to raise a foundling. And how Miss Havisham immediately said, "I will."

So I've grown up in her small house on the high street, close enough to the baker's that in the mornings I can smell the bread in his oven, and every morning before school Miss Havisham gives me a penny for a bun with raisins in it. I always share it with Pip while he walks beside me, carrying my schoolbag. I tell him I can carry it perfectly well myself, but he insists, so I let him. It's useful, but sometimes tedious, that he's been in love with me since we were both children.

If we stop for a moment and look back as Pip and I walk to school, you can see Miss Havisham's house, with its green shutters and window boxes filled with geraniums. Above it, you can see the downs among which our village is nestled, with sheep grazing on them. Sometimes you can see the herds moving like clouds, driven by a black-and-white streak of sheep dog. Over them runs the high road, to places I've never been—through fields and forests, joining with other roads. Eventually it reaches London, with its grand houses and shops and Buckingham

Palace itself. Sometimes I think about taking that road, traveling to the greatest city in the world. But then the school bell rings, and I turn and run after Pip.

I have started my story this way—by telling you about Miss Havisham and Pip and the bakery and the geraniums in the window boxes, so you will understand what our village was like before the specks appeared.

I first noticed them on a Sunday morning. All the respectable inhabitants of the village were in church. The less respectable were in the tavern, already worshiping John Barleycorn, as Mr. Henchard calls it. Miss Havisham and I were seated in our pew. In the box at the front, I could see mad Lady d'Urberville, who lives in the Hall. She always arrives in a brougham with her estate agent, Mr. Clare. He was sitting beside her, leaning toward her as though whispering a secret. I envied her red brocade and the red hat with egret feathers, however inappropriate it might be for Sunday service. She is the only woman in the village whose dresses do not come from Miss Tulliver's shop, but from a modiste in London. Miss Tulliver was there too, with her brother the miller and his large family. The Ushers slid into the pew in front of us, and Mr. Usher turned around to bow stiffly to Miss Havisham. I believe he eats only vegetables and wears some sort of patent undergarment. He always looks ghastly, as though he were recovering from an illness. Dr. Lydgate paused for a moment on the way to his own pew to take Miss Usher's hand. He put the fingers of his other hand on her wrist, above the edge of her glove—measuring her pulse, I suppose. She is said to be consumptive, although she looks healthier than her brother. Pip waved to me as though frantic for my attention, until Joe Gargery cuffed him on the head and he had to stop.

Then the organ started, and I had to stop looking around, which I have to admit is always the most interesting part of the service. What was the relationship between Lady D'Urberville and Mr. Clare? Would Miss Tulliver ever find herself a husband? Was Dr. Lydgate secretly in love with Miss Usher? These were the sorts of pious thoughts that kept me occupied, although Miss Havisham gave me a reproachful glance over her prayer book. I tried to pay attention, but Reverend Rivers was talking about our dark-skinned brothers in darkest Africa, who sounded as though they were doing quite well for themselves, with plenty of missionaries to eat. To keep myself from looking around, I studied the back of Miss Usher's thin, pale neck, where it showed beneath her bonnet and a few wisps of straggling hair. It was covered with black specks.

What could they be? They did not look like dirt, and anyway I could not imagine Madeline Usher having a dirty neck. Yet there they were. A symptom of consumption, perhaps?

Absorbed in this mystery, I said the Lord's Prayer, sang the same hymns I'd been singing since I was a child, and walked to the communion rail, all without thinking a single religious thought. As I held out my hands for the Host, I noticed a pair of hands beside mine—large, masculine, with black specks on the palms. I glanced up surreptitiously to see who it was, and saw Dr. Lydgate.

After that, Reverend Rivers could have announced the arrival of Armageddon and I would not have noticed. Once we had all filed out of the church, I looked around and saw Dr. Lydgate walking among the gravestones.

"Estella! Do you want to go fishing today?" asked Pip.

"No," I said rudely. "I'm detecting." I have always fancied myself a detective, like the most famous inhabitant of our village, Mr. Holmes.

"What are you detecting?"

"Never mind right now. Just come with me and stay quiet."

I walked to the graveyard and stood beside a marble angel on a pedestal. "What are you thinking about so intently, Dr. Lydgate?" I asked. His hands were bare—he never wears gloves unless the weather demands it. I could not see the palms, but there were specks on the backs of his hands as well.

He smiled. "Nothing that would interest a young lady, I'm afraid, Miss Havisham. I was thinking about a new vaccine that would save lives like the one buried here. It was the measles that took him, and only six years old. Such a pity. And what are you doing in the graveyard on a fine morning?"

"Meditating on mortality," I said.

"A commendable, although unusual, activity for a healthy young lady like yourself."

"It's an assignment for school. Dr. Lydgate, you seem to have gotten some dirt on your hands."

He held up his hands and looked at them. "Have I? I confess, they seem clean to me, but young ladies have a higher standard of cleanliness than old bachelors like myself. I'll wash them as soon as I get home." He smiled again, indulgently. I could tell he hadn't seen them.

"What was all that about dirt on his hands?" asked Pip while he was walking me home from church.

"You didn't see it either?"

"See what?"

I sighed. "Did you see Mr. Holmes during the service? I tried to find him afterward, but he wasn't there."

"He was sitting behind Joe and left right after the processional. He said something about his bees needing him more than the Lord this morning."

It was a mystery, my very own mystery. I had half a mind to keep it to myself. But I was also worried—Pip had seen nothing. What if I was simply imagining the specks? It made sense to consult a real detective and make sure.

But first, I would go around the village and see if I could find any more of the black specks. After dinner, of course—my stomach was starting to grumble.

"See you tomorrow," I said to Pip when we had reached the front door. He opened his mouth, and I knew he wanted to ask if he could come detecting with me. But this was my adventure, and I wanted to go on it alone. When I closed the door, he was still standing on the step with his mouth open. I almost felt guilty—but after all, it was only Pip.

Sunday dinner consisted of an Irish stew and soda bread that Fanny had prepared. Miss Havisham always allows her to serve a stew so she can cook it beforehand and go to the service. Then she can just heat it up on the stove. I don't think anyone is as generous to their servants as Miss Havisham. Who else would allow Fanny to keep her child in the house? But Miss Havisham says that every child is a gift, whatever its origin.

"Estella," said Miss Havisham after we had finished, "you've been happy here, haven't you?"

"Of course I've been happy. You've been like a mother to me, and I've had everything I could have wanted—except the red brocade dress Lady D'Urberville was wearing today, and can you imagine the scandal I'd cause, wearing that?"

Miss Havisham laughed. "I'm glad. I've always hoped that with a proper home, and the right sorts of things—books, and friends like Pip, you would grow up to be . . ."

"What?"

"The sort of young woman you're turning out to be. Intelligent and compassionate."

I went over to her side of the table, gave her a hug from behind, and kissed her on the cheek. She always smelled nice, like lavender water. It's a comforting smell that reminds me of hurt feelings soothed, scraped knees bandaged, tears wiped away. I don't think my mother, whoever she was, could have taken better care of me than Miss Havisham.

"Thank you, my dear. Now, I'm going to do some knitting. Tell me what sort of adventure you and Pip have planned for this afternoon."

As she stood up from the table, I noticed that she moved more slowly than she used to, and she put a hand on the back of the chair to brace herself. Was Miss Havisham getting old? As long as I remembered, she'd looked the same: white hair under her lace cap and blue eyes that seemed to pierce right through you (she always knew when I had stolen from the jam jar), surrounded by lines that laughter had formed over the years. I have never known anyone kinder or more forgiving.

"Would you give me your arm into the parlor? I seem to be feeling my age today."

At the thought of Miss Havisham growing older, a chill settled about my heart. Somehow, I have never imagined such a thing could happen.

"Pip and I aren't doing anything this afternoon," I said. "Do you want me to read while you knit?" I could put off detecting for one day. Anyway, maybe I had just imagined the specks.

She looked startled, but said, "That would be lovely." So for several hours, I read from Gibbon's *Decline and Fall of the Roman Empire*, which I found tedious but Miss Havisham found fascinating. "Thank you, my dear," she said afterward. "That was the loveliest afternoon I've had in a long time."

That night, as I lay in bed under a quilt she had sewn for me, which had kept me warm since I was a child, I realized that the world I'd lived in all my life might change. I stared into the darkness, not knowing how to react to such a thought.

The next morning, there was a scattering of black specks over Pip's cheek and down his collar. I didn't mention it to him, although he probably wondered why I kept looking at him so intently.

When we reached the schoolhouse, I went over to the girls' side and sat next to Flora. There were spots on her pinafore, and her notebook looked as though she had spattered ink over it. I took out my schoolbooks. There was a black hole in my *School History of England*. It went through every page, as though a large worm had chewed right through it. The date of the Norman Conquest was missing, as were parts of the Duke of Wellington's victory at Waterloo and an engraving of Queen Victoria's coronation.

"Estella," said Miss Murray, "is everything all right?"

No, I wanted to tell her. *There are splotches of nothing on the map of the world hanging by the chalkboard.* But I just nodded.

"All right, students," she said. "I want the older girls to help the younger ones with their spelling. Estella, Pearl, Flora, and Nell, can you form them into a line and take them into the schoolyard? The weather is fine, and I want you to do your lessons out there while I test the boys on yesterday's Latin." There was a general groan from the boys' side of the room.

The rest of the school day was as busy as usual. But everywhere I looked, I noticed black specks, spots, holes. They seemed to be spreading.

After the bell rang to signal the end of the school day, I started detecting. Pip wanted to come, of course, but he had to work in the blacksmith's shop, which was for the best. I wasn't ready to explain what I was doing, or why.

I started at the far end of the village, at the cottage of the foreign ladies, Mrs. Rochester and her companion Miss Rappaccini. They had come to the village several years before. Mrs. Rochester is from the colonies and speaks English, but Miss Rappaccini is Italian. She answered the door, and I had to explain myself twice before she could understand what I wanted.

At every house, I would knock, and when the door was opened I would say, "I'm doing an assignment for school on 'How We Live in the Nineteenth Century.' Can I come in and look around?"

It's astonishing what people will believe when you look at them steadily and speak with conviction.

"Come right in, Estella," they would usually say, although Mr. Henchard grumbled about public education, which was nothing like in his time (thank goodness, or we might all end up as ignorant as he is), and Mr. Fawley apologized for the state of his parlor, which had piles of books covering the floor and on every armchair.

Our village isn't large, but I was offered tea several times and felt as though I had to accept. Being polite is a nuisance. By the time I was done, it was too late to visit Mr. Holmes, as I had intended. I would have to see him the next day.

I admit, it was beginning to scare me: all around the village, there were splotches of nothing, and they seemed to be growing. As I walked home, I could see them on the trees, like black lichen. On the flanks of horses in the pastures. I almost stumbled into one on the road.

How would you feel if your world were disappearing? Well, that's how I felt.

When I got home, it was a relief to notice no spots at all, not a single speck. There, at least, the nothingness had not yet invaded.

The next morning, I did not go to school. Instead, I asked Pip to tell Miss Murray that I was sick. He looked at me quizzically. The spots on his cheek were now larger, the size of pencil ends. "I promise I'll tell you soon, all right?" I said.

"All right, Estella. But I wish you would trust me." He turned reluctantly and headed toward the school.

I headed toward Mr. Holmes's house. The garden was a riot of flowers. Mrs. Holmes was cutting roses and putting them into a basket on the ground. "Hello, Estella," she said. "Are you here to see me or Sherlock?" She did not ask me why I wasn't in school.

"I'm here to see Mr. Holmes."

"You'll find him in the study. Can you tell him that I've left plenty for the bees? He always objects to my cutting flowers. But you can't have a dining-room table without fresh flowers on it, can you?"

"I suppose not." No one else in the village would have put cut flowers on a table, although Miss Havisham has wax flowers under a glass dome. But before her marriage, Mrs. Holmes was an actress in London. She wears her hair down, dresses in what Miss Tulliver calls the aesthetic style, and rides a bicycle through the village. Miss Havisham says she's unconventional. I think I'd like to be unconventional when I grow up.

I had been in the study once before, several years ago, when Mr. Holmes had been sick and Miss Havisham had brought over some beef tea. He'd been lying on the sofa under a blanket. She had talked to him, and I'd been able to wander around, looking at all the books, the scientific instruments on the tables, the weapons on the walls.

"Hello, Estella," he said as I entered. "Come look at this." He indicated the microscope he'd been looking through.

I went and looked. "What is it?" I asked.

"The hind leg of a bee. You can see the three segments. Can you see that the third segment is shaped like a basket? That's called the corbicula, where the bee carries pollen. I'm writing a monograph on the Apidae, on their anatomy and habits. Perhaps later I can show you my bees. They are fascinating creatures. If only men could work together as harmoniously! But I'm sure you haven't come here to talk about bees. Has Miss Havisham sent you?"

"No. I need to consult you myself. I've been seeing specks, black specks. Only some of them are spots, or holes. Some of them are quite large. On Sunday, I saw them on Miss Usher in church. Since then, I've been seeing them everywhere. You can actually put your finger, or even your hand, into them. They feel cold, like nothingness. Yesterday, I went around the village and wrote down where they were, and their sizes and depths. It's all in this notebook."

I handed him my school notebook. I had written all my findings down and then recopied them the night before. "But only I can see them," I added. "So you see, I may be going mad." I tried to sound logical, like a detective, but my voice trembled.

He gave me a sharp glance, then leafed through the notebook, methodically.

"Let's sit down, shall we?" I sat beside him on the sofa. "It seems to me that there are two possibilities. Either you are having hallucinations, in which case you need to see Dr. Lydgate. Or you actually are seeing black holes that no one else is seeing. Do you see any in this room?"

"Yes. There's one on the sofa, right beside your shoulder." It was the size of my finger. I put my finger right into it, up to the knuckle. I didn't want to tell him that there were specks on his chin, like the stubble of a beard, and down the front of his Norfolk jacket as though he had spilled ink on it.

"Fascinating," said Mr. Holmes. "I don't think you'll need to consult Dr. Lydgate."

"Why?"

"Because although I can't see a hole in the sofa, I just saw your finger disappear into the upholstery. I'm going to ask Irene for a glass of sherry. I think you need it."

He went to the door and called Mrs. Holmes. In a few minutes, he brought me a glass of liquor the color of garnets. It burned going down, and I coughed.

He sat back down on the sofa, putting his elbows on his knees and his chin on his clasped hands. "Have you noticed any patterns? Are there places where the spots are larger or smaller? I'm interested in whether they're spreading from a particular location."

I leafed through my notes. I should have thought of arranging the sightings by size. "They seem larger on the other side of the village. The largest one I saw was on the wall around Mrs. Rochester's garden. It was the size of a cabbage. And she told me that her terrier has disappeared. She asked me if I had seen him, and I didn't know what to say. Mr. Holmes, I'm afraid the world's disappearing. I only started to notice the specks on Sunday, but those larger spots—they've probably been growing for some time."

He thought for a moment, then asked, "Is there any place the spots don't appear?"

"Only at home. I haven't seen any there."

Why? Why hadn't I seen any spots at home, when I had seen them everywhere else? I'd been so relieved by their absence that I hadn't even bothered to ask. And there had been enough to worry about, with the revelation of Miss Havisham's frailty.

"Mr. Holmes, I have to go. I have to talk to Miss Havisham."

He nodded, looking concerned. "Yes, that seems indicated." Then he smiled, as though he could not help it. "So the game is afoot, Estella."

"Something like that," I said, handing him the glass of sherry.

Halfway home, I started to run.

"Miss Havisham," I said. "Can I talk to you?"

She was sitting on the parlor sofa, knitting what I suddenly realized would eventually be a sweater for me. Her fingers were as nimble as they had always been. The parlor looked just as it always had, with light filtering through the lace curtains, falling on the gleaming wood of the furniture and the rich colors of the Persian carpet. Not a single speck.

"Of course," she said. "Is it the dinner break already? I must have lost track of time. I seem to be doing that more and more, these days."

"No. I didn't go to school today."

She stopped knitting and looked up at me. She must have seen something in my face or heard something in the tone of my voice, because instead of scolding me, she sat perfectly still. As though waiting.

I sat in one of the armchairs and put the notebook on my knees. "Yesterday, I went around the village and—here. Look at this." I held out the notebook.

She put the knitting needles down on the sofa beside her, took the notebook, and leafed through the pages. Then, she turned back to the beginning and read each page again. Finally, she said, "I see. When did you first notice this?"

"On Sunday. But it must have been spreading for some time."

"Yes, I'm sure it has. Although I didn't think anyone here would notice."

Now it was my turn to sit, waiting. I was afraid of what she was going to say. I had no idea what it was, but she knew about the spots—that itself frightened me.

"Estella, I'm going to tell you a story." She leaned against the back of the sofa and looked down at her hands, as though suddenly not sure what to do with them. "I'm not used to telling stories, so I may ramble a bit. You'll be patient with me, won't you?"

"Of course. Just tell me." I sounded impatient, almost angry—but it was from fear. She didn't seem to notice.

"Once, there was a girl about your age who wanted to be a writer. Her parents didn't want her to be a writer—they wanted her to be a doctor or lawyer, something practical."

"Girls can't become doctors or lawyers."

"They can in this story," said Miss Havisham. She sounded different, somehow. Not like the Miss Havisham I knew, but like Miss Murray when she gives us a lecture on the suffrage movement. Was this the kindly old woman who had brought me up, taught me how to make jam and mend stockings? Who had brushed my hair at night?

"So instead of becoming a writer, she decided to become a college professor—and yes," she said, looking at me, "in this story girls can do that as well. She studied what other people had written—literature, that is, from medieval poems to modern critical theory. What she particularly loved was Victorian literature—Charles Dickens, George Eliot, Thomas Hardy, even American writers like Nathaniel Hawthorne. Anything written during that era."

What in the world was Miss Havisham talking about? I worried that she was going mad. She was making no sense, but I didn't dare interrupt.

"Their novels sometimes made her sad, because so many of them ended badly. She started imagining alternative endings, just before she fell asleep at night. She would imagine her favorite characters living together in a village, happily ever after—or as happily as possible.

She would imagine all the details of that village—the church where St. John Rivers could preach on Sundays, the main street with a blacksmith's shop for Joe Gargery and Pip, a shop where Maggie Tulliver could set up as a seamstress. And she imagined herself living in one of the houses—with a daughter." I was startled to see a tear run down her cheek. She wiped it away with her hand. "In her own life, she never married, never had any children of her own. Except the hundreds of students who took her classes, because eventually she became a professor of literature at a college in Vermont. Every night she would imagine the village—it became an important part of her life. It seemed so real to her."

"And then what happened?" I was beginning to understand. It was impossible—and frightening. But my book of aphorisms says you should believe six impossible things before breakfast.

"She began forgetting things. The date of the Indian Mutiny, her students' names. She had to go into a hospital, where the doctors looked inside her head. They can do that, in this story." She gave me a small, wry smile. How strange it was, listening to this new Miss Havisham. So direct, so unlike the Miss Havisham I knew.

"What did they see?" I asked.

"Black specks," she answered. "There's a medical term for it, of course. But that's essentially what they saw—black spaces where there was nothing, where the brain had died."

I sat staring at her, not sure what to say. Both believing and incredulous. "So what's going to happen to the village? And why am I the only one who can see what's happening?"

She looked down again, as though defeated, and that frightened me more than anything else. "I don't know. I'm sorry, Estella. I've tried every medication the doctors prescribed, and nothing has helped. The specks—the black spaces are growing. I don't know why you're the only one who can see them—perhaps it's because you've grown up with me. You're closer to me than anyone in the village. But there's no way to stop the memory loss."

"Then that's it?" I was almost shouting at her, but I couldn't help it.

"So what's going to happen to all of us? And me—am I just someone in a book?"

She leaned forward and took my hands. "Oh, my dear. You're my Estella. The girl who grew up in the village, playing with Pip and Flora and Pearl, learning history and arithmetics from Miss Murray. You're smart and sometimes selfish and obstinate, but a good friend. And you're my daughter. That's who you are, Estella. Hold on to that."

"How can I hold on to that?" Now I really was shouting. I'd never shouted at Miss Havisham in my life. "I don't even know who you are!"

I pulled my hands away, jumped up, and ran out of the room, then out the front door and down the high street, past the blacksmith's shop, running and running until I had left the village behind. I looked around—fields. I set out across one of the fields, toward the downs.

I walked and walked, grasses tickling me through my stockings, above my boots. I didn't stop until I was so tired that I could barely continue. Where was I?

By a copse of trees and a small stream. In the distance was the Hall. Had I really come that far? And then I saw something I had never expected, although I suppose I should have. Just above the chimneys of the Hall, on the blue of the sky, there was a scattering of black spots, like small moons.

"Hello, Estella."

I turned around, startled. There was mad Lady D'Urberville, in her red brocade gown. Had she been here all along? I had been so preoccupied, so frightened by what I had seen in the sky, that I hadn't noticed.

"Have you come here to dance? I often dance here myself. It's the fairies' dancing ground."

She picked up her skirts, curtsied gracefully, then started dancing to some music only she could hear. When she turned, her skirts spread around her, revealing black gaps around the hems that made them look ragged.

"Aren't you going to dance too, Estella?" she asked, holding out her hand.

"I don't feel like dancing," I said. For a moment I watched her as she turned and spun, then asked, "What would you do if you found out that the world you lived in was—some sort of dream?"

She stopped and stood, considering.

Suddenly I heard a shout: "Tess, where are you?" I looked around. Her foreman, Mr. Clare, was walking toward us from the direction of the Hall.

"I'm coming, my angel!" she called back. Then, leaning toward me as though she did not want anyone else to hear, although no one was close enough, she said, "*All that we see or seem is but a dream within a dream.* Remember that, Estella." She blew me a kiss and danced away over the field to where Mr. Clare was waiting.

I looked around me, at the fields and the downs beyond them, at the Hall in the distance. At the damaged sky. I looked back toward the village. I could just see the church spire. Miss Havisham had dreamed the village. All that we see and seem. Was that other life of hers a dream as well? Was someone dreaming her—the professor in that world where girls could go to college and study literature? If so, who was the dreamer?

I imagined an infinite number of dreamers, all dreaming each other. It made my head hurt.

"Estella, are you all right?" It was Pip. Black spots were now scattered down the front of his smock.

"Where did you come from?"

"I saw you run by the blacksmith's shop. I had to run in and tell Biddy where I was going, but since then I've been trying to find you. Don't get mad at me—I know you don't like me following you around like a sick dog, as you once said. But I was worried about you. You've been acting so strange for the last couple of days, barely talking to me. And why weren't you in school?"

Poor Pip. Miss Havisham was wrong—I hadn't been a very good friend.

"I want to try something. Will you stay quiet while I lie down on the ground? You can lie next to me if you want." I tried to sound calm, although I was scared. Would I have to watch the world disappear around me? For a moment I wished I were anyone else, so I wouldn't know what was happening.

He looked puzzled, but nodded.

I sat down on the ground and then lay back. Stalks of grass tickled my neck.

Pip sat beside me. "What are you going to do?"

"I'm going to dream."

"Don't you need to fall asleep first?"

"It's not that kind of dreaming. Now hush."

I closed my eyes and imagined Mrs. Rochester's terrier, with its sandy hair and sharp, loud bark. I tried to remember everything about him. Then I imagined Mr. Holmes's sofa, and my schoolbook with the engraving of Queen Victoria's coronation, and the back of Miss Usher's neck—all the places where I'd seen the nothingness spreading. I imagined every part of the village where I'd seen specks, spots, holes, or gaps. In my mind, I repaired them all. I repaired the sky itself. Finally, I imagined Pip's face, which I'd seen every day of my life, with no spots on it. I imagined as hard as I could. *All that we see or seem*, I said to myself, repeatedly until it became an incantation. Until I saw the village, every detail of it, as though it existed in my mind. I was its mender, its preserver, its creator.

I opened my eyes.

Pip was leaning on his elbow, looking down at me. His cheek was smooth and brown and unspotted. Behind him, the sky was blue—completely blue, except where white clouds floated across it like sheep.

I shouted with pleasure and pulled him toward me. I had meant to hug him, but instead he put his lips on mine and kissed me. It was awkward and wet, but satisfying. My first kiss. Although I had never imagined that Pip would be the first to kiss me, I was glad.

"Estella, I love you. Will you marry me?"

"Don't be silly. I'm only fifteen, and anyway when I finish school, I'm going to London to be a writer."

If I could dream the village, then perhaps I could dream London? Or even the world? And perhaps I could dream it differently—perhaps it could be a world in which girls could go to college, as Miss Havisham had described. I would have to dream every day, I would have to repeat my incantation, my spell. Tomorrow I would go around the village and make certain all of the gaps were indeed gone. But I felt confident that if there were any left, I could fill them. I could save the village I loved. Could I save Miss Havisham? Perhaps the one who lived in the village, the one who had raised me. That other woman she had described—another dreamer would have to take care of her.

The thought of it made me sad. But the only world I could save was my own, the one I lived in, the one that was waiting. Maybe someday I would marry Pip—but certainly not yet. I had all sorts of adventures ahead of me.

"Come on," I said. "You look like a dog that's lost its bone. You've had one kiss, and if you can catch me, I'll give you another!"

Then I jumped up, laughing, and ran back toward the village, across the fields, under a blue sky with flying clouds.

PELLARGONIA:
A LETTER TO THE *JOURNAL OF IMAGINARY ANTHROPOLOGY*

DEAR COLLEAGUES:

We think that's the right way to start, because Julia's dad always started his letters that way. [Starts, not started. He's missing, not dead.—Julia] Starts. Anyway.

We [Julia, David, and me, Madison] [That should be I, not me.—David] are writing to you because we need your help. Professor Jorge Escobar is missing, and it's all our fault. We hope we're not going to get in trouble for what we're about to write. [But we're pretty sure we are.—David] See, we were the ones who created Pellargonia. We know it says Professor Escobar on the article ("A Brief History of Pellargonia," *Journal of Imaginary Anthropology* 12.2, Fall 2018). But we were the ones who wrote it and sent it in. He didn't even know about it, which is why Julia was so surprised when the letter came. [Surprised is an understatement.—Julia] It was on heavy cream-colored paper, with a crown and a coat of arms on top, all in gold. [Embossed.—David] The address was The Royal Society of Pellargonia, 12 Santa Eugenia Stras, Bellagua del Mar 1024. It came to his office at the university, and he brought it home to read to Julia's mom before dinner while Julia was doing her math homework at the kitchen table. He said, "Honey, I've been invited to give this year's keynote at their annual conference,

and they want to make me a Fellow of the society. What do you think?"
[Did I get that right?—Madison] [Mostly. But my dad speaks Spanish
at home.—Julia] [Well, I don't know Spanish, and some of our readers might not either.—Madison] That's the weirdest part of this whole
thing—even he thought, I mean thinks, that he wrote the article. But
it was us. [We.—David]

In case you don't believe us, I'm going to send photocopies of the
maps and all our notes. [I drew the maps.—David] They're pretty
messy—at least my handwriting is. David's is pretty neat, and Julia
types everything anyway. But I think you can be more creative when
you write by hand—you can sketch and doodle and stuff, and it sort
of sets your brain free. [Great, if you can read it afterward!—Julia]
And I'll tell you the whole story, how we created Pellargonia and lost
Julia's dad.

At first it was just a game we played between classes. The country
didn't even have a name yet—we just called it Country X. In Honors
Bio it was David's turn.

> The rebels are closing in on the capital. Cesar Fuent-
> es has set up his headquarters in the old Estrella Ceilo
> estate. They have AK-47s that they bought from the
> Russians, plus some rogue American military advisors.

He is really into military history. And weapons. [But not in a school
lockdown kind of way. My interest is purely theoretical. The only thing
I've ever shot is a Nerf gun.—David] Then Julia and I had Algebra II
while David went off to Honors Math. That was Julia's turn, because
she doesn't really need to pay attention in math. Her brain does that
stuff automatically. She could be in Honors Math if she wanted to,
but she says it's too much work, and her parents let her take pretty
much whatever she wants. I wish my mom was that way!

> Zoraida Delacorte, the mistress of King Leopold IV,

is about to assassinate him. She has the poison ready.
She will put it in the glass of whiskey he drinks every
evening before going to bed, so he won't even taste it.
After he drinks it, she will flee through the secret
passage to join Cesar Fuentes in the forest.

Then we split up: Me to French, Julia to Latin, and David to Spanish.
He wanted to take Latin too, but his dad didn't understand why he
would want to take a language no one else speaks. His dad manages
the main bank here in Lewiston. He wants David to become an accountant. [Over my dead, decrepit, and decaying body.—David] No
one wrote anything then, because you have to pay attention in language
classes. Anyway, we were all working on a language for Country X that
would be sort of like French, and sort of like Spanish, but with some
weird Latin stuff mixed in. Like declensions. Julia really likes declensions. But in AP World History it would be my turn.

Princess Stefania, who has never trusted Zoraida
Delacorte, switches his whiskey glass with that of
the Prime Minister, who wants her to marry Baron
Alfonse el Cerdo, who is at least twice her age. She
thinks with longing about her school friend, Clotilde,
and that kiss they shared on the day they graduated.
Will she ever see Clotilde again?

And then we had electives: art for Julia, cello for me, and pro-
gramming for David, not because he needed it—he's really good with
computers—but because his dad thought it would be useful.

After school, we would go to the library to study and hang out. The
lady who runs the YA and kids' section, Doris, who's known me pretty
much my whole life, would say, "Here come the Three Musketeers!"
Which is a pretty lame joke, but I kind of get why she says it. David
and I have known each other since we were kids and he lived next

door. He moved after his parents got divorced—now he lives with his mom on the other side of town, and his dad lives with his stepmom in a big house close to the reservoir. Mom and I still live in Grandma's house, which is close to the library, so she doesn't have to walk that far to work. We couldn't afford to move even if we wanted to, and anyway my mom says it's the perfect house, with an office for her by the kitchen and a bedroom for me up in the attic. I could have moved down to the second floor after Grandma died, but I like it up there. It's like a nest. And I wanted to keep her bedroom the way she had left it, with her celluloid brush and nail buffer on the dressing table. I never knew my dad—I was just a baby when he died in Afghanistan—but at least I had a long time with Grandma.

Anyway, I've known David for most of my life, and Julia moved to Lewiston the year after he moved across town, when her dad started teaching at the university. In ninth grade she was behind me in homeroom, and we got along right away—Julia's the sort of person who can be friends with almost anybody. She's naturally curious about people. At first David was kind of standoffish with her, but then they discovered they both liked graphic novels and tabletop RPGs, and that sort of made them non-enemies, even though David liked World War I reenactments and Julia was into classic D&D. And then they discovered they liked a lot of the same books, and also disliked a lot of the same books, including everything we were assigned in school, from *The Catcher in the Rye* to *The Great Gatsby*. I actually like *The Great Gatsby* myself, and that's where I got the idea for Fitzgerald G. Scott, the American who bought up that land on Mount Floria and built a casino resort, which Cesar Fuentes took for his headquarters when the revolution started. [OMG you are so rambling.—Julia]

Anyway, I wasn't really into all the stuff David and Julia were into—you know, games and fantasy and sci-fi. I prefer history and romance, which is why I know who the Three Musketeers are. But when Julia got the idea for Country X, it was like, okay, let's try it. It had war for David, and lots of drama for Julia, and we were going to write it down, not just make it up, which is what got me interested. I want to be a writer and create books, not just sort and catalog them like Mom.

So Julia and I biked over to David's house, because he has a game room in the basement, and we planned it all out. I mean the basics—how Country X had been founded by one of the Gaelish tribes [Gaelic.—David], and then the Romans came, and then it was part of Spain for a while, and then part of France, and it sort of went back and forth until finally it became its own country. We decided it had to be on an ocean, so we could have lots of trade and immigrants. We wanted it to look like us—you know, diverse. Like David being African American, and me being mostly just white but part Polish, which I guess counts for something, and Julia being a mixture of lots of different things, including Native, which is the way she says people are in Argentina. And all different religions too, although the three of us aren't very diverse that way. David's family is Methodist and my mom isn't really religious—she says she's spiritual and goes around smudging things when there's bad energy around. Julia goes to Mass every Sunday with her parents, which I guess is sort of different, at least for Lewiston. Anyway, we wanted it to be as different from Lewiston as possible. Mom once said that living in Maine is sort of like eating Wonder Bread for lunch every day, which isn't totally true—we have some kids in school from Somalia and Bangladesh, and we have a girl in homeroom from Thailand. I don't know her that well because she's a cheerleader, and they tend to hang out together. But it's still pretty boring here. I mean, people go bowling or to miniature golf on dates, and the biggest social event of the year is homecoming, although Pride Day is getting bigger every year. [Hello, my dad is still missing. Can we get back to talking about Pellargonia?—Julia]

On the earliest map [I labeled it Figure 1.—Julia] you can tell we didn't even know which ocean it was on. The wavy bit is just labeled "Ocean." That was last fall. We were still getting used to tenth grade, and taking an AP class, and our parents starting to talk about college. We were taking PSAT prep tests and comparing our results. [I'm the one in Honors Math, and Julia still gets the highest math scores.—David] [The PSAT is just another way high school indoctrinates us, so we can be become cogs in the industrial machine of late capitalism.—Julia] [Ok, but you still have to take it. Your mom said so.—Madison]

It was Julia who first told us about the *Journal of Imaginary Anthropology*. I think it was around Columbus Day [Indigenous Peoples' Day.—Julia], because that was the last long weekend before Thanksgiving. Her parents live in the university dorms—I mean, they have a regular apartment, but it's in a dormitory on campus, and her mom and dad do a lot of advising and stuff, like when students are sick [You mean drunk.—Julia] or have problems with their classes. So the university is sort of like her neighborhood—she knows all the buildings and a lot of the people who work in them, and everyone knows she's Professor Escobar's daughter. One day she was in her dad's office in the anthropology department, waiting to talk to him about a problem from school [The bio teacher said she would fail me if I didn't dissect a fetal pig.—Julia] [Julia is vegan and eats those weird fake burgers.—David] [You eat chicken embryos. How is that less weird?—Julia] and she saw a copy on his desk. She was leafing through it and when he came in, with his hair all rumpled from teaching [He always runs his fingers through it, so you can't tell if it's gray or just chalk.—Julia], she asked him what it was.

"Nonsense," he said. "A bunch of nonsense. Written by a group of grad students who should know better. This is what happens when you take postmodern literary theory too seriously. You start thinking that if you can *write* reality, you can *create* it. Bullcrap." [He was going to say bullshit, but he tries not to swear in front of me, even in Spanish.—Julia] "Now, what's this about bio, and did you really call Mrs. Ellerton a carnivorous fascist?"

The next day, we went to the university library. I mean, wouldn't you, after what Julia's dad said? If it was bullcrap, we wanted to find out what kind of bullcrap it was—we wanted to know what imaginary anthropology was, and if it was as interesting as the real kind. Julia

had her own UMaine-Lewiston library card, but you can't take journals out, so we sat on the floor of the stacks, with the bookshelves all
around us, reading the back issues. There weren't that many, since it
was a new journal. We spent the next couple of hours sitting on the
cold floor—I don't know why they have don't rugs, like in the regular library—telling each other about the different countries, their customs,
the people who lived there. It was as good as reading a history book.
And some of the articles talked about theoretical stuff, too, although
we didn't understand all of it. But that's how we learned about the
Tlön hypothesis, and Cimmeria, and Hyperborea, and Zothique.

It was David who said, "We should make Country X real. It deserves to be real. Mount Zamorna, and Cabo del Alexandrion, and
Santa Petra Bay."

"And that little town where Hemerosa first met Alonzo Lorca,"
said Julia. "The one in the poem he wrote. I mean that Madison wrote
for him. And Karolus Ludvig University, and the Bellagua Botanical
Gardens."

"And the Berengaria Mental Hospital where they locked up Zofia
Montague until she agreed to marry her cousin, King Leopold II. And
the Livia Sagrada School for Noble Ladies, where Princess Stefania
met Clotilde." I wanted that school to be real. I wanted Stefania and
Clotilde to be real. It was going to be the greatest romance in the
history of Pellargonia. [Greater than Hemerosa and Alonzo?—Julia]
[Oh, definitely.—Madison]

But how were we going to make it real?

"We have to start writing about it," said David. "Like on Wikipedia
and stuff. We need to write an entry for . . ." That's when we realized
our country didn't have a name.

It was Julia who came up with it. I don't think even she knows
exactly where it came from. [No clue.—Julia] But later, when I was
looking it up online to see how many entries it had, I noticed there's a
flower called pelargonium. So maybe that had something to do with
it. [But I don't know anything about flowers. Anyway, pelagic means

"of the sea," and Pellargonia is on the sea.—Julia] [There's also "ar-chipelago." Like those islands off the coast where Federico the Red hid when Leopold II was trying to get rid of all the pirates.—David]

There were other names suggested—Mossimore was one. So was Elsivere. We made a list of names—you can see the list in our notes. At one point we started playing around with spelling. Dajuma, Juma-da, Majuda. But we thought they all sounded fake, and we wanted Country X to be real.

Pellargonia was the one that stuck. And then we had to figure out where it was going to be. Because of the language, the obvious place to put it was between France and Spain. But it had to be on the ocean because of the pirates who pillaged around the Arroz Islands. That left only two choices: either on the Mediterranean or on the Bay of Bis-cay. I wanted the Bay of Biscay, because it sounded romantic, but Julia wanted the Mediterranean because of the *Odyssey*, and David said it was better for pirates. And on the map we found a little country called Andorra, right in the Pyrenees mountains. It was so much like Pel-largonia that we figured someone else must have had the same idea we did and put it there. I mean, you can tell it's one of the imaginary countries, like Ruritania and Liechtenstein.

First we wrote the Wikipedia entry, with a history of Pellargonia back to the Stone Age. David wrote the ancient stuff about the tribes that had lived there, fishing and hunting, and the cave art they left in cliffs around the Ruata river basin. Julia wrote from the Roman occupation through the Middle Ages, when Ottaker converted to Catholicism, and made everyone else convert too so he could marry Princess Magdalena, the youngest daughter of the French king. He became Otto I, the first king of Pellargonia. David covered from the conquest by the Umayyad Caliphate to the Reconquista, and then Julia took over again, because she had learned about the war between Aragon and Castile in Spanish class, and Pellargonia became part of Aragon for a while. I took over from the Renaissance through the nineteenth century, including when Louis XIV claimed Pellargonia for France as part of the War of Spanish Succession. I also covered the Industrial Revolution and a bunch of other revolutions—real ones, I mean. The Pellargonians rebelled a lot too, especially when Julia was bored in math class. We worked together on the War of Independence and the Treaty of Bellagua, when Pellargonia finally became its own kingdom again. Well, queendom technically, under Queen Zofia since Leopold II died in mysterious circumstances just after their wedding. Then David did the twentieth century, because he really likes the World Wars. [I don't *like* wars. I like studying wars. That's totally different.—David] He did the modern stuff, like Pellargonia being in the EU and Schengen and all that.

We made Wikipedia pages for all the important figures, from Amalia Croce, who started the 1883 Women's Revolution and got the vote for women, way before we got it here in America, to Cesar Fuentes, the leader of the Pellargonian National Front, who may be holding Professor Escobar captive. You can tell it was us because we're listed as the earliest editors: JuliaE@lhs.edu, Maddie@lhs.edu, and superyoda@gmail.com. Julia was worried about the people who were there already. "What will happen to them? I mean, some of them are French and some of them are Spanish. Will they go on being French and Spanish, and just sort of move to make room for Pellargonia?" To be honest, I hadn't thought about that. She's more socially conscious than me and David [David and I.—David]. She doesn't even wear leather shoes.

"They'll just become Pellargonian," said David. Anyway, that's what we hoped would happen. Like, one day they would start speaking Pellargonian, and their passports would turn into Pellargonian ones. It was still in the EU, so they would be fine, right? It's not as though we would really be changing very much. Just, like, the street signs, and they would have a new king, but Leopold IV was a constitutional monarch. He was mostly there for opening hospitals and riding a white horse down Santa Eugenia Stras on Liberation Day. Pellargonia was still a representative democracy. Finally even Julia decided it was all right, because the French and Spanish had colonized so many other people, they deserved to be colonized a little themselves. Anyway, we wouldn't actually be hurting anyone. To be honest, we didn't think about it as carefully as we should have. I mean, exams were coming up. And we only half believed it would work. Could we really create a country just by writing about it? Maybe it was bullcrap, after all.

After we put everything up on Wikipedia, we divided the social media stuff. I posted on Facebook, because I still have an account so I can share funny cartoons with my mom. Julia posted on Instagram. She took photos around Lewiston and photoshopped them, putting in castles and villages from tourist agency ads. She had to add a lot of sunlight because Lewiston isn't exactly on the Mediterranean. She painted a bunch of historical figures herself. [Sort of. Digital painting on top of older stuff. Like, Queen Magdalena is really Leonardo da Vinci's *Lady with an Ermine*, but I changed it to a dog, because who keeps an ermine as a pet? That's as bad as wearing fur.—Julia] And David did whatever you do on Reddit, because he's the only one of us who's actually been on Reddit. I don't even know what it is, to be honest. [Because you're not a nerd.—David]

We filled the internet with Pellargonia. It took a lot of time, because we still had to study and eat and sleep and stuff. And Julia had soccer. Lewiston High was as close as it had ever gotten to the state championship, so she had to go to a bunch of away games. [We came in second, after one of the big Portland high schools.—Julia] Just when David and I thought we'd done enough, Julia said, "You know, we need to write an article. For the *Journal of Imaginary Anthropology*. It won't be real without that."

Of course, none of us knew how to write an academic article, so we spent most of Thanksgiving break in the university library. We looked at all those articles from the *Journal of Imaginary Anthropology* again and wrote down sentences we could use. Not to plagiarize, we know that's wrong, but so we could sound like professors. We learned words like Industrial Capacity, Agricultural Sector, Balance of Payments. [Those are phrases, not words.—David] We realized that we'd thought a lot about the history of Pellargonia, but we hadn't really thought about how it would fit into the modern world. We knew it used euros, that was easy. But was it a member of NATO? [Yes, it joined at the same time as Spain.—Julia] And we wrote a lot of footnotes—we noticed journal articles had a lot of footnotes. David was especially good at those. He sort of talks like a footnote anyway. [There's nothing wrong with being articulate.—David] [See what I mean? I would never have used the word "articulate."—Madison]

I wrote the first draft, except for the footnotes. Then Julia revised it and added a lot more. Then David revised it, because he sounds the most professory, and then I revised it again to take out some of the professoryness, because we wanted it to be readable. [It was readable. And what's wrong with saying "articulate"? Just because you have a limited vocabulary doesn't mean the rest of us have to.—David] [I don't have a limited vocabulary. I just happen to talk like a normal person.—Madison] We also added a bunch of maps and charts [Those are Figures 2–12. I drew all the maps.—David] [You already said that.—Madison], including the dates of the different kings and queens, since women can be heads of state in Pellargonia [Damn straight.—Julia], ever since Saint Eugenia, the youngest daughter of King Ludovic I, became queen in 1306, after her two older brothers were assassinated. The Pellargonians were out of possible kings, so they just went ahead and made her queen—plus she had a divine vision that she was chosen by the Virgin Mary herself. [I put that in. Maybe it was a real divine vision, maybe not. We'll never know!—Julia] Then we formatted it all correctly for submission to the journal, the way it said on the website.

The last step was putting Jorge Escobar, PhD on the first page, right below the title. I remember at the time we all thought it was pretty funny—and harmless because Julia's father would never find out. I mean, how could he? He doesn't have a subscription to the *Journal of Imaginary Anthropology*—remember, he thinks it's bullcrap. And even if he did, no one actually reads academic journals. They just download the articles from JSTOR. We figured only a few people would ever see the article, but with all the other stuff we were doing, it would make Pellargonia real. Then we decided we should add his name to the Wikipedia page, as an expert on Pellargonian history—after all, he had written the definitive article on Pellargonia, right? Of course, now we wish we hadn't done it. But if wishes were horses, beggars would ride, as my grandma used to say. [What does that even mean?—Julia] [It's a proverb.—David] [That doesn't mean it makes sense.—Julia]

We got a reply back only a month later. I mean, Professor Escobar got it, but Julia was checking his departmental mailbox, and she took it before he noticed. We opened it together, not really expecting anything. Julia handed the letter to David, who read it out loud—our article had been accepted![1]

---

1   This is, of course, an extraordinarily short period of time for acceptance to a peer-reviewed academic journal. Although the writers of this letter could not have realized it, we were at the time receiving very few submissions—the situation in Gondal was at its most tense, and there were some voices calling for an end to the imaginary sciences, saying that imaginary anthropology, archaeology, geology, and the nascent field of imaginary astrophysics imperiled us all. Others pointed out that some respectable fields—xenobiology, for example—had always been at least partly imaginary, and that reality was not more relative and conditional now than it had ever been. The history of cartography, for example, consists entirely of imaginary maps that can never accurately depict the territory. I remember when this article first crossed my desk. I shared it with my office mate (also an adjunct at Southern Arizona State, teaching a 4/4 schedule with one class per semester in the anthropology department, the other three freshman comp). It had some mistakes that I put down to hasty composition and corrected in proofs, but I had no reason to believe it was not by Professor Escobar. Reviewer 1, my office mate's ex-girlfriend who had also gotten her PhD in our department and who was now an Assistant Professor at Mary Margaret Wentworth College in Virginia, said it was fine. Reviewer 2, who had been my thesis director, said it should refer to his seminal work, *Imaginary Anthropology: Theory and Practice*, which he says in every review, and which I felt was not applicable in this particular case. So the article was published as it was sent to me, with only minor alterations.—Ed.

After that, things got really busy for us. There was Christmas break [Winter break, technically.—David], and then studying for the AP exam. Our AP World History teacher wanted all of us to take the exam that year because he said it didn't really count. Since no college gave AP World History credit anyway, he thought it would be good practice. So as soon as school started again, we started taking practice tests. Julia was working on an online graphic novel in Spanish, posting a chapter a week. David was practicing for the jazz ensemble (he plays the trombone, but he said he was getting tired of marching band). [Too many football games.—David]. I had decided to join the girls' basketball team. I'm not great at basketball, but I'm tall, and that counts for a lot. We still worked on Pellargonia when we could—I mean, we didn't want to leave Zoraida Delacorte in trouble, and there was a whole revolution going on. [As usual.—Julia] Plus I really wanted Princess Stefania to meet up with Clotilde again. There was a girl on the basketball team who looked a little like Clotilde, and I wondered if she might like to go to the mall, to get bubble tea or something. But there wasn't much time.

One day, Julia grabbed me in the hall as I was heading to lunch. (That quarter, she was in a different lunch period, so David and I ate together.) She was all jumpy, the way she is when she gets excited, like a jack-in-the-box. "I got a Google Alert!" she said. "Look at *this*! And tell David."

This was an Air France flight to Pellargonia. CDG to BDM, it said: Charles de Gaulle airport to Bellagua del Mar. On sale for 80 euros in economy.

When I got to the cafeteria, David was already sitting there, with tater tots on his tray. He has tater tots every single day, with ketchup. That's it, just two servings of tater tots. [It's the only edible thing in the cafeteria.—David] I got a rectangular pizza and the obligatory vegetable, probably spinach because it was green and slimy, like seaweed. [You should get tater tots. They count as a vegetable.—David] If Julia had been there, she would have brought something from home, like a tofu ham sandwich or one of those rolled up nori things.

When I showed David what Julia had shown me, he took out his cell phone and said, "Siri, how can I get to Pellargonia?" He's the only one of us with an iPhone, which his dad bought him. I just have my mom's old Android with a dented case, and Julia has an ancient Black-Berry. [Didn't the dinosaurs use those?—David]

"There are two ways to get to Pellargonia," said a mechanical female voice. "Would you like to go by plane or by train?"

My phone doesn't have a fancy voice, but while David asked about flights, I looked up train routes on Google Maps. There were trains to Bellagua del Mar from Barcelona and Montpellier. The one from Barcelona stopped in Girona and Figueres. The one from Montpellier stopped in Perpignan. Once you arrived in Bellagua del Mar, it looked like you could get around Pellargonia pretty easily. There was a highway from Bellagua to Magdalena, in the northern mountains, which is sort of a resort town. That's where Fitzgerald G. Scott built his casinos. It's also the center of the revolution. There were a lot of smaller roads to towns we had named, and towns I had never heard of. Who had created them? And there was a dotted line from Mallorca to the Arroz Islands.

"That's a ferry service," said David. "It runs three times a day." He showed me his phone, which had all the times, 40 euros round-trip. He swiped to show me the train schedules, and then the Air France website. "Would you like to book a flight?" asked Siri.

Pellargonia was real.

David said, "And look at this." He swiped again, and there was YouTube, with PTV-1, the Pellargonian state TV channel, broadcasting the news in Pellargonian. I could sort of understand it, a little. We had made up the basic stuff, like verb tenses, words for things like sun, moon, cat, dog, tree, flower, traitor, king, succession, assassination. Conjunctions and propositions. But this was a real language! We just sat there staring at each other, until Ms. Patel told us to hurry up and put our trays in the rack, because lunch was almost over.

She's usually the gym teacher, but she was monitoring lunch that day. Lunch only lasts twenty minutes—I don't know who can eat in twenty minutes, even if it's just rectangular pizza. David shoved the rest of his tater tots into his mouth. Then we heard the bell, and we had to rush to AP World History. At least the three of us had that class together. We were talking about Europe during the Cold War—we had just gotten to the "Modern World Order" chapter in our history textbook.

"Yes, David?" said Mr. Delacorte. We named Zoraida Delacorte after him, although she's a former ballet dancer and spy, while Mr. Delacorte is a short man with a halo of white hair who's been teaching history at Lewiston High since my mom went there. To be honest, I wasn't really paying attention. I mean, there was the whole Pellargonia thing, but also I had a basketball tournament that week, and I was visualizing my jump shot. Ms. Patel, who is also our coach, has us do a lot of visualizing—she says that's how players in the WNBA get so good. First they visualize, and then they practice what they visualized over and over. It helps with cello, too. [That is so not important right now.—Julia]

"What about the little countries?" asked David. "Like Luxembourg and Montenegro and stuff. What happened to them during the Cold War? Or like Pellargonia, just for example."

I sat up in my seat and looked back at him. He had such an innocent expression on his face, like he had just happened to think of Pellargonia right then. David can do that—he never looks guilty, no matter what he does. That time he cut my hair and then swore he didn't do it, my mom believed him, even though he was standing right there, holding the scissors. I got sent to my room, and it took a year for my hair to grow back. [We were *five*. You've got to let that go.—David]

I was ready for Mr. Delacorte to ask him what he was talking about, to say there was no country called Pellargonia. But instead he said, "Well, these little countries, David, tend to be heavily influenced by the larger countries around them. Luxembourg, surrounded by Belgium, France, and Germany, became a wealthy banking center. Montenegro is not really that small. It was part of Yugoslavia, which we covered last week, so I'll refer you to your notes from back then. It's still dealing with the effects of ethnic conflict. And Pellargonia, which borders on the Catalan-speaking part of Spain, is in the middle of a civil war between those who want to remain part of the EU, speaking New Pellargonian, and the nationalistic Euroskeptic Old Pellargonian speakers. Evidently, it's going rather badly for the central government, and there's talk of deposing the king. Not that he has much power anyway, but fighting in the north has created a refugee problem on the French border from people trying to escape the fighting, and they're looking for someone, anyone, to blame."

A civil war? We had thought of it as one more romantic revolution—I mean, Pellargonia had a history of revolutions. It had been about Cesar Fuentes, and Zoraida Delacorte, and King Leopold IV, and Princess Stefania. We hadn't really thought about the political consequences. Or, you know, people dying. All that stuff about Old Pellargonian was just a footnote. David wrote it because we thought there should be some kind of history about how Pellargonian had changed over the centuries, like from Old English to regular English. Julia and I thought it was a cool idea at the time. [We were kind of dumb.—Julia] [We didn't really believe in it. I mean, it was like a game, like when you're the Dungeon Master in D&D. I thought it would be interesting to have a different language for the northern part, around Mount Zamorna. I never thought anyone would have a war about it.—David] [We're not making excuses for ourselves, just trying to explain.—Madison]

But what were we supposed to do? We were just three kids [Young adults.—Julia] living in Lewiston. We weren't politicians, or anything like that. And the Tlön hypothesis says that, once you create a country, it takes on a life of its own, and then it's not yours anymore. That's supposed to be the coolest thing about it. Except I guess it's not cool if people are fighting and dying, for real.[2]

We stopped playing at Pellargonia after that. It wasn't a game anymore. Anyway, school ended and the summer vacation began. David went off to math camp [Which was like math class all day, every day. I started having nightmares about being chased by quadratic equations.—David], and Julia went to her grandmother's in Los Angeles. I was left by myself in Lewiston. Well, not exactly by myself, because I was volunteering at the library, so I got to spend time with Mom. But you know what I mean. Every once in a while, we texted each other:

> Did you see that there's a truce between the Pellargonian National Front and the Social Democrats?—Julia

> There's a story in *El Mund* saying the Prime Minster might have been poisoned. Do you think they'll figure out it was Zoraida Delacorte?—Madison

> Fighting has broken out again around Magdalena.

---

2   This is, of course, the problem with imaginary anthropology. People and the political systems they create are inherently unpredictable. You never know what they will do. The situation in Ruritania is a case in point. You can't really blame David Ignatious and his group at Harvard for the autocratic regime of General Szarkov. I mean, you can, and this journal issued a very stern warning for all imaginary anthropologists to be particularly careful when creating former Soviet Bloc countries. That configuration seems to have inherent instabilities. The Harvard group was out of its depth, but what do you expect from a bunch of Ivy League grad students? They're convinced they can walk on water. Each of them wants to, individually, be God. What I have learned in the imaginary sciences is that reality has its own imagination, and we are all only a small part of its creative power. I will be expanding on this hypothesis, with Pellargonia as one of my examples, in a paper to be given at the Imaginary Anthropology Symposium at the University of Glasgow next summer.—Ed.

I saw it on PTV-1.—David

They just announced that Princess Stefania is going to assume the throne. King Leopold is stepping down on Friday.—Madison

The referendum was 57% remain in the EU. But that still means a lot of people want to leave, and they're mostly in the north.—Julia

They found Cesar Fuentes's headquarters at the casino, but he had already fled. I hope Zoraida is with him.—Madison

Hey Mad, did you see the cover of *Vogue France?* There's a blonde woman with Princess Stefania. Is that Clotilde?—Julia

OMG can someone send me Oreos? The only cookies here are these weird chewy things with flax-seed, because they say it's brain food. I'm going to die of starvation. Oh and BTW someone tried to bring a bomb into the Catedral dela Santa Eugenia during the coronation. It was hidden in a camera—he was pretending to be a journalist for *El País.* I'm glad they caught him.—David

Queen Stefania made a statement on PTV-1. She's going to try to negotiate with the PNF. I hope it works.—Julia

But mostly we focused on other things. We couldn't think about Pellargonia all the time. And we figured, now that it was real—now that it was part of the world—there wasn't much more we could do. It was like we'd created Frankenstein, and now it was going to go off by itself, doing whatever it did. [Frankenstein is the scientist. The monster doesn't have a name.—David] [The scientist *is* the monster.—Julia]

Until the letter came for Julia's dad.

It came just before school started, after David got back from camp [Six weeks of math and mosquitoes! I thought I was going to die.— David] and Julia got back from the art program she had gone to after Los Angeles. [We painted from a nude model. A *male* nude model. My mom kind of freaked out when I told her.—Julia] It was all we could talk about, even though we were going to start eleventh grade and there was so much to catch up on. This year we were going to be taking the SAT, and all our teachers had decided to assign summer reading—before the first class! I was thinking about asking my friend Audrey (the one on the basketball team) out on a real date. David had a crush on a girl from math camp. [I wouldn't call it a crush. It was a mutual attraction.—David], and Julia had started selling some of her art on Redbubble, on mugs and things. [I'm JuliArt.—Julia] But all we could talk about was Julia's dad and the letter.

We'd thought about visiting Pellargonia ourselves someday. Like when we were in college backpacking around Europe together, staying in hostels and stuff. Julia's mom had done that with some of her friends, when she was young—I mean younger, since she's not really old, although she has gray hair. [Most hair dyes have chemicals that can give you cancer.—Julia] Anyway, it sounded pretty cool. But now Julia's dad was actually going!

Why had they invited him? Because he was an expert on Pellargonian history, of course. After all, he had written the definitive article— it said so on Wikipedia. [I told you no one ever reads the actual journals.—Julia] How was he going to get there? Air France. Where was he going to stay in Bellagua del Mar? The university had a guest house at the Estrella Ceilo estate. Would he meet Queen Stefania herself? He had no idea, and Julia was asking so many questions that he told her to please stop pestering him, because he had a keynote address to write.

Of course we were a little worried, because we knew that Queen Stefania's offer of amnesty had been rejected, and the PNF was still active in the mountains around Magdalena. "He'll be fine," Julia said. "He's just going for a week to some academic conference. He goes to conferences all the time."

But it wasn't fine. You know that—I'm sure you've seen the footage on PTV-1, and it was even on CNN. Just as Queen Stefania started her welcome address, the rebels burst into the auditorium. They had Kalashnikovs, flash grenades, and tear gas, and David says he even saw a rocket launcher. [The video was blurry, but I'm pretty sure that's what it was.—David] They wanted the queen, of course. Well, they didn't get her, but after all the smoke cleared, three of the people who had been sitting beside her on the dais were gone: Dr. Otto Lenker, the president of the Royal Society; Dr. Amélie Beaulieu of Lyon University; and Julia's dad.

It's been three months. The PNF made a deal with the French government, and Dr. Beaulieu was released. Dr. Lenker and Julia's dad are still being held captive. There was an offer to exchange them for two of the rebel leaders being held in prison, but the Pellargonian government said it didn't deal with terrorists. We think he's still alive—I mean, we know he is. [He is.—Julia] Julia's mom got in touch with Senator Mitchner as soon as she heard the news, and he says the US government is doing all it can. She's pretty frantic, and she keeps talking about flying to Pellargonia, just so she can be there. I mean, she needs to be here to take care of Julia, but she's asked for a leave of absence from the clinic she works for, and she thinks another therapist can cover for her, for a while. [Sometimes I can hear her crying at night.—Julia]

So we've started a GoFundMe to get her and Julia to Pellargonia. I mean, we *made* Pellargonia. Maybe there's something Julia can do, and maybe David and I can help, even from Lewiston? But we're just three kids. [Young adults.—Julia] You were probably in high school yourself at some point. [Everyone has to go through high school at some point. It's like the common cold.—David] So you must know what it feels like—everyone tells you that you're almost an adult, so you're supposed to be responsible, but no one *treats* you like an adult or takes you seriously. When I tried to talk to Mom about what had happened, she said, "Sweetheart, you can't make up a country. Pellargonia has been around for a long time. You can look it up on Wikipedia."

The GoFundMe has about $700, mostly from David's stepmom and his band friends. We thought, maybe the *Journal of Imaginary Anthropology* could send an email to its readers, or post something on the website? We need money, but also, we need someone to go with Julia and her mom—someone who really understands imaginary anthropology, and might be able to fix things? Like one of the authors who wrote those theoretical articles. If there's someone like that out there, who can actually help us find Julia's dad and maybe stop the civil war, please contact us at Professor Escobar's university address with a letter of intent, your CV, and two references. [Does that sound right, Jules?—Madison] [Yes, that's the way it's usually done.—Julia] We look forward to hearing from you.

Sincerely,
Madison Kowalski, David Lewis, and Julia Escobar

Editor's Note:
I have published this letter in full, exactly as I received it, from Madison, David, and Julia, whom I have since communicated with by email. I am convinced that they did, in fact, create Pellargonia—a remarkable feat for a group of high school students, considering that the Stanford group failed to create any country whatsoever after two years of trying. This supports a pet theory of mine that creating a country is not, finally, about expertise but

imagination and the *capacity to believe*, or at least not *dis*believe. Davidson et al. started out as skeptics. No wonder it didn't work. More importantly, I'm including this letter in the current issue instead of my usual introduction in the hope that our readers will support the Save Professor Escobar fund. I intend to travel with Julia and Dr. Gabriela Escobar myself. I don't know if there's anything I can do, but as editor of this journal, I feel a sense of responsibility.

Since I received the above letter, conditions have improved in Pellargonia. Queen Stefania is considerably more popular than her father, and her economic policies are expected to help the poorer northern districts, including Floria and Zamorna. Her personal appeal to Zoraida Delacorte on PTV-2, the fashion and lifestyle channel, was both an effective political move and good PR. Hopefully the current cease-fire and the resumption of negotiations between the government and the PNF will help us free Professor Escobar. Whatever happens, I hope to document our trip and my observations in a future article in this journal. I will call it "Pellargonia: A Case Study in the Problematics of Imaginary Anthropology."

LOST GIRLS OF OZ

DEAR DOTTIE,

This will be a long letter, because I'm going on a trip, and such a trip! You won't believe me when I tell you! But don't tell Mamsie, because you know how she worries when she thinks either of us girls is doing anything the least bit—well, she would call it dangerous, but I'm going to call it adventurous.

But I do want to tell you about it, because I want you to know where I am in case anything goes wrong. That makes it sound dangerous, I know—but please don't worry about me. I'm perfectly capable of taking care of myself, and I wouldn't be an intrepid girl reporter if I didn't follow my story wherever it took me. And this is quite a story, my dear. I'm so glad that I came to San Francisco, even though it meant leaving you and Mamsie. I would never have gotten a story like this, or the Ogilvie murders either, if I hadn't left sleepy old Sacramento for the big city.

Do you remember how much Mr. Leavis liked my story on the murders? I spent months researching those girls, and when they actually caught and arrested Ogilvie, based on the evidence I had uncovered, it was quite a coup for the *Ledger*, I can tell you!

This morning, Mr. Leavis called me into his office, which always reeks of cigar smoke, and said, "Nell, you know these girls that have been disappearing?" Well, of course I did—they've been in all the papers, and there was a story on them in the *Ledger* last week. You remember the clipping I sent you—girls from respectable neighborhoods, gone missing and no bodies found. Quite the opposite of Ogilvie, who strangled them and left them in alleys. "I want you to look into it," he told me. "You did good work on the Ogilvie case—under my direction, of course." As though he'd had anything to do with it! Honestly, sis, the way he takes credit for everyone's work is just sickening. "The Langs have agreed to be interviewed. We can run a story on the poor, grieving family and at the same time launch our own investigation. How about it?" Well, of course I said yes! Imagine if I could find out where those girls had gone—I would be on the front page again, but this time I would insist on my own byline! No more "by Eleanor Dale and Edward Leavis," thank you!

After lunch, I went to see the Langs. At first, I wasn't sure if I was going to get the interview after all. Mr. Lang was obviously drunk and refused to let me in, but his wife pleaded with him, saying it was "for our Mary." So we sat on the sofa and had a very stiff interview indeed. Luckily, Mr. Lang passed out in the middle of it, and then Mrs. Lang really opened up. Poor woman! She was the one who had called the police, and then the *Ledger*—her husband hadn't even wanted to file a missing person report. "He said Mary had run off with some boy, but I don't believe it," she told me. "Mary was always a good girl." She talked about how much she missed her daughter, what a help she'd been around the house and with the little ones. And she let me look around Mary's room. She even showed me Mary's diary. There wasn't much in it, just an account of her daily life, but every once in a while I came across a curious entry: "Father angry today." Or "Father especially angry today."

Fathers do get angry, but it was the reoccurence of the phrase that caught my attention. And there were mentions of a best friend, a Sally Russell. I asked Mrs. Lang if she could give me Sally's address. It was only a couple of blocks away. I walked along streets of placid houses surrounded by white picket fences. They seemed to be sleeping in the California sunlight. (Do you like that description? I'm going to use it in the story.)

Sally Russell was a tall, lanky girl with freckles and straw-colored hair. She wasted no time in telling me what was what. "Of course Mary ran away!" she said. "No, she didn't have a boyfriend—Mr. Lang would never have let her. He used to beat her something awful—and her mother too, but her mother never did anything about it. And he was going to do worse . . . He wasn't Mary's real father, you know—her father ran off, and then Mrs. Lang married Mr. Lang and had two more children. Mary could never go anywhere, because she had to take care of them. The little imps, she used to call them. I think it was the school nurse who told her—one day when she was afraid Mr. Lang had broken her wrist, it was so swollen, and she just couldn't hide it anymore. The nurse told her that there was this underground—that it could get girls to Oz."

Well, you can imagine how I responded to that! Everyone knows you can't get to Oz anymore, not since the borders were closed. No one even knows where it is, now. It could be in the middle of the sea, or a great desert. And even if you could find it—what if you ran into Nomes, or Wheelers, or Flying Monkeys? I told her, quite sternly, that Mary had probably been tricked, and could be in a lot of trouble. She grew frightened at that. There was something she hadn't given the police—it was an address where Mary had said she could send letters. Well, she gave it to me, after I promised that I would investigate and make sure Mary was safe. I promised her I would do it myself and not turn the address over to the police. It was an easy promise to make—I didn't want to be scooped!

I took the address and looked it up on a map. It was in an older, run-down part of the city. The trolley took a while to get there, and it was already dark when I arrived. But that allowed me to sneak around the back of the house and look in through the windows. Only one room was lit, and in it was a man, rather old and stooped, sitting at a table and writing something in a book.

Well, he didn't seem terribly frightening! And I knew what to do next. Just a few blocks from the house, close to the trolley stop where I had gotten off, was a diner. I asked the waitress if she had any rubber bands, then went into the bathroom and washed all the makeup off my face. I put my hair in two pigtails. When I came out, she looked at me curiously.

"I went to a party with my boyfriend," I told her. "He's in college— he doesn't know I'm just in high school. But someone took my school uniform. I don't know what to do. If I go home like this, my mom is going to kill me."

"I used to do that," she told me, sympathetically. "Here, why don't you take my sweater? And I've got some shoes you can borrow. You can tell her that someone accidentally took your uniform at gym, and you had to borrow clothes from another girl."

"I could just kiss you!" I told her. Then I traded my hat and jacket and pumps for her sweater and a pair of rubber-soled shoes. I looked at least five years younger. It's a good thing I carry a leather postman's bag instead of a silly little purse! In the dark, I thought it would look enough like a schoolbag.

When I knocked on the door, the old man answered it and said, "Yes, my dear? What is it?"

"Mary Lang told me to come here," I said, looking fearfully around, as though afraid someone might have followed me. "She said you could help!"

"Oh, goodness, come in, come in quickly," he said. "Along that hall-way to the back, where we can't be seen."

Well, I was alone in the dark house with him, but I wasn't afraid. He looked so old, and not particularly strong. And you know I've taken jiu-jitsu.

I followed the hallway and found myself in a room at the back of the house. When he turned on the light, I saw that the curtains were drawn. There was a bed along one wall, and a dresser, and a table with two chairs. Really, it was a perfectly ordinary room.

"You must be hungry," he said. "What would you like to eat? Ask for anything—anything at all." Laughing at him a little—surely this funny old man couldn't produce anything I asked for—I said I would like a pork chop with mashed potatoes and peas. And then—you won't believe this, Dottie, but it's true—he pulled out a wand from inside his jacket, and waved it over the table, and there it all was! With a glass of lemonade to drink. Of course, I knew who he was immediately.

"You're Oz, the Great and Terrible," I said.

"Oh, I don't go by that name anymore," he said, smiling modestly. "I just go by Oscar, or Mr. Diggs if you prefer. To make up for the terrible deception I practiced on the Ozites, I spend my life helping Ozma in her great work."

"And what work is that?" I asked.

"Why, helping girls like you and Mary," he said. "By royal decree, any girl who asks for refuge in Oz is granted it. What did you say your name was again, my dear?"

I hadn't said. "Sally Russell," I told him. "Mary gave me your address so I could send her a letter. She didn't know I would need it myself! But my uncle—he lives with us, and he's such a frightening man! He—"

"You don't need to tell me, my dear," said the Wizard. "It's a story I've heard many times, from girls very much like you. But there is a place and a purpose for you in Oz. Finish your dinner, and sleep here tonight—there is a nightgown under your pillow—and tomorrow we shall go to Oz!"

"How will we get there?" I asked him. "Aren't there terrible dangers in the way?"

"Oh, we have our methods," he said. "Don't you worry. Just get some sleep. We have a long journey tomorrow."

Well, Dottie, you can imagine what was going on in my mind! This was undeniably the Wizard: he had made a dinner appear before my eyes, and a very good dinner too! And he was taking girls who had run away from their families to Oz. That's where all the girls were going. What a story this would make! It would be on the front page, to be sure. Imagine if I could go to Oz and interview Mary Lang!

I ate a bit of everything he had given me, then waited half an hour to see if it contained a sedative, but I felt perfectly fine, so I finished my dinner. Now I am sitting at the table, writing this letter to you. As soon as I finish it, I'm going to sneak out through the window and post it in a letter box I saw down the street. Then I'll get some sleep. I don't know what tomorrow will bring, but this is quite the adventure, isn't it?

Don't worry about me, my dear. But I do want you and Mamsie to know where I've gone. Just in case something does happen to me (but it won't). Love you, little sis! I'll write to you again when I can.

Your own,
Nell

Dearest Dottie,

I don't know when or even whether this letter will reach you. Once I finish writing it, I'm going to give it to a woman I met at the Great Market in the Emerald City. She's a traveling merchant who brings rugs to sell in Oz from beyond the Deadly Desert, crossing the sands on one of the ships that sail across it, blown by the wind. There is no way to get to Oz except across that desert, and anyone who touches the sands turns into sand himself! Of course, there is no other way to leave Oz either . . .

Yes, I'm in Oz, in a camp outside the Emerald City. As I sit in my tent, writing you this letter, I can hear the other girls outside, talking and laughing. Girls from all over the country! In this tent there are six of us: two from California, one from Kentucky, one from Oklahoma, and two sisters who ran away together from Massachusetts. The others are outside right now, probably roasting marshmallows, which grow on the marshmallow bushes down by a swampy area close to the city walls. The fields outside the walls are gay with tents and banners: red and yellow and purple and blue, the colors of the four countries of Oz. All of us girls have been assigned to a particular division: the six of us are in the Quadling division, so our tent and uniforms are red, which I think goes quite well with my hair! But I can't explain where I am without telling you the whole story, from the last time I wrote.

After climbing out of the Wizard's window and mailing you my last letter, then climbing back in again undetected, I had a good night's sleep. The next morning, the Wizard woke me and conjured a breakfast of toast and butter and marmalade and eggs sunny-side up, with a mug of coffee. I have to admit that it was delicious. But his car! It was a Model A that looked as though it had come through the war. Wouldn't you think a wizard could conjure a better car than that? I asked him, but he said he didn't know that kind of magic. We drove down toward San Jose, and then east past Fresno. Slowly, the verdure faded from the landscape, to be replaced by the dun-colored hills of eastern California. (Isn't that a good line? Frances—one of the girls from Massachusetts—used the word verdure earlier, when we were talking about the gardens in the Emerald City, and I liked it so much that I wanted to use it myself.) At some point, I must have fallen asleep: it was so dull, driving through the desert. The car jounced along, making it hard to talk, and the Wizard was not a particularly good driver—every time I asked him a question, he turned to look at me, and I was afraid he would swerve off the road.

We stopped under a sign that said "Welcome to Nevada" and had a picnic lunch: ham sandwiches, apples, and more lemonade. It's quite useful having a wizard along when you're traveling! Although I wish he could have conjured up an electric fan. At that point, I was too awake to sleep. I kept staring at the miles and miles of sand and scrub, wondering how in the world we were supposed to get to Oz. Maybe the Wizard, although undoubtedly a genuine wizard, at least as far as ham sandwiches were concerned, was also a crazy old man who drove girls into the desert and murdered them, leaving their bodies to rot on the desert sands? When I looked over at the Wizard, I couldn't bring myself to be scared of him. But maybe that was part of his plan, to seem so harmless? Well, if he was a murderer, he wouldn't find me easy to kill! I went through my jiu-jitsu moves in my head.

Just as the sun was starting to set, we came to a town in the middle of the desert. Well, town is too fancy a word for it—it was just a gas station, the first we had seen for hours, and a general store with a "Closed" sign in the window, and some houses that looked as though they might collapse at any moment. Next to the gas station was a motor lodge, and that at any rate was still open, because there was a "Rooms to Let" sign out front and a car in the parking lot, in considerably better shape than ours. We pulled into the parking lot and got out of the car. I was so sore from sitting and jouncing! The rooms were arranged in a semicircle around the parking lot, and one of the doors opened. Out came a girl about my age, who waved at us.

She was dressed all in green: a green blouse, with hearts embroidered on it, and green trousers over which she wore thigh-high green leather boots. Around her waist she wore a gun belt, with silver pistols in the holsters. She had short green hair that stood up in spikes all over her head.

"Jellia Jamb!" said the Wizard. "It's so good to see you. I've brought a last-minute addition to our party."

"I have two more in the room," said Jellia. "And the Shaggy Man telephoned to say he will be here tonight, with another three. We'll leave in the morning and meet Nick Chopper at the second rendezvous point."

"My friend Nick is a fierce fighter, although no man has a kinder heart," said the Wizard, turning to me. "We'll need his help getting through the Nome Kingdom."

I nodded, not quite knowing what to say. It was like walking into a fairy tale, or a film studio—you know how often Mamsie would tell us about the famous people of Oz, before it was cut off from the world.

The Tin Woodman and the Scarecrow and the Cowardly Lion and Scraps, the Patchwork Girl . . . And here I was going to meet them! Until that moment, I had not truly believed that we were going to Oz. But now I knew we were.

In the room at the motor lodge, I met the other two girls. Joan was also from California. She had run away from home to be a film star, and had ended up living on the streets of Los Angeles. Ingrid was from a farm in Oklahoma, and she would not talk about why she wanted to run away. She spoke with an accent—I think her family was Swedish or something like that. I told them about being Sally Russell from San Francisco, and about my friend Mary Lang. We sat on the beds and talked a little, but mostly listened as the Wizard and Jellia leaned over a map on the table and made their plans. Jellia said the Nomes had been especially troublesome lately, which was why Nick Chopper was joining us. Once we made it past the Nome Kingdom, we would be fine. "The last time the Growleywogs and Scoodlers bothered us, we had the Hungry Tiger with us, and we showed them what for!" said Jellia. "I don't think they'll be bothering us again soon." Once we reached the third rendezvous point on the border of the Deadly Desert, we would be transported to Oz.

"How will that happen?" I asked.

"Don't you worry," said Jellia. "All that will be taken care of."

Because we were all hungry, the Wizard conjured up some ice cream, the flavors we liked best—I asked for strawberry and chocolate. I was amused to see that Jellia asked for pistachio. Just as we were finishing, we heard a knock on the door. It was the Shaggy Man.

He was exactly the way I had expected: shaggy everywhere, all his clothes in rags although they weren't really. If you looked carefully, you could see that the cloth had been carefully cut to appear ragged. And his hair and beard were separated into a number of small shags, all tied with ribbons. His clothes were so colorful that he looked like a rainbow. He had brought three more girls: Lula Mae from Kentucky, who immediately started talking to Ingrid about milking cows, and Frances and Enid, two sisters who had run away from a fancy boarding school in Massachusetts. At first I didn't have a lot of sympathy for them, but during our journey they earned my respect. None of us could build a fire as fast as they could, or put up a tent like they did so it wouldn't blow over during the night.

"Well, Jellia my dear, and Wizard, my good friend, I'll take the first watch," said the Shaggy Man. As I fell asleep, in the bed I was sharing with Joan and Ingrid, I saw him standing in front of the motor lodge, holding what looked like a machine gun out of a gangster film.

The next day, we drove across the desert in a caravan, Jellia's car in the rear because it was the most heavily armed. By evening we had reached the second rendezvous point, where Nick Chopper was waiting for us.

I saw him as soon as I stepped out of the Wizard's car: a man made all of metal, gleaming in the light of the setting sun. He was armed with an axe and, although he had a jolly enough smile on his metal face, I would not have liked to make him angry! Next to him stood a boy about my age. He looked as though he had been training for one of the strong man contests at the state fair: his biceps bulged out of his shirtsleeves, and blond hair flopped over his eyes. Behind them was a van armored all over with metal plates.

"Will you look at that," said Joan, who was standing next to me. She was staring at the boy with the muscles. I was more impressed with the Tin Woodman.

"This is my friend Nick," said the Wizard. The metal man made us an awkward bow.

"I've brought Button-Bright," he said. "The last caravan we sent through the Nome Kingdom was attacked. They've gotten bolder since Ruggedo III ascended the throne. They don't dare attack Oz itself, not while Ozma has the Magic Belt. But they want to annoy and harass us as much as they can."

"Is that Button-Bright?" I asked, pointing to Mr. Muscles.

"How-dee-do," he said. "They call me Button-Bright because I'm as bright as a button."

"Oh, do they?" I wondered what kind of button they, whoever they were, had in mind. He sounded as thick as his thighs.

"Did you bring ammunition?" asked Jellia, ignoring Button-Bright. I guess she didn't have much use for him either.

Nick Chopper opened the back of the van. It was filled with stacks of cardboard flats—filled with eggs. "As many as we could bring," he said. "And I brought a secret weapon."

Out of the back of the van stepped . . . a chicken, with yellow feathers and a red comb. "This is Belinda," he said. "She's one of the grand-daughters of Billina herself. She generously agreed to accompany us."

"Oh, it's so good to see you again, Belinda," said Jellia. She knelt and embraced the chicken.

"Well, you don't need to squeeze me quite so hard," said Belinda. "I'm not a stuffed chicken, you know!"

"It's a great pleasure to see you again, my dear," said the Wizard. "I haven't seen you since you were quite a young chick and used to hide in my pockets!"

"Well, doesn't that beat all," said Joan, low enough so only I could hear her. "A talking chicken."

"What, they didn't teach you about Oz in school?" I asked. "All the animals talk there."

"I dropped out after sixth grade. We never got to talking animals."

We would all be grateful for those eggs and the talking chicken before long. The third rendezvous point was beyond the Nome King-dom, in the Land of Ev. That night, we slept in the tents for the first time. You wouldn't believe how the Shaggy Man snored! I could hear him all the way across the camp.

The next morning, we crossed the border.

The Nome Kingdom was rocky, and the road was in bad repair. It ran between steep cliffs, and several times boulders came crashing down, hitting and sometimes denting one or another of the cars. Now I knew why they all looked so battered!

"They're watching us," said the Wizard, grimly. "Waiting to attack."

Ingrid, who was riding in the back next to me, reached over and held my hand.

The attack came on the third day. We had stopped to rest and eat our lunch in a gully. Suddenly, down the rocky faces of the cliffs came the Nomes—so many of them that the cliffs looked as though they were covered with large black spiders. That's what the Nomes look like, with their spindly arms and legs, and their round, fat bodies. Ingrid and Lula Mae screamed and held on to each other. Nick took up his axe and the Wizard raised his wand. Button-Bright and the Shaggy Man both aimed their guns. Jellia threw open the back of the van and said, "Girls, to me! Form a circle and throw eggs, as many as you can!"

Well, I would have thought that the farm girls, at least, would have been too scared to fight. But all of us followed Jellia's orders. I don't like to remember what happened next. Do you know what happens to Nomes when they are hit by eggs, Dottie? They *explode*. There we stood in a circle, lobbing egg after egg until our arms were aching, while all around us Nomes were bursting as though they were balloons filled with horrible green goo. Imagine the smell of smashed eggs, of Nome goop, of our own sweat! It was horrible, but we worked together as a team. Meanwhile, the Tin Woodman was chopping their limbs off left and right, and the Wizard was turning as many of them as he could into pebbles, and Button-Bright and the Shaggy Man were shooting into the mass coming at us. Bullets don't hurt the Nomes. But the Shaggy Man and Button-Bright did slow them down so we could pelt them with our eggs.

We were so tired, and the Nomes just kept on coming! I could see one standing up on a rock, with a hideous crown on his head. He seemed to be directing the others, and didn't he look triumphant to see us girls getting too tired to aim well?

"They've got me!" shouted Nick Chopper. Sure enough, the Nomes had managed to wrench away his axe and were now trying to pull him apart limb from limb.

"It's time!" shouted Jellia. From the rear of the van flew Belinda, straight at the Nome with the crown on his head. He uttered a high-pitched shriek when he saw her coming and tried to crouch down, but she made straight for his head and beat him with her wings.

"My eyes, my eyes!" he screamed. "Retreat! Retreat, all of you worthless fools!"

Suddenly, the Nomes began to scurry back into the rocks, and in another minute we were the only ones in the gully. We all looked bruised and battered, especially the Tin Woodman, whose left arm was nearly wrenched off.

"Well, at least it's the left one," he said. "I'm a much better fighter with my right."

"I don't think rotten old Ruggedo will be attacking us again soon," said Belinda.

"Why, what did you do?" asked Jellia, smoothing her ruffled feathers and lifting her back into the van.

"Pecked out one of his eyes." She sounded satisfied with herself.

After that attack, the word must have gone around, because we were not attacked again. It took several more days to cross the Nome Kingdom, but finally we reached the border of Ev. There the landscape changed: the rocky cliffs gave way to green meadows and pleasant gardens. As we passed each farmhouse, families came out to ask us about our journey through the Nome Kingdom and praise us—especially Belinda—for our bravery.

At the end of that day, we reached the third rendezvous point: a farmhouse on the border of the Deadly Desert, where yet more girls were waiting for us. They had arrived several days ago, some of them with Aunt Em, Ojo the Lucky, and the Scarecrow, who had come through Noland, and some with Polychrome, Johnny Dooit, and the Cowardly Lion. "They had an even more dangerous journey than we did," said the Wizard. "Not even Ruggedo is as dangerous as Queen Zixi. She is a sorceress almost as powerful as Glinda, and although she is hundreds of years old, she has learned to maintain her youth by eating the hearts of young women. You can imagine how much she would like to capture any of our girls!"

After dinner, I went out and looked at the place where the green meadow ended and the Deadly Desert began. "Hello, my dear," said the Wizard. I had not heard him come up behind me.

"What now?" I asked, looking at the endless expanse of sand that would turn you to sand yourself as soon as you stepped on it.

"Don't you worry about that. Now that we're all here, Ozma can wish us over the desert sands with her Magic Belt. She can only make one wish a day, but tomorrow after breakfast, we will gather in the farmyard and you will see the Emerald City for the first time!"

The next morning, after a breakfast of pancakes with maple syrup, we gathered together in the farmyard. Some of the girls looked scared, and some held each other's hands or put their arms around one another's waists. At nine o'clock exactly, the Wizard made a particular sign—and the next thing I saw was a great palace, all of white stone with turrets and parapets and whatever else palaces have, including great archways flanked by stone lions with emerald eyes. It was the most magnificent thing I had ever seen—even more than San Francisco! Standing on a balcony above us were five girls. The tallest one, who had long black hair and looked like a film star, said "Welcome to Oz. I am Ozma, and these are Dorothy, Betsy Bobbin, Jinjur, and Trot."

And then she told us.

Have you been wondering, Dottie, while you've been reading this letter, why all these girls are being taken to Oz? Well, I wondered that too—wondered as I lay in my tent, listening to the Shaggy Man snore at night. Wondered as we traveled day after day through the Nome Kingdom. Why all these girls? Ozma told us.

Standing up on that balcony, she told us about how she had been taken as a baby to the witch Mombi, and how Mombi had turned her into a boy, and made her work, and beaten her. "I never want another girl to be beaten the way I was," she said. "So any girl who wants to come to Oz is welcome. She will find refuge here, with me. But we have to save all the other girls, don't you see? That's why I invite any girl to join my army. It will be an army of liberation, sent from Oz to conquer all the lands around, and then the rest of the United States of America. But we're not just going to conquer and rule the country, girls. We're going to transform it too, so it becomes like Oz." She held out her arms to us, and I don't think Mary Pickford could have looked more appealing. For a moment, even I wanted to sign up right away, to save all those girls—even if it meant conquering the United States. Of course I did sign up—I mean, Sally Russell signed up. We all did.

Are you laughing, Dottie? At the thought of an army of girls—all those runaway girls—fighting our military, with their guns and tanks? Well, you can stop laughing now. After Ozma's speech, which was short—she probably gives it every day, as more and more girls arrive—Dorothy showed us the camp. That's General Dorothy—she, Betsy Bobbin, Jinjur, and Trot are the generals of Ozma's army. Each of them leads a division of the army that is associated with one of the countries of Oz. Joan, Ingrid, Lula Mae, Frances, Enid, and I were put in the Quadling division. We were given our uniforms, and then Dorothy, our General, talked to us about what we would be doing now that we were soldiers.

We stood on a hill, looking down at the camp, which was covered with tents as far as the eye could see—red and yellow and purple and blue.

"Time works differently here than it does in the outer world," said Dorothy. "We've been gathering soldiers for ever so long. If a girl doesn't want to join Ozma's army, she doesn't have to—but almost everyone joins. Who wouldn't want to fight for Ozma and Oz? Anyway, the girls who come here know what it's like out there. I remember what it was like in Kansas—never enough to eat, and people passing through who had no place to call home. They were just trying to get to California, where they thought things would be better. Well, here in Oz, if you don't have enough to eat, you find a lunch-pail tree!"

"But there are wicked people even in Oz," said Enid.

"Yes, what about old Mombi?" asked Lula Mae.

"Of course," said Dorothy. "But Glinda finds out about them, and they're punished."

"And do you really think a bunch of girls can conquer the American army and air force?" asked Frances, dubiously.

"Oh, but we don't just have a bunch of girls," said Dorothy. "We also have the Jack Pumpkinheads, and the Woggle-Bugs, and the Tik-Tok Men. Come on, I'll show you." And she showed us, all right.

The Jack Pumpkinheads are grown in fields in Gillikin Country, where Ozma created the original Jack when she was a boy. At least, their pumpkin heads are. Their bodies are made of wood, and after they are put together, they're sprinkled with the Powder of Life. "It's mixed up in large vats in Gillikin Country," said Dorothy. "We can sprinkle it on anything we like, of course. But the Jack Pumpkinheads are good soldiers. They can't be killed, and they just keep on going unless you chop them up into small pieces. If they lose a limb, they can replace it with any old pieces of wood."

The Woggle-Bugs come from hatcheries in Winkie Country. "They reproduce so quickly that we have lots more than we need," said Dorothy. "When they're born, they're just the size of a pea, but if we need them to fight, we highly magnify them. They're pretty scary, aren't they?"

I have to admit, if I had an army of Woggle-Bugs coming at me, I'd turn around and run! They look sort of like cockroaches, but when they're highly magnified and standing on their hind legs, they're the size of a man.

"The Tik-Tok Men are made in a factory in Munchkin Country," said Dorothy. "They're just about indestructible, and the machine guns are built right in."

You've never seen anything like the Tik-Tok Men, Dottie! When I saw them, I realized they would plow our soldiers down and keep on marching. For the first time, I was scared. What if I never escaped from Oz? But there's no time to be despondent when you're an intrepid girl reporter, is there? Instead, I tried to estimate the size of the Oz forces.

"But the girls are the most important part," said Dorothy. "Girls are a lot fiercer than most people suppose. All these girls—they've come to Oz because of how they were treated out there. I ought to know—I was like them until Uncle Henry and Aunt Em took me in. They can fight themselves—we've been training them. And they can direct the Jack Pumpkinheads and Woggle-Bugs and Tik-Tok Men, who haven't much brains of their own."

I remembered how we had all fought the Nomes together. Maybe Dorothy was right. Maybe girls don't fight in the world out there because they've never been taught how. As we walked through the camp, between the colorful tents and banners, I saw girls everywhere: some of them were practicing a kind of jiu-jitsu, some of them were loading and unloading their guns, some of them were listening to lectures on how to blow up trains. They looked busy and serious, but also festive in their colored uniforms, as though they had gathered for some sort of outing. I began to see that Ozma's army was nothing to laugh at.

"Ozma doesn't want to kill anyone," said Dorothy. "She doesn't even like to swat flies! She says they are as much her subjects as any creature in Oz. She'd be much happier if everyone just surrendered. That's why she's sending the army of Oz first. But things have to change, don't you see? If the army doesn't work, she'll use the Magic Belt. She can wish whole countries dead, if she wants to."

"Will that work outside Oz?" asked Ingrid. She sounded shocked at the thought of such destruction.

"Of course," said Dorothy. "Magic is like electricity. It works the same everywhere."

So you see, Dottie, I've got to get my story out! Don't you tell anyone any of this, because I don't want to be scooped. I'm going to stay here long enough to figure out the size of Ozma's army, and then I'm going to cross the Deadly Desert—I don't know how yet, but if a rug merchant can get across, so can I. And then I'm going to break the largest story the *Ledger* has ever seen!

Your loving sis,
Nell

My dearest Dotts,

I've asked the Shaggy Man to bring you this letter. When you've read it, I want you to tell Mamsie the whole story—from when I first started investigating Mary Lang's disappearance. Make sure she's sitting down on the parlor sofa, and tell her slowly. It's not good for her to be startled or upset. But she was the one who always told us stories about Oz, so maybe she won't be as startled as you or I would be.

Once you've told her, I want the both of you to pack whatever you need—but only what you need. The Shaggy Man will bring you back to Oz, and there isn't much room in the Gump. Do you remember the Gump? Ozma made it when she was a boy, out of two sofas lashed together with palm fronds for wings, a broomstick tail, and a head that looks as though it once belonged to a peculiar sort of moose. It's the most sarcastic creature, but quite safe to fly in. It will carry you across the Deadly Desert and to the Emerald City. The Shaggy Man will make sure you arrive safely.

You might be surprised by this letter, after the last one I sent you. But when I sent it, I had just arrived in Oz, and I didn't understand how important this war is—how it must be waged and won. (That's pretty good, isn't it? Waged and won. I think I'm going to use that in my next article.) Ozma has appointed me Royal War Correspondent of Oz, and I'm proud to fulfill that role. Once the war starts, it will be important for you and Mamsie to be safe—and no place will be safer than the Emerald City.

But I'd better tell you what changed my mind about this war. About a week after we had begun our training, General Dorothy came into our tent. She said, "Sally and Joan, you've been chosen to join Glinda's personal guard. Are you willing?" Joan and I looked at each other in amazement. Glinda's personal guard is an elite unit in the army—it contains the bravest, best-trained girls from our division. We both nodded. "You'll be going down to Quadling Country," said Dorothy. "There, you will continue your training with Glinda herself. Make me proud, girls!"

That afternoon, we packed our kits and set off, about a dozen of us. It took us several days to reach Glinda's palace, but the journey was pleasant—we walked through green fields and sunlit forests, mostly following the road of yellow brick, and had no trouble at all from Hammer-Heads or Fighting Trees. Sometimes we slept in tents, sometimes we passed farmhouses where we were given food and beds for the night. When the Quadlings heard we were joining Glinda's personal guard, they bowed and curtsied with great respect.

Glinda's palace is not as large as Ozma's in the Emerald City, but when I first saw it, with its spires glowing in the light of the setting sun, I was impressed! Instead of tents, we were put in barracks made of marble and rare woods, with the most luxurious baths I have ever seen, and given new uniforms of rose silk.

The next morning, we began the most intensive training we had yet received. Do you know, little sis, how to kill someone with a pocket comb, or a mirror, or even a handkerchief—everyday items that a girl might carry in her purse? Do you know how to pick any lock with a hairpin, or make a bomb out of ordinary household ingredients? Well, I do! Glinda's guards aren't just soldiers—they're spies. We were trained by a roly-poly sergeant who could flip any of us on our backs before you could say "Boo!" I can tell you that we gave each other many bruises! At the end of the day I would lie in one of the baths, in rose-scented water, to ease my aching muscles.

When we had been at Glinda's palace for about a month, we were told that Glinda herself wanted to see us. I thought we would be taken to a throne room of some sort, but instead we were shown into a pleasant parlor. There were sofas and armchairs upholstered in rose chintz, and on the low tables were trays with heart-shaped cookies and chocolate cake. There was also a cut glass bowl of strawberry punch. As we stood in that room, not quite sure what to do with ourselves, Glinda herself entered. She looked about our age, although I've heard that she's more than a thousand years old. She wore a long rose-colored gown and a gold crown on her head. She was not as beautiful as Ozma—at least, she looked less like a film star and more like a Sunday school teacher, with calm gray eyes. She said, "Girls, please pour yourselves some punch and take some cookies and cake. And then sit down and make yourselves comfortable. I've asked you here because I like to get to know my new recruits."

I piled cake and cookies on my plate—the training had made me hungry! We all sat, some of us on sofas, some in armchairs, some on the floor. When we were all comfortably seated, Glinda said, "Girls, I'd like to hear your stories." So we went around the room and all told where we had come from, before we came to Oz.

Oh Dottie! What some of those girls had gone through. I felt ashamed of myself, telling the made-up story of Sally Russell. Some of the girls cried and held each other, and I could see that sometimes tears flowed silently down Glinda's cheeks, although she remained silent.

"Thank you, girls, for sharing your stories," she said when we had all spoken. "You have gone through pain and loss and grief. I hope that here, at my palace and in Oz, you will find what you have so often missed in the outer world—a sense of sisterhood, and of family." Before we left, she embraced each one of us.

"I feel so much better now," said Joan when we were back in the barracks, sitting on our bunks. "As though my heart were lighter. Listen to me! Can you believe I just said that?" And you know, it was the first time I had seen her actually smile.

That night, I couldn't sleep. I lay awake in the darkness, remembering the stories those girls had told—one had shown us cigarette burns up and down her arms.

The next morning, before the other recruits were awake, I went to the sergeant's quarters. She was already awake, of course, doing her calisthenics. "I need to talk to Glinda," I said.

She looked at me for a moment, keenly, then nodded. "Glinda will be in her study," she said. "If you're not sure of the way, ask one of the porters."

I did have to ask one of the porters, a girl in a rose-colored dress and ruffled apron who was mopping the marble staircase. She led me to Glinda's study and opened the door. Glinda sat at her desk, doing whatever sorceresses do in the mornings. I walked up to her, boldly enough, and said, "I'm not Sally Russell."

"Who are you, then?" she asked, with a kind look on her face.

"My name is Eleanor Dale, and I'm a reporter for the *San Francisco Ledger*. I came here under false pretenses, so I could figure out where all the missing girls had gone. Are you going to have me court-martialed?"

Glinda smiled. "My dear, I knew all this long before you arrived at my palace. I was waiting to see if you would tell me."

I stared at her. "How did you know?"

"I have a book that tells me everything that happens, all over the world. It told me you were coming here as soon as you thought of it yourself. The words appeared on the pages of the book, as though written by an invisible pen. I do wish it had an index—it can be most unwieldy to use."

"But then why did you let me come into Oz, and come here from the Emerald City?"

"Because you're a brave girl, and I thought we could use you on our side. Anyway, if your letters had fallen into the wrong hands, Ozma could simply have wished them to disappear. But you're willing to fight for us now, aren't you, Eleanor? To fight for Oz and everything it represents?"

I nodded. "Should I go back and join the others in the barracks, then?"

"No," said Glinda. "I let you train with my guards until you were ready to tell me the truth, but now that you've shown your honesty and loyalty, I have a more important task for you. We need someone to write about the war effort, to create leaflets and pamphlets and articles for the *Emerald City Daily,* and all the smaller newspapers in Munchkin Country and the other countries of Oz. You'll be syndicated, my dear."

Well, you can imagine what I thought of that!

So here I am, sitting in my office in Ozma's palace, in the Emerald City. Later today, I have an interview with Professor H.M. Woggle-Bug, who developed the Woggle-Bug strategy, and then I'm reviewing the troops with General Betsy Bobbin and touring a Tik-Tok Man factory. And I'm meeting Scraps the Patchwork Girl for dinner, but that's just because we're friends. Oh, and you won't believe this—I found Mary Lang! She's in the Munchkin division, and is becoming a demolitions expert. She says she's happy here in Oz, and looking forward to contributing to the war effort. She wanted to let the real Sally Russell know that she was all right, and I said the Shaggy Man could post a letter for her.

I can't wait to see you and Mamsie again! I have a lovely apartment here in the Emerald City, which I'm sure you will both love. And I will be glad to know that you're safe in the coming months, as Ozma begins her invasion of California. I'm looking forward to covering the siege of San Francisco! Remember, the Gump is perfectly safe, and the Shaggy Man will be with you the whole time. See you soon, darling!

Your loving sis,
Nell (Royal War Correspondent of Oz)

TO BUDAPEST, WITH LOVE

I AM SEVENTEEN. I am in Budapest, and it is the Communist era. When I flew into the airport, there were Russian soldiers with Kalashnikovs patrolling the runways. Only one airline flew to Budapest, the national airline Malév. There were few passengers. I stopped at passport control and showed my American passport. It contains a photograph of me next to my American name. I also have a Hungarian name, but I have not used it for a long time, since my mother changed our names so we could be more American. The passport control officer looked at me suspiciously. For a moment I couldn't breathe. I felt a tightness in my chest, as though my lungs were being squeezed by a giant hand, like the beginning of a panic attack. Then I reminded myself, he probably looks that way at everyone.

That day, my grandparents, whom I am visiting, let me leave the apartment by myself for the first time. When my mother was seventeen, teenage girls did not walk around the city alone, but I am bored and restless. After all, I've been walking myself home from school and letting myself in the front door, then making myself Campbell's tomato or cream of mushroom soup from concentrate, since I was twelve. So I am allowed to descend two flights of stairs to the ground floor, and cross the street, and walk in the park around the Nemzeti Múzeum. As I walk under the linden trees, I smell something I've smelled before:

the linden flowers. And I remember holding someone's hand, and then a swing set, and then flying high in the air, and a song that starts with the words *hinta-palinta.*

But I also want to walk in the streets, to see more of Budapest, so I do. Just a block because I don't want to get lost in this strange city, where no one speaks the only language I understand. The apartment buildings around the park are covered with soot from Trabants and Yugos. There, walking down the street, I feel something for the first time that I will feel again many times in my life. Suddenly, it's as though I am in a spaceship high above the city, looking down on it from above. I can see myself walking along the street: I am so small, inconsequential on this planet spinning through space. It makes sense that I should be in a spaceship looking down, because I only recently became an American citizen. Before that, I was an alien. A legal one, but still.

Looking down at myself walking along the city street, I think, that poor girl. She doesn't belong anywhere.

This is a love story, but not a happy one, and I don't know how it ends.

It begins when I am a child, the one swinging into the sky under the linden trees.

For a long time, I had a green card, which meant I was not yet American.

But I was no longer Hungarian either. I had lost my ability to speak the language. I went to an American elementary school. After school I watched *He-Man* and *Jonny Quest* cartoons. At home, my mother did not insist on Hungarian because how was I going to assimilate unless I spoke in English? So we spoke in English.

According to the *Oxford English Dictionary,* assimilate means to "make like" or "cause to resemble." I needed to be made like an American child. I needed to at least resemble one. But the word also has a second-ary meaning, to "absorb and incorporate." It was not enough to change me on the outside. I must be changed inside as well. I must become American.

Years later, I watch *Star Trek* on television. The Borg Queen says, "You will be assimilated," and I think, yes. That's exactly how it happens. It will take me a long time to realize that, ironically, the Borg are supposed to represent Communism.

When I was eleven, I started reading science fiction. I read about aliens, but not like me. These were science fictional aliens, from other planets. They invaded Earth or they were invaded by Earth. Sometimes they enslaved human beings, sometimes it was the other way around. They wore either spacesuits or primitive clothes that looked like Speedos and bikinis, but you know, gold. They were sometimes green, and sometimes resembled cats. Giant space cats. Sometimes they had the cure for all of Earth's diseases. Sometimes they brought diseases that devastated humanity.

They never came to Earth and worked in hotels or opened restaurants, although that would have been more realistic.

There is one constant in alien stories. The alien and human are always in opposition to each other.

What does that make me, I wonder.

I started understanding Hungarian again the day I realized it was the opposite of English. Whatever I wanted to say in English, in Hungarian I had to say the opposite. Trying to reason from English to Hungarian always got me into trouble.

In Hungarian, tegnap is yesterday, not tomorrow.

Bor is wine, not beer.

Nyolc is eight, not nine.

In Hungarian, át does not mean at, but across or through.

Subject–verb–object, I tell my American university students. That is the basic structure of an English sentence.

But in Hungarian, it's object–verb, and the subject is often implied. If I am in Budapest, Budapesten vagyok. I exist only in a case ending.

I am thirteen. My best friend Amy and I are swinging on the apartment complex swing set. She does not feel human either. Years later, she will write from college to tell me she is in love with another woman, that at some level she has always known she is gay. Marriage equality will still be many years in the future. That day, we talk about how a ship will come down from the sky to take us home. Our home planet is much more exciting than Earth. There, we are princesses. We fly genetically engineered dragons. We save entire civilizations. We wear clothes of silver mesh, with boots that come up to our thighs. We fight sky pirates.

Then we kick our legs higher and higher, so we can feel as though we are flying.

She writes her name Aimée because it's more exciting. I am still legally Dóra but I write my name Dora because it's more American. That's how I've been told to write it.

I continue to not feel human. I am, in fact, not feeling human now, as I sit here looking out the window at the trees in the park around the Nemzeti Múzeum. There is a bird somewhere, making a sound like castanets. At first I thought it was some sort of machine.

I am forty-seven years old, and I have been back many times. I still do not feel at home here, but then I do not feel at home anywhere else either. This is as close to home as I think I'm going to get. Unless a spaceship comes for me, of course.

Don't laugh. It could happen.

When I am twenty-five, I go back to Hungary for the first time since the Berlin Wall fell. Now there are no longer Yugos and Trabants on the road. Now there are Mercedes Benzes parked outside Russian casinos, and beggars sleeping on the streets. Budapest has become a frontier town in the get-rich-quick dreams of the West.

The last time I saw her, my city was dressed in sackcloth and ashes. Now she parades topless beside the Danube in a show called *Girls Sexx Girls*. I don't know what to think of her.

We have not talked for a long time, and she has become so different. This is called alienation of affection, I think. Someone has taken her away from me, tempted her with money and fame.

"What happened to you?" I ask.

Girls Sexx Girls, she answers in neon light.

The *OED* tells me that alienation has several meanings. First, it is the "state of being estranged." I have become a stranger to Budapest, and she has become a stranger to me, even though I was born here. I know because it's the only thing I can read on my birth certificate.

It also tells me that in Marxist theory, alienation means the "condition of workers in a capitalist economy, resulting from a lack of identity with the products of their labour and a sense of being controlled or exploited." Do aliens feel that way, I wonder. Do the Borg ever lament their alienation from the methods of production? They mostly seem to run around shouting "Resistance is futile."

What about the alien in *Alien*? Does she feel discontented? Does she want something better for herself? For her children? Is the entire movie really a metaphor for the revolution, about how if the proletariat don't get what they want, they will find their way inside the power structure and burst out of its chest? Or am I overthinking this?

A year after *Alien* appears in theaters, Ronald Reagan will be elected president. He will call on the Soviet Union to tear down the

Berlin Wall. Once the wall is down, aliens will start invading Western Europe. I don't know, the timing seems significant.

When I return from Hungary, I ask my mother why she brought me to America. After all, I've lost my city, my country, even my grandparents, who are once again behind the Iron Curtain. When I send them letters, I have to be careful what I write, because my letters will be opened by the police.

She says, "To give you opportunities you could not have had there."

So maybe it's more like Kara Zor-El's mother putting her in a spaceship and sending her to Earth, where she can become Supergirl. Except I don't have any superpowers. I can't fly, and I'm certainly not bulletproof. I'm not even proof against the ordinary teasing and gossip of high school girls. I don't think I'll be defeating supervillains anytime soon. I mean, I barely survived calculus.

Each time I come back, Budapest is different. By the time I am forty-five, she has returned to her old self—a courtesan whose best days may be behind her, still beautiful despite her wrinkles and age spots, basking in the sun beside the Danube.

"Vienna is richer than you are," I tell her.

"You don't care about Vienna," she answers, smiling. "You come back, over and over again. You don't care if I'm dirty or poor. The air here is the only air you can breathe without effort. Everywhere else, you have to wear an invisible mask, a filtration system. You can't adjust to the atmosphere. Here, the sunlight is the right color. Here, food tastes the way it should."

"I'll leave you and never come back," I say.

She answers only, "I'd like to see you try."

In Hungarian, when you are in a country or city, you are either -ban or -ben. Amerikában. Bostonban. But you are on Hungary, Magyarországon: the suffix is -on or -en. That's because to the Magyars, Hungary was the world, and they rode their short, sturdy horses across it, from one horizon to the other. It's the same for Budapest. When I am there, I am Budapesten. I am standing on Budapest, and from here I can see everything.

By the time I am thirty-three, I've become a hyphenated American. This is a new century. Multiculturalism is an important topic at my university, and suddenly we are all hybrid, interstitial. I am Hungarian-American, but what does that actually mean? If I'm not fully American, but I'm not fully Hungarian either, where do I fit? Not on either side of the hyphen. Then perhaps I am the hyphen?

I imagine inhabiting a two-dimensional planet, an immigrant Flatland where I have no substance or shadow. I exist only on a straight line *between*.

As I write this, which is neither a story nor an essay, perhaps a hyphenated story-essay, I am in Budapest, and the birds that perch on the roof are clicking like castanets. I am leaving in the morning. Great Britain has just voted to leave the European Union, and I'm suddenly afraid that time will go backward, and soot will descend on the buildings, and there will be Yugos in the streets again.

I thought the future was going to be like *Star Trek*, with all of us living together as one human family. We got our communicators, right? Later I will call my daughter and talk to her, just waking up in the morning, six hours behind me. I will see her face, with the confident grin of a typical American teenager, on the small screen of my cell phone. "See you tonight," I'll say, and then I'll fly across the ocean to have dinner with her in Boston. Surely it's not that far from here to the *Enterprise*.

But today the future feels as though it's turning into something by William Gibson. *Neuromancer*, maybe. Except that novel's most famous metaphor is already out of date. Most of my students can't imagine a sky like a television tuned to a dead channel. They've never seen a dead channel. They watch television on their cell phones. Someday, I suspect, cellphones will be implanted in them directly, and they will simply have to close their eyes. They will have become cyborgs. That's another way of being assimilated, but also alienated. In that future, we will all be aliens, right here on Earth.

When I am seven, I see America for the first time through an airplane window. It looks like stars, far below me in the darkness. I am told those stars are the lights of New York City.

It's difficult becoming American. I must learn to eat new foods. Will I be able to survive in this strange place on Wonder Bread, which you can scrunch up into a ball and bounce on the kitchen table? Campbell's soup from concentrate? Cap'n Crunch? The atmosphere here is different, heavier than on my home planet. The sun is not as bright. This planet must be farther from its sun.

I watch *The Brady Bunch*. Perhaps if I become like Marcia Brady, the inhabitants of this strange place will accept me as one of them.

When I am twenty-one, I watch *Alien* on my boyfriend's VHS player. I sympathize with the alien. She's a mother, after all. She's only trying to protect her children. Find a better life for them, one with more opportunities. What mother would do less?

Imagine what it's going to be like for those little aliens, growing up in a world inhabited by human beings. They'll probably need to disguise themselves as human, learn how to eat human food, how to speak

English. They might try to look like Marcia Brady. In fact, the entire Brady Bunch may be a family of aliens trying to pass as human. That would explain a lot.

Nevertheless, they'll probably be teased in school. It's not easy being a creature from outer space. Trust me, I know.

If I am at home anywhere, it is here, in Budapest speaking a language I only fitfully understand, in a city I will probably never inhabit.

The Hungarian language is not related to any other language in Europe. Finnish, maybe, but even that is a tenuous connection. I once saw a chart on which the languages of Europe were represented as a tree. Hungarian was off by itself, a branch growing from the trunk, unconnected to any other branches. I wondered if it was lonely.

It sounds like something made up for a television show, like Klingon. Except I think Klingon is probably easier to learn.

It sounds like something spoken by an alien species. Perhaps it was taught to the Hungarians by the same aliens who built Stonehenge, and Machu Picchu, and the Egyptian pyramids. Or perhaps Hungarians are aliens. That would account for the prevalence of high cheekbones.

On a Swissair flight over the Atlantic, I watch *John Carter of Mars* on the small screen on the back of the seat in front of me. It's in English, but somehow I've managed to turn on the Chinese subtitles, and I don't know how to turn them off. I decide the movie is actually better with Chinese subtitles. It adds a sense of dislocation that seems entirely appropriate.

During World War II, a group of Hungarian scientists emigrated to the United States. They were Jews fleeing the Nazi occupation of

Hungary, and when they arrived, they joined the Allied war effort. Among other things, they helped to develop the atomic bomb. Because of their religion and strange accents, they were not immediately accepted into American society. One of them, the physicist Leó Szilárd, jokingly referred to them as "the Martians." The name stuck, and the group is still known by that name. If you don't believe me, go on, look it up on your communicator.

When asked about the possibility of alien life, Szilárd responded, "They are already here among us: they just call themselves Hungarians." See, what did I tell you?

When the plane took off, I remember thinking, *hinta-palinta.*

When I am a fifteen, I realize with satisfaction that alienation can be written alien-nation. I come from an alien nation.

Like a typical teenager, I hate everyone, including myself. I am alien-nated. Does that "nated" come from the same root as native, nativity, natal? Does it mean I am alien born?

Well then, I am an alien born.

The *OED* says that "alien" comes from the Latin *alienus*, which means, among other things, "of or belonging to others, unnatural, unusual, unconnected, separate, of another country, foreign, unrelated, of a different variety or species, unfamiliar, strange, unfriendly, unsympathetic, unfavourable, inappropriate, incompatible, distasteful, repugnant." Repugnant? That's a bit much.

In its fourth definition of the word, the *OED* mentions its use in science fiction: "of, belonging to, or relating to an (intelligent) being or beings from another planet; designating such a being; extraterrestrial." I'll take intelligent over repugnant, thank you. Even in parentheses.

In the Budapest airport bookstore, I find a copy of *The Little Prince* in Hungarian.

Back in Boston, everything seems wrong. I've flown from one ancient city bisected by a river to another, but that river is the wrong color, and the sky looks like a television tuned to a dead channel in the 1980s. I can't taste the food: it's as though I'm chewing on cardboard. My stomach hurts. I have a perpetual headache. Somehow, I seem to have wandered into an alternate reality, the one in which time travelers failed to stop World War II.

Every morning, to practice my Hungarian, I read a chapter of *The Little Prince*, or more accurately, *A Kis Herceg*. It's exciting to recognize words I know. Bolygó: planet. Repülőgép: airplane. Róka: fox. Rósza: rose. Óriáskígyó: boa constrictor. I learned that one at the Budapest zoo. The little prince comes from egy kisbolygó, a small planet, as I come from a small country. He's also searching for home, answers, the cure for a broken heart. We've both felt the sting of a fickle rose, although mine is an entire city.

Maybe I can find a friendly fox. Or, you know, aviator.

It occurs to me that I will be leaving Budapest for the rest of my life. As though we are in one of those movies with Richard Gere or Diane Lane where two people meet for a month each summer until they are old and one of them dies. I will die before Budapest, which is reassuring.

What will happen to her? In a future I won't see, will she grow into a city of steel and glass? Will spaceships from Mars and beyond dock at her towers? Will aliens from other worlds eat gulyásleves and somlói galuska in her restaurants? Will they sit in her bars drinking pálinka, speaking alien languages, like a scene out of *Star Wars?* Will they go shopping on Váci utca?

Or will she drown when global warming raises the Danube? Will her buildings, crumbling by then, be flooded by jade-green water? Will her inhabitants develop gills and live beneath its murky surface?

Or will she be bombed again in World War III, as she was the last two times? Will her buildings and bridges burn? Please, I think, let me not see that happen.

When I am fifty-three, when I am seventy-five, when I am ninety-one I will return, assuming I'm still around. Who knows, by then I might be half machine, or half green gilled woman in a gold bikini. I will go back and stand in the park around the Nemzeti Múzeum and think, this is me spinning through space, but it does not matter, because for now, for a little while, I am Magyarországon, Budapesten. At least I am standing on my own ground.

I can smell the linden flowers . . .

Someone asks me why I write stories about space aliens, alternate histories, dystopian futures. Stories that could be classified as science fiction. I answer, because I'm a realist.

CHILD-EMPRESS OF MARS

IN THE MONTH OF IND, when the flowers of the Jindal trees were in blossom and just beginning to scatter their petals on the ground like crimson rain, a messenger came to the court of the Child-Empress. He announced that a Hero had awakened in the valley of Jar.

The messenger was young and obviously nervous, at court for the first time, but when the Child-Empress said, "A Hero? What is his name?" he replied with a steady voice, "Highest blossom of the Jindal tree, his name is not yet known. He has not spoken it, for he has as yet seen no one to whom he could speak."

The Ladies in Waiting fluttered their fans, to hear him speak with such courtesy, and I said to Lady Ahira, "I think I recognize him. That is Captain Namoor, the youngest son of General Gar, who has inherited his crimson tongue," by which I meant his eloquence, for an eloquent man is said to have a tongue as sweet as the crimson nectar of the Jindal flowers.

Lady Ahira blushed blue, from her cheeks down to her knees, for she had a passion for captains, and this was surely the captain of all captains, who had already won the hearts and livers of the court.

"Let the Hero's name be Jack or Buck or Dan, one of those names that fall so strangely on our tongues, and let him be tall and pale and silent, except when he sings the songs of his people to the moons, and let him be a slayer of beasts, a master of the glain and of the double adjar." The Child-Empress clapped her hands, first two and then four, rapidly until they sounded like pebbles falling from the cliffs of the valley of Jar, or the river Noth tumbling between its banks where they narrow at Ard Ulan. And we remembered that although she was an Empress and older than our memories, she was still only a child, hatched not long after the lost island of Irdum sank beneath the sea.

"Light upon the snows of Ard Ulan, he is indeed a slayer of beasts," said the captain. The Ladies in Waiting fluttered their fans again, and one sank senseless to the floor, overcome by his courtesy and eloquence. "He wounded two Garwolves who approached him, wishing to know the source of his singular odor. He wounded them with a projectile device. They are in the care of the Warden of the reed marshes of Zurdum."

"This cannot be," said the Child-Empress. "The Hero must go on his Quest, for that is the nature of Heroes, but he must not harm my creatures, neither the Garwolves singing in the morning mist, nor the Ilpin bounding over the rocky cliffs of Jar, nor the Mirimi birds that nest in the sands of Gar Kahan, nor even the Sloefrogs, whose yellow eyes blink along the banks of the river Noth. He must not bend a single wing of an Itz. Let us give him a creature to speak with, who can learn his name and where he has come from. Let us send him a Jain, and with her a Translator, so that he will perceive her as resembling his own species. Is there one of my Translators who would travel with the Jain to meet the Hero?"

All three of the court Translators stepped forward. From among them the Child-Empress chose Irman Adze, who was the oldest and most honored, and who signaled her willingness to make such an important journey by chirruping softly and nodding her head until her wattles flapped back and forth.

The Child-Empress said to Irman Adze, "Your first task is to remove his projectile device and replace it with the glain and the double adjar, so that he is suitably equipped but can cause no great harm to my creatures and the citizens of my realm." Then she turned to the court. "And let us also send an Observer, so that we may see and learn what the Hero is saying and doing." The Observers whirred and flew forward. She selected one among them and entered its instructions.

"And you, Captain," said the Child-Empress, turning to Captain Namoor, "because of the pleasure you have brought us in announcing the arrival of a Hero, you shall be permitted to wear the green feather of a Mirimi bird in your cap, and to proceed after the Chancellor on state occasions."

His training prevented Captain Namoor from blushing with the intensity of his emotions, but he must have blushed inside, for not one in a thousand receives the honor that the Child-Empress had bestowed upon him. Lady Ahira squeezed my upper left hand until it went purple and I winced from the pressure.

"What beast shall he slay, great . . . green feather of the Mirimi bird?" asked the Chancellor, in his ponderous way. He fancied himself a poet. The Ladies in Waiting hid their ears with their fans, and even the Pages giggled. His words were so trite, and not at all original.

"What beast indeed?" asked the Child-Empress. "Since I have said that none of our creatures must be harmed, let us send our own Poufli." Hearing his name, Poufli rose from where he had been lying at the Child-Empress's feet and licked two of her hands, while the other two stroked his filaments.

"Go, Poufli," said the Child-Empress. "Lead the Hero on his Quest, but allow him eventually to slay you, and when you have been slain, return to me, and I will think of a way to reward him that is appropriate for Heroes."

The next day, the Jain, with the Translator strutting beside her and the Observer whirring and darting around them, left for the slopes and caverns of Ard Ulan, where the Hero had awakened. Poufli bounded off in the opposite direction, to where the Child-Empress intended that the Hero should encounter his final Obstacle.

We watched, day after day, as the Hero traveled across the valley of Jar. The images transmitted by the Observer were captured in the idhar at the center of the Chamber of Audience. I preferred to watch in the mornings, when the mist still hung about the bottoms of the pillars but the dome high above was already illuminated by the rising sun, and the Mirimi birds were stirring in the branches of the Gondal trees. I would splash water on my face from one of the sublimating fountains, eat a light breakfast of Pika bread spread with Ipi berries, drink a libation made from the secretions of the Ilpin that were kept at court, and then sit on one of the cushions that the Child-Empress had provided, watching, with the other early risers, as the Hero performed his ablutions and offered his otherworldly songs to the gods of his clan.

As the Observer transmitted, the Translator interpreted for the Hero and simultaneously showed us what he saw, so we were confronted with our own landscape made strange, like the landscape of another world. The Ipi bushes, the yellow Kifli flowers that grew at the edges of the reed marshes of Zurdum, the waters of the marshes, all were flatter, as though they had lost one of their dimensions, and they lacked many colors of the spectrum. The Jain had become tall and pale, although the Translator did not disguise her undulations. The Observer had become organic. It bounded rather than flew, and was covered with a fine brown fur.

"Dog! Come here, dog!" we heard the Hero say, and "Would you like something to eat?" to the Jain, whose articulations he listened to with care, as though she were speaking a language he did not understand.

I preferred these quieter, intimate moments, although each day, in the late morning or early afternoon, the Child-Empress sent the Hero an Obstacle: once, a swarm of Itz to sting him, so that he swelled up and the Jain had to cover his arms and legs with the leaves of an Ipi bush soaked in marsh water; once, two Habira that he fought off with the glain and clever use of a flaming reed; once, a group of warriors from the town of Ard, so that he would know he was approaching the towns and cities where the citizens lived. Once, the citizens came out of a town to offer him welcome, placing a garland of pink Gondal flowers around his neck and giving him cups of the intoxicating liquor that westerners make from an iridescent fungus they call Ghram, which grows on the roots of the Gondal tree. Once, he was placed in a cage at the center of the town, and the citizens came to see him, until he said a word that was the name, they told him, of an ancient god who was still secretly reverenced.

As court Poet, it was primarily my responsibility to create the events and Obstacles of the Quest, although the Child-Empress was an enthusiastic collaborator. After my morning viewing, I would go to her chamber. However early I went, she was always lying upon her couch, absorbed with matters of state, attending to the well-being of the citizens. But she would put aside her work, waving away the Chancellor and the Courtiers that were gathered around her, and say to me, "Good morning, Elah Gal. What have you thought of for my Hero today?"

The morning that the Hero reached the court of the Child-Empress, the Translators occupied themselves with interpreting us to the Hero. We looked at ourselves in the idhar, translated. We were still ourselves, yet we were no longer ourselves—Lady Ahira still blushed blue, although her knees were stiffer, and an entirely different shape. The Courtiers were stiffer as well, more angular—and silent. I must admit that I did not miss their chirring. Many of us were only partly visible, and the Translators themselves appeared only as a shiver in the air. The Pages still ran back and forth behind the cushions where we sat, but on two slender legs, like Ilpin. I had to remind myself that they would not fall—they were only translated.

The Child-Empress was still herself, still a child, still an Empress, and yet how different she looked. Substantial parts of her could no longer be seen, and when she clapped, it was with only two hands.

"That must be what a child of his species looks like," whispered Lady Ahira, and would have whispered more had not the Hero walked in, with the Jain at his side and the Observer, grown positively shaggy, by his feet.

"Welcome, visitor from another land," said the Child-Empress. "Do you come from far Iranuk, or fabled Thull? Tell us what land you come from, and your name."

"No, ma'am," said the Hero. "My name is Jake Stackhouse, and as far as I can make out, unless the stars are lying to me, I'm from another planet altogether. What planet is this I've landed on?"

"Planet?" said the Child-Empress. "This is Ord, the crimson planet. Have you truly learned to travel across the darkness of space? You must be a great wizard, as well as a great warrior."

"No, ma'am," said Jake Stackhouse. "I've got no idea how I ended up on your planet, though I sure would like to find out, so I can go home again. And I'm not a warrior or a wizard, as you call them. I'm just a ranch hand, although I've had a few knocks in my life, and learned how to take care of myself."

"You do not know your way home?" said the Child-Empress. "I am sad that you are not able to return to your clan, but what is a misfortune for you may be fortunate for us. I have heard that you fought the Garwolves and defeated the warriors of the western marshes. Surely you are the most courageous man on Ord. I ask for your aid. We are threatened by a fearsome beast, called a"—I suddenly realized that when we had created this encounter, the Child-Empress and I, we had not given our beast a name—"a Poufli. This beast is ravaging our eastern cities and towns, eating and frightening our citizens. If you will defeat this beast, I will give you ten hecats of land, and one of my Ladies in Waiting to be your mate."

Captain Namoor, who stood next to the Chancellor, turned orange down to the tops of his boots. Let him, I thought. A little jealousy would do him good.

"I don't want a mate, ma'am. Just this girl here, who's traveled for the last three days, the strangest days of my life, at my side. She's saved my life a couple of times, I reckon. I don't know her name, so I call her Friday."

"You would have that female for your mate?" said the Child-Empress. "Then know, Jake Stackhouse, that she is a priestess of her people, the Jain of Ajain, from the far north, where the river Noth springs from the mountains of Ard Ulan. To mate with her, you must win her in battle with the glain and the double adjar. Are you willing to fight for her, Jake Stackhouse?"

I could not help blushing pink with surprise and appreciation. What an improvisation this was, not the words we had created together and so carefully rehearsed, but the Child-Empress's own, created at that moment. Around me I heard a scattering of applause as the court realized what had just happened. I applauded as well, pleased with her spontaneity. How honored I was that my Empress, too, was a poet.

"All right," said Jake Stackhouse, "I'll fight this Poufli for you, and then fight for the girl I love best in all the world. I never thought I'd marry a green bride, but underneath that skin of hers, she's as sweet and loyal as any woman of Earth."

"It is well," said the Child-Empress. "Defeat the Poufli for me and I will give you ten hecats of land by the upper reaches of the river Noth, where the soil is most fertile, and I will ensure that the Jain becomes your mate. Now, take some refreshment with us, Jake Stackhouse."

The Pages brought platters of the roasted fruit of the Pandam tree, and a sauce made from the sap of the Pandam, and stuffed roots, and the sweet lichen that grows on the roofs of the houses of Irum, in the south, and Ghram that had been brought from Ard for the Hero's Feast. The Hero sat on a cushion, with the Jain beside him and the Observer at his feet, and told us stories of his planet and the place he had spent his childhood, the Land of a Single Star. He spoke of towns in which warriors battled each other with projectile devices, thieves who stole from transport vehicles, and herds of creatures that stretched over the plains so you could see no end to them. He spoke of females so beautiful they were given the names of flowers. The Ladies in Waiting were so eager to hear his stories that they listened without respiring, and some of the more delicate Pages swooned or emitted the scent of marsh water. I myself, Elah Gal, the court Poet, listened and recorded, so that these stories of another planet could be placed among the Tales of the Heroes, which my ancestress Elim Dar had begun when the Child-Empress herself was only a dream of her parent's physical manifestation.

Grief and consternation spread throughout the court on the day the Observer transmitted the tragic news: the Hero was dead. His body was brought back to the palace, and three Healers examined him to determine the cause of his death. They reported their findings to the Child-Empress. Poufli was not to blame. He had played his part both enthusiastically and with care. The Hero's wounds were minor. But his dermal layer, when they examined it, had been covered with red spots. He must have had a reaction to Poufli's emissions, or perhaps to the touch of his filaments.

But Poufli was not to be consoled. He lay submerged in one of the palace fountains, beneath the translucent fish from Irum, refusing to eat, refusing to sleep, as had been his custom, at the foot of the Child-Empress's couch.

The court grieved. The Courtiers put on their white robes of death, and I myself put on the death robes that my mother had worn when her spouse of the second degree had chosen to demanifest. The Ladies in Waiting would not blush. Lady Ahira postponed the celebration of her union of the fourth degree with Captain Namoor, for which luminous mosses had already been grown on the walls of the Chamber of Audience. The Pages stood silent, neither giggling nor emitting scent. By orders of the Child-Empress, the murals on the walls of the palace were muted, until only faint outlines reminded us of their presence. The palace Guards wore mourning veils, and drifted around the halls of the palace like gibhans of the dead. The Jain was inconsolable, and filled the halls with the mourning wail of her kind. A cold wind seemed to blow through everything.

I sat beneath the Jindal tree in the palace garden and tried to create a poem about the Hero, but how can one commemorate defeat? The Child-Empress herself would not leave her chamber. I went in once a day to try to consult with her, but she simply sat by the aperture, looking out at the garden. I did not wish to interrupt her contemplations. Even the Chancellor stood by her couch without stirring, waiting for her to emerge from her grief.

On the seventh day, she came into the Chamber of Audience. She wore robes as red as the Jindal flowers, and she had adorned her arms with bracelets of small silver bells, which jingled as she moved. Poufli was at her side, pushing his noses into her robes.

"Citizens and creatures," she said, "you are sad because the Hero has died. We cannot now celebrate his victory, nor follow with fascination the story of his life here on Ord. Is this not so?"

The Ladies in Waiting, the Courtiers, the Guards, the Pages, all nodded or waved or emitted to signal their assent.

"But we should not be sad," she said. "To watch the triumph of the Hero would have been like listening to a poem by Elah Gal, or watching the blossoming of the Jindal flowers, or attending the union of Lady Ahira and Captain Namoor. It would have been most satisfying. But there is another sort of satisfaction, when Elah Gal pauses and there is silence, or the blossoms fall from the Jindal tree, or lovers part in sorrow after their time together has ended. Do we not take satisfaction also in the passing of things, which we can no more control than we can control the way of the Mirimi bird in the air, or the way of two loves once they are mated? The death of the Hero reminds us of our own demanifestations. This too is a poem, perhaps a greater poem than the Hero's triumph would have been, because it is more difficult, and to understand it we must become more than ourselves.

"Let the Hero, whose physical manifestation our Healers have so artistically preserved, be placed on a pedestal of stone from the quarries of Gar Kahan, beneath the branches of the Jindal tree in the garden, where their blossoms will fall upon him. And let us celebrate the death of the Hero! Let us celebrate our own demanifestations, which are to come. Let the Jain be returned to her clan so she can differentiate and deposit her eggs, and let her offspring be raised at court, in recognition of the service she has performed for us. Let Elah Gal create a poem about the Hero, a new kind of poem for a new time, and let it be included in the Tales of the Heroes. And let us all celebrate! Come, my friends. Let song and laughter and blushes return to the palace! But I shall withdraw, for I have important work to do. Tonight, as the moons rise over Ord, I shall begin to dream, so that, in your children's children's lifetimes, another Child-Empress will be born."

For a moment, there was silence around the Chamber of Audience. Then, the murals on the walls began to glow. The Ladies in Waiting began to clap and laugh and blush. The Pages leaped into the air and landed again on their toes, emitting the scent of Kifli flowers. The Guards cast off their veils and clashed their disintegrators on their shields, so that they rang through the halls. Everywhere, there was the sound of joy and of wonder. I myself could not keep my orifices from misting. To live at a time of the dreaming! The Hero had indeed brought us something greater than we could have imagined.

I wondered, for a moment, if I would become one of those poets who are celebrated for having created what no other poet could have— if I would create the poem of the Child-Empress's dreaming, of her becoming no longer a child but the full essence of herself, until eventually she emerged in the perfection of her nonphysical manifestation. But then my humility returned. Such poems were still to be created. The first of them would be about the Hero, of how he had died and yet fulfilled his Quest.

But today was a day of celebration. We sang and danced in the

Chamber of Audience, celebrating the union of Lady Ahira and Captain Namoor. At the height of the festivities, the Child-Empress withdrew. But we knew now that it was not to contemplate her grief but to begin an important new event in her life. And we leaped higher and turned faster with joy, while the Musicians played their kurams and their dharms, until night fell and the mosses illuminated the ancient murals, and the moons rose, and the Jindal flowers spread their fragrance over the palace.

LETTERS FROM AN
IMAGINARY COUNTRY

Dear Dr. Goss:

Thank you for sending us a copy of *Under the Northern Lights: Folk and Fairy Tales of Farthest Thüle*. We plan to review it in the spring issue. Will you be attending the International Conference on Folk Narratives in March? Both our editor-in-chief, Paula Cisneros, and I will be there, and we would love to meet you. To be honest, I wish the conference were somewhere other than Oslo this year! There are plenty of folk narratives in warmer climates. But I'm looking forward to Dr. Elsa Aarne's keynote. If you plan to attend, please let us know when you might have some free time. The coffee is on us, and I hear there is a dessert called trollkrem that we really should try. Apparently, it's made with lingonberries, which are a special favorite with the trolls . . .

Hoping to meet you in person,
Jennifer Reed, Reviews Editor
Journal of Fairy Tale Studies

From: animarta@gmail.com
To: theogoss@bu.edu

Dear Professor Goss:

My name is Anika Martok-Taylor, and I'm currently ABD at the University of Alabama, finishing my dissertation on Baba Yaga in Russian folklore. I hope you don't mind that I'm writing to you? I got your address from the Boston University website. First, I'd like to thank you for your wonderful book on the fairy tales of Thüle. It was one of the required texts for my course on folklore in translation with Professor Sandra McGinty. She says you were in graduate school together? When I told her I wanted to write you a letter, she said to say hello.

Your book was especially important to me because my mother actually comes from Thüle. She immigrated to the United States after the 1972 revolution. The only thing she brought with her, other than some clothes and a photograph of her mother at Lake Vialka, was a book of fairy tales that her grandmother had given her. Unfortunately, I can't read Thülian—my father was born in Alabama, and we always spoke English at home, though sometimes my mother would talk to herself in her native language. But she used to show me the illustrations before I went to sleep at night and recount the stories in her own words. I remember "Fair Evána," and "Death Comes for Jánki," and the one where King Ottokar turns into a bear. My favorites were the ones about Ama Yaníga, which is probably why I started researching Baba Yaga. Of course, now I realize that my mother left out some details to make the stories less gruesome! For example, she never told me about Mik, Mak, and Ratoshka, the Hounds of Fate who eat human souls. Finding a copy of these stories in English translation was so meaningful to me that I bought your book for my little brother as well. (His name is János, and we call him Jánki. Now he knows who he's named after!) So first, I just wanted to thank you for your wonderful book.

Second, I hope you don't mind me asking, and please feel free to say no, but would you be willing to serve as an outside examiner on my dissertation committee? I'm asking not just because I loved your book so much, but because my department only has two professors who study folklore, or fantasy at all (Professor McGinty and Professor John-Paul Ricardo, who specializes in gothic and modernism). My other option would be a Shakespeare specialist who doesn't believe folklore should be included in the literature department at all—he keeps saying it belongs in anthropology. Again, I hope you don't mind me asking, and I'm sure you're very busy with research and teaching, but I thought it couldn't hurt to write!

With all best wishes,
Anika

Dr. Prof. Ülla Pálev
Department of Languages and Literature
National University of Arts and Letters, Brázlov, Thüle

Dear Dórika,
Yosefína and I met at Kafé Gustav yesterday after her seminar, and we missed you so much! I remember when M. Gustav called the three of us the Weird Sisters from *Macbeth*—or perhaps their younger, more chic versions. At least, you and Yosefína are still young, while I am rapidly becoming an old woman. If age wasn't turning my hair white, this government would be!

Honestly, it's getting worse every day. They already controlled the radio and television stations. Now they've taken over the main opposition website by the particularly modern expedient of purchasing it. Viktor Yurgi's nephew owns it now, and it's turned into a mouthpiece for nationalist propaganda—when it's not obsessed with celebrity gossip. At least in the old days you could see the censorship in action. In my childhood, if Luchenko wanted to shut down a newspaper, he would send in the police. The editor would be put in prison, and we would stand outside the prison walls, chanting and holding candles—or flowers. It was flowers during the day, and candles at night, if I remember correctly. But that was so long ago, before you and Yosefína were born. Did I tell you that I met my Üwe, rest his soul, at a protest rally?

This new blend of capitalism and authoritarianism is particularly *toxic*, as you would say in your American slang. How do you fight it? Or rather, how do we fight it? Because I'm quite certain that it's coming for the universities next. There are already rules about what can be taught in the primary and secondary schools. Soon they will start focusing on the university curriculum, and tenure will not save an old radical like me. I told Yosefína to get out while she still can. What kind of career could she possibly have here, as long as this God and Motherland party is in power? Goddamn motherfuckers, is what I call them, but only to you and Yosefína. Because I am too old to go to prison. Although I will continue to teach the history of Thüle, good and bad, as long as they let me.

I wish I could do more, like in the old days, when Üwe and I had our underground press and distributed pamphlets through cafés and radical bookstores. But the young people must do it now. It is their turn to fight, if they can get off their TikToks or whatever else they are doing. You know, just yesterday I had to take away two mobile telephones from students who were using them in class? I'm sure they will mention that on course evaluations.

Well, I'll stop complaining. The real reason I am writing, of course, is to send you the enclosed newspaper article. I thought you might find it amusing. Ever since a farmer said he saw King Ottokar in a barley field near Dombrátz, there have been sightings of that crazy old tyrant—usually in rural areas. At least one of the opposition candidates (from the Greener Thüle party, I think) claims Ottokar is returning to clean up the corruption in government. If only he would! Of course, our charming Deputy Prime Minister (that's Yurgi's other nephew) says these sightings show that Ottokar is blessing their version of illiberal, EU-skeptical, NATO-reluctant Thüle with his presence. He wants to commission an Ottokar rock opera for Foundation Day. It's exactly the sort of ridiculousness I would expect from the current government, but I thought you, as a folklorist, would appreciate it.

I hope you are well, my dear, and that you will be able to come next summer as we planned—if the political situation doesn't deteriorate further. But I'm very much afraid that it will, and I fear for my students and colleagues.

With love,
Ülla

Ministry of Culture, Ottokar kír Palatz
Brázlov, Thüle

Dear Dr. Prof. Theodora Goss!

It is our great pleasure to recognize your achievement in publishing *Under the Northern Lights: Folk and Fairy Tales of Farthest Thüle*, which makes the traditional tales of Thüle available to an English-speaking audience, with the King Ottokar Award. This award is given annually to those who have advanced the cause of Thüle in scientific, artistic, or commercial sectors. The award comes with a prize of 500 zloty, and is given at an award ceremony in Brázlov. The government of Thüle will be pleased to pay for your travel expenses, to include one economy-class ticket and two nights at the Brázlov Intercontinental Marriott. The award will be given at the recently refurbished Opera House. If you choose to attend in person, please be prepared to make a speech of no more than five minutes. If you cannot attend in person, your speech may be recorded and sent directly to the Office of Cultural Affairs, which will place it online with a recording of the award ceremony. In either case, please send the proposed text of your speech to Miss Isola Járvinen at the Office of Cultural Affairs at least five days before the ceremony for approval, keeping in mind that the award ceremony is not an appropriate forum for political discourse.

Again, congratulations on your significant achievement! We hope to see you in Brázlov.

Sincerely,
Bozram Ifik, Undersecretary for Cultural Affairs
On behalf of President Viktor Yurgi

From: yosefinag@brazlovuni.te
To: theogoss@bu.edu

Dear Dóri,

I understand how you feel about the award ceremony—absolutely I do. You would certainly be justified in refusing to accept the award and publishing your op-ed in the *New York Times*. I agree with it completely. Nevertheless, I ask you as a friend to do what is against your nature—to come and accept the award, even to make a gracious speech approved by the government censors. And not to publishing anything—at least not now, not yet.

Remember when we traveled together in that rented Citroën, with its bottom almost rusted out? Remember the little villages in the mountains, and that time our auto sank into the mud, and we thought we would have to spend the night under the oak and pine trees of the Bírkenséa? Then we saw a fox with its eyes gleaming in the darkness, and help came to us so unexpectedly. I will never forget the strangeness of that night. I petition you in the old phrase, *by the bones of my mother and her mother before her,* please come. I will explain later, but not in an email—a university email account is not as private as it used to be. You ask how things are going here. What can I say? Ülla is still smoking those terrible brown cigarettes that will certainly be the death of her, if her heart does not kill her first. Certainly events at the university have not lowered her blood pressure. Mikkel has given up teaching altogether. We used to talk about having children, but how could we bring a child into the world, as it is now? Still, the apricot trees are starting to blossom again in Saint Kinga Park. Spring always comes again, no matter how dark and bleak the winter.

When you come—please come—we will sit beneath them again, the three of us, drinking coffee and complaining about the state of the world. I look forward to that.

With a kiss from me, and one from Ülla,
Yosi

From: rachelc@nyt.com
To: theogoss@bu.edu

Dear Theo,

Of course I'm disappointed that you want to pull the op-ed, but I understand. One of our reporters, Jordan Kirov (his father is Thülian), is on the ground in Brázlov, and he thinks the situation is particularly volatile right now. He says the students are organizing protests, and once they start, the teachers' unions will probably follow—he expects government crackdowns. Obviously I don't want you to put your friends at the university in danger.

But I really object to this idea of going to pick up the award in person. Judging from Jordan's emails, it's NOT SAFE, not even for an American. He's thinking of getting out himself and establishing a base just over the border in Ruritania. At least that's in the European Union, or is it the Schengen Area, I always forget. Seriously, don't do it—I'm begging you. Charles and Leslie and I want many articles from you on Eastern European politics, and folk festivals, and whatever you want to write about—hell, write an article on Thülian cuisine! We'll fit it in somewhere. I can talk to the cooking and lifestyle editors. Just don't risk your life in a potentially dangerous situation—not to pick up some stupid, or even not-so-stupid (I know it's an honor, yada yada), award. Just don't.

Love and a big hug,
Rachel

Rachel Cohen, Opinion Editor
The New York Times

Dr. Oksana Mákinen
Department of Languages and Literature
National University of Arts and Letters, Brázlov, Thüle

Dear Dr. Goss:

I'm sure you never heard of me, but I am Oksana Mákinen, and I am a postdoctoral student of Dr. Yosefína Güell. I am very sad and sorry to write that Yosefína and her husband, Dr. Mikkel Güell, have been taken to prison. You have probably heard that she participated in the demonstration with the students in front of the parliament building during the Foundation Day celebration, when you received the Ottokar

Award. Excuse me, but I do not think you should have accepted the award. Yosefína said you had a good reason to do it, but I believe such gestures only empower the current administration. While you were inside the Opera House with the politicians, we were outside in the streets of Brázlov, standing up to the police. My friend Marika had to go to the hospital afterward because one of them struck her on the head with a stick—I think you call it a baton, and the leaders of the student union were questioned, or rather interrogated—I think that is the right word—for hours. They are free for now, but how long until they are dragged away like Yosefína and her husband?

I was supposed to meet her yesterday morning at their flat, and I found the door broken in. Everything was a chaos—the books pulled off the bookshelves, clothes pulled out of the wardrobes and scattered on the floor, furniture overturned. Even the porcelain figures that belonged to her mother had been taken out of the vitrine, and some were broken. I went to her office in the department, and they had gotten there as well. The drawers of her desks had been pulled out, and all the papers—all her notes and research material—were missing. You can imagine how worried I was for her! It took a few days for us to find out where she was being held, and then a few days more until I could see her. Fortunately, my father is a lawyer and we are not living in a complete autocracy—yet.

She said she was all right—that she had not been beaten or otherwise mistreated, but she has not been able to see Mikkel, who is accused of being a traitor because of his research casting doubt on the idea of a historical Greater Thüle and his support for EU membership. She says there is talk of prison camps in the north, near the Bírkenséa. She is afraid he may be sent there.

I do not know why she wanted me to contact you, but she said, write to my colleague Dr. Goss and tell her that I am here. Can you do anything to help Yosefína and her husband? You are far away, and a foreigner, and perhaps your interest in Thüle is purely intellectual. Perhaps all you care about is our fairy tales of King Ottokar and

Clever Jánki. But if you can possibly help in this, please do so, I beg of you.

With regards,
Oksana Mákinen

57 Prinzessin Eugenie Strasse
Vienna, Austria

Dear Dorochka,

I am writing a brief letter to let you know that I am in Austria. Thank you again for the use of your identity documents. Really I think we do not look so much alike, but then the border guards never look too closely, do they? And they would not stop an American from leaving the country. Did I ever tell you, that night we met in the Bírkenséa, that you resemble your great-grandmother? It was one of the first things I noticed about you. I am very sorry to hear about Yosefína, who knew such beautiful stories about me. Some of them were probably true.

Vienna is quite different from when I was last here, but that was in the time of one of the Hapsburg emperors, I don't remember which— they all looked alike, so dreadful, all chin and nose. Ülla fusses over me as though I were her granddaughter. I have to tell her that yes, I know how to use a stove! Yes, I can cook dinner for us, and even go to the grocery store and pay with money, although I will never understand why you put so much faith in bits of paper. Such sorcerers you are, with your strange creation of whatever gods there be. In the old days, you believed in Ingvar and Inválla. Nowadays it seems to be some bearded old man, or is it some rock star on the television? Oh yes, I understand television as well! I tell you, Dorochka, in all the time I have been on this earth, I have never seen a god, not one. Only Mother Night and her children, the stars. The spirits of the trees and rivers, the mountains. Mála combing her long gray hair, and the golden bird, and of course the trolls, and Ama Yaníga. She is as real as anything, the realest thing in this strange world. I do not know if there is a realm of the spirits high above us, but if so, I have never been there, nor seen any sign of it.

All I know comes from the earth, and lives on the earth—you and I and even Viktor Yurgi, curse him for destroying my homeland. Ülla has gathered a group of Thülians in exile, and we shall do what we can to end his vile dictatorship—the petroleum deals with Russia, the construction contracts given to his family and friends, the destruction of newspapers and radio stations and universities. He is worse than Kilaman, Ottokar's son, and I was there. I remember what a bastard he was.

I tell you, it is not only the students and intellectuals who are against him. It is the grandmothers whose sons might be conscripted into his military, the farmers afraid of losing their land to his schemes for attracting foreign investment. It is teachers in the rural schools who do not want to teach the new curriculum or put a portrait of Yurgi up in their classrooms. The trees and stones of Thüle reject him. Even the trolls hiding in their underground caverns whisper their hatred of him. When they can, they disable the engines of his military trucks or pull fallen branches across his logging roads. The foxes piss on his statues.

I do not know how I can help Ülla, exactly. I can make apple and pear trees blossom, or summon all the birds from the sky, or speak to the waves of the ocean and bid them be still—I am not a revolutionary. But she seems to think I am a symbol of something, I suppose of Thüle itself. Perhaps that is a way of helping.

I am sad to be so far away from the land that made me, but we will do what we can, from where we are, to save Thüle from this despoiler.

With my blessing,
Evána

24 Karl Kalmán Platz
Brázlov, Thüle

Dear Theodora,

Rachel gave me a heads-up about your revised op-ed. I have to warn you that it's going to make you *persona non* grata with the governing powers in Thüle. I'm happy to tell you that your friend Yosefína Güell was released from prison several days ago, but her husband is still in custody. There will be some sort of trial—my sources tell me there's not much hope, since the new law was passed forbidding any criticism of the government or its official version of Thülian history, with the glorious reign of King Ottokar, etc. etc. This is a dangerous time to be a history professor, or to have opinions about contemporary issues. Mikkel Güell wrote too many articles for the opposition newspapers before they were shut down for the current administration to just let him go. I have to be honest with you, I think he's headed for a prison camp.

Honestly, I was worried we weren't going to be able to get you out, after you lost your passport. Thank God for Mike Gallagher at the Embassy. I think I mentioned that we were at Columbia together. Anyway, he's a genius at greasing official wheels, and I'm trusting him to get me out if there's a revolution. There will be if the students get their way, but Yurgi's been building up the military, and whatever happens won't be pretty. It's better if you stay out of it. I strongly suggest that you stay away from Thüle, at least for the foreseeable future. That would be good advice for me too, but I've never listened to good advice yet, which is why I'm a journalist! And who knows what the unforeseeable future will bring? Except Ama Yaníga, says Thülian folklore, and she ain't talking!

All the best,
Jordan

Jordan Kirov, International Correspondent
The New York Times

Office of Senator Emily Warner
Boston, Massachusetts

Dear Ms. Theodora Goss:

I'm writing to assure you that Senator Warner is doing all she can in the matter of Dr. Mikkel Güell. The senator is deeply committed to supporting democratic institutions throughout the world, including in Thüle. As a former teacher herself, she is also particularly committed to academic freedom.

Unfortunately, there are limits to what the United States government can do in a situation like this. However, Senator Warner, together with Senators Amy Lewis of New Hampshire and Alberto Martinez of Arizona, has proposed Senate legislation that would impose sanctions on the government of Thüle to match those recently imposed by the European Union, which would significantly affect its ability to do business with American companies.

Our records indicate that you contributed to Senator Warner's reelection fund in her previous campaign. Thank you for being one of our valued supporters! If you sign up for Senator Warner's newsletter at www.emilywarner.senate.gov, we will keep you updated on this important legislation and Senator Warner's other official endeavors.

Thank you again for your support!

Sincerely,
Mike Lombardi, Legislative Aide

From: sandymcg@ua.edu
To: theogoss@bu.edu

Dear Dora,

First let me say thank you for serving on Anika Martok-Taylor's committee. She is one of the most promising graduate students I've had in years, with a genuine love of folklore and Eastern European languages—she's currently working on her Thülian, which I understand is a sort of distant cousin of Latvian or Estonian. I don't know how much that will mean in the current job market—last year I could count the tenure-track openings for folklorists on the fingers of one hand, *nationally*. My department won't have an opening again until one of us dies off—our expert on Nordic folklore is eighty-two and shows no sign of retiring. I'm afraid Anika will end up like most of our folklore graduate students, deep in the mines of freshman comp. But anyway, I appreciate your help so much!

Second, I like your idea of a special session on Thülian myths and fairy tales at the next Conference on Folk Narratives. It would definitely be topical, considering what's happening in Thüle right now. "Folklore in Peril" is a great title, and I would love to contribute a paper coauthored with Anika. It would focus on how figures from Thülian folklore are being used by both the government and the protesters to claim and define national identity. Anika was showing me some videos from CNN of students carrying effigies of Efa Evána, which she tells me means something like Fair Evána in both senses of the term, beautiful and just, and of course King Ottokar's crown is on government uniforms, vehicles, etc. The paper would draw on Anika's familiarity with Thülian folklore and my work on the political uses of folk motifs. We would each present for about ten minutes, with a PowerPoint. Does that sound like the sort of thing you're looking for?

I'm hoping we can expand and publish it in the journal of the Folklore Society. I just wish your colleague Yosefína Güell could be there. Have you heard anything more about her husband? What a world we live in, where university professors are jailed for expressing their opinions! I would like to say, oh, that's Thüle, a small former Soviet republic in northeastern Europe. But you and I know it could happen anywhere.

I have to run and teach my graduate seminar! Dennis says hello. Allison is starting middle school in September. Can you believe it? It's been way too long since we've seen each other! Hopefully at the conference . . .

All the best,
Sandy

5 Olga kírina Strasz
Brázlov, Thüle

To the charming Dóra!

Yosefína has made me sit at this desk and write a letter—not the first one I have ever written, I believe I wrote one many years ago to Queen Elgína, the wife of King Aleksánder the second or third, I don't remember which. She had hair like a wheat field, and eyes like cornflowers, and I was terribly in love with her—as I am with you, my swallow who always flies away from me, but you know this, for I have told it to you in poetry and song. You beautiful women are all alike, you break a man's heart without a second thought. To be honest, and I am always honest, you are not quite so beautiful as Queen Elgína, for whom the River Dün changed its course so she would not get her boots wet. But you have pretty eyes, and I hope that sometimes they cry for your far-away Jánki, who may die in this war—Yosefína, who is also charming but cruel, reminds me that I cannot die, but what does she know? If I am immortal, it simply means that I can die a thousand times, more than any mortal man.

For a long time I waited for you, or some other beautiful woman to love me, but alas, I wandered alone among the mountains of Thüle, with only trolls and the occasional rucksack-wearing hiker for my companions. But now I have taken my broken heart to the battlefield, to fight for my country against my ancient foe—yes, King Ottokar has returned from wherever he was buried, whether under a stone, or at the bottom of Lake Mála, or among the stars. I shall fight him with every weapon I have, whether my two fists, or my clever wits, or—

Yosefína says I should stop romanticizing and tell you quite plainly that Ottokar has returned and is collaborating with the regime of Viktor Yurgi, and that I am working with the leaders of the student faction, and that Evána is abroad somewhere, trying to raise funds for our cause—the liberation of Thüle from tyranny! Freedom for the people, freedom for the nation.

Dóri, excuse me for asking this idiot to write a letter but I've been so distracted by Mikkel's court case that I didn't have time to do it myself. At least you have a sense of what's going on here from the above, embroidered as it is with unnecessary verbiage! Jánki is looking over my shoulder and objects to being called an idiot, so I will say that in all fairness, he is clever in the ways that count. It was he that planned the yarn attack on the parliament building—imagine a bunch of old women knitting and crocheting all night in so many colors, then hanging what they had made over the doors and windows of parliament, like politically motivated Arachnes! So the politicians could not get into the building without cutting apart these rainbow webs, and Yurgi immediately became a laughingstock for trying to arrest a bunch of grandmothers.

And then the next day, there were flower paintings on the military vehicles! But I must run, because I have to meet with Mikkel's lawyer. There is very little hope, but I must, or I would go crazy . . .

As I was saying before I was so rudely interrupted—but I have forgotten what I was saying. I hope the next time you return to Thüle it will be a country liberated from tyranny, where every peasant will have his loaf of bread and a jug of wine, and the students will have—whatever they want, I'm not entirely certain. They are a talkative and rather tedious lot. I remember students being much more interesting in the days of King Aleksánder.

I send you my kisses—however many times you refuse them. You know that I am entirely devoted to you, and scarcely notice the female students with their short, very short, skirts.

Your humble servant,
Jánki, sometimes called The Clever

General Consulate of Thüle
New York, New York

Dear Dr. Prof. Theodora Goss!

I write to notify you that your visa to visit Thüle, whether for business or tourism, is hereby permanently revoked. If you wish to appeal the revocation of your visa, please contact Commissioner Gregori Yurgi of the Brázlov Metropolitan Police.

Sincerely,
Brüno Krigov, Consular Assistant

From: llevinelit@gmail.com
To: theogoss@bu.edu

Dear T, you'll be as surprised as I was to learn that Mount Auburn Press has agreed to everything—a signed limited edition of *Under the Northern Lights*, in hardcover and illustrated by Viktória Krebo, who was lucky enough to be in Paris when the uprising started. They'd never heard of her, but I told them she was the most important children's book illustrator in Thüle. All proceeds will go to a fund for Thülian refugees who have fled the country. It's great publicity for the press, but I wasn't sure they would see it that way—these old Boston publishing houses are so conservative. Neither of us will make money on this, which is too bad, considering that Sasha's tuition bills at Swarthmore are killing me, but I'm proud to be your agent.

They're also interested in the new proposal, but to be honest I'd rather shop it to some larger publishers. I think one of the big five would be interested in your travels around Thüle collecting stories, as long as it's more of a memoir than an academic book. I mean, you can put the information in there, but talk about what you ate, what you saw, what you *felt*. Didn't your great-grandmother come from Thüle, or something like that? Can you play up a family angle? If you can draft a new proposal that focuses on a popular audience, that's relevant for this particular moment, etc. etc., I can send it out and see if we get any bites. What do you think? And when could you get it to me? I really think this could be your breakthrough into the mass market.

As for the limited edition, give me a call and let's talk about the timeline. I want to start thinking about how to turn this into a publicity bonanza for you. And the refugees, of course.

Ciao,
Larry

Levine Literary Agency
Brooklyn, New York

Bírkenséa, Thüle

Troublesome child!

I knew, as soon as I saw you and Yosefína Güellina at my door on that dark, wet night, when the rain came down as though it would never stop, and the trees of the Bírkenséa gleamed black in the moonlight, that trouble was coming. I could smell it in the air, like electricity from the new powerlines they have built through the forest. And I am not at all pleased about those either.

Of course, I don't blame you for the revolution. I blame that son of a mangy she-goat, Viktor Yurgi, and his insufferable sons. I remember when he was one of the revolutionaries himself, standing up against the Soviets. How time changes everything—except, perhaps, me. Efa Evána says she is in Austria raising money for the revolutionaries. Kopik Jánki is in Brázlov—who knows what mischief he is up to there. And Ottokar kír, that old idiot, is working with Yurgi's men, or so I hear, and I hear everything, from the acorn that sleeps underground, dreaming it is an oak, to the hawk that glides over the mountain valleys, searching below for a mouse stirring among the grasses.

However, when I saw you that night, dripping wet, looking just like your great-grandmother when she came to me, asking for a way to escape the marriage her parents had arranged for her because she wanted to marry Ivó, the village blacksmith—that is, your great-grandfather—I knew the world had changed yet again, and soon, whether in five years or fifty, there would be another revolution. If a daughter of Thüle had returned, looking for the old stories, then something had changed in the world beyond the Bírkenséa, and that change would come even to my cottage door.

I remember Evána, still half fox, already half woman, when she brought you to my door. It was a peaceful night that you and Yosefína Güellina spent here, listening to an old woman telling stories. May there be a peaceful night again, when all this is over.

Jánki has asked me to search for Mikkel Güell, who was transported to a prison camp at the foot of the mountains. Well, I have found him. He is alive, although not well—the ravens tell me he is coughing and has a pain in his chest, for he holds his hands there, above his heart. Still he talks and laughs with the other prisoners as they break the hard ground to dig for potatoes. But winter is coming, and I know what winter does to prisoners. Do what you can to get him out soon. I have power in the forests of Thüle, in its valleys and mountains, wherever its rivers flow—but not in government buildings or prison camps.

Evána has asked me to do more than this sort of reconnoitering—she has asked me to let loose Mik, Mak, and Ratoshka. Do you know what that would mean, child? They have not feasted since 1972, when the Soviets came with their tanks. They are hungry, and they miss the taste of blood. But Evána says the students are already being slaughtered.

The old stories say that I can foretell the future, but it is not true. I see it only dimly, like the web of a spider stretching into the darkness, each raindrop on that web reflecting something, some small fragment of what is to come. I do not know who will win this fight, only that revolutions will come again and again, seemingly without end, as long as some men want power over others, and other men want to be free. So they have come, time out of mind, since I have lived in the Bírkenséa, and I remember when Lake Mála stretched from Brázlov to the mountains. I am as old as the shells schoolchildren sometimes find among the rocks.

Should I do it, Dorochka, daughter of Ána, daughter of Galína, daughter of Irma who married Ivó? Perhaps it is better to let loose the hounds of death and destruction, perhaps it is sometimes necessary, I don't know. I would like to see Mak sink his teeth into Viktor Yurgi's throat.

As I write this, they pace beside me, eager to join the fight. For years they lay by my fire, sleeping peacefully, going into the forest only to relieve themselves and hunt rabbits. But now—

When you visit Thüle again, come and see me. Come to my cottage and sit by the fire, and I will tell you more stories, enough for another book, about wise owls and thieving foxes, and when Kilaman, Ottokar's son, fell in love with Evána and she escaped by turning first into a doe that ran away from him, and then a dove that flew away, and then a toad that he threw away in disgust. And when Jánki had to marry Balgíta, the queen of the trolls, I have not told you that one. When I look into the future, along the spiderweb, one of the raindrops shows you here in my cottage, listening, listening.

May it be so.

Ama Yaníga

THE SECRET DIARY OF
MINA HARKER

SINCE THE DISCOVERY of Mina Harker's secret diary in a walnut writing desk on an episode of the British television series *Antiques Roadshow*, there has been significant controversy over the diary itself as well as its authorship. This controversy mirrors the late nineteenth-century debate surrounding the publication of *Dracula*, the manuscript compiled by Mina and published in 1897. In his concluding note to the manuscript, Mina's husband Jonathan Harker writes, "None shall believe us," and that has largely, although not completely, proven to be the case.[1] *Dracula* has generally been regarded as a clever fraud incorporating actual events, such as the wreck of the ship *Demeter* off the coast of Whitby, within a nest of falsified narratives—or as an instance of mass hallucination.[2] At the time of its publication, it ruined the reputation of the men who featured in its pages. Arthur Holmwood, later Lord Godalming, became a laughingstock in Parliament and retired to his

---

1   All quotations from *Dracula* are from the scholarly edition edited by my dissertation advisor, John Paul Riquelme.

2   However, Marianne Vermeulen argues that Mina should be seen as an early modernist writer, and that *Dracula* is an example of bricolage—a monstrous assemblage that contains a monster. For Vermeulen, Mina is a precursor to experimental women writers such as Virginia Woolf and Gertrude Stein.

estate, where he lived the rest of his life as a recluse. Dr. Seward lost his medical license and ended his life as a patient in the mental asylum where he had once been director. Professor Van Helsing, whose methods were already being questioned by the Viennese authorities, lost his university position and spent the rest of his life in Central Europe, advertising himself as a freelance vampire hunter. Jonathan Harker left his legal practice in London for a small town in Yorkshire.[3] Mina moved with her husband to Yorkshire and founded a school for local farm girls. She apparently died at the age of fifty-four, shortly after her husband, and was buried beside him in the churchyard of Christ Church, Huddersfield. After his mother's death, their son Quincey Harker, whose birth is mentioned at the end of the manuscript, sold the film rights to the American movie star Charlie Chaplin, whose silent film version of *Dracula*, with himself as the Count and Mary Pickford as Mina, is still considered a masterpiece of early cinematography.

The diary was discovered in the sort of concealed drawer common in nineteenth-century writing desks. The provenance of the desk itself is impeccable. It was sold at auction by the estate of Elsie Harker Hallo- way, Jonathan Harker's grandniece, who inherited the desk from her mother. The diary is contained in a small leather notebook with *Household Accounts* stamped on the front cover, and the first eleven pages are indeed household accounts—apparently from when the Harkers were first married, because they record the purchase of items that newlyweds would typically need, such as kitchenware and bed linens. Analysis of the paper and ink conducted by the British Library confirms that the document was indeed written in the late nineteenth century, and a comparison of the handwriting with a typed manuscript of *Dracula* in the library archives, which contains handwritten corrections as- sumed to have been made by Mina, strongly suggests that both were written by the same author. Scholars generally accept that the secret

---

3   As we learn in the manuscript, the final member of the vam- pire-hunting band, the Texan adventurer Quincey Morris, died in the final attempt to dispatch Count Dracula.

diary was indeed written by Mina Harker. A notable exception is Gerald Bottheimer, who argues that neither the manuscript corrections nor the diary were written by Mina.[4]

If we accept, as I do, that the secret diary is by Mina herself, what do we make of the discrepancies between the official manuscript of *Dracula*, which must have been approved by the so-called band of brothers (Holmwood, Seward, Jonathan Harker, and of course Van Helsing) before publication, and the diary concealed by Mina in her writing desk? The two accounts give us significantly different versions of what are already ambiguous events. The diary starts on the twelfth page of the notebook, dated September 30th, the date on which Van Helsing first tells the band of brothers that Count Dracula is a vampire and enlists their aid in dispatching him. In the manuscript, Jonathan immediately agrees, speaking for both himself and Mina. This sounds as though husband and wife are in accord, but Mina never actually agrees to destroy the vampire. In the diary, the entry for that date reads, "They are determined to kill him. What shall I do?" It seems clear that the official manuscript of *Dracula* and the secret diary present us with two versions of Mina Harker. Which is the real one?

The next day, October 1st, the diary entry begins, "I told him he was in danger. He laughed at me. 'I fought the fiercest armies of the Ottomans,' he said. 'Why should I fear five men?' *Because you are only one man*, I wanted to tell him. *You have no armies here.* He trusts in

---

4   Bottheimer's argument that Jonathan was the author of both documents is unconvincing. Why would Jonathan, at that point a busy London lawyer, have taken the time to both correct the typed manuscript of *Dracula* and handwrite a secret diary that directly contradicts the manuscript? Furthermore, the handwriting is in the sort of late nineteenth-century school script Mina would have taught to students at the Newnham Ladies' Academy where she first met and mentored Lucy Westenra, rather than the clerical script a lawyer like Jonathan would have used. I was in the unfortunate situation of being on a panel with Bottheimer at a Gothic Studies Association conference. He kept addressing me as "young lady," and several times he put his hand on my knee under the table.

his powers—too much, I sometimes think. He laughs at Van Helsing, with his crosses and wafers and holy water. 'I'm a good Catholic,' he says. 'I saved the Holy Roman Empire. Do you think such things have any effect on me?' As though he fought off the Ottomans single-handed! I live between two worlds, one of the day and one of the night—both dominated by boastful men."

Judith Browne points out that Mina's voice in the secret diary is quite different from the voice we hear in the journal she was keeping at the time, which she eventually incorporated into the manuscript of *Dracula*. In her journal, Mina repeatedly describes the vampire hunters as good, brave men saving modern civilization from the Count. By contrast, in the diary, Mina's October 1st entry ends with, "I have no desire to endanger his life—but how can we allow them to get away with their crime? Damn them for what they did to Lucy, the bastards." This discrepancy has led scholars such as Bottheimer to dismiss the diary and reject what it suggests: that Mina is in league with Count Dracula.

Bottheimer sarcastically asks why, if Mina was in league with the Count, she recorded his vampiric attacks in her journal. Why not keep secret that the vampire is drinking her blood? The obvious answer is that Dr. Seward witnessed Mina and the Count together in her bedroom. Since he saw them together, Mina had to write about it—and she had to characterize it as an attack.[5] But crucially, in Seward's narrative, it is Mina who is drinking from the Count's chest while Jonathan lies beside her on the bed, in a seeming stupor. Although Seward describes the Count forcing Mina to drink, does this reflect what he actually sees, or his preconceived notions?[6] Horrified by what he has

---

5   Am I suggesting here that Mina basically "faked" entries in her journal to deceive the band? Yes, I am.

6   Seward tells us that the Count holds Mina to his breast like "a child forcing a kitten's nose into a saucer of milk to compel it to drink." What he does not want to see here is an act of both reproduction and breastfeeding. The vampire nourishing its newborn in this way is a normal part of the vampiric reproductive cycle.

witnessed, he summons the rest of the band. The Count apparently cowers before their religious paraphernalia, then turns into vapor and drifts under the door. If we ignore Seward's interpretation and look at what actually happens in this scene, we see the Count and Mina in what counts for vampires as a sexual encounter, while her husband lies drugged beside her. Who drugged him? The most obvious possibility is that Mina has given him the sleeping draught prescribed for her by Seward himself.[7]

When Jonathan regains consciousness and is told what happened, Mina physically holds him back and says he must not go after the Count because she fears for his safety. Soon after, she calls herself "unclean," insisting that she must touch and kiss her husband no more. She both prevents Jonathan from pursuing the Count and declares that they must no longer act as husband and wife. Hmmm—I don't know about you, but this seems pretty suspicious to me. Even before the discovery of the secret diary, John Paul Riquelme suggested that Mina was acting as a double agent.[8]

When the secret diary was discovered, I was in Budapest, teaching on a Fulbright grant at Pázmány Péter Catholic University. I was teaching two classes, one on the American Gothic tradition and one on fictions of the American South. I had applied for a Fulbright to escape from yet another semester of teaching rhetoric and composition as an adjunct professor in Boston, where my income from teaching two classes a semester, plus an online writing course to students completing certificates in criminal justice or paralegal studies, barely covered the rent on my studio apartment, and partly to reconnect with my Hungarian heritage. My mother's family had left Hungary in 1956, after the failed revolution. They had settled in Belmont, Massachusetts, where there was already a Hungarian community. My mother had

---

7   Which is in fact what happened. The draught in question consisted mostly of laudanum.

8   See his note "Mina Harker, Double Agent" in the special vampire issue of *Modern Fiction Studies*.

gone to Wellesley and then gotten a Master's in Education. I had gone to the high school where she still teaches ninth and tenth grade English. My father was, as he called it, Boston born and bred. His ancestors had come over from Ireland in the late 1800s, around the time immigrants were pouring into the melting pot of America—except some of them wouldn't melt. My father was proud of his Irish heritage. "You know, the first vampire novel was written by an Irishman," he said when I told him I was going to write a doctoral dissertation on vampire fiction.

I didn't tell him that, in fact, the first vampire novel in English was written by John Polidori, the son of an Italian immigrant. The Irishman Sheridan Le Fanu's *Carmilla* would not be written until fifty years later. But I did tell him it was another Irishman, Bram Stoker, who would dramatize Mina Harker's manuscript. *Nosferatu*, the play he wrote for the Shakespearean actor Henry Irving, would become the template for all later theatrical and cinematic versions of *Dracula*. The Chaplin film version is based mostly on Stoker's play, although it makes Mina's encounters with the vampire more melodramatic. Mary Pickford is a sweet, innocent Mina unwillingly seduced by the charming vampire, who turns increasingly horrific with the help of early Hollywood makeup and special effects.

"How exactly is writing about vampire fiction going to get you a teaching job?" asked my mother.

In the end, it didn't, not really. In his role as my dissertation advisor, John Paul had warned me. "You'll need to sell yourself as a Victorianist. They'll want to know if you can teach George Eliot." Well, I didn't know how to teach George Eliot—there were no vampires in her novels, unless Rosamond Vincy counts.[9] But it didn't matter much

---

9   In the finale of *Middlemarch*, we are told that Tertius Lydgate "once called her his basil plant; and when she asked for an explanation, said that basil was a plant which had flourished wonderfully on a murdered man's brains." Rosamond doesn't suck blood, but she is a spiritual vampire. I wish I had thought of this during my one and only interview for a tenure-track position.

anyway, because the year I graduated, there were exactly three jobs for Victorianists in the entire country. I applied for every position I was remotely qualified for and ended up, as so many of us do, as an adjunct rhetcomp instructor.

In Belmont, I had grown up with a combination of Hungarian and American customs. Some presents were brought by the Baby Jesus on Christmas night, some by Santa Claus on Christmas morning. On Easter, my mother sprinkled me with water and recited poetry I barely understood. We painted eggs with Hungarian embroidery designs. On Saint Patrick's Day, my father and I wore green. We ate corned beef and cabbage with soda bread, and when I was old enough, we always had a Guinness together, although I don't actually like beer. We celebrated my name day on February 6th, the festival date of Szent Dorottya, even though my American birth certificate says Dorothy Nolan.

So when my friend Ildikó Balogh said, "You really should apply for a Fulbright. We always need teachers, especially of American literature. We can't pay enough to keep them—you would not believe how little the government pays university professors," I decided to go for it. Why not? I'd never been to Hungary, and my Hungarian was elementary at best, but the Fulbright program would pay for my housing, and I would have a semester to *not* grade first-year writing.

I had barely settled into my apartment in the 8th district of Budapest when I received an email from Judith Browne.[10] "Dodo," she wrote, "I think you'll want to see this. But don't show it to anyone else, at least not yet—it's top secret at the moment. The publicity department wants to make a big deal of it when it's published."[11]

---

10   Judy, who also studied under John Paul, defended the year after me. She was smarter than I was—she wrote her dissertation on James Joyce, called herself a modernist, and was immediately offered a tenure-track position at Boston College. As long as she offers a survey course on Irish literature every year, she can teach whatever else she wants—last year, she taught "Science Fiction from Shelley to Le Guin" and "Medusa's Daughters: Female Monsters in Popular Fiction."

11   Dodo was a joke between the two of us—from *Middlemarch* and

This was a typescript of the secret diary of Mina Harker, which Judy had received because she was going to write an introduction to the American edition, scheduled to come out from Bedford—a real publisher, not a university press.

"You should write about this in your book," she said. She meant the scholarly book I was supposed to be writing based on my dissertation—which I didn't have time to write because I had to read thirty-six iterations of what ChatGPT thought about Octavia Butler's "Bloodchild."

I read the manuscript in one night, staying up too late, eating grocery store rétes.[12] When I told Ildikó about it, she said, "You should talk to Magdolna Tóth. She's a professor emerita—she retired a few years ago. But she had some sort of theory about Mina Harker. I'm sure she would be happy to talk with you? Perhaps you could start by writing an article on this diary—for example, how it helps us interrogate the official narrative of *Dracula*."

If you look closely, there are quite a lot of places where that narrative interrogates itself.

First, Mina's journal was obviously written to be read—and by whom? By the band of brothers, judging by how often she calls them good, brave, strong—really, it's so over the top that I wonder how they bought it. But then, nineteenth-century men had very high opinions of themselves. So what was Mina's agenda in writing her journal?

On October 2nd, in her secret diary, we get this cryptic message: "I have become the bride of night, of a darkness so bright that it outshines the sun. It runs in my veins and illuminates—everything."

In her journal, she had to convince the band that she was the vampire's victim, but also their ally in defeating him. This was particularly

---

a grad student party where we both got slightly drunk. You had to have been there.

12 Rétes is a Hungarian pastry that usually contains a fruit filling like sour cherries, although it can also contain poppy seeds, sweet cheese, etc. If you've had it, you know how good it is—even the grocery store version. If you haven't, I won't torture you by describing it. I'm not a monster.

important because she had begun to visibly transform into a vampire herself.[13] On October 6th, she goes to Van Helsing and tells him that she has a great idea—if he hypnotizes her, she will use her psychic connection with Dracula to reveal his location and plans. She assures Van Helsing that at certain times, the psychic connection works in only one direction—they can listen in on the Count, but he has no knowledge of what they are doing. Van Helsing agrees, confident that he controls her connection with the vampire. But does he?

The secret diary makes clear that Van Helsing's knowledge of vampires was limited and in some cases incorrect. Most of the vampire "rules" he describes in *Dracula* come from medieval texts on vampirism, such as Herenberg's *Philosophicae et Christianae Cogitationes de Vampiris,* which is basically nonsense. Relying on these sources to fight vampires is like trying to do chemistry by reading the alchemical writings of Sir Isaac Newton.

Why does Mina come up with the idea of acting as a psychic telephone? The diary makes that clear. On October 3rd, Mina writes, "I've convinced him to leave England. I want him safely back in his own country, his own castle. And later—I don't know, I can't think. My head is bursting, as though fireworks are going off inside me. Is this how caterpillars feel, when they turn into butterflies?"

But Van Helsing will not leave well enough alone. When Mina, under "hypnosis," assures him that Dracula is leaving England, he insists that the band of brothers follow the Count. Mina asks why they need to follow the vampire once he has left the country. "Because," Van Helsing tells her, "he can live for centuries and you are but a mortal woman. Time is now to be dreaded—since once he put that mark upon your throat." Here, for once, Van Helsing is correct. After

---

13   A mature vampire looks exactly like an ordinary human being. But the transformation process involves some physical changes, such as pallor and lethargy, not substantially different from having a bad flu or a case of Covid. And of course, the vampire's bite is visible until the extraordinary immunity associated with vampirism kicks in.

vampirism is introduced into the blood, there is no cure. Mina will inevitably continue her transformation. Van Helsing erroneously believes that killing Count Dracula will halt that transformation—but then, in the late nineteenth century, scientists did not fully understand the process of infection. The germ theory of disease was still controversial.[14] We can't blame Van Helsing for misunderstanding certain medical aspects of vampirism. Whether to rescue Mina or for personal aggrandizement (likely both), he is determined to pursue the vampire to his castle.[15]

When the band of brothers gives chase, Mina insists she must go with them so they can continue to protect her against the vampire and she can continue her psychic reportage on his movements. During the voyage, she is the band's primary source of information on the vampire. In the official manuscript of *Dracula*, Mina insists she knows nothing of what happens when Van Helsing "hypnotizes" her; however, the secret diary reveals she is both fully aware in her hypnotic state and transmitting information to the Count. In one entry she writes, "I have told them he is sailing toward us, but he is the master of storms. He will not let them catch him like a rabbit in a trap." Sure enough, a storm blows the ship in which Dracula is traveling off course, and on October 28th he lands in Galatz instead of Varna.[16]

Once Dracula lands, the manuscript records a race across Transylvania between the band of brothers and the Count. Will they catch

---

14   The miasmal theory lingered into the 1890s, and still exists in certain parts of the American South—Louisiana, for example.

15   Van Helsing later advertised himself as "The slayer of Count Dracula, greatest of the Vampires."

16   Of course, not every diary entry is so significant. Some entries show us the ordinary details of a woman's life in the nineteenth century. For example, on October 15th, Mina writes, "Arrived in Varna. The Orient Express is not as comfortable as I had expected. The hotel is adequate, but I had to wash my undergarments in the sink, as there was no laundry service. It would never occur to Jonathan that, it being my time of the month, I might need flannel, hot water . . . Well, I was able to clean everything with the help of the maids. Soon, such things will no longer concern me."

him before he reaches his castle, guarded by his followers, his animals, even his forest? There, everything is on his side.

On October 28th, Seward records that Mina looks more like her old self again. He takes it as a sign that she is no longer under the influence of Count Dracula. Instead, of course, it means she is further along in the transformation process. That day, she makes a presentation—Mina's TED Talk—in which she tells the band of brothers what she believes the vampire will do and how they can catch him. From that point on, Mina dominates the action of *Dracula* while giving all the credit to the band. They do the chasing, but it is she, through the messages she delivers under "hypnosis" and her own suggestions, who tells them where to go and how to get there.[17]

Meanwhile, the entries in the secret diary focus on the landscape of Transylvania. Only here and there do we get indications that something else is going on.

October 31. The hotel at Veresti was rough but good—clean sheets. I could not eat the food—Van Helsing is convinced this is significant, but actually it was just too spicy for me. I seem to have become more sensitive to everything. The sunlight sparkles off the ice on the trees as though they were covered with diamonds, and I am almost blinded.

November 1. The roads are very bad, and we can barely get through.

---

17   As Felicia Fitzroy has pointed out in a blog post, this was the strategy suggested in conduct manuals for young women in the late nineteenth century. "A wife should never *opine* but merely *suggest*," states *A Mother's Advice to her Daughters* by Lady Charlotte Guest. "It is by sweet promptings and insinuations that a woman should make her preferences known. A husband who may instinctively disagree with outright statements or requests, will often be humoured into acquiescence with an indirect manner and liberal praise of his generosity" (qtd. in Fitzroy). Mina is directing the band's action using techniques that would have been taught to upper-class female students at Newnham Ladies' Academy.

The landscape is blanketed with white, as though Mother Holle had shaken out her counterpane. I remember telling Lucy that story—it was her one of her favorites. Sometimes we ride through forests of dark pines whose tops resemble white tents. I can hear a hare stirring under the snow, a fox chuffing as it lopes under the branches, the wings of an owl as it hunts, pine needles falling on the sod. It is as though I have never seen nor smelled before. I am born again.

November 2. We are driving into the Carpathians. As a school-teacher in Newnham, I could never have imagined that I would see such sights. Or was the Mina I am now always in me? Has he mere-ly uncovered the butterfly that was always potentially inside? Snow blankets the earth for miles around us. The villages are few and far between. The inn last night was rude and simple, but I slept well. I al-ways sleep well now. The clothes of the women have pretty embroidery on them. I asked one about a pattern on her blouse, and she drew it for me on a piece of paper. I reproduce it here.[18]

November 2, later. Slowly the land rises. I think we will reach the Borgo Pass today—and then?

November 3. I can hear my sisters calling me. I could travel through this countryside forever, it is so peaceful. This is what I imagine Heav-en looks like—the rocky mountains rising around us, the life of the forest on either side, the sky clear and white and cold, the endless si-lence. Sometimes great falls of snow slide down from the heights with a sound like thunder. How beautiful, how splendid, how sublime.

The chase ends in two acts of horrific violence: the murder of Drac-ula's "brides"[19] by Van Helsing and the killing of Dracula himself by

---

18   The pattern is of tulips shaped like hearts—a common one in that part of Transylvania.

19   This term vastly oversimplifies the vampire family structure. Vampires reproduce asexually, which is not to say that the reproductive

Holmwood, Seward, Morris, and Jonathan Harker.

On the evening of November 4th, Mina is visited by those brides, who materialize by the circle of holy wafers Van Helsing has made around her. That visit is described in the official manuscript. He tells her that within the circle she should be safe, although he fears for her. Mina assures him there is no need to worry. She knows the brides are not there to attack her, and indeed, the November 4th entry in the secret diary reads, "I have always wanted sisters. To think that poor, sweet Lucy could have been like them."

On November 5th, Van Helsing leaves Mina behind in the wafer circle and makes his way to Dracula's castle, where he stakes and decapitates the "brides." He tells us, "hardly had my knife severed the head of each, before the whole body began to melt away and crumble into its native dust."

This is an excellent example of where the official manuscript of Dracula deconstructs itself. We were told, much earlier in the narrative, that vampires are capable of dematerializing, of turning into dust, mist, vapor—let's just say small particles of *something*. We were also told that they must be completely decapitated so they cannot regenerate. The murder of Lucy Westenra in her tomb is described as both time-consuming and thorough.[20] The decapitation of the "brides,"

---

act is not sexual. A vampire, male or female, spreads vampirism through the exchange of blood, creating a new vampire that could be considered its offspring. The blood exchange is also a sexual act, so the vampire offspring is also, in some sense, the vampire's mate. However, although the movie versions always include three vampiric "brides," it is more accurate to call two of the female vampires Dracula's "daughters" and the third his "mother." I should also add that vampire clans are usually matriarchal—despite Dracula's flamboyance, he is not the leader of this particular vampire family.

20   She is first staked while Biblical verses are recited over her, then completely decapitated and her mouth filled with garlic. This final gesture is another grotesque and laughable example of Van Helsing's pseudo-expertise. Many, but not all, vampires love garlic. The only part of this horrific ritual that is at all accurate is the decapitation. The head of a vampire must be completely separated from the body so that the vampiric superimmunity

however, had "hardly happened" before they dematerialize.

Are they actually dispatched, as Van Helsing claims?[21]

A similar question can be asked about the climactic incident of the novel, the killing of the Count. The moment of the killing itself is described by Mina, who is watching it through a pair of binoculars. Dracula is traveling in his usual dramatic fashion, lying in a coffin.[22] Jonathan Harker and Quincy Morris pry open the coffin lid with their knives. Jonathan slashes through Dracula's throat, Quincy Morris thrusts a knife into his heart, the vampire crumbles into dust, and the sun sets on Castle Dracula.[23] Here we have exactly the same problem we had with the incident of the vampire brides. Vampires don't turn into dust when they *die*. They turn into dust when they *escape*.

The clues are all over the manuscript compiled, typed, and revised by Mina. She gathered the various narratives in the final manuscript, deciding which to include and which to leave out. There is evidence that she also altered the contents—Seward's accounts, in particular, do not read like exact transcriptions of phonograph recordings, and of course the original wax cylinders were burned by Dracula, along with all the early documents gathered by the band of brothers. Mina's records are the only ones we have.

If Dracula was not killed by the band of brothers, what then? The

---

cannot operate. If the head is reattached within the first fifteen minutes to half an hour, the vampire's white blood cells may be able to heal the site of separation, just as an ordinary person's body can heal a cut.

21   Gizella is currently living in Prague, where she has become quite a famous artist. Szilvia is one of those YouTube polyglots who makes videos about learning multiple languages, which hardly seems fair—she's had five hundred years to learn them. And Irina works at the Nemzeti Múzeum in Budapest, restoring medieval and Renaissance paintings.

22   This is not, in fact, a necessary mode of vampiric transportation. Vampires can ride in carriages and motorcars, and on the metro, just like everyone else. Some vampires just like to show off.

23   It was John Paul who first pointed out to me how completely unconvincing this is. We don't need the secret diary to tell us that this is not the way to kill vampires.

secret diary gives us one possible answer: in her entry of November 6th, Mina writes, "This is the end. This is the beginning." The rest of the diary records the journey back to England. After that, there are some entries describing life in London, a reference to the birth of Quincy Harker, and then a gap of six years. On the next page, a new entry starts, "We are going to Transylvania. After so many years. What will he think of me now?" The following entries are simply travel details, until one that reads, "Finally. It has been so long. I would like to show him his child."[24] And then, "Tomorrow we go back to England. I told him it might be a long time before I could return again. He said he would wait for me until the stars fall from the sky. Typical romantic nonsense."

There is one final entry in the diary, written years later in ballpoint, which had become a popular replacement for the old-fashioned fountain pen. It is dated April 3rd, 1921, and it says only, "Finally." Later that year, Mina died and was apparently buried next to her husband.

But was Mina Harker buried in the churchyard of Christ Church, Huddersfield next to Jonathan? That is the question I asked myself as I boarded the tram to Buda, where Magdolna Tóth lived.

I got off at Móricz Zsigmond körtér and walked the rest of the way. Professor Tóth lived in a much nicer part of the city than I did, on my Fulbright housing stipend.[25]

"This is Dorothy Nolan," I said into the intercom. "Ildikó Balogh sent me?"

---

24   The child referenced here must be Quincy Harker. In what sense is Quincy also Dracula's child? Vampirism passes through the blood. The internal evidence of the text suggests that Mina's blood already carried the vampiric strain when she became pregnant with Quincy. It would have passed through the placental barrier to her fetus. Quincy's status as the son of both Jonathan Harker and Dracula is typical of the ambiguous, paradoxical nature of vampirism.

25   The stipend is actually quite generous, but rent has gone up so much in Budapest that even American money is no longer enough. As Karl Marx pointed out, the ultimate vampire is capitalism.

The front door buzzed open.

The elevator, an ornate metal cage that probably dated to the early twentieth century and lurched a few times on the way up, took me to the second floor.[26] Before I could knock on the only door on that landing, it opened.

"Come in, come in," said what I would describe as a little old Hungarian woman if she were not a professor emerita of English literature. She looked like an illustration of Baba Yaga, with gray hair coiled in a braid around her head and a crocheted lace shawl around her shoulders. She had dark eyes as piercing as those of a falcon or an academic search committee chair. "I will get you some house shoes," she said. Her accent was much stronger than Ildikó's. "I hope these fit?"

I took off my shoes and put on a pair of felt slippers. They were very warm. I wondered if I should thank her in Hungarian, but suddenly felt self-conscious about my own strong accent, so I murmured a thanks in English.

"Ildikó told me about your so interesting project—this article you intend to write on Mina's diary. And she said you have a copy in PDF? There is someone I would like you to meet. Come, I made pogácsa. Do you like pogácsa? But you must—Ildikó said your mother is Hungarian."

Someone she would like me to meet? I had assumed I was there to meet *her*.

"Once," she continued, leading me down the entrance hall, "I thought of writing a monograph on *Dracula* myself, from a Central European perspective. But at the time it was almost impossible to present at foreign conferences, and difficult to research anything in English. You and Ildikó have no idea know how much easier it is for you, with this internet. Although research is difficult even now from Hungary! Yesterday I was attempting to download an article from JSTOR but the computer said it was not included in the university's—what is it called? Subscription, its subscription. Can you imagine?"

---

26   Third floor, for Americans.

I was not sure what to say. Here I was, following a character from a fairy tale, and she was talking about JSTOR access.

"In here, please," she said, waving toward an arched doorway. "I will go get the coffee."

I stepped into what was obviously Dr. Tóth's living room, although it seemed to function more as a combination office and library. There were bookshelves on every wall, up to the high ceiling. They were filled with books and entire series of academic journals. A sofa and two armchairs were mostly covered with file folders of notes and photocopied articles, so you could barely see their brown corduroy upholstery. Near two tall windows was a wooden table covered with an embroidered cloth and set for an afternoon snack, Hungarian style—with cheeses and cold spreads and pickled salads, and the savory biscuits called pogácsa. It was the only surface in the room that did not have research materials on it.

Beside the table stood a man, somewhere between thirty and fifty, with ginger hair and an equally ginger mustache, dressed in a tweed jacket over jeans—typical professor wear.

"Dr. Nolan?" he said. I was startled to hear him speak with a British accent. "I'm Quincy Harker."

This is the point at which Peer Reviewer #2 will reject this article. Peer Reviewer #1 gave up on it long ago, when I first started describing my childhood. This isn't what an academic article should sound like, is it?[27]

"Dr. Tóth tells me you have a PDF copy of my mother's diary. We heard that the British Library purchased it at the Sotheby's auction. I tried to contact someone there and was told there might be some sort of special exhibition next year, but no one seems to know for certain.

---

27   When I asked Mina for permission to write this article, she said, "Go right ahead, my dear. First of all, no academic journal will accept it, and second of all, no one will believe you, just as they didn't believe what I wrote in my manuscript. Women writing about monsters. Who would listen to us?"

And it seems they are planning to publish the diary. Do you happen to know when?"

"Quincy Harker?" I said. "Are you a descendant—"

He smiled. He had a rather charming, lopsided smile.

"I did some research on you, Dr. Nolan. There was a profile of you in a university article on your work with ESL students. Since your father is Irish and your mother is Hungarian, you should be able to believe seven impossible things before breakfast. Or at least one."

"I don't understand," I said. Although I did, sort of. I mean, I'd written an entire doctoral dissertation on vampires, so I couldn't plead innocence—I wasn't Mary Pickford. I just didn't want to slip completely out of the ordinary narrative of everyday life unless I had no other choice. I didn't want to sound insane unless it could be proven that insanity was the new sanity.

"My mother knows she can't get the diary back, although she hates the idea of her private thoughts belonging to someone else, even if it's the British Library. But she would like to look at the diary again before it's made public in case it contains anything that could be dangerous for our family. She has an excellent memory, but she can't remember exactly what she wrote over a century ago. She would like to know if you would be willing to show her the PDF."

I stared at him, not sure what to say. On one hand, I had always believed there were things in the world outside our ordinary reality, or I would not have gone into Gothic Studies. On the other, I had not expected them to be so prosaic. Mina Harker's son standing in the middle of a typical professor's book-strewn living room, in jeans and a tweed jacket, was a bit much. I suspected some sort of trick, but who would go to so much trouble to get a PDF of a document that was going to be published in a few months anyway?

"Here is the coffee," said Magdolna Tóth, carrying three miniscule cups on a silver tray. Clearly, this was going to be straight-up espresso. Well, I needed it. "Now, you must sit and eat. The pogácsa is fresh—I bought it at the market it this morning."

"Magdi néni," said Quincy, "Dr. Nolan is understandably skeptical. How can I prove to her that I am who I say I am?"

"You know how," she said, then added disapprovingly, "but don't get blood on my books."

"I hope you don't faint easily," said Quincy. "This may be a bit unpleasant."[28] He took off his jacket and rolled up one sleeve. Then, he took a pocketknife out of his jeans pocket, and before I could tell him not to do whatever he was about to, he cut a long slit down one forearm. The blood welled and oozed out of the cut—but did not spill. Before it could, the cut healed itself again, as though someone had zipped up his arm. There was no scar.

"All right, that's impressive," I said. "I sort of believe you. Mostly."

"Then you'll email me a copy of the PDF? It's quincy dot harker at gmail dot com."

"No," I said, shaking my head for emphasis. My mother says I'm too impulsive and sometimes don't stop to think. But I had been thinking furiously throughout his demonstration. "I won't email it to you, but I will print a paper copy and give it—personally, I mean—to your mother."

He looked at me as though surprised, and then laughed. "Half Hungarian, half Irish. I should have known you would be trouble."

"I am both trouble and hungry," I said. "Dr. Tóth, thank you, everything looks absolutely wonderful. Could you tell me about your research? And how you came to meet Mr. Harker?"

It did, in fact, turn out to be a wonderful meal, with the best pogácsa I've tasted in Hungary. I particularly liked a ewe cheese spread flavored with paprika, as well as the little crescents filled with ground walnuts.[29] Quincy Harker had only coffee, which was as strong as I had anticipated.

---

28 This statement, more than anything else, would have convinced me that he was born in the nineteenth century. Women don't generally faint nowadays—unless they're intermittent fasting.

29 These are called kifli.

"I knew his mother before I met him," said Dr. Tóth. "When I was a young academic first doing research on *Dracula*, I gave a presentation at a conference, and afterward she came up to me—this very elegant woman, very educated, with quite good Hungarian. She corrected some of my interpretations. Then we became friends, and we even wrote a paper together. I can email it to you, but it's in Hungarian. As you may imagine, it was very useful for my research, having such a friend—although unfortunately I could not cite her as a source. Take some more—your plate is almost empty. Or more coffee?"[30]

"Mr. Harker still hasn't told me whether he intends to introduce me to his mother," I said.

"More coffee for me, please, Magdi," said Quincy Harker. He looked at me with an expression of wry amusement. "First, call me Quincy, and second, do I have a choice?"

That evening, I prepared for a trip to the mountains—I put a sweater into my bag in case it might get cold and added an umbrella in case of rain. The next morning, Quincy picked me up in a gray Mercedes that looked like every other gray Mercedes on the streets of Budapest.

"I brought a picnic," he said. "Mostly for you. It's a long drive, and we should stop along the way."

A picnic? Surely this wasn't a *date*. And then he smiled at me in a way that made me wonder if perhaps it might be. He was an attractive man, particularly considering his age. He looked very good for a centenarian.[31]

---

30   Hopefully, once my Hungarian is fluent enough, I can translate some of Dr. Tóth's papers into English. They're better than most of the material I read on the gothic, and they deserve to be read by an English audience. It's an impossible language, but I have a lot more time now that I'm no longer teaching, and Szilvia is helping me.

31   Quincy thinks I put that in to tease him. And he's right, of course.

When we reached the foothills of the mountains—the Mátra mountain range in the north of Hungary—we stopped at the ruins of a medieval church for a picnic. We had driven what Hungarians call "far" and what Americans call their morning commute. It was a beautiful spring day—in Boston, in April, I would still have been wearing a winter coat, but in Hungary the wild cherry trees were already in bloom. We sat on the remains of what had once been the paved floor of the nave. Here and there, grass and clover poked through the paving stones, and there were violets growing by the stone walls.

He had packed bread, butter, pickles, and slices of mangalica ham.[32] He put slices of ham onto his own plate.

"So vampires do eat," I said.

"People with vampirism," he said.[33] "And yes, we do eat—in our own way. Think of me as an obligate carnivore, like a cat. Or as someone with coeliac disease, except the list of things I can't eat is infinitely long. That caused a lot of problems, when I was a child growing up in Yorkshire. My mother had to tell my teachers that I was allergic to everything."

"And do you really drink blood?" This seemed like an insane conversation to be having on a peaceful April morning, with the sun shining down on the ruins, casting their shadows on the grass. Bees were buzzing among the clover flowers.

"Yes, really, although it's a lot more boring than it sounds, mostly leftover blood from the meat processing industry. It doesn't have to be

---

32   Mangalica ham comes from a special breed of Hungarian pigs that are basically wild boars—or they look like wild boars, with their thick, curly coats. One good thing about being a vampire, I suppose, is that you don't need to worry about getting heart disease from eating fatty cured meats.

33   This was him teasing me, although I wasn't sure at the time. Most people with vampirism prefer to be called vampires. The most accurate way to think about vampirism is as a blood-borne pathogen that results in a chronic disease. On one hand, it gives the bearer what we might consider superpowers. On the other, it changes the bearer's physiognomy in a fundamental and sometimes detrimental way.

human blood, no matter what you learned watching *Buffy the Vampire Slayer*. You would have seen than in America, yes?"

I nodded, although by the time I watched *Buffy*, it was streaming on Netflix. When it first came out, my idea of a vampire was Count von Count on *Sesame Street*.

"But tell me about yourself, Dr. Nolan."[34]

"Like what? You already know I live in Boston. I'm an adjunct professor of freshman composition, I'm here on a Fulbright—"

"Not those sorts of things. What's your favorite book? Or your favorite food? What do you like to do when you're not teaching? Do you have hobbies? By the way, I hate the word hobbies. It used to come from the word hobbyhorse, and meant something you ride without getting anywhere."

Seriously, this was the conversation he wanted to have? All right, then. I made myself a bread, butter, and ham sandwich. "I don't have hobbies—I used to crochet, but I was never any good at it. Not compared to my mother. She can make all sorts of things, like that shawl Dr. Tóth was wearing." The sandwich was good, better than I had expected.[35] "What else? Oh, my favorite book—I don't have a favorite. But I've read the Oz books a million times—all of the L. Frank Baum ones. And my favorite food—chocolate? Or cherries. Or chocolate with cherries.

"Ah, *The Wizard of Oz*—about a magical, inaccessible land. Do you think that's because of your name, or because you come from an immigrant family? In a sense, you've returned to Oz."

"Thank you for the psychoanalysis, Dr. Harker!" I was not particularly interested in being analyzed in this way. I was the one with the PhD in literature. I could do my own analyzing, thank you.

"Dr. Harker is my mother—I'm a humble BA myself. My favorite book is probably *The Wind in the Willows*, which I read over and over

---

34   Teasing again. We were already on a first-name basis. That had been established during the drive.
35   I had grown up with the American assumption that ham sandwiches should be topped with mustard.

again as a child. My favorite food—I don't know. Can you have a favorite food when all you've known is a diet appropriate for a hunting dog? I could say that my favorite is rabbit, but in the end it all tastes the same. You know, I didn't choose this condition. When I was growing up, I tried desperately to eat the sorts of things other children ate. But I threw it all up—Yorkshire pudding, steamed spinach, stewed prunes, vanilla ice cream. Nothing stayed down and everything made me sick." He sounded bitter.

"I'm sorry," I said. And I was—imagine a childhood without ice cream.[36]

"I told you, vampirism is a disease. At least, that's the way I've experienced it." He stared at the ground—either he was contemplating his strange childhood or he had taken a sudden deep interest in clover. He was definitely no longer flirting with me. I finished my sandwich to the sound of bees buzzing in the sunlit silence. When I was done, he stood up and offered me his hand. "Come on, Dorothy. From here we have to drive up into the mountains. Let's go meet my mother."

"Mountains," by the way, are an exaggeration. The Mátra are not mountains in the way the Carpathians are. They are mountains relative to Hungary, which is generally a flat country, with hills here or there to vary the landscape. We drove up and up on winding roads carved out of the forested hillsides. On my passenger side, I could see a wall of earth and rock where the mountain had been sliced through to make the road, held together with the roots of trees that grew, stubby and gnarled, at the tops of the steep road cuts. Between those twisting brown roots grew stunted shrubs and tough wildflowers with white blossoms like stars. On the driver's side, the ground fell away. I could see a forested valley, across it the distant hills, and above them a blue sky with puffed white clouds floating on empty air[37]—the same empty

---

36   And sports. Despite loving football (the European kind), Quincy could never participate on school teams or even pickup games because if he were injured, he would heal too quickly.

37   They reminded me of the whipped egg whites floating on custard

air we would be floating on if the car swerved across the road and pitched down the cliff. Unfortunately, I have an overactive imagination and a fear of heights. But Quincy drove safely enough—I could feel the Mercedes hugging each curve. He drove without speaking, except once to point out, on a rare bit of road that ran between two equally flat and forested sections, a doe and her fawn in the undergrowth.

Up and up we drove, until at last he said, "Almost there." He turned into a gravel drive I had not noticed between the trees and drove for another minute or so through the forest, with the wheels crunching on gravel.

There was at the end of the drive, which emerged from the forest and made a doughnut-shaped circle in front of a house. It was an old stone house, almost a castle in miniature with gothic, or more likely pseudo-gothic, details. Its diamond-paned windows caught the after-noon light. In front of the house, on the steps leading down from a portico, stood a woman in a dark knee-length dress.

"Mother always knows when I'm coming," said Quincy. "Psychic connection, you know. It was one of the worst parts of my twenties. Imagine being twenty and having your mother always in your head. I did quite a lot of drugs to avoid it. Heroin, mostly—you could buy it in the drug stores, in those days. I don't know if I should have told you that, Dr. Nolan."

I didn't know what to say—except *Stop calling me Dr. Nolan*, which would have been obnoxious after such a confession. Clearly a vampiric childhood was the sort of thing one needed therapy for— maybe a century's worth of therapy.

After parking in front of the portico and trying to open the car door for me—I was already halfway out when he came to the pas-senger side—he greeted the woman on the steps with a kiss on both cheeks. "Mum, I've brought you Dr. Nolan, who is holding the man-

---

in a dessert called madártej (which means bird's milk) that my mother used to make for Hungarian Christmas.

uscript of your diary hostage. Here she is—and I suggest you watch out, because she's tougher than she looks. She has been listening to me so patiently that, in a lapse of common sense and good taste, I've been boring her with sad tales of my underprivileged childhood."

The woman on the steps looked at me intently, as though making some sort of judgment. She had dark brown hair caught up in a bun at the nape of her neck. What I had thought was a dress turned out, on closer inspection, to look very much like a navy Chanel suit, somewhat frayed at the cuffs but still elegant.[38] She looked about her son's age—I would have put her closer to fifty than forty, simply because there was a look around her eyes that seemed to say, *We've seen a lot.* And if this was really Mina Harker, I bet she had.

"You're going to have to forgive Quincy, Dr. Nolan," she said. "Sometimes, especially when he's been emotional about something, he talks the most complete nonsense, like a character out of a Monty Python sketch. I think it's a British response. Please come in, and excuse me—I was on a Zoom call. I'm on the board of a foundation—we fund artists, often ones that speak out against the Hungarian government, and we had a meeting this morning. Can I get you some tea?"

"She's right, you know," Quincy whispered. "So please ignore me about fifty percent of the time. The other fifty percent, I'm relatively sensible." I gave him a skeptical glance and shook my head—this was no time for banter. Then, I followed his mother into a room that looked like a medieval hall turned into the living room of an English country house. It had a stone fireplace with two sofas on either side, covered in faded burgundy brocade. On one of them lay a large white dog—a kuvasz, I later learned.[39]

"Lila, off!" said Mina. The dog turned its head and stared at her, then with obvious reluctance, as though protesting eviction from its rightful place, climbed down from the sofa with deliberate slowness.

---

38   It was, in fact, a Chanel suit, from when Chanel meant Coco herself.
39   The kuvasz is a Hungarian breed used to guard flocks—and people.

"Please, sit down. Or would you like to explore a bit? This house is very interesting. It's an early nineteenth-century imitation, of course, but quite a good one—with a secret staircase in the library. Most of the real medieval buildings in Hungary were destroyed long ago. The history of this country consists of almost incessant warfare. Or you might like to see the garden? Quin, show Dr. Nolan around."

"Please, call me Dorothy," I said.

"Show Dorothy around while I change into something less official, and I'll bring the tea. I know I don't need to dress up for Zoom calls, but I still feel as though I should, somehow. Is Lady Grey all right? I prefer it to Earl Grey myself. Once upon a time we had servants. Now I have an administrative assistant, and her job is much more important than mine—among other things, she keeps all the computers talking to one another. I'll be back in a few minutes."

"We've been given our orders," said Quincy. "Excuse my mother— she's the boss, so she's used to being bossy. Shall I give you the grand or not-so-grand tour?"

"Not-so-grand for now, please," I said. "At the moment I'm feeling a little overwhelmed. Although I would like to see the secret staircase at some point. I always wanted one of those."

"Then come this way, Dorothy-not-Dr. Nolan." He smiled at me— he looked quite handsome when he smiled, and he seemed in a better mood than he had on the drive. It occurred to me that living for more than a century might make one deeply cynical. Immortality might not be a gift after all.

I followed him through several other grand but somewhat shabby rooms. In one of them hung the portrait of a man in what looked like a hussar's jacket made of black fabric with a lot of gold cording, as well as a fur collar and cuffs. He had thick, curling black hair that hung down to his collar, fierce black brows, one of those Roman noses, and a black mustache.

"My father," said Quincy. "One of my fathers. He's currently in Belgium, meeting with some committee of the European Parliament. I don't follow politics as closely as I should, which is the one thing he, quite rightly, shouts at me about. But like Lila, his bark is worse than his bite. Of course, he doesn't go about so gorgeously arrayed anymore."

"So he didn't die—" I said.

Quincy looked at me with surprise. "You never believed that, did you?"

"No, I never did. It just never made sense."[40]

"Well, let's leave my édesapa[41] to stare at dusty furniture and go out into the garden. That sounds sarcastic, but we're actually on very good terms. We get on better than I did with the father who gave me the genes for orange hair and green eyes, like one of those marmalade tomcats. We were always quarreling. Oh hello, here's Zita. How are you, girl?"

Zita was a white dog that looked exactly like Lila, and just that minute Lila came out to join us—the two white dogs greeted each other, nose to nose. Then Zita sniffed me up and down. Clearly, of the two, she was the more conscientious guard.

"They're sisters," said Quincy. "Strictly speaking, to present a properly vampiric image, we should have wolves loping around the property. But I don't think the Hungarian government would appreciate our keeping endangered animals as pets. So the two of you will have to do, won't you, Zita?"

She looked at him and barked, almost as though she understood—or as though she wanted a treat. When one was not forthcoming, she turned toward the open doorway and looked back at us, clearly expecting us to follow her.

"You had the same thought, did you?" said Quincy. "Then the garden it is."

We followed Zita through a mudroom with pairs of dirty boots

---

40   See my analysis of Count Dracula's death earlier in this article. Nevertheless, I was glad to have Quincy's confirmation of what I had believed ever since taking "Modes of Gothic Fiction" with John Paul.

41   Hungarian for "dear father."

lined up by the wall, and then out the door. After the dimness of the house, I blinked in the bright sunlight. The walled garden directly behind the house had once been formal, with straight stone paths between flowering beds, but it had been allowed to grow wild. Perennials spilled over the paths, their leaves and flowers forming haphazard arrangements. Annuals had reseeded themselves wherever they wished—in the middle of the perennial beds, in the cracks of the walls. At the center of the garden was a stone fountain presided over by a nymph holding a water jar, although the fountain was empty and the nymph no longer spilled her water into its stone basin, which was now covered with moss. To one side, close to the wall, was an ancient pergola covered with wisteria just starting to bloom. It must have been as old as the house—its vines looked almost too heavy for the iron lattice that bore its weight. Under the pergola was a table surrounded by four chairs with the sort of all-weather cushions sold at a home goods store like OBI.

"This is beautiful," I said. "It's all beautiful."

"And no bats," he said, "except at twilight. You'll see them then, catching mosquitoes. Shall we sit or go on? There's a gate at the end of the garden that leads to a very nice view."

"Let's sit," I said. "Your mother promised us some tea."

"And so I did," said Mina. I jumped a bit—I had not noticed her walking up behind us.[42] "Lady Grey, with milk and sugar for those who consume."[43] She had changed into a striped blue-and-white sweater over a pair of blue jeans. She looked the absolute least you could look like a vampire—more like a fancy soccer mom.

"Served by Countess Dracula herself," said Quincy.

"Are you, actually?" I said. "Countess Dracula, I mean?"

She set down the tea tray she had been carrying, which looked

---

42   In literature, vampires are notoriously quiet—they sneak up on you. In this case, Mina was just wearing sneakers.
43   Vampires can drink both tea and coffee, but milk and sugar are off-limits.

quintessentially English, with a silver teapot, matching sugar bowl and creamer, and three porcelain cups. "Stop it, Zita. Dogs don't get tea around here, and the biscuits are for Dorothy. If you're a jó kutya,[44] I'll give you a treat later."

Mina sat in one of the chairs and crossed her legs. "Technically, I suppose I am. We did get legally married at a government office in Budapest. In those days, a woman automatically assumed her husband's citizenship. During the Socialist era there was a much greater emphasis on having the proper papers. I didn't want to be deported, so I put on my best suit—what they call a kosztüm here—and pillbox hat, with a little veil, and we promised to love and honor each other until death do us part. If it ever does. My marriage certificate says I'm Drakula Vladimírné, which sounds ridiculous, doesn't it? You should have sold film rights to that, Quin—*Bride of Dracula*. Wouldn't that make a good movie?"

"You could have been played by Ava Gardner," said Quincy.

"I think *not*," said Mina. "Audrey Hepburn for me, thank you very much. Now, I'm going to pour out—milk or sugar for you, Dorothy? Or both? And if you don't think it's terribly rude of me, I'm going to get down to business. What would you like for that manuscript?"

I stared at her in surprise. "I don't want anything for it. You know it's going to be published anyway, right? All I can give you is an advance copy. I just wanted to meet you, that's all. To see if you were really real."

Mina smiled, clearly amused. When she smiled, I could see the resemblance between mother and son. "Am I really real? Sometimes I'm not sure myself. Well, it seems I misjudged you, my dear. I've seen quite a lot of the worst of humanity, including more greed and cruelty than I care to remember. I'm used to people wanting things from me— including immortality. Quite a lot of people want to become vampires

---

44   Good dog, in Hungarian. Zita is generally a good dog, but she can't resist human food. And, unlike a vampire, she is not an obligate carnivore.

until they realize what it actually entails. Then, they mostly go home to live their ordinary lives. Once, I asked Magda if she wanted to become a vampire. She told me her husband is waiting for her in Heaven, and she's looking forward to seeing him again. Basically, no thank you. So if you don't want anything—"

"Here you go," I said, pulling the PDF I had printed out of my bag. "It's a little creased—I accidentally sat on a corner of it during our picnic."

She took it from me and looked at the first page—*The Secret Diary of Mina Harker*, edited and introduced by Judith Browne, Bedford Books, 2025. Then she flipped past the pages of household accounts. "Incredible how cheap linen pillowcases were in those days," she said, as though to herself. "This brings back memories." She was silent for a moment, then looked up at us. "Children, have your tea and enjoy the garden. I'm going to read this in my office. I'll call you when I want you."

"Well, that's Mother," said Quincy after she had elegantly left us, taking the manuscript with her. "After tea, would you like the rest of the tour?"

About an hour later, we had explored the house from top to bottom, including the secret staircase, followed by Zita, who had either decided that she liked me or that she could guard the house from me by constantly butting against my hand so I would scratch her head. We were in the library looking at a collection that seemed to range from medieval Bibles to modern science fiction, in Latin, German, and Hungarian.

"I like you, Dorothy Nolan," he said, looking at me almost too seriously. "I can be a terrible misanthrope sometimes—but I like you very much." Then he looked up, like a hunting dog that has just smelled a rabbit, and said, "Mother wants to talk to you. Psychic telephone. Go down the main stairs, turn left, and you'll find her office."

I like you too, Quincy Harker, I thought. *You're a bit of a mess, but then so am I, and I don't even have to deal with being a vampire.*

Mina Harker's office was the least gothic place I could have imagined, within the context of a pseudo-gothic castle. It looked onto the garden through diamond-paned windows with pointed arches, but the wallpaper was a cheerful blue with butterflies on it, and the furniture was both practical and comfortable. There was a large desk with a desktop monitor and keyboard, a printer stand with a combination printer/scanner, several file cabinets, and bookshelves filled mostly with modern art books interspersed with file boxes. In one corner was one of those deep armchairs that are so perfect for reading, with a blue linen slipcover. It looked as though it had come from IKEA.[45] The armchair was occupied by Lila, curled comfortably next to an embroidered throw pillow shaped like a large multicolored butterfly.[46] She lifted her head when we entered.

"Come in, Dorothy," said Countess Dracula.[47] She swiveled around in her ergonomic desk chair. The PDF was in her hand. "Take a seat, if you don't mind some dog hairs. If you do, I can put a blanket over the armchair. It's my reading chair, and after I sit in it, I always find a sprinkling of them on my outfit—like doggy snow."

"I don't mind," I said, thinking that my blouse and jeans, which I had chosen as a compromise (blouse in case the picnic was indeed a date, and jeans because we would be sitting on the ground), could scarcely be considered an *outfit*. I patted Lila on the head as she relinquished her place in the armchair. Mina had not commanded her to give it up—unless she had done so psychically?[48] The kuvasz looked back at me reproachfully as I took her place.

---

45   It had. With the dogs, Mina later told me, washable slipcovers are absolutely necessary.

46   The Fjäril pillow from IKEA.

47   Actually, she hates it when I call her that, and I'm doing it here only because the contrast struck me as so ironic: the vampire in her Pinterest-worthy home office.

48   Vampires can in fact form psychic bonds with animals. But Lila is very smart, smarter than her sister. She knew when she was not wanted and politely, although reluctantly, showed herself out.

"Then please sit. I have a question I want to ask you."

Like the elephant's child in that story by Kipling, I have insatiable curiosity. But I didn't want to say *Sure, ask away.* Mina is not the sort of person one is flippant with. I sat in the armchair, which smelled a bit like *eau de dog*, and waited.

She put the PDF on her lap and leaned back in her chair. "First, I want to thank you for bringing me this, although it was painful to read—it brought back the past so vividly. I can still remember those little inns along our route through the Carpathians . . ."

"Quincy said you were worried it might contain something dangerous to your family," I said, meaning of course her vampire family. "Does it?" I hoped the question wasn't too personal, but I had to satisfy at least part of my insatiable curiosity.

"No, not in the way you're thinking." She looked at me intently for a moment, then said, as though making a confession, "The truth is, I was worried there might be something in the diary—something I wrote long ago—that could hurt Vlad or Szilvi or Rina, or even Gizella, although she's pretty tough. She's been through more than the rest of us, including the disintegration of Pannonia, the Roman province that predated the coming of the Magyars.[49] And I was worried about Quin, of course. He's more sensitive than he seems. Under his sophisticated cynicism, there's a child who was bullied in school for being different from his classmates. It's a strange thing that no matter how long you live, you don't become any less yourself. All the Minas I have ever been are still in me. Including the one who, several lifetimes ago, fell in love with a young lawyer named Jonathan Harker. But it seems I didn't write as much as I feared—the important entries are rather cryptic.

---

49   Vampire families are too dispersed and decentralized to keep official records, but as far as I know, Gizella is the oldest vampire still in existence. Despite the popular notion that vampires are immortal, the average lifespan of a vampire has historically been only about two to three hundred years. In addition to dying in various vampire hunts in the days when people still believed in vampires, they tend to participate in wars and politics, which are easy ways to get even a vampire killed.

English professors will have a wonderful time trying to interpret them. No offense." She smiled.

"None taken," I said. "Anyway, I'm an adjunct professor. That's almost a different species."

"Yes, I know. That's why I'd like to ask—" She hesitated. "You see, I would like to tell my version of the story. The real version, or as much of it as I can. This may sound narcissistic to you, but I've watched every film version of *Dracula*. I think Winona Ryder does quite a good job of being me—she's a lot like I was, at that age. I've read all the modern novels that try to retell the story—several from what is supposed to be my point of view. I've even read the scholarly articles on *Dracula*, although there's nothing quite as tedious as academic prose, unless written by someone like Magda, whose primary aim is clarity rather than tenure. There's one scholar—Bluebottle, Bottfly, something like that. I found him especially infuriating.[50] So many interpretations, and none of them correct."

"In what way—" I started to ask.

"For example, this great romance between Dracula and Mina in the Francis Ford Coppola version. It wasn't a great romance, not at first—he was attracted to Lucy, and she to him. How could he not be? She was so smart, the best student I ever had. Her parents had arranged her marriage to Arthur—Lord Holmwood. But Lucy wanted more than to be a society hostess. She used to talk about women travelers who had gone to all sorts of places—who had climbed the Himalayas, or ridden across the desert in Egypt. She wanted those things for herself, and Vlad promised she could have them. She chose vampirism because it seemed preferable to the conscribed society life her parents had relegated her to."

"Then the letters she wrote to you, the ones you quoted in *Dracula*—"

"Oh, Lucy didn't write those," said Mina, smiling. "I modeled them

---

50   I'm quite sure Mina meant Bottheimer.

on some popular novel—I don't even remember the title. Something like *Estella Makes Her Debut*, one of those novels about young women in society.[51] Absolute trash. The students at Newnham Ladies' Academy weren't allowed to read novels, but of course they snuck them into the school and shared them around. I knew that everything I put into the manuscript of *Dracula* was going to be read by Jonathan and the others, especially that sadist Van Helsing. At every point, I tried to misdirect them, outwit them—to save the people I cared about. In those letters, I manufactured the perfect Lucy they wanted her to be. But she was nothing like that. She was brave and adventurous. Vlad saw that in her, and of course she was very beautiful as well. He's more of a family man than you would expect, but he has always appreciated beautiful women.

"And then, when Jonathan told me what he and those *good, brave* men had done, how they had murdered her in the most grotesque and horrifying way while she was still in the middle of her transformation—really, like killing an infant—I could have torn them apart myself with my bare hands.

"That was how we began, Vlad and I. We both wanted revenge. Infecting me with vampirism was part of his revenge on the men who had killed Lucy, and I welcomed the infection if it would give me the power to take my own revenge against them. Everything after that, we planned together. But in England, he did not have the necessary resources to deal with the vampire hunters—for him, it had begun as a business trip, and he was not prepared for battle. We thought, perhaps if we could lure the men to Transylvania, we could take our revenge there. As we collaborated, something grew between us. At first, it was

---

51   I was able to locate this book on the Internet Digital Archives. It's actually titled *Estella Fitzgerald*, by "A Lady," published in 1886 by Blackwell's. In it, the titular Estella, the daughter of an impoverished gentleman who can't provide her with a dowry, makes her debut, entrances society with her beauty and goodness, becomes engaged to a Lord Dervish, and writes a series of letters about how grateful she is for his regard. She marries him and becomes Lady Dervish, then dies beautifully of consumption.

a sort of camaraderie, since we had both cared for Lucy and lost her. Then came friendship and the desire to protect each other—I did not want them to hurt him, he did not want them to hurt me. Then finally, something more. He's an attractive man, in a completely different way to Jonathan, whom I thought I had known and loved until he murdered my friend. With Vlad, I experienced a part of myself I had not known existed."

She smiled. "Sorry, that might be too much information, or TMI, as the younger generation calls it. I try to keep up with contemporary slang—it's easier now, with YouTube and TikTok. At some point we realized we had fallen in love. Then the important thing was not revenge anymore, but being together. We talked about living in his castle, about having a life there among the mountains. I told him we needed a new plan. I would help him escape from England, and we would make the vampire hunters believe he had been destroyed. Then, after they had been thrown off the scent, I would join him in Transylvania. At least, that was what we planned, then . . ."

Mina looked down at the PDF in her lap, as though remembering.

"But you didn't, did you? You had a whole life with Jonathan." I leaned forward in the armchair. "Why—"

"Because three months after the Count was supposedly destroyed, when I was back in England with Jonathan, pretending to be a dutiful, ordinary wife, I found myself pregnant with Quincy. That wasn't supposed to happen. Vampirism is the best contraceptive—it disrupts the human reproductive cycle.[52] I don't have an explanation for how it happened, except that it was still early in my transformation—I had been infected only a few months before. But here I was, pregnant with a child—I could not simply take him away from his biological father.[53]

---

52   Magda says that for female vampires, this process resembles menopause, although without the hot flashes.
53   Technically, Count Dracula is also Quincy's biological father, since vampiric reproduction is a biological phenomenon. But I understand what Mina meant here.

And once Quin was born, even in those first few weeks, it was clear that he had particular weaknesses, particular sensitivities and needs. I could not simply travel with him across Europe. I did take him, once, to see Vlad—he was about six at the time, too young to understand who the man in the black cloak with the mustache was, although I think he understood *something*. He was always an observant, intelligent child.

"Then, when I thought Quin might be old enough, war broke out and it became impossible to travel. So I lived my life with Jonathan, the man who had participated in murdering Lucy and believed to the end of his life that he had been heroic in ridding the world of Count Dracula. Soon after he died, Quin held a lovely funeral for me. I watched it from behind a black veil, and then I left for Transylvania."

"How old was Quincy when you told him?" I asked. My own childhood had generally been free of trauma, except for the usual problems of a bookish child who liked to read and was bad at sports, the perpetual victim in dodgeball. I had never felt as though I belonged anywhere except in books, but that's a common feeling among future literature majors. It was hard for me to imagine what Quincy's childhood must have been like, let alone his teenage years. Being a teenager is hellish enough without the extra burden of vampirism.[54]

"Fifteen, sixteen? I had to explain to him why he had so many allergies, why he was anemic, why he could hear things bats could hear, smell things dogs could smell. Why when he scraped his knee, it healed so quickly. He didn't take it well. He rebelled for a long time—you should have seen him in the punk scene in London in the 1970s. He had his hair in a mohawk for a while, and he would get angry because

---

54   Contemporary young adult fiction, for example the *Twilight* series, has created an image of the romantic teenage vampire. In reality, there are very few teenage vampires—all the ones I've met were infected as adults, and even the few infected in their teens wouldn't stay teenagers for long. In YA novels, the "teenagers" are hundreds of years old. Their "romances" with ordinary high school students are pedophilic and predatory. There is very little romantic about vampirism—in Quincy's unusual situation, growing up with vampirism was like having a chronic and sometimes debilitating illness.

whenever he pierced his ears, eyebrows, whatever, they would immediately heal. His body rejected the dyes in tattoos, and the images would disappear within days. He didn't speak to me for about thirty years."

"But you seem on good terms now," I said.

"Well." She smiled. "That took a lot of therapy, both by himself and with me. For a while, we went to a very smart woman in Budapest—do you know family systems therapy? She modified it to deal with our very unusual family . . . but that's his story to tell. What I want to do, Dorothy, is tell *my* story. So what I want to ask is—"

"Yes?" Finally, I was going to find out what this was all about.

She looked down at the PDF for a moment, then said, "I'd like to write my memoirs, and I need an assistant. Partly to help with research and editing, because the foundation takes up so much of my time. It's been a long time since I've done anything like this—most of my writing now is grant applications. But mostly—to be my mask, my disguise. I can't just write as myself, whatever that self is—Mina Harker or Wilhelmina, Countess Dracula. I can't contact an agent, work with a publisher, go on a book tour. Can you imagine me signing books at Waterstones? Here I am, Countess Dracula. Go ahead and test my blood." She smiled, but it was an ironic smile—at that moment, she looked very much like Quincy.

Where was she going with this, and where did I fit into her plans? I was almost afraid to hear what she might say next—I had a sense, sitting there, that it would fundamentally change my life. And although I did not particularly like how my life was going, it felt as though I was at my limit of impossible things for one day.

"What I want is something like *The Memoirs of Mina Harker*, as told to Dorothy Nolan.[55] And when the interviewers ask whether you

---

55   Mina later told me that she had gotten this idea from Anne Rice's *Interview with the Vampire*, in which the vampire recounts his life to a reporter, as well as Princess Diana's memoir, which is one of those "as told to" affairs. "I always admired Princess Diana," she said. "Her marriage was as much of a trap as mine, and we both found a way out. May she rest in peace."

really interviewed a vampire, you can say of course you did, so they're convinced it's a work of fiction. But at least the truth will be out there. *My* truth."

"But I've never done anything like that before," I said. "Don't you want a professional writer, someone who's written novels or even short stories? I would think—"

"That's exactly what I don't want," said Mina. "A professional writer would want to dramatize—that's what professional writers do, what they're trained to do. I want to tell the truth, ordinary as it is. I googled you, Dorothy. While you were walking around with Quin, I skimmed the first chapter of your doctoral dissertation. You're a clear and careful writer, a trained researcher. Then I called John Paul Riquelme and asked him about you."

"You called John Paul?" I asked, incredulous. Somehow, two parts of my life were coming together in a surreal, incongruous way, like tectonic plates crashing into each other. This was definitely over my impossible things limit.

Mina smiled. "I met John Paul many years ago at a conference. I was there to see what professional scholars were saying about my manuscript—about *Dracula*, I mean. For the most part I was not impressed, but during a Q&A session—after that Bottfly person read his paper— John Paul made some very interesting points. Something about how the text deconstructs itself, which is more or less what I had been going for. I wanted to leave clues, so anyone who read carefully would know that the story I was telling wasn't the real story. At the time, I encouraged him to write more about *Dracula*."

"He did," I said. "He wrote several articles, and he edited the Bedford edition. I was his research assistant. But he never told me that he had met you—I mean, *the* Mina Harker."

"I swore him to secrecy," said Mina, as dramatically as Mary Pickford

---

Needless to say, *Interview with the Vampire* is in fact a work of fiction—yet another inaccurate and romanticized account of vampirism.

might have, if her captions could have been translated into sound. "Or rather," she added in her ordinary voice, "I asked him as a personal favor not to mention it to anyone, and he was considerate enough not to. After all, who would have believed him?"

I certainly wouldn't have. And I probably wouldn't have chosen as my dissertation advisor a man who claimed he had spoken with Countess Dracula.

"But the important thing is, when I told him I was interested in hiring you for this project, he gave you an enthusiastic recommendation. So, Dr. Nolan, would you like to help me with my memoir? I can offer you the same salary as you're getting for the Fulbright. The foundation has a small apartment you can use—it's not fancy, but it's close to the Ervin Szabó library. And you're a dual citizen, so you can apply for national healthcare. Of course, the Hungarian healthcare system is a disgrace—the pay is so low that our best doctors and nurses go to Germany. There are so many problems in this country, and in Central Europe. Perhaps after all, you would prefer being an adjunct professor in Boston?"

I'm fairly certain that at that point, I was staring at Mina like a goldfish staring out of its bowl. I had prepared myself for the extraordinary—I had not expected the utterly mundane. When I had left my apartment that morning, I had certainly not expected getting a job offer.

"Well," I finally said. "It can't be much worse than the American healthcare system."

Sitting in that office, with its file folders and butterflies, I thought about the fact that the Writing Program would not tell me whether I was teaching fall semester classes for another two months, since adjuncts were always the last to be assigned classes. I thought about how it had taken two years for me to get a shared office—before that, I had met with students at a desk in the Writing Center. I thought about how the rent was going up on my studio apartment, and I had been planning to ask if there were any extra online courses I could teach so I wouldn't have to move back in with my parents. I thought about how taking this job with Mina Harker might destroy my academic credibility—the Gerald Bottheimers and Marianne Vermeulens of the world would never take me seriously. But would they have anyway?

What I would help Mina produce would be postmodern, recursive, referential. It would be literary criticism by another means. It would be both an interpretation and an interrogation—you could throw all sorts of other Lit Crit words in there, like liminal and simulacra. We could get John Paul to write an article about it.

I could see my future spooling out in front of me, like the road back to Budapest. Quincy and I would drive back down through the mountains—I would tell him to take the curves more slowly this time. In my apartment, I would call my parents and tell them that I was staying after the Fulbright to work on a research project. My father would ask me what in the world I was thinking, but my mother would tear up a little when I told her I was planning to practice my Hungarian. Then I would send an email to the director of the First-Year Writing Program to tell him that I wouldn't be teaching in the fall, and an email to Ildikó to tell her I would be staying in Budapest, if she needed me to pick up some extra classes—I could be an adjunct professor as well here as in Boston.[56] And then, just maybe, I would go down to the café around the corner from my apartment and have a medium cappuccino and a slice of almás pite, which was almost as good as my mother's.[57]

"All right," I said, leaning back in the blue armchair, as though some tension had gone out of me. And I added, in my best academic interview voice, "Thank you. I accept your very kind offer."

———————————

56   Of course, I also sent an email to John Paul. I won't repeat here what I wrote him or what he wrote back. Some things are between a PhD candidate and her former dissertation advisor.

57   Almás pite is the Hungarian version of apple pie, but much better.

Note: I tried submitting this article to *Gothic Studies* and *The Dracula Review*. Reviewer #1's comments for *Gothic Studies* were particularly dismissive: "I have no idea what the writer was thinking, submitting a work of fiction to a peer-reviewed academic journal. I suggest submitting it to one of those pulp science fiction magazines that one sometimes sees in the racks at Barnes & Noble, below *Granta*." So I'm posting it on Academia.edu.

As Mina said, no one will believe it anyway. Who's going to believe an article about imaginary beings like vampires and adjunct professors?[58]

Then, I'm going out into the afternoon sunshine of Budapest, to the park around the Nemzeti Múzeum, where Quincy is waiting for me. We will walk under the shadows cast by the leaves of the chestnut trees, then stop at Auguszt Cukrászda for ice cream, although I'm the only one who can eat it.[59] I don't intend to give up ice cream or mortality anytime soon—but it feels good to have joined the vampires.

Update: *The Memoirs of Wilhelmina, Countess Dracula* will be published by New Moon Press next August. Everyone who preorders through the publisher's website will get a vampire bookplate signed by Mina herself.[60]

---

58   Mina predicts some readers will think I wrote this entire article as publicity for the memoir, which is fine by me. To paraphrase Jonathan Harker, we ask none to believe us. As long as you buy the book.

59   Quincy insists this isn't rude. Vampire etiquette allows the non-vampire to eat even when the vampire is incapable of joining in.

60   Or, if you don't believe in vampires, "Mina" herself.

STORY NOTES

The Mad Scientist's Daughter

I have a strange habit of writing shorter things that turn into longer things—poems that I rewrite as stories, stories that I rewrite at novel length. This is a story that became something very long: The Extraordinary Adventures of the Athena Club trilogy of novels, which include *The Strange Case of the Alchemist's Daughter*, *European Travel for the Monstrous Gentlewoman*, and *The Sinister Mystery of the Mesmerizing Girl*. I think of those novels as the pursuit of my doctoral dissertation by other means. My dissertation, which was titled *The Monster in the Mirror: Late Victorian Gothic and Anthropology* (catchy, right?), focused on nineteenth-century gothic fiction. Think *Carmilla*, *The Strange Case of Dr. Jekyll and Mr. Hyde*, *The Island of Dr. Moreau* . . . As I read and wrote about those novels, I noticed something: female monsters were considered more dangerous than male monsters, and they always died. They were just too dangerous, so they always had to be dispatched in some way. Just as importantly for me, even if they lived for a while, they never got to tell their own stories. So I decided to let them speak through me. It was very interesting, finding out what they wanted to say.

Dora/Dóra: An Autobiography

In some ways, this is a fairly simple story. It starts with something I have often wondered about: what would my life have been like if I had grown up in Hungary instead of in the United States? Perhaps this is why I have always been interested in doubles and doppelgangers. On the other hand, doubles are inherently interesting, from the wicked shadow in Hans Christian Andersen's "The Shadow" to Mr. Hyde. Of course, Dora is no more me than Dóra, although I have used some real elements of my life in constructing her—this story is a contradiction in terms, a fictional autobiography. My favorite part of this story is that I was able to give Dora and Dóra something very few stories about doubles have—a happy ending.

Cimmeria: From the Journal of Imaginary Anthropology

If you're familiar with the work of the Argentinian writer Jorge Luis Borges, you already know where this story came from: his "Tlön, Uqbar, Orbis Tertius." In that story, a secret society creates the history of an alternative, or perhaps completely other, world. As pieces of that history come to light in various texts, artifacts from Orbis Tertius start appearing in our world—our world slowly starts turning into the imaginary one. My story started with the idea of creating reality by writing about it—that's what the imaginary sciences (imaginary anthropology, archaeology, geology, etc.) do. But I also wanted to write a story that could be flipped inside out, about some American graduate students who "create" a society, and are then told by members of that society that no, those graduate students are deluding themselves—the society has existed for millennia. Who is right? And don't anthropologists in a sense "create" the societies they study, in ways those societies might push back on and question? Couldn't members of that society look at academic papers in journals and say, "This is my culture, and I don't recognize the way you represent it"? It's also a story about relationships, and whether you ever truly know the person you love—about how we all have shadow selves that even we may not completely understand.

England Under the White Witch

This story started with the idea of Jadis in London, although there are White Witch figures scattered throughout European literature—I don't mean my White Witch to be Jadis specifically. She is equally Hans Christian Andersen's Snow Queen. "Who is Jadis?" you might ask if you have not read C.S. Lewis's *The Magician's Nephew*. If you haven't, go read it now, and you will encounter Jadis in all her glory. In that novel, she comes to London, and I thought, what if someone like that, someone like the Snow Queen or another of the White Witch figures of English literature, really did appear in London? What would her reign look like? She would, of course, be an authoritarian figure, colonizing not just the city but also the imagination. Some of the details of Jadis's reign come from my having grown up hearing stories of communist Hungary and other Eastern Bloc countries—stories of coercion and betrayal. How can love exist in a society like that? I'm not sure . . .

Frankenstein's Daughter

The thing is, people change their minds all the time. So why not monsters? When Frankenstein's monster vowed that, after Frankenstein's death, he would make his way to the Arctic and there immolate himself, did you believe him? Well, I didn't. After all, where there is life, there is hope, and Frankenstein's monster is, after all, a Romantic hero. I think he would keep wandering around, and eventually find people who might not be as aesthetically picky as nineteenth-century Europeans. After all, if you're strong and smart, as the monster is, maybe a native tribe would value your skills over your appearance. Maybe you would marry a woman of that tribe, who would love you for what you are, not reject you for what you lack. And maybe you would have a daughter together. The Frankenstein's monster of this story is not the same as the one in the Adventures of the Athena Club novels. Mary Shelley's creation is such a fascinating creature that I wanted to explore him from a number of angles, and I don't think I'm done writing about him yet. But here, the important thing for me was the daughter who loves and believes in her father—she would have a very different view of him than the annoyingly incompetent Robert Walton. And she would have her own life, her own ambitions and point of view.

Come See the Living Dryad

This story starts with a place and a video. The place was the Hunterian Museum in the Royal College of Surgeons in London, where I was doing research for the first of the Adventures of the Athena Club novels. In that museum are housed anatomical specimens from the nineteenth century—thousands of them. There are also skeletal remains, as well as photographs and paintings, of famous "freak show" performers. I had initially become interested in late nineteenth-century "freak shows" because I was teaching a class called "The Modern Monster," in which we discussed how human beings had defined the "monstrous" throughout history. I was also interested because in the Athena Club novels, several characters make their living in such displays. Famous "freak show" performers, such as General Tom Thumb; Eng and Chang, who performed under the name "The Siamese Twins"; and a large number of Bearded Ladies, could be exploited by the show circuit, but could also gain economic wealth and a measure of freedom through their performances. It was a fraught, but also fascinating, area of study. The video, I happened upon accidentally as I was doing research for my class. It was called "The Man Turning into a Tree," and it was about an Indonesian man, Dede Koswara, with a rare autoimmune condition that allows warts caused by the human papillomavirus to grow uncontrollably on his extremities, so that he appeared to be turning into a tree. I tried to imagine what it would have been like for someone to have this condition in the Victorian era, when he or, in my story, she would certainly have been displayed as a "freak." I find some comfort in the fact that nowadays, we have a greater understanding of some of these conditions, and that we no longer have such an exclusionary understanding of what is considered "normal."

Beautiful Boys

As a teenager growing up in Virginia, I went to a typical American high school, which is rather strange, if you think about it—that the cliché could be so real. There were nerds and jocks and theater kids, and they really did sit in different places in the cafeteria. Of course I was one of the nerds. My high school was rather small, so all the nerds were in the AP classes, which meant that they essentially spent the entire school day together, except that some of them were taking Latin and others were taking band. (I was taking Latin.) It was like one of those movies from the 1980s with Molly Ringwald, except without Molly Ringwald—we were real teenagers, which meant that we had acne and the dialog was not as well written. In that environment, the popular kids genuinely did seem to exist in a different society.

The captain of the football team dated the girl who was voted home-coming queen. She was tall and beautiful, with perfect curling-iron rolls on either side of her head, like Farrah Fawcett. For those of us who were nerdy girls, especially, the popular boys might as well have been aliens, from a different planet. This story is partly a thought experiment—what if some men really are aliens? And of course you could flip it over—what if the narrator is, you know, kind of nuts? I like stories that have two sides, like coins.

Pug

For this story, I have to either thank or blame (or both) Professor Julia Brown of Boston University. During my PhD, while I was still taking classes, I took her course on the novels of Jane Austen. The first writing assignment was a paper analyzing one of the minor characters—the more minor, the better. I am fascinated by characters who don't get to speak—my impulse is always to give them a voice. So I wrote an entire paper on poor, maligned Anne de Bourgh, who does not say a single word in *Pride and Prejudice*—she just sits on the sofa and looks ill. But she was probably expecting to marry her handsome cousin Darcy. How does she feel? What does she think about all this? Anne gets absolutely no sympathy from Austen, and it is actually Austen's ruthlessness that makes us love her, that has made her last—she is the master satirist of English literature, who sees human nature as clearly as though we were made of glass, with our squashy interiors showing, and whose humor cuts like glass shards. I love Austen, but she has very little pity for human foibles. After writing that paper for Professor Brown, I wanted to write a story from Anne's point of view, and I also wanted to ask a question: might Austen have had some sympathy for her minor characters? Might she have given them a way out? The other impetus for this story was of course Pug, Lady

Bertram's pet dog in *Mansfield Park*, and E.M. Forster's distinction between round and flat characters. Could a flat character ever become round? I wanted to find out.

A Letter to Merlin

This story is ultimately the fault of Jonathan Strahan, who asked me for a time travel story, but I had been thinking about the idea for a while. The center of the story is the old tale of Arthur and Guinevere. I had always thought that if I were Guinevere, I would have fallen in love with hardworking, well-intentioned Arthur, not the glamorous fighter Lancelot. Arthur was much more my type. But if I had actually been able to go back in time, to be Guinevere, I would have had to betray Arthur, in order to preserve the timeline of history. Because Camelot needs to fall, to create the legend of Camelot—no fall, no legend. That would be a terrible situation, of course—to be a time traveler, doomed to betray the man you love. But a terrible situation makes for a good story. And of course it's always fun to play around with the end of humanity. I suppose that's the way my imagination works, putting bits and pieces of incongruous things together, like one of those old quilts made from scraps of skirts and blouses and aprons that when sewn together hopefully result in a unified whole.

Estella Saves the Village

Victorian literature is pretty depressing. Characters die, their ambitions are thwarted, the course of true love never does run smooth . . . It's not a genre that provides a lot of happy endings. When I wrote this story, I had somewhat recently read *Great Expectations*—within the last five years or so. I was also thinking about becoming a professor of Victorian literature and how depressing that might be, teaching Charles Dickens and George Eliot and Thomas Hardy every semester. Don't get me wrong, I deeply admire them, but for the most part, I don't read them for fun. At some point, I thought, *I wish I could give some of those Victorian characters normal, ordinary lives, with everyday happiness.* So I wrote a story about a literature professor who does that, and a young woman who realizes that her world is constructed—and that she has the power to reconstruct it when it begins to disintegrate. By now, you can probably tell that I'm deeply interested in how we create reality through language. Perhaps all of these stories are just variations on that theme.

PELLARGONIA: A LETTER TO THE *JOURNAL OF IMAGINARY ANTHROPOLOGY*

After writing "Cimmeria: From the *Journal of Imaginary Anthropology*," I didn't want to give up the imaginary sciences. They have such potential! I thought, *maybe it's not just graduate students who can imaginatively create other societies.* Maybe even children can do it. (I'm pretty sure the Brontës' Gondal and Angria exist somewhere.) But imaginatively creating a society is also necessarily dangerous—it's always dangerous to mess around with other people's lives. In these stories, I'm saying something about how writing both is and is not powerful. I wrote "Pellargonia" before reading Yuval Noah Harari's *Sapiens*, in which he argues that through writing, human beings create an "imagined order" that includes things like nations, corporations, money . . . basically, the majority of our "reality" in the modern world. And yet, the "reality" we create, which affects our lives deeply, is still nevertheless not as real as the actual reality of plants, animals, seasons, death—all the things that, in the end, truly affect our existence on this plant, and some of which our imaginative order is actually endangering. (Except death.

We seem pretty good at spreading and perpetuating death.) This story also suggests that children can be smarter than academics, which I think is certainly true.

LOST GIRLS OF OZ

When I was growing up, I read the Oz books written by L. Frank Baum, all fourteen of them. I loved their wit and wonderful imaginativeness. Every corner of Oz seemed to be inhabited by strange and interesting creatures, all of whom were accepted as long as they did not harm or seek to impose their world views on others. One of my favorite aspects of Oz was that, after the first book and for most of the series, it was essentially ruled by girls. There was Ozma of course, who was the rightful ruler of Oz. She was advised by Glinda the Good Witch. Dorothy, who eventually became a princess of Oz, was joined in Ozma's castle by Betsy Bobbin and Trot, and of course there was lovely Polychrome, the Rainbow's daughter. I suppose it wasn't the most realistic depiction of female political power, but then what was, when I was growing up? Certainly, it seemed a better alternative than Margaret Thatcher. I wrote this story because John Joseph Adams asked me to write a story about Oz—the land in the books, not the film version. So I thought, what is the central thing I know about Oz? That it's a land for girls, a land where girls can go . . . just as I went there in my imagination as a young reader.

TO BUDAPEST, WITH LOVE

What can I say? I love Budapest. It's the city where I was born, and a city I go back to as often as possible. My grandparents had an apartment there, overlooking the park around the Nemzeti Múzeum, which is the National Museum of Hungary. When I wrote this story, I had not yet inherited that apartment—I was going back to Budapest only intermittently, as I could afford it, during summer vacations. I was struggling to relearn the Hungarian I had lost as a child (which is an ongoing struggle). The story is both a love letter to the city and an exploration of what it means to be an immigrant—someone who is, metaphorically at least, an alien in both America and Hungary, never fully at home in either place. I suppose that experience of alienation is why I became a writer of fantasy, science fiction, fairy tales—whatever you call what I write. I call it the stuff I *can* write, the stories I *can* tell, the literature of the liminal spaces that I grew up inhabiting.

Child-Empress of Mars

This story is mostly the fault of John Joseph Adams, who is directly or indirectly responsible for several stories in this collection. John asked me to write a story for an anthology he was editing set on Barsoom, or Mars—where Edgar Rice Burroughs set his John Carter novels. I had never read what I came to call the "of Mars" novels, so I started on *A Princess of Mars*. I found it delightfully pulpy, and I had no idea what to write an "of Mars" story about until I fell back on my habit of writing from the point of view of a character who does not get to speak. In this case, it was Woola, John Carter's fiercely loyal guard calot (basically, his Martian dog). Everyone else on Mars was telepathic, so I thought, why not Woola? I gave him his own thoughts, his own goals, even his own side quest. But this is not that story. This is the story I wrote after that one. While reading *A Princess of Mars*, I had laughed out loud at one line, where John Carter is amazed that he could find true love with his Martian princess, Dejah Thoris, "who was hatched from an egg." Nevertheless, she appears in all particulars identical to a mammalian Earth woman (you know what I mean). This was surreal enough, but shortly afterward, on a Swissair flight from Boston to Budapest, I watched the movie *John Carter of Mars*. For some reason, it started playing with Chinese subtitles. I could not figure out how to turn them off, but anyway the movie seemed to make more sense with subtitles in a language I don't know how to read. It seemed to me that if John Carter or any other human had actually met Martians, they might have been so utterly different from him that he might not have been able to fully perceive them—it might have been like meeting bees, who can see wavelengths of light that we can't. And the Martians might have been as entertained by John Carter as I was. *That* is where this story came from.

Letters From an Imaginary Country

When I was thinking about what to call this collection, I decided to call it *Letters From an Imaginary Country*. Then I thought, if I call it that, I should actually write a story called "Letters From an Imaginary Country," so it could be included in the collection. Somehow, the story started to take shape in my head, with characters and a country and a political situation, all the things that make up both stories and our reality. In a way, all of these stories are letters from the imaginary country that exists inside my head, which looks something like America, and something like Hungary, and a whole lot like the history of literature, in English and otherwise.

The Secret Diary of Mina Harker

This story is Jacob Weisman's fault—the story only exists because he asked me for one more story, a monster story, to put into this collection. I'm sure he didn't expect one this long, or with footnotes. And after all, who is the monster in this story? I don't know, although a higher educational system that treats adjunct professors as disposable faculty members is one good candidate. But this is a story about vampires, right? Right. I will tell you a few secrets about this story: almost everything in it is made up, but John Paul Riquelme was very real. He was my dissertation advisor, and I would not have made it through my doctoral dissertation—I would not be Dr. Goss—without his patience and generosity. He did actually edit a scholarly version of *Dracula*. I was his research assistant, which is why I could later write the second of the Athena Club novels, *European Travel for the Monstrous Gentlewoman*, from a position of having read much of the nineteenth-century literature on vampires. He passed away several years ago, so I don't know if it's fair to put him into a story, because he can't give permission. But this is my way of mourning a professor and mentor who made my academic career possible. It seems that for me, vampires are inextricably bound up with research and academia and footnotes. I did not intend this story to have footnotes—they just appeared. I should add that the Mina Harker in this story is not the same as the Mina in the Athena Club novels. Like Frankenstein's monster, she is a character that I find endlessly fascinating, and I want to explore various sides of her—various situations and timelines in which she could exist. But she is also not *not* the Mina in the novels, if you see what I mean. She could be? But we would have to ask her, and for that, you would have to come to Budapest. I will have some coffee and pastries waiting.

THEODORA GOSS was born in Hungary and spent her childhood in various European countries before her family moved to the United States. She is the World Fantasy, Locus, and Mythopoeic Award-winning author of short story and poetry collections *In the Forest of Forgetting, Songs for Ophelia, Snow White Learns Witchcraft,* and *The Collected Enchantments,* as well as the novella *The Thorn and the Blossom,* debut novel *The Strange Case of the Alchemist's Daughter,* and sequels *European Travel for the Monstrous Gentlewoman* and *The Sinister Mystery of the Mesmerizing Girl.* She has been a finalist for the Nebula, Crawford, and Shirley Jackson Awards, as well as on the Tiptree Award Honor List. Her work has been translated into fifteen languages.

Goss has a BA in English literature from the University of Virginia, a JD from Harvard Law School, and an MA and PhD in English literature from Boston University. She is also a graduate of the Odyssey and Clarion writing workshops. She has taught at the Stonecoast MFA Program in Creative Writing, the Odyssey and Alpha Writing Workshops, and at Readercon, Boskone, and WisCon. Currently, she teaches written, oral, and visual rhetoric in the Boston University College of General Studies.

Jo Walton has published fifteen novels, most recently *Or What You Will* (2020). She has also published four poetry collections, two essay collections, and a short story collection. She won the Astounding Award for Best New Writer (formerly called the John W. Campbell Award) in 2002, the World Fantasy Award for *Tooth and Claw* in 2004, the Hugo and Nebula awards for *Among Others* in 2012, and in 2014 the Otherwise Award (formerly the Tiptree Award) for *My Real Children* and in 2015 the Locus Non-Fiction award for *What Makes This Book So Great*.

Walton comes from Wales but lives in Montreal where the food and books are much better. She is a columnist at Reactor Mag, and founded International Pixel-Stained Technopeasant Day. She gets bored easily so she tends to write books that are different from each other. She also reads a lot, enjoys travel, talking about books, and eating great food. She plans to live to be ninety-nine and write a book every year.